FINDING ZASHA

RANDI BARROW

SCHOLASTIC PRESS / NEW YORK

Copyright © 2013 by Randi Barrow
Map by Peyton Rosenthal and Whitney Lyle

Library of Congress Cataloging-in-Publication Data

Barrow, Randi G.
Finding Zasha / Randi Barrow. — 1st ed. p. cm.
Prequel to: Saving Zasha.
Summary: Twelve-year-old Ivan has escaped from the Siege of Leningrad, but when the town he has taken refuge in is occupied by Hitler's troops, he sees his chance to help the partisans he has met—and to rescue two German shepherd puppies, Zasha and Thor, from the cruel Commander Recht.
ISBN 978-0-545-45218-2
1. German shepherd dog — Juvenile fiction. 2. World War, 1939–1945 — Soviet Union — Juvenile fiction. 3. World War, 1939–1945 — Underground movements — Soviet Union — Juvenile fiction. 4. Soviet Union — History — German occupation, 1941–1944 — Juvenile fiction. [1. German shepherd dog — Fiction. 2. Dogs — Fiction. 3. World War, 1939–1945 — Soviet Union — Fiction. 4. World War, 1939–1945 — Underground movements — Soviet Union — Fiction. 5. Soviet Union — History — German occupation, 1941–1945 — Fiction.] I. Title. PZ7.B275677Fi 2013
813.6—dc23
2012030834

10 9 8 7 6 5 4 3 2 1   13 14 15 16 17

Printed in the U.S.A.   23
First edition, January 2013
Book design by Marijka Kostiw and Whitney Lyle

ALSO BY RANDI BARROW

SAVING ZASHA

FOR MY SISTERS
SUSAN, CINDY, SALLY,
AND ELAINE —
BRAVE, BEAUTIFUL
WARRIORS

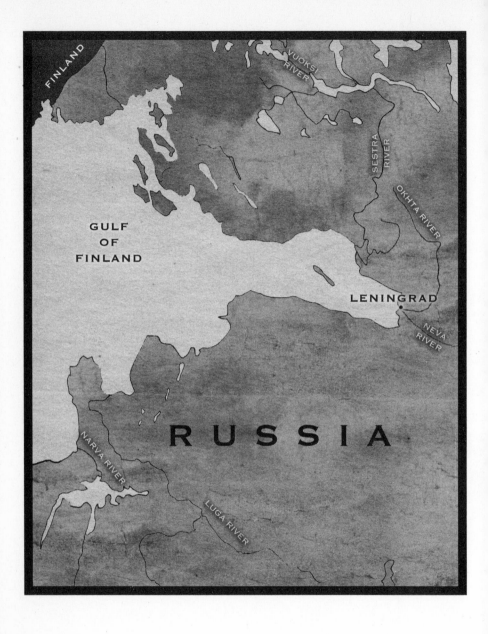

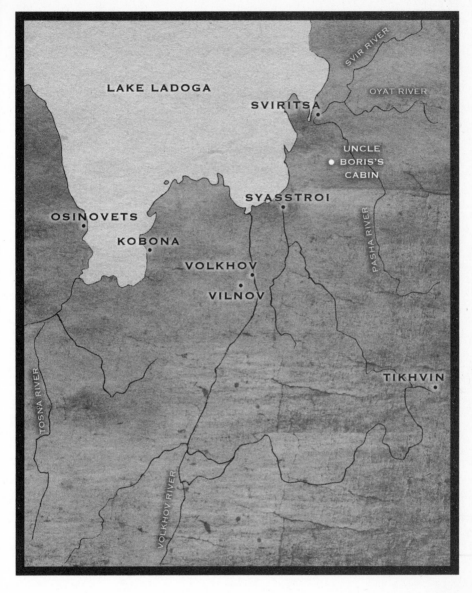

THIS MAP SHOWS LENINGRAD AND THE SURROUNDING CITIES THAT ARE IMPORTANT TO IVAN'S EXTRAORDINARY JOURNEY. IT IS NOT INTENDED TO EXACTLY REPRESENT THE DISTANCES BETWEEN CITIES, NOR DOES IT SHOW THE ENTIRETY OF RUSSIA.

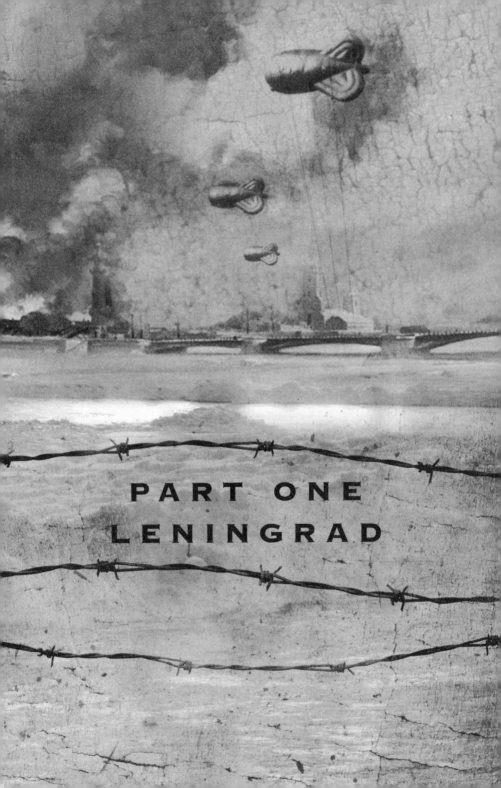

PART ONE
LENINGRAD

CHAPTER 1

I GRABBED HITLER FROM BEHIND BY THE HAIR AND WOULDN'T LET GO.

"OW! YOU'RE HURTING ME," HE CRIED.

"Coward! Baby! Nazi pig! You'll pay for what you've done to Russia! Now turn around. And if you make one false move, this bayonet goes right into your gut."

"Be careful. You could hurt me," he whined.

"Don't tempt me," I snarled, poking a stick into his back.

"Why do I always have to be Hitler? Why can't I be the Russian general for a change?" Misha asked. It was a fair question. His brother, Alik, and I made him play Hitler all the time. We blamed it on his dark hair; we said it matched the mustache made of brown cloth we pasted on his upper lip.

In truth it was because he was eleven years old and we were twelve, and we could always talk him into it. Alik liked playing Stalin, the boss of all Russia, while I preferred to call myself General Ivan, mostly because I liked the sound of my name with a fancy title in front of it.

"Do you know who I feel sorry for?" Alik asked. "Blondi, Hitler's dog." We'd seen pictures of them once in the newspaper. She was a beautiful German shepherd.

"Poor Blondi," I agreed. "Can you imagine having to lick his hand all the time?"

"Ewww!" groaned Misha. "I'd bite it right off!"

"Or having to do what he told you to do or be punished?" Alik continued.

"I'd run away," I said. "Hey, that's an idea. Let's pretend Blondi ran away to Leningrad. She's here now, lost in our city. We have to find her before Hitler does. Come on!"

Misha ripped his mustache from his lip, yelling, "I'm not Hitler anymore!" And off we ran. Life had never been more exciting than it was since the war began three months ago. Mothers worked in their factories eleven hours a day now instead of eight. Fathers were at the front, and schools were closed — or in our case, destroyed by a bomb.

"We are so lucky that happened!" we said when we were alone. If adults were near, we said, "We are so lucky that happened on a Saturday when no one was in school." Either way, we had a freedom we'd never experienced before.

That's not to say we weren't busy. All through the summer of 1941 we proudly filled sandbags, collected bottles, planted vegetables, and sewed bandages for the wounded. We were fascinated by the searchlights that scanned the sky at night. They were like giant swords of light that could protect us from anything.

The war had its difficulties, too. Food rationing had started immediately after the Germans invaded Russia in June. For growing boys who could eat five meals a day and still have room for dessert, this wasn't what you'd call good news, but no one went hungry.

There had been a few bombing raids, like the one that destroyed our school, and by early September the Germans were close enough to shoot artillery at us from the south. Yet somehow it was all tolerable. We had no doubt we were ready for the Germans and whatever they had planned for us.

That all changed on September 8, 1941, the day Leningrad

was surrounded, cut off from the rest of the world. That was the night the Germans began teaching us what bombing really meant.

★ ★ ★

That evening, Alik and Misha, who lived next door, had come over to play. My mother's shift at the Kirov Works factory had ended, but she wasn't home yet. Alik and I were practicing a new song on our concertinas, little accordion-like instruments. Misha didn't play an instrument, but he shook a tambourine every once in a while as accompaniment.

"Sit down, Ivan," Alik demanded after he'd missed his chord change and we had to stop and start over again.

"I play better standing up," I said.

"You show off better standing up."

"Maybe I do!" I twirled around, squeezing the luscious sound out of my concertina. "You should try it sometime."

"Let's start at the beginning again." He sighed. "I know what the notes are, I just . . . forget."

"Sure." I sat down across from him on a wooden chair in the room that served as our kitchen, living room, and my bedroom. "Watch my left hand; do what I do. We sing in unison for the first four lines," I reminded Alik. He nodded. We played a brief introduction and then sang.

My dear sunflower,
With your golden hair,
Sing to me
In the evening air.
Your dark eyes sparkle over skin so fair. . . .

The front door opened abruptly and in came Olga Osipenko, followed by her small black dog, Oskar. I loved Oskar and had taught him several tricks.

"Here, boy," I said, clapping my hands. He jumped into my lap but slid off because there wasn't room for both him and the concertina. Misha bent down, picked him up, and laughed as Oskar began to lick his face. I watched them jealously. We'd never been able to have a pet because my mother sneezed and sniffed if she petted a dog or cat, or was around one for very long.

"Don't you have work to do?" Olga demanded, addressing the three of us, leaving the door open behind her. She was thirteen and in charge of the children's work duties in our apartment building. Although a good group leader, sometimes she was very bossy.

"Did you forget how to knock?" I responded.

"We're practicing a new song. Do you want to hear it?" Alik asked with his natural kindness.

"That's a waste of time when there's a war going on."

Oskar jumped down from Misha's arms and began to explore our apartment.

"It's called culture, Olga." I stood up and began playing my concertina. Maybe Olga didn't understand, but I knew music was important for telling our stories and keeping our history alive.

She put her hands on her hips. "Did you complete your fire-watch hours on the roof?"

"Yes. Look at the paper hanging next to the door; we signed in and out," Alik informed her as he played the melody to "My Sunflower."

"What's your assignment tomorrow?"

"Address removal," I answered.

"Alik and Ivan and me — we're painting all the addresses in Leningrad white, and the street signs, too," Misha said in one long breath. "If the Germans get in, they won't know where to go!" He slapped his tambourine for emphasis.

Alik began to play our sunflower song from the beginning. In full voice, Misha, Alik, and I sang, *"My dear sunflower, with your golden hair, sing to me in the evening air."*

In through the open door came the tiny ancient woman known to the children in our building as Auntie Vera, or simply Auntie. She lived in the apartment above us. After my father died when I was three, she'd been a great help to my mother, acting as a friend and babysitter. She stopped in almost daily to visit or to share a meal with us.

Her small shoulders were already moving up and down to the song, a smile spreading across her face. "Beautiful," she murmured. "Don't stop." She put a lumpy cloth bag on the table, which I guessed held her rations. She stretched out her arms. "Dance with me, Olga?"

The girl shook her head; Auntie Vera was unfazed. "Misha?" He put down his tambourine and joined hands with her. Alik and I both began playing more enthusiastically now that we had an audience of sorts. Even Oskar sat down in front of us as though to listen. I imagined how wonderful it would be to play for a room full of people one day. It was my secret dream to make my living by playing music. Well, either that or doing something with dogs — I could never quite make up my mind.

Then, at the open door, smiling at the scene before her through her weariness, was my mother. "Mama!" I called, continuing to play. "How do you like our new song? Come dance for us!"

She laughed as she set her heavy bags down on the kitchen table. "The only dancing I want to do is in my sleep! Hello, everyone. Hello, Oskar." Oskar looked up at her and wagged his tail, although he knew by now she never petted him. After work my mother usually stopped at one or two stores to get our rations. She had to do this almost every day, as most stores stocked only one item: this one for bread, that one for cheese or butter, another for a small bit of meat. Precious hours she could have spent sleeping or home with me were wasted standing in line. It was a new demand of the war, but my mother was strong, and only a few years over thirty. Thankfully I was able to help her by standing in some of the food lines now that school was suspended.

I smiled as I looked at my friends, my mother, our cozy apartment, my little world. Rising out of my chair, I tried to infuse my music with the joy I felt.

"Ivan," my mother said, "I like the new song you and —" She stopped talking and her head tilted suddenly to the side. She ran to the windows at the front of our apartment, stuck her head out as far as she could, and scanned the skies. I stopped playing and heard what she'd heard — a low drone, steady, getting progressively louder. The notes from Alik's concertina faded; Auntie and Misha stopped dancing. Olga froze; Oskar ran to her side.

"The Germans," I murmured, rushing to the window, leaning out to see if I could catch a glimpse of the planes.

"Yes," she said, "but something's different." As if on cue, the sound of the incoming planes seemed to double. The air-raid sirens, wired into almost every street in Leningrad, began to scream their warning. I spun around and saw my fear reflected in the terrified faces of my friends.

"Alik," I cried, "where's your mother?"

"At work," he answered, as if he could hardly catch his breath.

"I'm going home!" Olga shouted, and she ran through the open front door, with Oskar close behind.

My mother took charge. "Ivan, help me put the covers over the windows. Auntie, take Misha and Alik and go into the bedroom. There are chairs in the closet. Wait there for us." Auntie held out her arms to shepherd the two brothers into the closet we'd prepared for just such an emergency.

I leaned out the window again. The sky was dark with a dozen or more low-flying planes on their way to bomb us. The noise was triple what it was a minute ago, the air-raid sirens relentless.

"Ivan!" my mother shouted. "Help me!" She had picked up one of the large pieces of wood we had to cover our main windows in case of an air attack and was struggling to slide it into the slots we'd made to hold it. I grabbed the end nearest me, and we had it in place in seconds. The sound was a monstrous roar now; it felt like it was on top of us, under us, surrounding us, a violent hurricane of noise.

Just as we lifted the second piece of protective wood, a bomb hit nearby. "Hurry, Mama!" I cried as we tried again to slip the cover into its brackets. Another bomb hit and our building shook. We fell to the floor only seconds after we'd maneuvered the covering into place.

My mother jumped to her feet, grabbed my hand, and ran with me into the bedroom. We were thrown into the closet by what felt like a shock wave, landing on the laps of Alik and Misha. I slipped down to sit on the floor; my mother settled herself into the chair next to Alik and put her arm around him protectively. Auntie prayed the old Russian Orthodox prayers quietly. It was dark in the closet, but I could see everyone until my mother said, "Ivan, close the door all the way." Then it was as dark as death.

The bombs were falling in such rapid succession that I lost count after the sixth or seventh one. Misha began to whimper. I leaned against my mother's legs in the dark. The building groaned; the air seemed to be seeping out of my lungs; there was pain in my ears. Then a bomb hit so hard, I was sure it had landed on our building. The bodies of my friends were thrown upon me, pushing the air out of my chest. I tried to yell "Get off me! Get off me!" No sound came out. I couldn't see. I couldn't move.

"Is anyone hurt?" It was the distraught voice of my mother. I felt someone being lifted off of me; air rushed back into my lungs.

"Alik," I heard my mother say, "are you all right?"

"Yes," he answered faintly.

"Misha?"

"Yes," he said, sounding as if he'd begun crying, and the weight became less.

"Auntie?"

"I'm here!" she said almost cheerily as the last of the bodies slipped off my back.

"Ivan," my mother said softly, fearfully, as she touched my shoulder and turned me over.

"I'm okay," I said faintly, coughing as the fine dust that covered my lips seeped into my throat when I spoke.

"Sit up." She pulled me into a sitting position and then onto the chair next to her, holding me to her. More bombs exploded in the distance; the planes had dropped our share of their loads on us and moved farther into the city to try to destroy someone else.

"Can we open the door, Mama?" I asked, desperate to have even the smallest bit of light in our cramped closet. The bedroom windows were small, and on the other side of the room, but they were uncovered. She hesitated.

"Just an inch," she said, fumbling for the doorknob in the dark. The comfort that slice of light provided calmed the terrible fear in me. I saw Misha most clearly, slumped in the chair, eyes wide open, his thumb in his mouth.

I smelled a pungent, sour odor. "What's that?" I said, half to myself, understanding at the same moment that it was Misha wetting his pants. No one answered.

"Where do you think they are now?" Alik sounded frightened.

"I don't know," my mother answered calmly.

"Will they come back?" Misha asked, not bothering to take his thumb out of his mouth.

"I think they're done for the day," Auntie said with assurance, as if trying to cheer us up. "It will be dark soon. They won't be able to aim very well in the dark."

"Can I go and look, Mama?"

"No. We wait fifteen minutes after the last bomb. If we don't hear any planes, we can go out again." The echo of air-raid sirens lingered, but they were coming from other neighborhoods now. I felt claustrophobic and sweaty; it seemed there was just barely enough oxygen for the five of us.

"Look at the bright side," Alik added after a minute. I waited, unable to imagine a bright side to a German bombing raid. "Olga went home." I laughed in spite of myself; so did the others. It would have been unbearable with one more person in the closet, even if she did come with my favorite dog. Suddenly I didn't feel so bad. *This is how soldiers must feel*, I thought, proud (and relieved) at having made it through an air raid in one piece.

After fifteen minutes had passed, my mother let us leave the closet. We looked ghostly, covered in the fine, dusty powder that had fallen from the tiny cracks that opened in the wall and ceiling as the bombs did their work.

"It's all right, Misha," I heard my mother say softly to him. "I'll take care of it."

"Do you think my apartment is still there?" Auntie asked us with a forced laugh.

"Ivan, why don't you boys walk Auntie upstairs?" my mother said. "Make sure everything is okay. I'll go out front in a minute and see what was done to our building."

I agreed, but watched her as she surveyed our living area, picking up the small framed photograph of my father off the floor and putting it back in its place. "The glass cracked," she murmured sadly.

"Our concertinas!" I exclaimed, having forgotten they lay unprotected.

Alik picked his up, shaking it gently to get rid of a light coating of gray dust. "I think they'll be fine. I can't see them too well." The wooden window covers were still in place, adding a gloominess to our usually cheerful home.

Auntie stood in front of a wall mirror that hung askew, brushing the dust from her shoulders and her hair, retying the small blue head scarf she wore. There was a tremor in her hand. Alik and I slipped the heavy window covers off, letting in an eerie, smoky light. My mother soaked a dish towel in water, going back to the closet to clean up after Misha. Under normal circumstances, Alik and I would have teased Misha mercilessly for his accident. That night, both of us pretended the dark, wet spot on his pants wasn't there.

"What do you say, boys?" Auntie asked, picking up her bag. "Are you ready to take me home?" All I really wanted to do was pretend everything was normal and be alone in our apartment with my mother and have her listen to the details of my day while we ate dinner.

I was watching Alik pack his concertina in its case and Misha wipe his tambourine with his shirt when I heard the planes once more. "Mama!" I cried. "They're coming back!"

"Get in the closet," she yelled. "Everyone!" The five of us ran for our cramped shelter. There was no time to cover the windows again. The air-raid sirens shrieked just as we closed the door.

We banged around in the cramped space as if we were in a car that kept hitting tree after tree after tree. The war had finally reached Leningrad.

CHAPTER 2

AUNTIE VERA UNLOCKED THE DOOR TO HER APARTMENT. A CUPBOARD DOOR HUNG OPEN, AND SEVERAL GLASSES LAY SHATTERED ON THE FLOOR; BOOKS HAD BEEN THROWN FROM their shelves. Whitish-gray dust frosted every surface. Her apartment looked much like ours, but worse because Auntie's home was stuffed with furniture, animal figurines, a large birdcage, and lots and lots of books. Her belongings looked like they'd been shaken in a jar and thrown out like dice.

"Oh, dear." She sighed, pushing the door open fully and taking a step inside. Alik, Misha, and I peered around her at the mess.

"Look," I said, pointing up and into the corner of her front room. The darkening sky shone through a hole between her ceiling and the floor of the one above it. If Auntie could see the sky, much of the ceiling of the family's apartment above hers had to be gone, because they were the top floor. "The roof!" I exclaimed as I remembered. "We're supposed to check for fires." All the boys between ten and fourteen who lived in our building were required to report to the roof after any hostile activity. I'd almost forgotten because the bombs had never been this close before. "Auntie, why don't you wait in our apartment?"

She nodded. "I hope it doesn't rain," she said with one last upward glance, making an effort to smile as she followed us out into the hall and closed the door behind us. "Go, boys. Hurry, but be careful."

When we arrived, a half dozen or so people were already there, carrying long, oversize pliers in their hands, the ones with the

14

four-foot-long handles that allow you to pick up incendiary bombs. The sole purpose of incendiaries was to start fires. They were about the size and shape of my arm from wrist to elbow. The Germans dropped thousands of them on their city raids along with their regular bombs. Even if they missed their primary targets, they could still be assured that they left countless fires behind them.

Flames were already festering on the roof of the building across the street. I stared, giving a silent thanks that it had missed our apartment house, feeling guilty for such a selfish thought. When I turned away, I was more fiercely determined than ever to protect our homes, our city, my friends, and their families.

We boys had two jobs: to spot the incendiaries for those with pliers and to provide buckets of sand and water for them to put the bombs into. The roof of our building was flat, which made many easy to find. Still, there were plenty of places the small incendiaries could be overlooked between the chimney pots and air shafts that dotted the roof.

I saw Olga; a metal helmet hung loosely over her dark braids. "Olga, what do you want us to do?" I called.

"Go over there." She pointed to the northwest corner of our building. "Make sure the sand and water buckets are full. Then start at the center of the roof and look for incendiaries." I was relieved to have Olga as our leader at a time like this.

We ran quickly but found that two boys who lived on the ground floor had already filled every available bucket and pail. "Let's find the hole in the roof over Auntie's before we look for incendiaries," I said. "We don't want anyone to fall through." Three bare bulbs on poles lit just three corners of the large apartment building, leaving many areas obscured.

"Ahhh!" someone near us screamed. "There's one!"

"Can you reach it?" another called. "Is it burning?"

"Not yet." There was a flurry of activity off to our left, the clank of metal on metal as the long pliers were used to grab the bomb and carry it with great caution to a nearby bucket of sand. I'd been told that sometimes just the pressure of the pliers on an incendiary could make it burst into flame. How brave those people were; the very thought of it made me shiver with fear.

The light changed as the fire in the building across the street grew. It provided the extra light I needed to get my bearings and find the damage we were looking for. There it was, not far from the edge of the roof: a savage-looking, bed-size hole. No wonder Auntie could now see the sky from her doorway.

As I looked around for Olga to tell her about it, an incredible explosion made us all jump. To the south and the east, flames poured up into the sky, higher and brighter than any I'd ever seen. I stared at the terrifying sight.

"Is it the Kirov?" Alik asked, looking at me in fear. I shook my head, knowing that whatever was in flames was near my mother's factory, but it wasn't the Kirov. I knew its position well.

"Oh," I gasped as another boom thundered over us and giant tongues of flame shot into the sky, surrounded by billows of black smoke. "It's the Badayev! The food warehouses are on fire!"

"Oh, no," Alik whispered. The Badayev warehouses held almost all of Leningrad's food supplies — flour, sugar, meat, lard. If they burned, we would starve.

"Come on!" I cried, running toward the door that led to the stairwell. "We have to help!"

CHAPTER 3

AS WE RACED DOWN THREE FLIGHTS OF STAIRS, WE ALMOST
RAN INTO MY MOTHER, WHO WAS ON HER WAY BACK UP TO
OUR APARTMENT. "WHERE ARE YOU GOING?" SHE STEPPED
toward the wall as if we might not be able to stop.

"The Badayev is on fire," I answered breathlessly, continuing
my run down to the ground floor.

"Ivan!" I stopped, not sure what I'd do if she forbade me from
going. She'd taught me to be strong and independent after my
father died by letting me take risks, but there were limits. "Do
exactly what the men at the Badayev tell you to do. Help if you
can. If they say to go home, come back immediately."

"Will you tell Mrs. Bukova that Alik and Misha are with
me?" I called from the bottom of the stairs, so grateful for her
understanding.

"Of course. But don't forget the curfew," she warned, leaning over the stairwell as we reached the front door. "You can be
arrested if you're not home by ten. And be careful!"

"I promise," I cried as the three of us stumbled to a halt only
seconds after we were outside. Our street had been cratered in at
least two places; the cement the impacts displaced was strewn
in a thousand pieces over cars, trucks, and lampposts. A huge
pile of rubble filled the sidewalk on our left. The street was full
of people, all moving quickly as if their panic and fear pro-
pelled them.

"This is bad," Alik murmured, glancing at me.

"Not as bad as the warehouses burning. Let's go." The three of us ran east. The rest of our street, Rizhsky Prospekt, looked even worse than our block. Fires burned in a half dozen storefronts, rooftops, and apartments. Alik fell over a piece of concrete, and I slipped twice near a gushing water main. We had three long blocks to cover before we reached Moskovsky Prospekt, one of Leningrad's main streets that runs north and south. A turn to the right there would bring us within a mile or so of the Badayev warehouses. The complex of wooden structures that stored our precious food supplies was spread over nine acres. It seemed unlikely that all of them had been hit by bombs or incendiaries, but fires spread quickly.

"What now?" Alik asked me when we reached Moskovsky Prospekt. I looked up and down the broad avenue; a streetcar lay on its side like a beast shot dead, air-raid sirens rang off and on. The column of smoke from the Badayev seemed even bigger than before. I was sure of only one thing — that I would not be deterred by the awful things we'd seen and that still surrounded us.

"Look!" I said. "What's that?" I pointed to our left. A tall man with a gray beard stood up on his horse-drawn milk cart, reins in one hand, gesticulating with the other. He was yelling something, and a few men were lifting themselves into the open back of the wooden vehicle. His horse trotted toward us, and we finally understood what the man was saying.

"Brave men of Leningrad! Come now and save the Badayev! Come now or we will starve!" We needed no further encouragement and ran toward him. The men already inside the moving cart reached out their hands and helped lift us over the sides and into the back. Within minutes the cart was overflowing with men and a few other boys. The cart driver finally sat down and stopped yelling for volunteers once the cart was full and a dozen others ran alongside us. He urged his lean, sway-backed horse on. The horse seemed as intent as the rest of us on getting to our destination quickly, despite the heavy load.

The tower of flame and smoke was our beacon. Once we crossed the canal into the more industrialized part of the city, we were within blocks of the inferno. There were people everywhere, along with cars and fire trucks, all headed for the warehouses. I hated to admit it, but the smells coming from the Badayev were fantastic, a complex mix of burning wood, caramelizing sugar, roasting meat, and melting butter. But they were poisoned by intermittent infusions of acrid smoke and the fine black ash that was already raining down on us.

We rounded the corner that led to the front entrance of the Badayev. The huge gates were wide open; the driver pulled his panting horse to a halt. "Come on, boys!" he yelled as he jumped from the cart, tied the reins of his horse around a tree, and ran toward the entrance. We didn't hesitate to follow him. There were already countless men there to fight the fires, men with hoses, buckets, and shovels, all of them in motion.

The wooden structures holding the food supplies were connected by narrow roads and alleyways. It looked like the worst fire, the one with the towering flames, was toward the rear of the complex. The driver rushed to the man who was directing the group of firefighters nearest to us. After a few seconds of conversation, the driver turned to us. "Anyone under sixteen, stay here and help this group. The rest of you, follow me."

Alik, Misha, two other boys, and I stood ready, waiting for further instructions. The burly man in charge yelled to us above the chaos and sirens. "See that shed? Go get some shovels. Shovel as much dirt as you can on any cinder you see in this area." He waved his arm to indicate the wide empty spaces in front of the two nearest buildings. Wiping soot and sweat off his face with his sleeve, he turned away and started calling out directions to another group.

There were only three shovels and two rakes left in the tin toolshed, the back of which was the security fence surrounding the complex. The older boys, who entered first, took two shovels, leaving us with one and two rakes.

"You're the strongest," Alik said, handing me the shovel. "These rakes will do the job, anyway. Let's get out there."

It became clear quickly that the cinders and bits of burning debris that fell were dangerous. Not to us, but to the buildings that surrounded us. They were like the incendiary bombs the Germans dropped, only very tiny, and they never stopped coming. The ground was composed of dry, half-dead grass and dirt. I pounded the smoldering cinders out with the back of my shovel or dumped dirt on them. Not once did any of the cinders that dropped into the area under our control fan into flames. After about an hour, I stopped for the first time to catch my breath; Alik and Misha noticed and did the same. An hour and a half later, now soot-covered, sweaty, and exhausted, I motioned to my friends to follow me. They did, and although I think we all felt a little guilty about it, we went into the toolshed to rest before continuing.

"I need water," Misha said.

"We'll get some before we leave," I assured him.

"What time is it?" Alik asked, looking concerned. "We can't forget the curfew."

I heard the sound of angry voices outside and held my finger to my lips to indicate to Misha and Alik that none of us should speak. Being nearest the door I leaned as close as I could get to the small opening between it and the door frame.

"I don't care what the boss says," a man said loudly. "I'm not going back there."

"There's nothing left; why should you?" his friend agreed. "What does he expect you to do — walk into a wall of flames to save a sack of flour?"

"Yes!" the other man said. "But there is no flour. No sugar, no . . . nothing. It's gone. All of it."

"You can't tell anyone," his friend warned him.

"Why not? The entire city can see the warehouses are burning."

"I know, but they probably think there's more somewhere else. If they knew there was only enough food for one or two weeks, there would be riots."

I glanced over my shoulder at Misha and Alik, wondering how much of the conversation they could hear. The look of worry on their faces told me they'd heard it all.

"Let them riot! Maybe then the idiots who thought it would be a good idea to store *all* of the food in the city in *one* place, in *wooden* buildings, will get what they deserve."

"They never get what they deserve."

The men were silent for a moment.

"Let's get out of here."

"We can't just leave."

"Why? This is useless. There isn't one building that will be standing in the morning."

"There's hardly one building standing now." The men sounded genuinely anguished. "But where will we work? How will we eat?"

"I saw the manager of warehouse seven loading sacks of something into a car just after the fires broke out."

"Let's go find him. Whatever he's got will be worth its weight in gold soon."

"I won't let my children go hungry while he makes a fortune! Come on. I know where he lives." That was the last thing we heard from them, and we didn't wait more than thirty seconds before we left the shack. The heat had been building, and I could feel that all of us were getting nervous about it.

I saw the scene with new eyes as we emerged into the noise, chaos, and danger of the fires. "Look!" I cried, pointing to the roof of one of the buildings nearby. It had caught fire during our brief absence. I stood silently, staring, imprinting the moment forever in my memory. No matter how hard these men tried, their cause was lost. The complex was on fire; no one could put it out, and it would destroy everything. What the two men we'd overheard said was true. Our city was now in a struggle for its very life. And so were we.

CHAPTER 4

WHEN ALIK, MISHA, AND I GOT HOME FROM THE BADAYEV — DIRTY, SWEATY, EXHAUSTED — IT WAS ALMOST AN HOUR AFTER CURFEW. OUR MOTHERS AND AUNTIE WERE WAITING in our apartment. They turned as one, looking hopeful and fearful as I opened our front door.

"It's about time!" Mrs. Bukova exclaimed, storming up to her sons and grabbing Alik by his left ear. "Are you trying to kill me? First the bombing, and now this?" She whacked Misha on the shoulder with the back of her hand while continuing her tirade. "Is this what I work for? To see my sons disrespect their mother and her rules? I should be asleep right now, but no, I'm waiting up to see if my boys are dead or alive!" She stopped for breath and spied me. "And you, Ivan Savichev, I thought you were smarter than this. How did you think three boys were going to help with the Badayev fires? I've been worried half sick."

"But we did help! We —" Mrs. Bukova, never at a loss for words, had much more to say on the subject and didn't let me finish. She kept up a steady flow of outrage after crying, "Home, now! March!" Grabbing her two sons by the backs of their collars like a feral cat mother might do, she half pushed, half dragged them out of our apartment and into their own next door. We could hear the muffled sounds of her reprimands even through the wall.

I turned to my mother, who stared at me. "I told you to be back by ten o'clock," she declared firmly.

"Yes, Mama, I know. But it was impossible." My mother was as unlike Mrs. Bukova as day from night. While my friends' mother would yell, scold, and give her boys a solid smack on their backsides, my mother punished me with the weight of her expectations and her disappointment. I almost wished she would have yelled instead.

"Why was it impossible?"

"The Badayev is so far away —"

"I know where it is."

"— and we had to walk all the way home in the dark."

"The curfew is serious, Ivan. Anyone can be put in jail for violating it, even a child."

"I know," I mumbled.

"Alik and Misha look up to you. If you don't behave responsibly, they won't, either. You saw Mrs. Bukova. Isn't it bad enough that her husband is at the front? Do you think she needs the extra burden of worrying about her children's safety?"

"No, ma'am."

"I'm very disappointed. You're old enough to have learned these lessons already. You shouldn't have to learn them again and again."

I stared at my battered shoes. I hated upsetting my mother. My usual way of making up with her was to try to make her laugh, but I couldn't come up with even one joke about the awful things we'd witnessed. If laughter was unavailable, distraction was my second line of defense.

"I see Auntie is still up. Should I walk her to her door and make sure she's comfortable for the night? We saw a hole in her ceiling and —"

"Auntie will be staying with us for the time being."

Auntie smiled briefly and looked at my mother.

"That's good," I answered. "May I help her bring some of her things down from upstairs?" I looked at them, hopeful that this would end my chastisement.

"That's what the three of us did while we waited for you," she said, but in a tone that told me she was ready to stop being angry.

"I'm sorry, Mama; it won't happen again." She sat down in one of our four kitchen chairs, and I realized how weary she was, how strained, and probably still shaken from the bombing.

"Why don't I make tea?" Auntie suggested, picking up the kettle and carrying it to the sink. My mother nodded her assent with a tired smile. "Oh, and Ivan, while the water boils I'd like you to come upstairs with me. There's one more thing I need help with. We'll be back in a few minutes, Elena," she assured my mother, settling the kettle over the flame on our sturdy stove. I got up and followed her to her apartment just above us. Once inside, she turned on the overhead light, and I saw that most of the mess left by the bombing had been cleaned up. Closing the door, she turned to me.

"Ivan, I need to talk to you." The serious look on her face made me nervous. "You're twelve, almost thirteen, and I'm going to speak to you bluntly, like you were an adult." I nodded. "Everything I tell you must be our secret. Will you agree to that?"

"Yes, Auntie."

She took a deep breath and glanced briefly around her overcrowded apartment. "Our lives are going to be different from now on."

"What do you mean?" I'd half expected her to lecture me about obeying my mother and was taken by surprise.

"Leningrad has been surrounded by the Germans. There is no longer a way in or a way out of our city. Ivan, do you understand? *No one and nothing can get in, and no one can get out.* The food warehouses have burned. We've had food rationing for two and a half months. It will now become severe." Her words scared me. She continued, "I lived through our revolution in 1917. I lived through the time when the government took over all the farms and industry in this country." She looked pained by the memories, her face pinched and tense. "I survived because someone talked to me as I will now talk to you. Sit down." I pulled out one of the kitchen chairs, never taking my eyes off of her. "Look around you. What do you see?" She was confusing me; I didn't know what to say.

"Well?" she prompted me.

"I . . . I see lots and lots of furniture. Too much! And pictures on the wall, several small rugs. Your birdcage by the window, a stove."

"What else?"

"I don't know — your cupboards are full of dishes and glasses. The table, three chairs, your sofa, and the comfy chair you like to read in. Books. Lamps. Very little walking space." I glanced back at her, knowing I wasn't understanding whatever it was she was trying to tell me.

"I survived because I prepared for the worst." I nodded, but only because I had nothing intelligent to say. "You see a room, an ordinary room. I am going to show you what you don't see. It may save our lives. If anything happens to me, you must continue to use whatever is left."

"You're scaring me, Auntie."

"You can't afford to be scared, Ivan. From now on, your attention must be focused on survival." Tiny Auntie Vera walked to the birdcage at the front window, its gray prongs sculpted gracefully to a point at the top, its door destroyed long ago since she didn't believe in caging birds. Instead she kept a small houseplant inside it. The bottom rim of the cage was about three inches high, a simple scored piece of metal. "Come here. Watch me," Auntie commanded.

Just under where the door once fastened was a small, round, buttonlike protrusion. She pushed it, which allowed the rim of the birdcage to slide about eight inches to the right, revealing an empty space of about three inches under the bottom of the cage floor. Auntie reached in and pulled out a gun. I gasped.

"Is it real?"

"Very real." She handed it to me. "The bullets are in a bag in back of it." She reached in again and pulled out a black cloth drawstring bag the size of a large bar of soap and placed it on the table. My mouth fell open; I was amazed.

"Do you know how to use a gun?"

"A little," I said, having taken some rifle training with a boys' camping group one summer.

"The enemy is at the gate, Ivan. The gun is to be used only for protection of your family and loved ones. Do not touch it under any other circumstances. Now . . ." She looked around briefly. "My table. Help me turn it on its side."

At this point I wasn't surprised by such a strange request and quickly put the gun and bullets on her sofa and helped her turn her smallish wooden table on its side. Auntie pulled a butter knife out of a drawer.

"Do you see these pads on the bottom of the legs?" I nodded, fascinated that my diminutive neighbor had a side to her I'd never dreamed of. She pried one of the wooden pads off to reveal that the leg had been hollowed out. Reaching into it with her index finger, she gently pulled out a thick roll of bills.

"Rubles! How much money is that?" I looked at her in astonishment. She smiled broadly.

"If there is one thing I learned during the revolution when the tsar was overthrown, it is not to expect help from the authorities in a time of chaos or war. You have to be responsible for yourself and your family. The other three legs are the same." She laughed lightly as she straightened up. "And all of us became hoarders."

"Hoarders?"

"If you've ever lived through a time when there was no food, afterward you become like a squirrel. You bury food to see you through the next crisis. You hide it, you preserve whatever you can, so that you never have to face that kind of hunger again." There was a haunted look on her face as she told me this, while continuing to peruse her apartment. "Let me show you something."

Near what I called her comfy chair, where I'd often seen her reading, Auntie pulled back two small, worn rugs. Again using the butter knife, she pried loose a board from her wooden floor. "Take a look." I wasn't sure what I was seeing at first. It looked like a row of silver-colored circles until I realized they were the tops of cans. With a little groan, Auntie reached down and pulled out a can of navy beans. She held it up with a smile like a farmer might have as he proudly showed off a prize tomato.

"This is amazing!" I said with a laugh. "What next — a tank hidden under the bed?"

"This area," she said, motioning to a six-by-six-foot area in front of her chair, "and the space between my bed and the window in the other room are full of cans like this."

"All beans?"

"They'll keep you alive and nourished better than most things."

I sat back on my heels, looking at her in admiration. "You have food, money, protection . . . there's nothing else you need!"

"You need fuel. All this furniture and these books can be burned to keep you from freezing to death." That was almost too much for me. I didn't like school, but I loved to read; the idea of burning a book was sacrilegious. "And your papers," she continued. "You keep your identification papers and your ration card hidden at all times. Where do you and your mother keep yours?"

"In a drawer in the desk in the living room."

"You'll have to change that immediately."

"Why?"

"People will be desperate soon. Very soon," she said quietly. "Their behavior will change. They will do things they never imagined they were capable of." She gazed intently at me as she said this.

"Like what?"

"They will steal your ration card knowing that means starvation for you. Some will even kill for them." She must have sensed the growing fear and confusion in me because she reached out and touched my shoulder. I thought of the men I'd overheard at the food warehouses and how they said there was food enough to feed the city for only a week or two. "From now on you must keep your door locked at all times."

"Even in the day?" I was incredulous.

"As I said, things are going to be different now. Food will be all that matters. It will be more valuable than gold." She reached in the pocket of her skirt and pulled out a small brown leather coin purse; from it she produced a long silver key. "This is the key to my apartment; there's another one hidden in the hall that I'll show you on our way out. You need to know where it is in case something happens to me."

"Don't talk that way, Auntie."

"That's something else we must all learn at a time of war."

"What?"

"You accept the truth of your situation. Immediately. If you don't" — she gave a little shrug — "you can't take the actions you need to survive."

"Have you shown my mother these things?"

She shook her head. "No. Your mother carries the battle on her shoulders eleven hours a day at the factory. It's up to you to take care of her, to protect her, to be ready."

I sat quietly in thought for a moment as I felt my new role taking hold of me. "I'm short, Auntie, like you," I teased. "But I'm also strong. I can do this."

"Strong is good," she said with a kind smile. "You must also be clever. Together they will give you at least a chance at staying alive. Come," she said, glancing at the clock on the kitchen wall. "We must go."

"What about the gun?"

"Put it and the bullets back in their place, then close the little door. Let me see you do it." I did as she requested, still marveling at all she'd told me, at the hidden secrets in her simple room, feeling exhilarated and amazed by all I'd experienced in one day.

"Remember, you may tell no one of what I've just shown you — not Alik, not Misha, not even the police. Understood?"

I nodded, knowing I could keep a secret.

As we locked the front door, she silently pointed to the baseboard near it and lifted off a five-inch piece of wood from the top, revealing the hiding place of her other key. She slipped the wood back in its place. You would never notice it unless you knew it was there and you were looking for it. Finally, we descended the stairs to my apartment, where my mother was opening the door.

"I was just going to go looking for you two! The tea's ready," my mother said.

"Ivan helped me do a little cleaning up," Auntie Vera lied.

"Yes, Mama, just a little . . ." I hesitated, remembering what Auntie said, that my mother's burden was already great enough. ". . . a little cleaning up. That's all."

CHAPTER 5

So many things happened in the next three days, it felt like we were being punished for escaping harm in the first three months of the war.

The Red Star Creamery was bombed, and the last of the butter in Leningrad was destroyed with it. Dozens and dozens of fires burned throughout the city, the blue sky woven with black and gray threads of smoke marking their locations. Food disappeared from the shelves. The government began rationing electricity and cut personal phone lines, although the public ones were kept on. Those were bad things, but the news that felt like a knife in my heart came with a knock on the door, early in the morning, when I was still asleep.

It was Georgi from down the hall. He stood there silently, his eyes glassy with tears, his pet rat, Leonid, climbing in and out of his cupped hands.

"Georgi, what is it? Are you all right? Has something happened?"

His lower lip trembled, and he watched Leonid for what seemed like a long time before he looked up and said, "Betty died. They got her. The Germans got her with their stupid bombs during the night."

I gasped and fought the truth of his words. "No, not Betty."

He nodded, a tear falling onto his hands. "Yes, I'm letting everyone know." I stood motionless, watching as he crossed the hall. Just as he reached our neighbor's door, he turned back to me.

"And the roller coaster . . . It burned to the ground." As he turned back around, I closed the door softly and stood staring into space.

Betty, Leningrad's only elephant, was the pride of our zoo. She was a magical creature who got more beautiful with every visit. Our mothers had used Betty as a promise and a threat since we were toddlers. "If you're good, we'll go see Betty!" Or more likely, "If you don't stop fighting with your brother, I won't take you to see Betty!" And now, gone. Not dead of old age, but killed by a war that had nothing to do with her.

After Betty's death — or murder, as Alik later called it — I thought things couldn't get worse. I was soon proven wrong.

★ ★ ★

Nine days later, Olga led ten of the children from our apartment house to other apartment houses to knock on doors and collect bottles. The children of Leningrad had gathered almost one million bottles since the beginning of the month, our contribution to the factory that turned them into Molotov cocktails. That might seem like a primitive weapon to some — all you had to do was throw it and it burst into flame — but as the whole world now knew, Russia wasn't really ready for war, so we had to make the most of what we had.

After an hour knocking on doors, Alik, Misha, and I each had full canvas sacks, almost too heavy to carry, the bottles clanking against one another and making a terrible racket as we dragged them to the curb.

"The truck should be here," Olga said impatiently, looking up and down the street. The factory was supposed to have sent a truck for us to dump our bottles into and then follow along behind us the rest of the day. That way we could work efficiently — collecting, dumping, collecting, dumping.

"Here come the Germans." Tomik, at sixteen the oldest boy with us, said it casually, while stopping to light a cigarette made from dried leaves rolled in newspaper. We were being bombed daily, and after eleven days we were almost getting used to it.

"All right," Olga said with a sigh, as if she considered it just an inconvenience. "Get into the lobby of the building over there. Let's move."

I stared at the sky as I shuffled toward the nearby apartment building. This raid sounded different from the others, and soon I saw why. It was just three planes flying in fast and low, and dropping something, but it wasn't bombs. You could barely tell anything fell out of those planes at first except that the sunlight glinted on whatever it was until it almost looked like a waterfall, a silver waterfall, made up of a thousand unnamed objects.

A swarm of them fell near the end of the block. Every one of us, including Olga, ran for the area where the things landed. It was like a dump truck had unhitched its back gate and unloaded its contents right there on the street. We slowed down and stared, approaching with curiosity and wonder.

"Cigarette lighters!" Tomik said with a smile. "And look — pens."

"That's a ten ruble note," Georgi said in amazement. "It's tied to a lump of metal so it won't blow away."

"Ration cards!" Alik exclaimed. "They've dropped ration cards!"

"Stop!" Olga cried. "Don't touch anything. We'll report it to the police."

We prowled like a pack of tigers, walking slowly around our

target, getting ready to pounce. "There are toys in there. I saw them, I'm sure," Misha said excitedly.

Alik looked confused. "Why would the Germans do this? They try to kill us and then they give us presents?"

I shook my head, feeling wary and suspicious. "Maybe they think we're ready to give up. They're trying to make us like them or something."

"I know I saw a little dump truck in there," Misha said, taking a step toward the pile of riches.

"No!" Alik shouted, grabbing his sleeve. "Olga's right. We wait. Don't touch anything."

"Since when do you take Olga's side?" Misha snapped, but he stopped moving.

Tomik threw his cigarette butt to the ground. "There's money waiting to be picked up, and you fools are going to wait for the *authorities*? Not me."

"Tomik, don't," I said. He was always doing something to annoy people.

Ignoring me, he stepped forward and reached into the collection of miscellaneous things. "It's a pen, Ivan. Who cares if I take a pen?" He held it up as if to emphasize how silly I was. I grabbed it in a lightning-fast move and threw it about fifteen feet from us so that it landed in the middle of the pile.

"You're such a —" Tomik began, just as the pen exploded in a fit of fire and smoke. I barely registered the cries of the others, the shouts, the disbelief, as I stood frozen in shock.

"It's booby-trapped. It probably all is," Olga cried. "Don't touch anything else. Back away slowly and go stand where we left our bottles."

People were opening windows and peering out to see what had happened. "What do you want us to do, Olga?" I asked, knowing she'd soon be busy giving information to the police.

"Leave your bags of bottles at the curb," she answered. "I'll take care of it when the truck gets here. Just go home. Don't tell anyone about this yet."

I nodded, knowing that Olga was really upset, but out of all of us, she was the best person to handle this.

It was a long walk home for the group, and no one had much to say, even when we reached our apartment building and headed toward our own units. Misha and Alik stayed with me. I knew Auntie would be there and that somehow she would make things tolerable.

The door was locked, something I was still getting used to, but when I unlocked it, I was greeted by a smiling Auntie, an apron tied over her dress, the smell of something cooking wafting out from behind her. "Hello, boys!" she said enthusiastically, but she quickly saw something was wrong. "What happened?" She watched us slump listlessly into the room. I looked up at her, wanting to tell her how toys had been dropped for us with the express purpose of killing. Instead, I threw myself into her arms and held on tight, startled by the sound of my own sobs. She stroked my hair and held me until I was done. Misha and Alik didn't say a word.

Leaning back so she could see my face, she said, "I've got some soup on the stove. Let me get you boys some lunch." The three of us sat down, still stunned, saying nothing until we'd eaten. Very gently, Auntie said, "Do you want to tell me about it?"

It poured out then, each of us talking over the other, not just about the toys and the pen but about how hard it was to adjust to our new lives. "I'm even ready to go back to school," I said, which got an understanding laugh from Misha and Alik.

Auntie listened, nodded, and didn't interrupt. Finally she said, "How we behave during this terrible time counts just as much as winning."

"What do you mean?" I asked, not absolutely certain what she was getting at.

"I mean, if we lose our humanity during the fight, then we have lost everything."

Misha looked confused. "Lose our . . . what?"

"I think I understand," Alik offered. "You're saying we might die, but that before we die —"

"Be quiet," Misha said. "I am *not* dying."

"That if we *were* to die," Alik continued, "how we acted toward one another is as important as if we stayed alive."

"Yes," Auntie answered quietly.

"What does it matter how you acted if you're dead?" Misha challenged her.   ·

"Just remember my words," she said, getting up and beginning to clear the table. "Things may get very hard very fast."

★ ★ ★

Truer words were never spoken. The first deaths by starvation began by the end of September. People were shot without trial for stealing food and ration cards from others. Food became the only thing that mattered, just as Auntie had predicted. By late October there were four inches of snow on the ground. Fuel was scarce; people were found frozen to death in their unheated apartments. Others anguished about how they would survive if the siege didn't end soon.

That's how desperate life became, and that's how fast it happened. In the month of October, each citizen was given five and three quarters of a pound of food, mostly bread, to last them for *one month*. That equals almost three pieces of bread for the entire day. Nothing more. No fat, no vegetables, no meat.

The desperation to escape our surrounded, strangled, starving city created a kind of madness. For me, what happened next, in November, was almost worse.

CHAPTER 6

I STARED AT MY MOTHER'S FACE, GAUNT FROM THE LITTLE
BIT OF FOOD SHE ATE EACH DAY, HER HIGH CHEEKBONES
LIKE CHISELED ROCK. TO ME SHE WAS STILL SO BEAUTIFUL,
although in her eyes I saw weariness beyond words.

My mother, Auntie, and I sat quietly at the table one evening
in early November. By the light of two candles we ate thin bean
soup prepared by Auntie. There was still electricity in our apartment, but only sometimes, and we never knew when it would
arrive or when it would be shut off.

It had been a blessing that Auntie Vera had come to live with
us. My mother worried less about me, and Auntie stood in the
ever-growing food lines for our meager supply of bread. My
mother didn't know that a large portion of the food that kept us
alive came from Auntie's hoard upstairs, or that she sometimes
bought extras for us on the black market at exorbitant prices with
the rubles she had stashed around her apartment. Auntie and I had
decided long ago that my mother didn't need any more worries
on her shoulders. Part of our job, as we saw it, was to keep her as
healthy and calm as possible under our terrible circumstances.

"Ivan," my mother said softly, after she finished her soup, "I
want to talk to you about something very serious."

I felt an awful tightness in my chest. "Yes?"

"You know that many — most — of the factories in Leningrad
were moved to the Ural Mountains before the bombing started."

I nodded, trying unsuccessfully to jump two steps ahead and
see what she was leading up to.

"But the Kirov, well, we're so big, we make so many different things . . . only a few units were sent east. Much of our factory remained here."

Why was she telling me things I'd known for months?

"There's been some talk. . . ." She stopped, almost as if she didn't have the energy to continue. "Some talk of moving my section to the Urals as soon as it can be arranged."

I gasped as if someone had snuck up behind me and grabbed my shoulders. "What?"

She nodded. "I have no choice in the matter. If the factory goes, I must go with it. We're under martial law, Ivan. I can't leave my job without authorization, and no one's going to give that to me. And besides, who would take my place? Every available person is already working eleven hours a day."

I glanced around our cold, candlelit apartment. It might have been meager, but I loved it with all my heart. "But I don't want to go. This is our home."

My mother stared down at the table for a long time. Then, with what looked like great effort, she looked at me and said, "Parents with children have been told to" — and here her voice almost cracked — "make arrangements."

"Arrangements?" I repeated, confused. Then I saw the look on my mother's face and I started to understand what she was saying. Anger and fear surged into my veins. "I am to be punished because I'm a child?"

"Do you think I like it?" she said in a voice so quiet, I could tell she was making a huge effort to control her emotions. "You will be thirteen soon, Ivan; you're not a child. The management has made it clear there will be no exceptions."

I practically jumped to my feet. "I don't care what they say. I'm going with you!"

She shook her head. "I will be living in a dormitory on the factory site. They haven't even finished building it yet. It's impossible."

"Nothing's impossible. Isn't that what you've always told me?" Her clear blue eyes held mine, glossing over with tears.

"I want you to go stay with your uncle Boris."

I began walking back and forth, feeling like a caged animal. "No! I won't go anywhere without you. And Uncle Boris is . . . I've only met him twice. I barely know him. I don't want to live with him."

My mother sighed and gazed at Auntie as if for help. She opened her mouth to speak again, but I interrupted her. "Besides, Leningrad is surrounded. No one can get in or out." I sat back down, as if that were the end of it, staring at her defiantly.

"It's November. The authorities think that Lake Ladoga will be frozen in another week or so. Evacuations can begin across the lake."

I glared at her now as if she were my bitterest enemy. "The lake?" I repeated. "You want me to go across water that *might* be frozen and *hope* I don't drown?" I said the last word in full voice. My mother leaned on the table with her left elbow, covering her forehead with her hand. I was on my feet again, moving closer to her, angry, my hurt making me feel mean. "My father was a sailor and drowned, in case you don't remember."

"I know, Ivan. I remember quite well." It was a reprimand, but the thought that she might leave me made me so upset that the worst in me surfaced.

"And *even if* I don't die, what then? Uncle Boris won't know I will be coming because there's no mail service here. What if I arrive at his cabin and he's gone? I'll starve to death. I'll die then! And it will be your fault."

I wanted to hurt her for the first time in my life. I wanted her to feel the pain I was feeling. If the tears that fell and the silent sobs that shook her narrow shoulders were any indication, I was succeeding.

Auntie stood up. "Ivan, may I see you in the other room, please? I want to speak to you privately." With one last angry look at my mother, I followed her to the room where she and my mother slept. It was almost dark, lit only by the candle Auntie brought from the table with her. She set it down on the small table by the head of the bed and turned to me.

The look on her face was ferocious; she grabbed me by the shoulders. "Listen to me. You've said enough to upset your mother tonight." Her face was close to mine, but I looked away. "Look at me," she commanded. I reluctantly lifted my eyes to look into hers. "Haven't you been paying attention? What do you see when you leave the apartment?"

"What do you mean?" I said, not yet ready to give up what I thought was righteous anger.

"You know exactly what I mean. How many people have you seen in the streets, frozen in the snow where they fell, too weak to go on? Do you know how many sleds I saw yesterday? Seven. *Seven* sleds being dragged down the street, each one of them carrying a corpse wrapped in a sheet. Two of them children."

I looked away again, but this time because I was picturing

the horrors that were now commonplace. The daily bombing, the barely breathing wraithlike people who stood for hours in lines in the snow, waiting to be given their pitiful portion of bread. And to call it *bread* was an insult. It was made of sawdust and glues, maybe a whiff of grain, and a dash of the oil used to lubricate machines. Any one of those starving people who'd fallen in the snow awaiting their death could have been my mother or me if we hadn't had Auntie's help.

"What do you want me to do?" I asked, my anger replaced quickly by shame and a desire to be strong.

Auntie finally let go of my shoulders. "I want you to apologize to your mother. Then I want you to prepare yourself to cross the ice road, and for the possibility of not seeing your mother until the war is over."

A strangled cry escaped me. Auntie drew me to her. "I'm sorry to be so honest, Ivan. It's just . . ." She pushed me far enough away so that I could look at her. "You have to remember what I told you the night I showed you the gun." I nodded. "Your survival will depend on accepting the reality of your circumstances and making your decisions accordingly. If you indulge your wishes and your emotions, you will perish."

"I remember," I said.

"Your mother has to go, and so do you. You must prepare yourself."

"I know. I'll go apologize to her now," I told her, wiping my eyes, gathering my courage.

I emerged from the room to see my mother washing dishes at the sink, leaning against it as if the task were almost too great.

Putting my arms around her waist, I hugged her tightly. "I'm so sorry, Mama. I'll do whatever you want me to do." We hugged for a long time.

"Even if it means going to your uncle Boris's cabin?"

I nodded and managed to laugh a little.

"Do you remember my old nickname for you?"

"Of course. Ivan the Not-So-Terrible. It still suits me, don't you think?" I looked up into her smiling face, unable to imagine how life would be without her. I understood clearly for the first time in my life that I had only so many days, hours, and minutes to be with my mother. Every one of them had to count. If she had already lost my father to the sea and was willing to send her son over the water to protect him, then I had to be as strong as she was. "Mama, what about Auntie? What will she do?" We both glanced at Auntie, who stood watching us.

"I'm going with you, Ivan," she announced, much to my surprise. "At least as far as Vilnov, where my sister-in-law lives. From there you must travel alone to your uncle Boris's house." I wasn't sure if that was better or worse. Better because we would be together; worse because if the ice road didn't hold, we might both die. "In the next few days we'll have to decide what to take with us and what to leave behind."

"Yes, Auntie," I said. *What to leave behind*, I thought as her last words echoed in my ears. *I'm leaving everything and everyone behind! Alik, Misha, Olga, Oskar — even Georgi and Leonid.* "Alik and Misha . . ." I murmured, unable to imagine life without my best friends in the apartment next door, available at a moment's notice for play and adventure. Suddenly, I felt so tired, I could hardly stand. This happened to me several times a day now, since the last cut in our rations. This time it felt worse, as if the thought of leaving my friends would sap the last of my strength.

"Ivan," my mother said, "why don't you play a tune for us before we go to bed?"

I glanced at the box under the bed that held my concertina. "I haven't felt much like playing since . . . since the bombing started."

"I understand," my mother said, turning back to dry the few dishes on our counter.

"But," I said, trying to muster my energy and enthusiasm, "for you I would gladly play till dawn." My mother smiled like she used to smile: fully, happily. If playing my concertina for her would allow me to see her happy, then I would play until I could play no more. And that's just what I did.

CHAPTER 7

TWO DAYS LATER I WENT UPSTAIRS WITH AUNTIE TO HELP HER PACK FOR OUR TRIP ACROSS THE FROZEN LAKE. "WHERE ARE YOUR TABLE AND CHAIRS?" I ASKED, STARTLED BY THE empty space in her kitchen.

"We used them for fuel, Ivan," she said, locking the front door of her apartment behind us.

"You mean . . ." Auntie had been doing all the cooking for us on the wood-burning stove. I hadn't stopped to notice where the wood came from. It hit me that even with the war and rationing, I still took a lot of things for granted. "Thank you," I murmured. "I don't know how we would have gotten along without you."

She smiled. "And don't worry. I remembered to take the money out of the table legs before I burned them."

"Any surprises for me today?" I called as Auntie disappeared into the tiny hallway between the bedroom and the living area.

"Maybe a few," she called from the bedroom. I followed her when I heard the scraping sound of something being dragged across the floor. Auntie was pulling a chair from the bedroom toward the hall.

"Let me," I said, taking over for her. "Where do you want it?"

"In front of the closet in the hall." I carried it the few feet that separated us from the closet and opened the door. "Can you reach the basket on the top shelf?"

"Of course." I stepped up onto the chair and carefully removed a covered basket the size of a suitcase. It was surprisingly light. "Where do you want it?"

"Hand it to me." Auntie took it and carried it into the living room.

"What are you looking for?" I asked, joining her.

"Some things that belonged to my husband."

I studied Auntie Vera's face to find the young woman underneath the ancient one I knew, trying to picture her with a husband, a man who had died long, long ago. I peered over her shoulder into the deep basket. "Valenki!" I exclaimed as she held up a pair of the dark gray felt boots.

"They were Arseny's." She gazed at them with a half smile. "Barely worn. Here." She held them out to me.

"What do you want me to do with them?"

"Keep them, of course."

As she continued emptying out the basket, I said, "I can't accept them, Auntie. It's too big a present."

"Nonsense. A pair of perfectly good boots is going to waste. You'll need them when we cross Lake Ladoga. And especially when you go up to your uncle's place. They might be a little big for you. Try them on."

Valenki were traditional Russian boots made out of felt, worn mostly by country people. They kept your feet warm in even the coldest temperatures. They weren't waterproof so you had to wear galoshes over them, but valenki were so sturdy and invaluable that people were known to pass them down from one generation to the next. All the Soviet soldiers were issued valenki with their winter gear or their feet wouldn't have lasted through one of our winters. Many hoped that the lack of valenki alone would defeat the Germans once they experienced the severity of our winter.

I'd never owned a pair because we lived in the city. I only went outside in the winter to play with Alik and Misha or run errands for my mother. If my feet got cold, I would soon be indoors again, drying off in front of the stove. I slipped my shoes off and cautiously put first one then the other foot into the valenki. They came almost up to my knees.

Auntie nodded. "A little big, perhaps. Wear them with a few pairs of heavy socks until you grow into them." I walked around the room to get a feel for them. Arseny had worn them enough that they weren't stiff and hard as I'd heard they were when they were new.

Looking up at Auntie with a smile, I said, "With these I think our journey won't be as hard."

She threw me a pair of black rubber galoshes. "Put these on over them when you use them outside."

I caught one in each hand and slipped them easily over what were quickly feeling like *my* valenki. "Thank you, Auntie. But are you sure?"

"Of course I'm sure. Take good care of them. You'll be with your uncle Boris soon, and then a new chapter of your life will be opening for you."

For the first time I let myself feel a little curious about what it would be like to live in the country, even if it was with my uncle Boris. If only I weren't being separated from my mother, I might actually feel excited about it.

"I thought it was in here," Auntie murmured as she emptied the last of the contents onto the sofa.

"What?"

"The knife."

"What knife?"

"Oh . . . yes!" she said brightly, and disappeared into her bedroom. She reappeared with a shoe box, its lid gone, stuffed with an old pair of weathered-looking men's work boots. She took them out of the box, set them aside, and pulled back a piece of fabric to reveal two slender knives with plain wooden handles, sheathed in brown leather. She held one out to me handle first; I stared at it and then at her. "Take it!" The smooth, wood-covered handle slipped easily into my hand and fit well.

"It's Finnish," she said, pulling out the other, holding it, turning it over. "This one's a little smaller; I'll keep it. You take that one."

"For what?"

"Everything!" she said, looking surprised at my question. "Protection, cutting branches for fire, gutting fish. You can't go to the country, especially on your own, without one of these." Auntie Vera sometimes felt to me like she was a magician pulling endless rabbits out of her hat.

"So," I said, glancing down at my new boots, "you think we'll be crossing Ladoga soon?"

She looked at me, held my gaze, and said, "Yes. If we don't, it's more likely than not that we will die." I knew she was right; the words hardly surprised me. There wasn't a moment I wasn't hungry. It was rumored that thousands of people were starving to death every day. Hardly any of my friends wanted to sled or play like we used to — everyone was too weak from hunger. We were all using our energy just to stay alive.

"It's my turn to get our rations today," I said. "I should go." It was the last thing I wanted to do, waste hours in a long line in the cold afternoon air. The forecast was for snow by nightfall. At least I had new boots to keep my feet warm. I left Auntie's apartment feeling lucky and proud of my new valenki, even if I did walk a little clumsily because they were too big for me.

After stopping in our apartment to get our ration cards, I went next door to see if Alik and Misha would go with me. They still didn't lock their door in spite of Auntie's warnings. I found them lying on their unmade bed in their living room, playing chess. "Do you want to see me checkmate Misha?" Alik asked, glancing up at me. "He hasn't a clue it's coming."

"I do, too!" Misha protested. "And I'm sick of chess anyway." He began putting the pieces back in their box without waiting for Alik's consent.

"I have to go get bread today. Do you want to go with me?" I asked before the brothers could break into a squabble about their game. They agreed, and soon we were out walking as light snow flurries floated down around us.

Three blocks later we turned the corner and saw a line that stretched an entire block from the storefront where we received our ration of bread. We took our place at the end of it. Not two minutes had gone by when we heard a scream from somewhere near the front of the store. We ran toward it.

Two teenage boys, one with a knife in his hand, were trying to steal the purse of a woman who looked like she was Auntie's age. Of course it contained her ration card. She'd laced her hands together, her purse in the crook of her arm, and kept turning away from the boy who was trying to take it from her. The boy with the knife in his hand yelled repeatedly to the rest of us, "Don't try to help!" as he swung his weapon in a wide arc.

And no one tried to help, including us, because it was too dangerous. We all stared in horror as the unarmed boy became more and more frustrated that he'd been unable to wrestle the purse from the tiny old woman. He kept threatening to do terrible things to her if she didn't let go. Finally, three women from inside the bread store rushed out, each one carrying some sort of wooden stick — broom handles, maybe — and began to hit the boy assaulting the old woman.

The boy with the knife ran away as soon as they began to hit his friend. The other boy soon followed after receiving a few good blows from the brave women of the bread shop. As they brought the frightened old woman into the store, one of them turned to address the crowd who'd been watching the drama unfold.

"We are so sorry," she said. "We have to close the shop until we have spoken to the authorities." She quickly closed the door. No one said a word; no one moved. I stared at the long line of people, almost all women, and a few children our age, and realized even more deeply that hunger now governed everything. No one had the strength to fight the thieving boys or to argue with the women who closed the shop. Our bread rations meant another day of survival, and none of us could afford to risk losing it.

CHAPTER 8

THROUGH HER CONNECTIONS AT THE KIROV FACTORY, MY MOTHER HAD SECURED A PLACE FOR ME AND AUNTIE ON THE FIRST CONVOY OF TRUCKS THAT WOULD CROSS THE ICE road over Lake Ladoga. We would leave at five A.M. We planned a special farewell dinner for our last night together and invited Alik, Misha, and their mother to join us. Soup and bread was what we ate at every meal, but on this night Auntie surprised us with special additions: three apples and a small bottle of vodka.

"I went to the Haymarket," she said, referring to the hub of Leningrad's black market, "and traded a ruby ring that belonged to my grandmother for all of it." She said it proudly, as my mother smoothed out the red tablecloth we used on special occasions and laid matching napkins next to our plates.

"A ruby ring!" I exclaimed. "But, Auntie —"

She waved her hand at my protest. "You can't eat gold or rubies."

Our table looked festive. Auntie had brought down some of her animal figurines from her apartment. A bird, a bear, and a reindeer, all carved from wood, made our centerpiece. I hadn't seen a flower since September, but my clever mother cut some bare tree branches and arranged them artfully in a narrow vase.

"Mama, I have a surprise for you," I said, my empty stomach growling at the thought of our special dinner.

"You do?" She turned to smile at me. It was as if time stopped, and I captured the moment like I was a camera. My mother smiling, looking so happy.

"I've picked out some of your favorite songs, and Alik and I are going to play them for you after dinner. Misha says he's going to dance!" She put down the spoon she was using to stir the soup, walked over to me, and gave me a hug so big, it almost crushed me. When she pulled away I could see there were tears in her eyes.

"My Ivan," she said, wiping away a tear.

"The Not-So-Terrible," I added.

Auntie held up a plate of thinly sliced apples. "What do you think?"

"They look delicious," I said.

"The soup is hot," my mother said, reaching into a drawer for a ladle. "Run next door and tell everyone dinner is ready."

They were waiting for me. Mrs. Bukova wore a dark, loose dress for the occasion, and the hairnet that held her hair flat against her head when she worked was gone. Misha and Alik looked like she'd made them scrub their faces and put on clean shirts. I led them to our open door, where Mrs. Bukova hesitated before entering when she saw our welcoming table.

"It's been a long time since I've seen something so beautiful," she said, motioning toward the table with its red cloth and decorations. "Not to mention apples!"

"It's a special night," I said, "one we all want to remember."

Misha pulled his chair back from the table so enthusiastically that it fell backward onto the wooden floor. We laughed at the silliness of it, out of the joy I was sure we all felt being together.

When we were seated, my mother picked up the small bottle of vodka and poured some into each of the adults' glasses; we boys had water. She raised her glass in a toast. "To friendship, to new beginnings, and to safe journeys!" We clinked our glasses together, and for the next hour or so we ate, and talked, and laughed, and savored our special dinner. Even when we exchanged details of hardships, our shared experiences seemed to give us strength.

"This has been the happiest evening I've had for many months," Mrs. Bukova said. "You know . . ." She paused and looked down. "I wanted to do something special for you. Write a poem, or . . . I don't know. Something that would tell you how much I will miss you all." She pushed her chair back, stood up, and reached into the pocket of her dress. Pulling out a small square of paper and unfolding it, she said, "I found out I can't write poems — although I tried for an hour!" We laughed and watched her expectantly. "However" — she cleared her throat — "I was able to write a letter. It's called Good-bye to Dear Friends." She covered her mouth with her left hand. "I promise I won't cry." This was a side of my friends' no-nonsense mother I'd never seen.

"It's all right," my mother assured her.

"Read it to us!" Auntie exclaimed. Misha and Alik looked as excited as the rest of us to hear it.

Mrs. Bukova glanced around the table at us, shook her head as if to clear it, and began. "To Dearest Elena, Vera, and Ivan: When I think of all the years we have known one another, I can hardly believe it. So many memories we have shared. Elena, how can I thank you for all the times you have watched one of my boys when the other one was sick? Remember when Alik had the chicken pox? Misha lived at your house for at least two weeks. I think even Ivan was ready for him to go home."

We all laughed. And it was true. By the end, I had been a little tired of having Misha around all the time.

She continued. "Such a good friend you have been in every way. I will miss having you right next door."

Mrs. Bukova put her hand on her chest and breathed deeply. "Vera. You have made a huge impact on my life. Do you remember when you lent me *The Brothers Karamazov* and I lied to you and told you I read it?"

"Oh, yes. I remember," Auntie answered with a laugh.

"You guessed my secret. I couldn't read very well. With such patience you helped me until I could read just as well as the next person. Thank you for changing my life." She rubbed her eyes quickly with her free hand because tears were forming. I couldn't stop staring at this rough, tenderhearted person.

"Ivan." She caught my eye and smiled. "Sometimes I feel like you are my third son. And like my sons, you are part angel and part devil! Alik and Misha couldn't have a better friend. Even when all I want is for you boys to be quiet and play nicely — I will dearly miss the sounds of laughter, and fighting, and your duets with Alik."

"Thank you," I murmured, almost wishing she'd finish so I wouldn't end up crying, too. Alik, who was sitting next to me, reached out and put his hand on my shoulder, leaving it there as she continued.

"And so . . ." She stopped as her voice quivered with emotion. "I say good-bye to you, my dear friends. I have no doubt we will meet again. Alik and Misha and I will guard your empty apartments like they were our own until the day you return." She could hold back her tears no longer and held the paper up to her face, covering it, as if to hide her sadness. My mother and Auntie hugged her and told her how touched they were by her words.

"The evening's not over," I said, to keep our night from ending on a sad note. "We have a surprise for you." Alik ran to get his concertina and the tambourine from next door as I unpacked my concertina and warmed up a little.

"Music," Mrs. Bukova murmured, clasping her hands together. "It's so late when I get home, I rarely get to hear the boys play."

On my last night with my mother and my friends — for who knows how long — we played all of our mothers' favorite songs and every other tune we could remember. Most of them were well known or traditional, and the six of us sang those together, often repeating verses just to relish the feeling of the song on our lips. Alik and I roamed around the room as we played, serenading Auntie and our mothers. Misha attempted the traditional Russian dance that demands that you squat down and then kick your legs out while squatting. He managed at least four kicks before he fell back onto the floor. That didn't stop him from taking a bow, or stop us from applauding him.

The hours slipped away, and finally Mrs. Bukova said, "We really must say good night. It's an early morning for us all."

Looking around our apartment at my family and friends, I said something I think we all felt in our hearts. "I wish I could make this night last forever." It was the closest I came to crying. Alik and Misha had made jokes earlier about coming with me to Uncle Boris's cabin. But I knew they would never leave their mother unless they were forced to. I wouldn't be leaving if I had a choice.

When we'd said our last good-byes and I closed the door behind them, I felt a deep sorrow and sense of loss. My mother must have seen it because a few minutes later she handed me an unwrapped box.

"It's a going-away present."

I opened it slowly; it took me a minute to realize what it was. "This is Papa's shaving kit."

She nodded and smiled. "I know you may not need it just yet, but you will soon. Whenever you use it, think of me."

"I will think of you, and of Papa, every day . . . many times. Every single day." We hugged each other for a long, long time before we went to sleep under the same roof for the last time.

CHAPTER 9

THE NEXT MORNING I PUT ON ALMOST ALL THE CLOTHES I
OWNED, NOT JUST BECAUSE I'D HEARD THE TEMPERATURES
COULD BE TWENTY DEGREES BELOW ZERO ON LAKE LADOGA
when the wind blew hard, but because I'd have less to carry. I
wore the valenki and galoshes and tucked the Finnish knife neatly
into the side of them.

Auntie gave my astonished mother most of the canned food
and half of the rubles she had left. "Where did you get all of
this?" she cried.

"I've saved like this since the revolution!" Auntie answered.
"You'll see. When this war is over, you'll always live like another one
could be just around the corner. I packed food and money for our
trip, too. You never know when a can of beans might save your life!"

I looked around our apartment for the last time as my mother
put out the candles. I knew its every secret, its every crack and
corner, the way the light came in thick and golden on a fall afternoon, the way twilight lingered forever in June. I said good-bye to
it, with a promise that I would return.

Auntie and I were allowed one piece of baggage each. Hers
was a battered leather suitcase; mine was a dark canvas duffel bag
that contained little more than the clothes I wasn't already wearing, my concertina, some of the remaining canned food, and my
father's shaving kit. I picked them both up and waited in the hall
with Auntie as my mother locked the door. We walked down the
stairs and into the street to wait at the curb. My mother and I
stood holding hands, saying good-bye without saying a word. A

truck from the Kirov factory arrived almost immediately to take us to the lake, for which I was grateful. If our good-bye had gone on even a minute longer, I would never have had the strength to leave her.

The driver got out and opened a side door to the back of the enclosed truck, a high, narrow space with wooden benches on both sides. He helped Auntie climb inside. I squeezed my mother's hand and turned to her. Tears were streaming down her face.

"Be good, Ivan," she whispered. "Be strong." I nodded. "I love you." I threw my arms around her, not sure I would ever let go.

I reached up and kissed her on her left cheek, and then her right. With one last look into her tear-filled eyes, I turned and climbed into the back of the truck. The driver closed the heavy door and pulled away from the curb. Auntie reached out and covered my hand with hers.

Suddenly I panicked and rushed to the double back doors of the van. Peering out the small square windows, I could just barely see my mother in the darkness waving good-bye to us. I waved back, crying, "Good-bye, good-bye! I'll come back!" as if she could hear me. We turned a corner and she disappeared. I'd heard the expression *broken heart* all my life, but until then I'd never felt it.

As I sat back down next to Auntie, she said, "That's the worst part."

"Yes," I said, as though I agreed, but I wasn't sure how it could get any better while I was away from my mother.

★ ★ ★

We picked up a dozen more people, all women and children, each adult struggling with the one overstuffed bag they were allowed, until there was standing room only. The younger children, aged from about three to seven years old, were remarkably quiet. Maybe they all sensed the seriousness of the journey we were undertaking.

My mother had explained to me that first we would be taken to the Finland Railway Station. Then a train or truck would deliver us to a port on the western shores of Ladoga, probably Osinovets, about twenty-five miles away. From there we would begin our crossing of Lake Ladoga.

When we arrived at the Finland Station, it was chaos. It was only through the toughness of our Kirov driver that after two hours we were successfully loaded into one of the trucks that would actually drive over the ice road. All of the women and children from the Kirov transport remained with us. Although we exchanged friendly looks and a few courtesies, no one conversed.

Two problems became obvious immediately. One was that the ice road trucks were open on the sides with a canvas covering on top. We were expected to stand during the journey, exposed to the wind, snow, and cold. The second problem was our driver. With all the able-bodied men at the front, the army had to accept whomever was available to help them, I suppose, and so we put our lives in the hands of a driver named Yanik.

He looked like he was in his seventies. He smoked one after another of the cigarettes people made themselves of dried leaves wrapped in old newspapers. What was left of his front teeth pointed outward, like threatening yellow and brown projectiles. His attitude matched his look: sullen, angry, domineering. When he wasn't spitting brownish liquid, he was wheezing.

"Listen to me," he snapped as we heaved our baggage into the back of the open truck and began to climb in ourselves. "You hold on tight. If anything bounces out — including one of you — it's your bad luck. We're not going back to get you." We stole furtive glances at one another, shock registering on our faces. He spit on the ground.

"Once you're in the truck, there's no eating, drinking, or peeing." I noticed some of the women wince at his crudeness. "We drive from here to Osinovets; that's twenty-five miles. Then over the lake to Kobona. That's about twenty miles. If the Germans shoot at us, we keep going. If they hit somebody, we keep going. Understood?" Murmured sounds of assent came from his captive passengers. "Grab something to hold on to. We're leaving." He turned and got in the cab.

To my surprise and horror, the engine whined, it churned, but it didn't start. Yanik tried again until the rhythm of the engine produced a sound like that of a rickety freight train rolling by. On the third attempt there was only a groan, then silence. I could see Yanik through the window at the back of the cab. He hung his head, but his hand was still on the key. After waiting for what seemed like minutes, he turned the key again, and the truck started as easily as if it had rolled off the production line that morning.

A collective sigh from his passengers blew out into the cold morning air as the truck lurched forward. Several of us were thrown off balance and against the low wooden sides of the truck. It was easy to see how someone could fall out if we hit a bump. One mother took off her scarf, tied it to her child's belt, and then to one of the slatted wooden boards that made up the side of the truck; some of the other women saw her good sense and did the same.

We traveled along at a good pace and were quickly out in the countryside. Its expansiveness was almost overwhelming. The long empty stretches of land between farmhouses made it seem vulnerable rather than private. Unconsciously, I felt for the knife in my valenki. Auntie noticed.

"Ivan, I want to get something out of my suitcase."

I backed up a little so that she would have enough room to open it. With fourteen of us in the back, there was barely any extra space. She knelt on the rough wooden floor, clicked the metal findings of her suitcase open, and lifted the lid.

"What are you looking for?" I asked.

After a few seconds she held up a thick pile of red cloth napkins. "These!"

"Auntie, aren't those the ones that go with my mother's tablecloth? The one we used last night?"

"The very ones." She took them out, closed her suitcase, and stood up. Counting out three, she handed them to me. "Here. Put them in your pockets."

I was confused. Why would she take napkins of all things when she had only one suitcase for all of her valuables? "Why?"

"It stands out well against the snow." She saw my confusion and said, "Look around you, Ivan. Snow everywhere. Color can save your life. If you tie one of these on your head, or around your wrist, or simply wave it, you'll be noticed."

Leaning closer to her, I whispered, "What are you saying?"

"I'm saying that this lesson makes sense to you now that we're here, doesn't it, where you can see the white and red with your own eyes?" I nodded. "We've got forty-five miles to go before we reach the eastern shore of Ladoga, and twenty or more after that to arrive at my sister-in-law's house. Just put them in your pockets. For an emergency." I watched as she stuffed three of the large red napkins in her coat pockets, and then I did the same. I felt even bulkier, but was pleased to have learned my first survival trick. Looking out over the empty, flat land, I wondered what other lessons awaited me.

The sky was gray and leaden, and I guessed we'd have snow in the next few hours. I looked around at the women and children who were already showing signs of weariness, and must have been hungry and thirsty. Suddenly, the truck lurched to the left and began to spin in a circle. I lost my balance and nearly fell; Auntie tumbled against me. Children started crying; the women were distressed and tried to comfort them. Several fell to the floor.

The truck spun around three times before it came to a stop. Auntie knocked hard on the window of the cab. "What happened?" she shouted. Yanik's reply was inaudible, but we could see him searching the floor for something. When he sat back up, he had one of his home-rolled cigarettes in his hand; he pulled out a match case and lit it.

Auntie turned toward me, looking furious. Very quietly she said, "That idiot dropped his cigarette. That's why we went into a spin." She closed her eyes as if willing herself to remain calm. "Don't tell anyone."

"What if he does something like that on Ladoga?" I whispered in her ear.

"We're on our journey now, Ivan. The best we can do is pay attention to everything and be ready if there's trouble."

"Trouble?" I felt my heart tremble. "Like what?"

"Like nothing," she said sternly. "Come on now, turn around and keep an eye on Yanik."

Apparently he didn't drop anything else, because we arrived in Osinovets without another mishap. Unlike the Finland Station, which was filled with people and noise and surrounded by vehicles, it was a silent world we entered. After being stopped by two sentries near the lake's shore, we drove slowly to an area where five other trucks awaited, all filled with women and children just like ours. Someone in uniform directed us to get in line behind the fifth truck.

A few minutes later, as we waited in the idling truck, the engine died. I closed my eyes and felt the breath go out of me. To my surprise, it started back up on the first try. A man in uniform knocked on Yanik's window; we could easily hear his instructions. "Don't turn off your engine. Follow fifteen feet behind the last truck. No farther. There won't be anyone behind you. Good luck."

I looked around us, thinking there had to be more, but his words were our only instruction and guide. Lake Ladoga lay before us, a snow-covered expanse looking very much like the land adjacent to it, the largest lake in all of Europe. Somehow I'd thought the army would be here to take charge, which was just silly given that all the men were needed in battle.

"Take my hand," Auntie said. "Look in the direction we're going." I nodded, turned to face forward, and slipped my left hand into her right hand.

This was it. We were crossing the ice road. There was no turning back.

CHAPTER 10

As we got closer to the lake, I saw that a crude sort of dirt ramp had been built leading from the ground to the ice. The lead truck pulled forward slowly; I held my breath as it rolled onto the frozen surface. The five trucks behind him, including us at the rear, followed. Remarkably, snow had been removed from the lake, defining a narrow road just about wide enough for two trucks.

"Why don't they leave the snow on it?" I asked, with a sudden feeling of nervousness in my stomach. "Wouldn't that keep it colder? Wouldn't we be less likely to fall through the ice?"

"No, Ivan. It's the opposite. Snow warms things because it insulates them. Think of a snow cave or an igloo. Without the snow on top of it, the water is able to freeze more quickly and more deeply."

Five minutes passed, then ten, as we traveled slowly, steadily in our little convoy. If I read the speedometer through the glass correctly, we were going about fifteen miles an hour. "Did Yanik say it was twenty miles across the lake?" I asked.

"Yes." Auntie kept her eyes straight ahead. She reminded me of a carved figure on the bow of a ship.

"If we keep going at this pace, it won't take more than an hour and a half before we're there!"

That thought kept me content until I heard the familiar, heart-piercing drone of an airplane about thirty minutes later. The sound ripped through our little group like an evil wind, and guttural cries of fear erupted from some of the women, while others grabbed their children and covered them with their own bodies.

"What do we do?" I cried, scanning the skies.

"Look," Auntie answered, squinting and staring into the distance, "it's just one." She was right, and it was flying low. The convoy picked up speed; we were going twice as fast in seconds. It felt bumpy, as if there were suddenly fist-size rocks under the wheels. "This is bad," she whispered. "If the trucks go too fast, it creates waves under the ice. It makes it more likely to crack."

"What does it matter?" I cried. "The bombs will kill us first!"

"Listen to me. Kneel down, then bend over and cover your head with your duffel bag. Do it now!"

I dropped to my knees, even as the plane zoomed closer. The temptation to watch it was almost overwhelming. I grabbed my duffel bag and pulled it across my head and neck. The muffled sounds of Auntie's voice broke through as she yelled for the others to do as she'd instructed me. The rough wooden floor of the truck slapped against my cold face hard, and I tried to keep a few inches away from it. Children were screaming and crying, mothers yelled for them to get down, telling them everything was going to be all right. The malevolent presence of the plane felt like it hovered just above us.

I waited for the bombs to hit, wondering what they would sound like as they smashed into the ice. Or would they rip right through it and sink to the bottom?

The explosions never came.

I pushed the duffel bag away and got up on my knees. The plane was so far past us, I could hardly see it. I stood up. All six trucks were still moving. "We're safe!" I shouted. "Auntie, look —

we're safe!" She poked her head out from under her little suitcase. Everyone sat up in slow motion, with fear, relief, and disbelief on their faces.

But we were no longer a calm, coordinated convoy. None of the drivers slowed back down. They fought hard and recklessly for the lead position. After ten or fifteen minutes of weaving and bobbing along the narrow road, as Yanik tried repeatedly and unsuccessfully to pass the truck in front of us, our truck suddenly slowed down and stopped.

"What's happening? Why are we stopping?" We all asked these questions out loud at the same time. Yanik got out of the cab but left the engine running.

I pushed my way over to his side of the truck and yelled, "Where are you going?"

He turned his craggy face to see who was talking to him. "I've got to pee," he announced.

"No, no, come back!" I cried as he lumbered off.

"Go get him. Make him come back," Auntie told me. I clambered over the side of the truck and dropped to the ground.

"Yanik!" I called, running toward him through the snow. His back was to me, his shoulders hunched. "Please come back. The engine could freeze up. We'd all die out here."

He threw me a scornful look as he turned away and urinated in the snow as if I wasn't there. "You call this cold?" he said with a laugh as he buttoned up his pants. "It's not even snowing."

"But it looks like it will soon. It could cover the road and we'd be lost out here forever. We could die."

"One more cigarette," he announced.

"Let's walk toward the truck while you smoke it."

"Get away from me, little wasp," he said with a wave of his hand. "Go back to the women and children where you belong."

I glanced back at the truck where everyone was watching us, then noticed something behind them; it was snowing up ahead.

"Yanik, look over there." I pointed to a place I guessed was about a half mile from us. "It's starting to snow."

He looked from side to side. "Where?"

"There." I continued to point into the distance.

"I can't see it."

"You can't . . ." I stared at him in disbelief, shaking my head.

Suddenly, a brief expression of worry passed over his face. "Let's go." He trudged past me in the snow. I ran toward the truck without another word. We were no more than ten feet from the idling truck when the engine suddenly died.

Yanik rushed into the cab and cranked the engine. It sounded like it had the first time it had died when we were still on the shore of the lake. Unfortunately, this time it didn't start on the first try . . . or the seventh, or the tenth, or the twentieth.

"Start!" Yanik yelled as he pumped the accelerator and tried the key once more. It gave one last wheeze and moan. He stared straight ahead and then turned to look through the back window. We locked eyes, and I knew then there was no hope of the truck starting again.

I leaned in close to Auntie and said, "What are we going to do?"

"I was doing some thinking while you were talking to Yanik. I think we went seven or eight miles before the bomber flew by. After the trucks sped up, I'm guessing we covered another seven or eight miles. The distance across the lake is twenty miles. That means —"

"We're about six miles from the shore," I said, interrupting her as the weight of the facts fell on me. What do we do?" As if by agreement, we both turned to look at our truckload of fellow passengers. Every single mother was watching us, their faces full of fear.

"We can walk six miles, but we have to leave immediately. It's snowing up ahead. It could cover the road, and we'd freeze to death out here."

"What about everyone else?"

She smiled and touched my shoulder. "They're coming, too, of course." How children as young as three or four were going to walk that distance in the cold, fighting the wind and maybe the snow, I had no idea.

"What about Yanik?"

"He can do what he wants, but he's not in charge. Always remember that at times like this. If you want to live, you make your own plan."

The driver's door slammed and out came Yanik. "Listen up," he said, as though talking to a reluctant work crew. "We've got a problem with the engine. Everybody stay calm. We're going to wait here till somebody comes back for us. So settle down and stay put." He climbed back in the cab and slammed the door.

The women began to murmur and shake their heads. Auntie clapped her gloved hands. "Ladies, ladies . . . may I have your attention?" All heads turned in her direction. "It is my opinion that the safest thing for all of us to do is to walk the rest of the way across the lake."

"What?" a young mother exclaimed. "That man just said someone would come and get us."

"There is no assurance of that whatsoever. I figure that we have six miles to go; it may be more, it might be less. It's beginning to snow up ahead. That could easily obscure the road for Yanik or a rescuer. We must get out of this weather and go toward the shore." A woman in the back began to whimper. "If we walk at a normal pace, it should take us one and a half to two hours."

I thrust my hands in my pockets and pulled out the three red napkins Auntie had given me. "We'll tie these together like a rope," I said, "and the people in the front will carry it so we can be seen from a distance."

A young mother seated not too far from us with one of the youngest children said, "What if we want to stay?"

Auntie nodded thoughtfully. "That is your choice. But I implore you to come with us. If no one comes to rescue you, both you and your child will die." Auntie paused to give those words their full weight. "If you want to walk with us, take a moment and give yourself and your children a little something to eat or drink. We will leave in three minutes."

There was a flurry of activity as the women gathered their things and took sips of water and bites of bread and fed the same to their children.

"Open the back gate of the truck, Ivan," Auntie instructed me. "Help them get down."

I jumped over the side of the truck and slid the back bolt out of its locked position. The women began climbing out, their children scrambling into their arms after them.

"Hey!" It was Yanik, lunging out of the cab. "What are you doing? Get back in there! Get back in the truck!" he howled, seeing that everyone was ignoring him.

I held up my arms to help Auntie down after she'd thrown her suitcase and my duffel bag to the ground, then looked around the truck bed quickly to make sure nothing had been left behind. She walked confidently over to Yanik.

"We've all decided to walk the rest of the way. Would you like to join us?"

"You can't do that!" he fumed.

"Nevertheless, that's our plan. Are you staying here or coming with us?"

Yanik looked furious. "You can all freeze to death for all I care!" He yanked his knitted cap from his head and threw it on the ground in anger.

"As you wish," Auntie said. "But I'd keep that cap on if I were you. It's going to get cold."

He swooped down to snatch the hat, then stomped away from us and back into the cab, yelling, "Stupid women! Of all the idiotic ideas . . ." He was still yelling even after he'd slammed the truck door closed.

"Come on, Ivan," Auntie said. "Let's get our things. We have to get moving."

"Where are your red scarves?" one of the women asked as she held her young son to her side.

"Right here!" I began to tie them together. Once we added Auntie's three napkins, the red "rope" was about ten feet long.

Auntie, the oldest and most experienced person among us, gave quick instructions. "Ivan, you stand on the left side of the road and hold one end of the rope. I'll hold it on the right side. Ladies, two of you and your children come up and stand between us." We were now six abreast on the ice road, the red rope stretching at waist height from one side to the other. "Now," she continued, "let's get the last eight of you directly behind us." That was it: two lopsided rows of humans and their meager possessions marked by a bright red line.

"Does anyone have a watch?" Auntie asked.

"I do," one of the women answered.

"I want you to tell us every time fifteen minutes has gone by. We should be able to walk a mile in that time. Can you do that?"

"Of course."

"All right. Everyone ready?"

The women and even some of the older children eagerly responded "Yes!" and off we went.

A boy of about six years was on my right, holding his mother's hand and looking excited by the adventure. "Do you know any songs?" I asked him. His mother glanced at me gratefully as he nodded. "What song do you like best?"

" 'The Frog and the Fairy.' "

"Can we hear it?"

After a few seconds he sang:

There was an old frog
Who lived in a pond
A-way, a-way, a-way-o.
And a fairy he did come upon
One day, one day, one day-o.

With eyes so blue
And long red hair
On pink little wings

She flew through the air.
"Oh, dear little fairy, can't you see?
You should marry a frog like me!"

And so began our six-mile walk to shore, to the tune of "The Frog and the Fairy." Yanik caught up to us about ten minutes after we left. He said nothing, and no one spoke to him. The woman with the watch called out the time every fifteen minutes. The snow flurries we'd seen in the distance had moved on, a dusting of white the only sign they'd ever been there.

Gusts of wind hit us like invisible fists. The youngest child was knocked down by them twice. Perhaps to redeem himself, Yanik carried the child for a mile or so until she demanded to be handed to her mother.

I think the strain and effort hit us all hardest at the five-mile point, not quite an hour and a half after we started. We seemed to stop as one. Using as few words as possible to conserve our strength, we agreed on a five-minute rest. Most sat down on their bags or suitcases. Then we took our places, picked up our bags, stretched the red rope in front of us, and marched slowly eastward.

Auntie's calculations had turned out to be fairly accurate; it was another half hour before we saw the other trucks and some people milling about on the shore. When they saw us, a truck came roaring toward us. "We thought you were lost!" the driver declared with a grin. He explained that none of the trucks had enough gas to go on a rescue mission to look for us. If any of us had waited for them, we would have been frozen statues by morning. He drove us to shore. A lakeside house had been requisitioned by the government as a place for the new arrivals to revive themselves before setting off on the next leg of their journey.

"How do we get to Vilnov?" Auntie asked one of the three men in army uniforms.

"Vilnov? Are you sure you want to go there?"

"Why wouldn't I?" she asked with a frown.

The soldier made a clicking sound with his mouth. "There's fighting not twenty miles from there. Bad fighting. But that's the case anywhere between here and Moscow, so I suppose it's as good as any." He turned away as another person approached with a question.

Auntie looked at me for a long time. "What do you think, Ivan?"

I glanced around the wide room at my fellow refugees. Tired, hungry women and children and a few older people, who probably had as little idea about what the future held as we did.

"Well, we can't go back to Leningrad," I said, trying hard not to think of my mother and my friends. "The country is at war. No one knows what will happen. Let's go to your sister-in-law's house and see if you're welcome there. If not, or if it's too dangerous, we'll both go up to my uncle Boris's cabin."

Auntie smiled broadly. "Spoken like someone who's just walked on water. Let's see if we can find a ride."

PART TWO
ZASHA AND THOR

CHAPTER II

DUSK WAS FALLING; BY FOUR P.M. IT WOULD BE DARK. AUNTIE SPOKE TO EVERY PERSON IN CHARGE, BUT NONE OF THEM HAD AN ANSWER ABOUT HOW WE WERE TO GET TO Vilnov, about twenty miles away. The other travelers had disappeared. One group was driven away in an army transport; they must have had influential relatives. Others were met by friends or family. A few simply walked down the road.

"What are we going to do, Auntie?" I was so tired and hungry, I had little energy left. "Do you think they'd let us sleep here?"

She didn't answer right away. "I'm sorry, Ivan. Your mother and I didn't know what to expect on this side of the lake, but we thought surely there would be something in place to help us." We looked around the room, empty now except for two drivers talking quietly in the corner. Supplies and gasoline were being loaded into the trucks we'd arrived in so that they would be full when they crossed the ice road in the morning on their way back to Leningrad. I stood up and walked toward the front door, forcing myself not to think about my friends and family who were still there.

"I'm going to get some air, Auntie."

I walked down the front steps and stood in the empty road. Clouds covered much of the sky, but here and there a deep bluish-purple color peeked through. It would have been an inspiring sight if I didn't feel so uncertain about every minute of my future. As I stared at the western sky, I heard something I couldn't place at first, something I hadn't heard all winter — sleigh bells. They came from behind me, and I quickly turned to see a horse-drawn sleigh in the distance, coming from the north down the narrow lane that ran in front of the lake house.

The driver looked about Auntie's age. He had a full gray beard and wore a sheepskin cap with flaps over his ears, making his head look exceptionally large. He was smiling and called out to me, "Hello! Hello!" as the sleigh drew nearer.

I stepped back onto the porch of the lake house and out of their way as he cried, "Whoa!" The dark horse had a streak of white down her nose, and lifted her head and looked at me as if in greeting as she stopped.

"Hello, young man," the driver greeted me in a booming voice. "You must be from Leningrad!"

"Yes, sir, but how did you know?"

"Look around you!" he said good-naturedly. "Everyone has been waiting for the lake to freeze over for weeks now. It's all we talk about." He stood up and craned his neck to look behind me. "Where are . . . the others?"

"What others, sir?" All I wanted was to pet his horse, but I tried to focus on the stranger.

"Your fellow travelers. Where are they?"

"They've all gone, sir. All but Auntie and me."

He looked crestfallen and sat down wearily on the front bench of the sleigh. "I meant to come earlier, but Nesa needed grooming," he said, motioning toward his horse. "Well, I'm here now, ready and able."

"I'm sorry, sir — ready and able for what?" I inched nearer to his horse.

"I thought I could help people get where they're going. I mean, I would have to charge a small something, but I wanted to do my part."

The front door behind me creaked, and out came Auntie. "Good evening," she greeted the man. "I am Vera Raskova, and this is Ivan."

"Yes, I'm just making his acquaintance!" He certainly was the jolliest person I'd seen in months, smiling for no reason, looking happy just to be alive.

"What a beautiful horse and sleigh."

"Thank you, ma'am. I thought I could be of some use here today, but I'm late, as always."

"I think you're just on time," Auntie said with a smile. "Ivan and I are going to Vilnov. We have no way of getting there. Would you allow us to hire you and your fine horse to take us there?"

The man frowned slightly and rubbed his forehead. "Vilnov. That's quite a ways from here. I'd like to help, but it's a good twenty miles."

"I know it will be dark soon," Auntie said, "and we wouldn't want to impose, but it would be a great help to us. What would you consider a reasonable cost for such a ride?"

"Ten rubles?" he answered, as if asking a question.

"I'll offer you twenty rubles to take us to Vilnov. Make it twenty-five."

"Really?" he said, looking at her carefully. "Twenty-five rubles?" He laughed. "Where is your baggage? Let me help you!" We quickly loaded our two bags into his sleigh and climbed in after them, but only after he let me pet Nesa. It was exciting and a little frightening to touch so large and powerful an animal. She stood proudly and let me stroke her head and shoulders. She smelled of earth and hay and sweat. It was one of the nicest things I'd smelled in a long time.

"I am Vladimir, by the way," he said as he turned the sleigh around. "Now, there is no shortcut to Vilnov, but there is a more beautiful road and a less beautiful road. Which one would you like to take?"

He glanced over his shoulder and smiled at us as we tucked ourselves in on the back bench under three warm blankets. We answered, "The beautiful one!" in unison.

"Excellent! Come on, Nesa, time to go." He flicked the reins lightly, and Nesa trotted down the road; soon we turned and were heading east. The bluish twilight enveloped us as it grew darker. The snow emitted a ghostly light; it surprised me that I felt no fear of being out in the country as night fell. The farther we got from the water, the clearer the sky. I leaned back and watched as the first stars appeared.

The road cut through a small forest of birch trees. We emerged into an area I assumed was farmland because vast stretches of it were cleared, except for clusters of pines and other trees near what appeared to be farmhouses. Vladimir and Auntie shared stories of how difficult life had been since the war started and the different effects on people in the city and country.

"My wife packed some bread and cheese for me," Vladimir said, reaching under his seat and handing Auntie a metal lunch box with a rounded top and a handle. "Help yourselves. There's a little jug of tea in there, too."

"Are you sure?" Auntie asked. "You'll have a long journey home."

"Yes, I'm sure. Besides, my wife will have something warm waiting for me."

Auntie opened the lunch pail and revealed an enormous hunk of bread and a square of white cheese as big as my fist. We eyed each other in amazement: It was real food! She pulled the bread into three pieces, kept the smallest one for herself, and gave me the largest. The same with the cheese, although that was harder because it was kind of crumbly.

I held the cheese in my right hand and the bread in my left as Auntie poured the tea into a small metal cup. "Don't burn your mouth," she whispered with a smile. Auntie held the cup while I sipped it slowly, feeling first the cold metal cup against my lips and then the hot, strong tea. It felt as comforting as a hug.

"You take some, too, Auntie."

When she was sure I'd had enough, she took a small sip.

"Heaven," she declared. "Now eat your food."

The bread was real bread, the kind we used to be able to buy before the German invasion. It bore little resemblance to the rationed mess of sawdust, flour, and who knows what else that we'd existed on for months. My body recognized what it had been missing immediately in a sort of blink of pleasure.

"Thank you, Vladimir," I said as soon as I'd swallowed. "This is the best food I've ever eaten."

"I wish I'd thought to bring more. Miss Vera, perhaps once you're settled, you and Ivan would consider visiting my wife and me. You can tell us the news of what's been happening in Leningrad."

Auntie glanced at me; I saw the same look of pleasure in her eyes that I knew was in mine. "I think we'd like that very much."

I opened my mouth to tell him how much I'd enjoy a visit when I remembered. "I'm only staying with Auntie for a night or two. I'm supposed to go up to my uncle's house. It's southeast of Sviritsa, but past Syasstroy. In the country."

"Sviritsa," he repeated. "You have quite a journey yet to make, and it's in another direction. How are you getting there?"

"I don't know," I said glumly, having no interest in being separated from Auntie, or in seeing my uncle Boris again. Vladimir nodded and said nothing.

"It looks untouched out here," Auntie said.

"Oh, we've been touched, all right. The Germans bombed the boats on the lake all summer in case any of them was on its way to Leningrad. They kept it up for months."

"We thought they were going to bomb us on the lake today!" I exclaimed as I held the cup for more tea.

Vladimir shook his head. "Did they hit anything?"

"No. It was only one plane, and it just flew over."

As he turned around to speak to us, I saw a movement on the right side of the road. Before any of us could speak, three young men rushed up to the horse and grabbed her bridle. As soon as Vladimir realized what was going on, he cried, "Whoa!" and pulled Nesa to a quick halt.

The three men walked slowly up to the front of the sleigh, examining us all closely. One walked around the sleigh and stopped very near me.

"Good evening," the tallest one said. They were thin but

tough-looking, their clothes not much better than what you'd see on a poor man in Leningrad.

"Good evening, comrades," Vladimir answered calmly. "How may I help you?"

"We've been walking a long way," the man answered, then paused. "We're on our way to Tikhvin."

Vladimir nodded and said, "Ahhh," almost inaudibly, as if confirming something in his own mind. "And what can we do for you?" I was watching the man nearest me. The man caught me staring at him and winked his eye. I turned away, confused and nervous.

"If you had some food you could share with us, we would be grateful."

Turning around and motioning toward us, Vladimir said, "My friends here have just arrived from Leningrad. You know how bad things are there. I shared my supper with them. I'm afraid I don't have anything to offer."

I expected an angry or hostile response, but it was a flicker of disappointment that crossed the man's face.

"Excuse me, Vladimir," Auntie said, pulling the blankets off of her lap. "I saved a portion of the food for you. I couldn't let you travel home without anything to eat."

"You did!" He sounded surprised and almost mad at the same time. "That was for you and Ivan. I can wait till I get home."

She stood up and held out the bread and cheese. "I think it was a fortunate decision. Perhaps our friends would accept this small offering." Suddenly, they didn't look so tough, more like hungry adolescents.

"Thank you," the tall man said as the man nearest Auntie stretched his hands out to receive the food.

"There's even a little tea left, if Vladimir doesn't mind."

"Please," the driver said, "take it and warm yourselves." Auntie emptied the last of the tea into the cup and passed it to the man next to me.

"Thank you," he said with a smile.

I was no longer frightened, but I knew something was going on among the adults. It was like they were giving one another signals I couldn't understand. The man who accepted the tea drank some, brought it to their leader, who took a few sips and exhaled happily, then gave the last of it to the man who had taken the food from Auntie.

"Where are you headed?" the leader asked Vladimir.

"Outside of Volkhov. Not too much farther, but a nice country drive."

"I don't think your horse could carry the load of three more men."

What in the world is he talking about? I wondered. *Vladimir never offered them a ride.*

"Not if you climbed in the sleigh," he answered with a laugh, "but if you had skis you could hold on to the back and we could pull you."

The leader nodded slowly. "We have skis. We also have some other things we need to bring with us."

"Why not?" Vladimir asked with a shrug. "We have blankets."

I hadn't said a word since the men appeared, but I wanted to stand up and shout *What are you talking about?* But as Auntie had taught me, sometimes the best course is to watch, listen, and learn. I held my tongue.

"All right, then," the leader said with a smile. "We'll be back in a moment." The three of them ran to the side of the road they'd come from and disappeared into a thicket of trees.

I thought Vladimir might snap Nesa's reins and yell for her to run as fast as she could. Instead, he turned to speak to Auntie. "Thank you. It won't be for long. They'll drop off before we get too near the town."

"It's fine," Auntie said as she took one of the blankets off our laps.

Within a minute they were running through the twilight toward us with their arms full, each one with a short pair of skis under his arm. Vladimir looked around us as though to see if anyone was watching. The young men dropped the skis behind the sleigh and brought their other items to the front. They consisted of three sleeping bags and three rifles.

My eyes grew wide as I finally understood. These men were partisans, the name given to the men, women, and even children who fought the enemy secretly. All I knew was what I'd heard from an old man in our building in Leningrad. He'd been a partisan during the civil war, hiding in the forest, shooting the enemy, stealing their food, blowing up train tracks, stopping communications, wearing them down, and disappearing back into the forest. Until now I'd never been sure if there were such things as partisans or if he'd made it up to make his wartime experience seem more interesting.

The leader handed the rifles to Vladimir, who quickly passed them to Auntie. She laid them down on the floor of our sleigh and covered them with a blanket. It felt like electricity was coursing through my body as I looked over at Auntie. She studied my face and said softly, "It's a little like the day I showed you the secrets of my apartment." I nodded mutely.

The men slipped on what looked like handmade skis and positioned themselves in back of the sleigh. "Ready?" Vladimir called.

"Ready," they responded. In a second, Nesa was trotting down the road with three guerrilla fighters in tow.

They held on for about five miles, then one of them said, "Comrade, this is far enough." I had to tap Vladimir on the back and repeat it because apparently he hadn't heard it. The partisans had been paying attention, because the forest we'd been riding through was thinning and a stretch of farmland was opening before us.

They retrieved their sleeping bags and rifles and removed their skis. "I'm sorry I don't have more to give you," Vladimir said.

"Oh!" Auntie exclaimed. "I have something for you." She reached down, opened her suitcase, and pulled out two cans of beans, some of the reserve she'd kept under the floorboards in her apartment. She held them up triumphantly.

"Thank you, good mother," the leader said. "It's not easy finding enough food on the road." He took them and thanked her again.

"May God go with you," she said.

"If God would give us bulletproof jackets, we'd be more than happy to have Him with us."

Vladimir laughed. "Thank you, boys. Kill them all." He slapped the reins and off we went. I turned back to watch as they disappeared into the forest.

I sighed as I turned around, shaking my head and saying to Auntie, "That was amazing."

"What was amazing?"

"What just happened, those men —"

"What men?"

I stared at her, perplexed. She leaned near to me and said, "Nothing happened, do you understand? There were no men. No matter who asks you, no matter how insistent they are, you never *ever* admit to having anything to do with a partisan."

There, she'd said the word; I was right. They were partisans, the ghost soldiers.

"Why not?"

"Because," Vladimir began, startling us both, "the more people who know, the more vulnerable everyone is. If the Germans think the whole village knows the whereabouts of the partisans, then the entire village will be tortured or killed until someone gives them the information they want."

"If no one knows anything," Auntie continued for him, "no one can say anything."

"Wouldn't the Germans torture them anyway — just in case?"

Vladimir was shaking his big head back and forth. "They can and they do." His voice was gruff and angry.

"The less you know, the safer you are," Auntie added. "Forget everything you saw or heard tonight."

"Yes, Auntie," I said, but I knew that no matter how hard I tried, I would remember every word, every detail.

CHAPTER 12

VLADIMIR, AUNTIE, AND I STOOD SILENTLY AT THE DOOR OF A COZY, MODEST HOUSE, WAITING IN THE COLD TO SEE IF AUNTIE'S SISTER-IN-LAW STILL LIVED THERE. A RUMBLING thunder pulsed in the distance, as though a storm was on its way. I realized I'd been hearing it intermittently for the last half mile.

"It's been many years," Auntie admitted, "but she is a homebody. I think she'll still be planted in the same place." She knocked a third time. We'd been traveling for thirteen or fourteen hours since leaving Leningrad. If her sister-in-law didn't live here, I planned on asking whomever did if we could please stay for the night.

"Who is it?" a muffled voice asked from behind the door.

"Galina, it's Vera! Vera Raskova!"

A woman even older than Auntie opened the door. Her silver-rimmed glasses sat at the end of a strong nose; a halo of wispy gray hair had escaped from the bun at the nape of her neck. Before the door was half open, she exclaimed, "Vera!" and spread her arms to hug Auntie. "Come in, come in!" she cried, touching both me and Vladimir in a gesture of welcome while closing and locking the door quickly. "I'm sorry if I sounded unfriendly, but they're so close. Did you hear them?"

"Whom?" Auntie asked.

"The Germans. Can't you hear their guns? I'm so distracted, I . . ." Her voice trailed off. "But, Vera, I'm so happy to see you! Who are your friends? I'm Galina." She held out her hand and shook mine and then Vladimir's as Auntie introduced us.

"I'm just getting supper ready, so you can join me. Let me take your coats. Tell me all about your journey, and to what I owe this wonderful surprise visit."

Vladimir hesitated. "I should be getting back. My wife will be worried."

Galina, knowing nothing of our circumstances, glanced at him as she hung our coats on a rack, as if waiting for more, but Auntie said, "You'll be out in the cold for almost two hours. Please join us — if only to get something warm in you."

He didn't need much convincing. "Whatever you're cooking does smell quite delicious. . . ."

"This way," Galina instructed us. After living in an apartment all my life, to be in a house was exciting. It seemed so large, although the ceilings were low. We followed her into the kitchen, where a wood-burning stove filled the room with warmth and the deeply satisfying fragrance of a real fire.

"You have a cat!" I exclaimed as a small orange cat sat up nervously on a chair, jumped to the floor, and ran out of the room.

"I certainly do," Galina said as she tied an apron over her dress. "She keeps all the mice outside where they belong! I call her the Tsarina. Do you have any animals, Ivan?"

I stared at her blankly for a moment. How could I possibly explain that the starving people of Leningrad were lucky to be alive, and that most animals had succumbed long ago? "No, Miss Galina, I don't" was all I said.

Galina made us comfortable at her small kitchen table and generously fed us soup, bread, and tea. She and Auntie exchanged information about old friends, a little about Leningrad, and a few memories of Arseny. Finally Auntie said, "Galina, I have something to ask of you." The old woman adjusted the glasses on her nose and waited for more. "Life has become intolerable in Leningrad. We were lucky to get out. Ivan's mother is being transferred to work in the Urals." Galina nodded as if she understood. "What I want to know, Galina, is . . . is if I could stay here with you. It might be for a very long time. Maybe until the war is over."

"Of course!" she answered without hesitation.

"I also wanted to know if —"

But Galina interrupted her. "And what about you, Ivan? What are your plans?"

"My mother wants me to go stay with my uncle Boris, in the country southeast of Sviritsa. I don't want to go." It came out so strongly, I think I startled everyone.

"It's his mother's wish," Auntie told Galina, "but honestly, I'm not sure it's the best plan."

"With all due respect to my mother, it's a terrible plan. He doesn't even know I'm coming." I felt overwrought at the thought of leaving this warm place and being separated from Auntie. Without her, I was truly on my own. I'd have nothing of home left.

Vladimir reached over and patted me on the back. "I'm sure your mother knew what she was doing when she made this decision."

I shook my head. "I think she's sending me to Boris's because there's no other choice."

Galina opened her mouth as if to speak, then sighed loudly. "I hope you will understand what I'm going to say in the right spirit." My heart began to sink inside me at those words. "I hesitate to take on the responsibility of a child."

"It's all right," I said. "I under —"

"Wait, Ivan, let me finish. There's enough food, and there's enough fuel. We live in the country; we're able to be more self-sufficient than city dwellers." I forced myself to listen to her and willed myself not to cry. "But the Germans are very, very close. Many people have already left the village. Everyone's frightened. We've heard such terrible things. . . ." She glanced at me quickly, didn't finish her sentence, and closed her eyes. "What I'm trying to say is that our town may be occupied soon. None of us knows what that will mean. There's a chance I will leave for Kazan to be with my sister." Auntie reached out and held her hand. "I welcome you both, but I'm reluctant to expose a child to these terrible dangers."

I looked up at her. All I heard was *I welcome you both*. I thought, *Oh, please let it be true. Please don't send me away.*

"Miss Galina, would it be possible for me to stay here for a few days? Perhaps a week? Just enough to rest. Then I will go find my uncle Boris." I rushed on, "You'll hardly notice I'm here! I'll work very hard at whatever you want me to do. I can clean, I can . . . I can . . ." I stopped, feeling ashamed to be begging. I could see it was upsetting her, too.

Very quietly, Vladimir said, "You can come stay with my wife and me, Ivan — with Vera's permission, of course."

I was deeply moved. But before I could answer, Galina said, "No, no, no. I shouldn't have said anything. It came out all wrong. I'm just worried, that's all, and nervous. It's not that I don't want you, Ivan. It's that I would feel so much worse if something happened to you than if it happened to Vera or me."

"I understand, Galina," Auntie said, sounding upset. "This is my fault. But if you knew what we've just escaped from . . . I'm sorry. I've put you *and* Ivan in a difficult position by coming here. I should have taken him directly to his uncle's."

Galina was quiet for a moment and leaned back in her chair. "I just want you to know it could be very, very dangerous."

"Dangerous is something I know about," I said, thinking of the constant bombardment and hunger that hounded our waking and sleeping hours back home.

She reached over, smoothed my hair away from my face, and stared at me. "When did you leave Leningrad?"

"About five o'clock this morning."

"No wonder you look so tired." She paused. "Why don't we get a bed made up for you?"

She hadn't said definitely that I could stay, but she hadn't said no, either. I looked up at her with all the gratitude I felt in my heart and whispered, "Thank you."

CHAPTER 13

"WHO ARE YOU?" I LAY BARELY AWAKE, GAZING BLEARY-
EYED UP AT SOMEONE WHO WAS SITTING ON THE SIDE OF MY
BED, STARING AT ME. DEEP-SET DARK EYES SHONE FROM A
pale, smooth face, its cheeks pinched pink by the cold. Two thick
dark braids almost to her waist fell from under her fur-lined hat.
She looked about my age.

"I thought you'd never wake up!" She smiled as though I were
a long-lost friend. "I'm Polina."

"Ivan." I glanced around the room for a clock, but saw none.
"What time is it?"

"After eight o'clock. It will be light soon. Would you like to
go sledding with me?"

I nodded yes before I could even think about it. She rushed
to the door, saying, "Hurry and get dressed" as she closed it
behind her.

I climbed out of bed, thinking how much fun it'd be to go
sledding, wondering how big the hills would be, when I realized I
should have checked with Auntie and Galina before I made any
plans.

Polina started talking the minute I opened the door; we
walked toward the kitchen together. "Miss Galina lets me gather
eggs from her chickens. Have you met them yet? There are six.
Sometimes she gives eggs to my mother, who makes —"

"Good morning!" Auntie greeted us from the kitchen table.

Galina was at the stove. "You didn't wake him up, did
you, Polina?"

"No, Miss Galina," she answered solemnly. "He was ready to get up on his own." I wasn't sure how true that was, but whatever Galina was cooking smelled so good, I didn't want to waste time contradicting Polina.

It turned out to be porridge with butter. Imagine that. Even the richest man in Leningrad couldn't buy those things. Polina and I had two bowls each.

"Auntie," I said, knowing that to dwell on such thoughts would only bring sadness, "what are we to do today?"

Auntie sighed and said to me, "I wish there was a way to let your mother know that you're going to be here a few days." But there wasn't. We didn't even know where exactly she was going. "Well," she said, looking around her and then at Galina, "what can we help you with?"

Galina shrugged. "Polina collected the eggs already. I cleaned out the chicken coop yesterday. We always need wood. Maybe Polina and Ivan could chop some wood for us."

Polina practically jumped out of her chair. "I was thinking the same thing! Only I thought we could sled first, and then chop wood. We'll bring it back on the sled afterward."

Galina nodded and pushed her glasses up higher on her nose. "Why don't you show Ivan our town, Polina? Let him get his bearings, and then go sledding?"

Auntie nodded, but said, "We don't want to be a burden on you, Galina. Please tell us how we can repay you for your hospitality."

Galina reached out and took Auntie's hand. "I'm just glad you're here. It gets lonely sometimes now that so many families have fled."

"Where have they gone?" Auntie asked.

"Different places, but mostly to Moscow."

"Moscow?" Auntie said. "I thought the Germans weren't that far from Moscow."

Galina shook her head. "No one knows the best thing to do. Some people panicked. Others felt they had no choice. My neighbor over that way," she said, motioning behind her, "left because she's eighty-nine years old. She heard that the Germans shoot all the old people. Whether it's true or not, I don't know. She didn't want to find out the hard way."

At least that was one worry I didn't have; I knew my mother would be safe. The factories were relocated to the Ural Mountains because they were so far east, no German planes or troops could possibly reach them.

Polina was holding the back door open. "Get your coat," she said. She seemed anxious to be gone, so I quickly grabbed my coat and dashed out the door.

We ran down a few stairs to the snow-covered ground. The sky was clear, the light turning from a deep blue to a golden glow. I felt so alive. Maybe it was because I'd had more to eat in the last two meals than I'd eaten in a week and a half back in Leningrad. Maybe it was because I rested in a soft bed covered by warm blankets. Maybe it was because I hadn't heard the sounds of bombs and artillery fire every moment. Maybe it was because I heard birdsong for the first time in as long as I could remember.

Polina and I walked north as she told me all about the little town. "Those two families are gone." She pointed to houses on either side of us. "I go in them sometimes just to make sure the roof isn't leaking and no animals have set up their homes inside."

"Really? They let you do that?"

"Of course. They asked me to! Almost all of us know one another here. If we don't watch out for one another, no one will." I thought about how we tried to do the same in my apartment building, but it seemed so limited compared to an entire village looking out for one another.

"How many people live here?" I asked as Polina jumped next to the low-hanging roof of a house we passed to knock the icicles off. I did the same and felt exhilarated as they cracked and fell into the snow.

"Now? Maybe two hundred. Before, three or four hundred. Not too big, not too small. Just perfect." She jumped again and shattered three icicles with one sweep of her arm. She turned back to me and smiled. "I love the winter best. Everything is so quiet and beautiful. Every minute of daylight is so precious. Of course, when spring comes I like that best. There's nothing like that first bit of green on the trees and the ground. It brings the mud, but mud is so much fun!"

"Fun?" I imitated Polina as she ran on a deserted street and slid on the hard-packed snow as if it were ice.

"Yes, endlessly. Last spring I made an igloo out of mud."

"Really? Why didn't it collapse?"

"Because I mixed it with straw and grass. It didn't last in the heavy rain, but still, for ten days it was my second home."

We turned a corner and were on what was obviously Vilnov's main street. It was just two blocks from Galina's house, and hardly more than a block long itself. A grocery store and a general store were already open. It was shocking to see people going in and out casually, normally, almost as if there weren't a war going on. How would I ever make anyone understand how grim life had been in Leningrad when hardly seventy miles away there weren't even lines for food?

"A lot of stores have closed," Polina said, pointing to the biggest building on the street, a two-story brick structure that had been painted a pale yellow. "I know how to get in the basement. There's a long hall there, hard and slick. Good for shooting marbles. We can explore it soon, maybe tomorrow, if you want. That's the whole town," she said suddenly. "Now we need to go sledding."

I couldn't have agreed more. "And chop wood," I added, wanting to repay Galina for her generosity.

"Yes, come this way. We'll go to my house and get my sled and a hatchet."

Polina lived just a block from Galina, to the west. I met her mother briefly, who was so different from Polina, I would never have guessed they were related. She barely met my eyes and seemed preoccupied and closed-up. Polina must have seen the confusion on my face, because as we descended into the small basement under the house, she said, "My brother is on the front line. She worries."

I nodded. "Where is your father?"

"Siberia."

"What is he doing in Siberia?"

"He's at a labor camp."

I didn't understand. "Why?"

"Comrade Stalin thought his politics were faulty." She headed up the stairs with her sled in her hands.

"I don't know what that means."

Polina shrugged. "Neither did my father. Neither do I, for that matter. The police came one night and he had to go with them."

"When is he coming back?"

"We don't know."

She said it in a way that let me know the subject was closed. *I'll ask Auntie later*, I thought. She understood political things, and I did not.

"Ivan, just inside the door you'll see where we hang the small hatchets. Grab two for us, would you?"

On the back of the basement door in a neatly constructed rack were four hatchets, all with leather sheaths covering the cutting edges. I took two and closed the door behind me. Polina's mother made a sort of acknowledgment when Polina told her where she was going and when to expect her back. It made me deeply sad to see her mother ignore the daughter in front of her in her concern for a son not present.

There were a few houses in back of the area where Polina lived, but only one had smoke coming from its chimney. After that was a forest of the kind that had checkered the landscape we crossed yesterday in the sleigh with Vladimir.

"Do you see those cherry trees?" Polina asked, pointing to a cluster near the last house on that edge of town.

"Yes."

"Their branches make the best snowshoes."

"You know how to make snowshoes?"

"Oh, yes. Give me some twine and two branches, and I'll make you snowshoes." She trailed her sled behind her on a rope; I followed with a hatchet in each hand.

"What else do you know how to make?"

"I know how to make snow goggles out of birch bark —"

"You do?"

"— with little slits for the eyes so you won't go snow-blind on a bright day."

"What else?"

"I'm good at making winter fires."

I swung one of the hatchets in my hand, pretending I was hacking off branches as we walked. "Show me."

"Not now. But the thing to remember is to dig all the snow away."

I stopped, amazed, feeling like I knew so little about how to take care of myself, and Polina knew so much. "I can play the concertina," I said, anxious to show that I had some skill to offer.

Polina laughed and turned back toward me. "I know. I saw it in your room. Better be careful with those hatchets. You don't want to be a nine-fingered concertina player. Maybe you'll play for me when we get back."

"Yes. But tell me how you know all these things about . . . survival."

"My brother taught me. The one in the army. Plus, I . . . I have a book."

"Maybe you can show it to me."

"Maybe," she said noncommittally.

I looked around for the first time in a few minutes. "Polina, the land is so flat. Where will we sled?"

"You'll see in a minute."

She was right. All of a sudden, the earth seemed to fall away. It sloped down steeply at first, and then continued to run all the way to a stream. It was frozen nearest its banks, but still flowing in the center.

"Brilliant! But . . . but how do you keep from going into the stream?"

"It takes some practice," she answered with a smile. "Let's go down together a few times. I'll sit up front, and then you can try it on your own. Leave the hatchets here." I tossed them into the snow a few feet from us.

"And if we get too near the stream?" I asked, climbing on the sled in back of her and putting my arms around her waist.

"Jump off!" she cried as she pushed hard with her feet, sending us over the edge of the little cliff.

It was frightening and exhilarating and fun, and I knew I wanted to do it a hundred more times before the day was over. Even the walk back up the hill wasn't so bad. After about an hour, we sat on the sled near the creek and decided we should begin to cut some wood.

"Where do we start?" I asked.

"First, look around you. See if there is any dry wood to pick up." I sighed, thinking I was never going to get to use my hatchet. She must have understood, because she said, "Come this way," and led me to an area past the creek.

"All right. Let's start on" — she scrutinized the various trees near us — "that one." She pointed to a tall evergreen tree.

"Really?" I was surprised because its branches were covered with rich green needles and a dusting of snow.

"Yes. Give me a hatchet and watch me. You get on your back and crawl under the tree. There are lots of dry branches near the trunk, especially at the bottom." I watched as she disappeared under the wide apron of the evergreen. I waited for a minute or two, listening to the faint snapping sounds she made. I was ready to crawl in after her when I saw her boots emerging from the edge of the lowest tree branch as she used her heels to pull herself forward and out.

"Ta-da!" She lay on her back, and across her chest were several inch-wide, foot-long dead branches and lots of smaller branches that would make excellent kindling.

"That's amazing!" I cried as I ran to her, then lifted the branches off her and put them on the sled. She sat up looking pleased, hatchet in hand.

"Now you try. Do that one." She pointed to a tree about five yards away that looked similar to the one she'd been under. I ran toward it, unsheathed my hatchet, and got on my back at its edge.

"Anything else I should know?"

"Yes. Don't drop your hatchet or you'll hurt yourself."

I gripped it tightly and pushed myself in, legs slightly bent, using only my heels for propulsion. It was a wonderland under there. The smell alone filled me with happiness and energy. Although there was some snow on the outer branches, there was almost none under the tree, especially near the trunk. I banged my head once on a broken branch, and some dead pine needles fell on my face. It was amazing to see how many small branches and twigs really were dead and dry enough to be snapped off. I lay my hatchet down on my right side to think for a moment and to see where I should position myself to be able to cut the most dead wood possible. Polina was right: If you dropped your hatchet in this cramped space, chances are it would land on you.

Suddenly, I heard a man's voice and I froze. "Polina," he said, "what are you doing out here?"

"Nothing, I just —"

"We're having a meeting in the morning. Six A.M. Be there."

"Petr, my friend is here with me." Her voice sounded funny; even at that distance I could hear the distressed tone.

"Where?" The way he spoke that one word made me grasp my hatchet, hold on with my right hand to the few twigs I'd managed to cut, and begin to pull myself out with my heels. As I neared the edge of the branches, two strong hands grasped my ankles and yanked me out. I gasped in surprise and fear.

I lay there in the snow, gaping up at the bearded face of a man who looked none too happy to see me. "Who are you?" he demanded.

"Ivan Savichev from Leningrad," I said with as much dignity as my position allowed. I got up quickly, the hatchet still in my hand. The man grasped my wrist, squeezed it, and took the hatchet from me.

"What are you doing out here?"

I glanced at Polina, who looked nervous. She answered, "He's with me. We were sledding and chopping wood for Miss Galina."

The man Polina had called Petr grabbed the front of my jacket near my throat. "What did you hear me say to Polina?"

I can't explain it except to say that in a moment I understood it all. That understanding meant I had to make a decision. I knew what I had to do.

I swung my right hand up quickly and knocked his grasp loose from my coat, startling him. Looking him right in the eye, I said in a firm voice, "You said, 'We're having a meeting in the morning. Six A.M. Be there.' Did I get that right?"

He didn't answer. Polina looked distraught. I continued quietly, hoping my guess was right. "You're partisans. Both of you. There are more, and you're all getting together in the morning."

His face was blank, but I could see the intelligence in his eyes and the mind working quickly behind them. "I want to join you." There was silence, and then he laughed. Loud and long.

"For all you know, we're a hunting club, or ice fishermen. Maybe we like to knit! Partisans? *Pfff.* Get yourself killed fast being a partisan. And what are you, anyway, ten years old? Talking about partisans . . . better to shut your mouth, boy. It could get you into trouble."

I stepped closer to him. "I said I want to join you." I never took my eyes off of him. "I am almost thirteen years old. I've seen people die from starvation and sickness in Leningrad. I almost starved myself. I left my mother and my friends behind and crossed Lake Ladoga, partially on foot. I met three partisans yesterday who were on their way to Tikhvin. We pulled them with our sleigh to help them and gave them all the food we had."

Petr was still sizing me up, but listening carefully. I could tell he hadn't made his mind up about me.

"You think you've suffered out here in the country?" I continued. "Which one of you survives on four ounces of bread a day? In Leningrad we make do with pathetic rations. People are so desperate for food they'd stew a belt for soup, hoping to find some bit of nourishment in it from a long-dead cow. Or they boil wallpaper and gladly eat the paste, praying it will be enough to live another day." My hands were balled into fists, my eyes were stinging with tears of anger at the memories. "Which one of you endures constant artillery attacks, bombs day and night? I've had more to eat in my two meals here than I had the entire last week and a half in Leningrad." I let my words hang in the air, knowing that they were having an effect on a man who had a serious decision to make about whether I was friend or foe.

"Were the partisans that you helped armed?"

I could tell it was a test question. "They each had a rifle, a sleeping bag, and homemade skis."

His expression softened a little. "And just what do you think you have to offer a group of partisans, assuming we are one?"

I thought a moment before I answered. "I'm smart. I'm observant. I hate the Germans. And I'm short and I look younger than my age, you said so yourself. People ignore children. I could act as eyes and ears."

"Is that all?"

"No. I play the concertina."

He laughed again, this time with a genuine smile on his face. I glanced at Polina, who looked enormously relieved.

"What do you think, Polina?" Petr asked her.

Polina stared at me. "I think he's suffered a great deal. And he's like me — he looks young and innocent. Although not nearly so pretty." She smiled and let out a little laugh. "We can always use help. The Germans aren't that far away. We've all heard them the last few days. If they make it much farther north . . ." She left the thought unspoken, but I think we all knew the implications.

"So, Ivan Savichev from Leningrad . . . we'll see you in the morning." He started to walk away.

"My hatchet, please," I said. Petr turned slowly, walked back to me, and handed the hatchet to me, handle first.

"You know, Polina," he said with a hint of a smile, "I think this boy has potential."

CHAPTER 14

POLINA KNOCKED LIGHTLY ON MY BEDROOM WINDOW. I'D BEEN SITTING FULLY DRESSED ON THE BED WAITING FOR HER SIGNAL. WITH ONLY THE CREAKING OF THE WOODEN floor to betray me, I quickly left Galina's house through the back door and joined Polina at the bottom of the stairs. We walked silently until we'd passed all the houses and were well into the forested area not far from where we'd been sledding the day before.

It was dark, although the light reflecting off the snow allowed us to find our way without any problem. After looking over her shoulder to make sure there was no one around, Polina said, "Are you sure you want to do this?"

"Yes."

"After you meet the others there's no turning back."

"Turning back to what, Polina? Our country has been invaded by barbarians. They want us all dead. Now that I have a chance to do something about that — however small — do you think I could refuse?"

She shrugged and nodded her head. She'd told me something similar the day before on our way back home after our chance meeting with Petr.

I felt no reluctance about joining the partisans, although there were two potential problems: Auntie and Uncle Boris. I didn't want to keep my participation a secret from Auntie, but I wasn't sure what she'd do when I told her. Because she'd shown me the secrets of her apartment, including the gun, along with her references to living through the revolution, I thought she might have been part of a similar group when she was young. That still didn't mean she wouldn't forbid me to join them. Uncle Boris . . . well, maybe that wasn't a problem because I'd made a decision that I wasn't going to go live with him no matter what. Somehow I would find a way to stay with Auntie in Vilnov.

"This way," Polina said quietly as we neared the point where the creek turned and ran south. This was the area near where Petr had found us, but Polina kept going into a more deeply forested part where small hills and gullies slowed our progress. At the bottom of one such ravine, a house that was built halfway into the hillside revealed itself.

A thin stream of smoke floated out of a chimney, the only sign of habitation. Its two small front windows were caked with what looked like years' worth of rain and mud splatter; brownish curtains hung behind them.

As we neared the front door, Polina said, "No, this way." She led me around to the side of the structure where it had been built into the hillside, to a rough-hewn door hardly taller than us. She knocked just once.

"Yes?" a voice answered from inside the house. Polina knocked once again. It was apparently some kind of signal. *Smart*, I thought; *no one knocks just once. A normal knock is three or four knocks.* My attention was keenly focused this morning. I wanted to know all about these people and their secrets.

The door opened a crack. Petr peered out at us, then opened the door just wide enough for us to enter before he closed it behind us. The room was lit only by a small fire. Before my eyes adjusted, I sensed the presence of three or four other people standing against the front wall opposite the fire.

Now that I was at Petr's, my heart was pounding. It wasn't fear, exactly. Excitement? Yes, some. Perhaps the best comparison was to the way you feel when you dive into a cold lake. You wanted to be in the water, you dove willingly, but you knew that for a moment you were going to feel like you would die from the shock of the freezing water.

I closed my eyes to help them adjust more quickly to the dim space. When I opened them, I stared first at Petr, who knelt in front of the fire, poking among the embers. Harder to see were the people who leaned against the front wall; they were too far from the fire for me to see them at first. When two of them came into focus, I gasped.

"Auntie! Miss Galina! What are you doing here?"

"Not so loud," Petr warned me without turning around.

They smiled at me like two people sharing a good joke. They must have known how shocking it would be for me to see them there.

"We're doing the same as you," Miss Galina said. "I knew Vera would want to be part of this. Polina surprised me when she said you wanted to join us as well."

I was speechless.

"I like a good fight," Auntie said with a sly smile. "Haven't you noticed?"

"And who is that?"

Petr got up, turned toward us, and took charge. "All you need to know are first names. That is Yeshka." A young man of perhaps fifteen or so nodded in a friendly way.

Two old women, a girl, a twelve-year-old, a teenager, and an older man who was as disheveled as a hermit. These were the partisans? How in the world was this group going to have any effect on such a cruel and efficient army? I sighed more loudly than I meant to and shook my head before I realized it.

"You don't approve, Ivan?"

I felt embarrassed. "Oh, no. I didn't mean to suggest . . . It's just that I assumed that partisans were fighting men."

"Most men of fighting age are in the army and at the front."

"Of course," I stammered. "I don't, I don't know. . . ."

"Let me give you your first lesson in being a partisan. Never let people know what you're thinking. Right now, you're as easy to read as a book. Develop control over your facial expressions, and keep your mouth shut as much as possible."

"Yes, sir." I began right then by gazing blankly across the room, my eyes fixed on no certain spot. It made me feel sort of invisible, which may have been the deeper point of Petr's remarks — *make yourself invisible, listen, and learn as much as possible.*

Polina coughed nervously, rubbed her nose, and sniffed. "And learn how not to fidget and make noises," Petr added.

"Sorry," Polina muttered, putting her hands at her sides.

"Let's get started. Sit or stand as you wish." I would have welcomed a chair, but as no one else moved, I remained standing. "Yeshka, tell us the latest."

"I spent two nights with a small band of partisans north of Tikhvin. They were getting ready to go behind German lines." I wanted to speak so badly, to question him about the journey, about how they survived outside in winter conditions, about whether he'd seen any Germans. But practicing my first lesson of the day, I kept my face neutral and my thoughts and questions to myself. "Everyone seems to think the Germans will push the front line farther north. Volkhov, Vilnov, and several other villages are probable targets. The men I spoke to said we should prepare ourselves for occupation. They thought the main group would set up headquarters in Volkhov. They also said the Germans always have some kind of headquarters in even the smallest villages."

"Did they have a sense of when this would happen?"

"Yes, any day. The rumor is that the Germans are planning to take Leningrad by Christmas."

"Let them try!" I cried, unable to help myself.

"If you don't learn more self-control, you're going to be of more help to the Germans than to us."

"Yes, Petr." I bowed my head, staring at my damp galoshes, intending to bite my own tongue if need be to keep my big mouth shut.

"Are everyone's papers in order?" Everyone murmured yes, including Auntie and me. It was something my mother had insisted upon before I left: Auntie and I each carried our own papers. My birth certificate, health records, and a copy of my mother's work identification papers from the Kirov factory were all safely tucked into my traveling bag. If I was supposed to have other papers, I didn't know what they would be.

"All houses and yards comply with municipal law?"

Yes again from those who lived in Vilnov.

"Anything that would make your house stand out to a passerby?"

This time the answer was no, except for Galina, who said, "There are my chickens."

"Ah, yes — the chickens. How many of your neighbors have chickens?"

"Since people began to leave the village, I'm the only one in my neighborhood."

He flinched and was quiet for a moment. "It will make you a target once they're here. They'll take the chickens and whatever else they want."

"I know," she said softly. "But, Petr, I need those chickens. I sell all the eggs that aren't eaten."

"Why not offer them to the Germans? Then they'd leave you alone," I suggested.

Petr looked at me like I was thick in the head. "Because you never draw attention to yourself."

"Then why are we even talking about the chickens? You just said they *will* draw attention, so they have to go."

Before Petr could say anything, Polina stepped forward. There was an intense expression in her dark eyes, and her voice sounded more like that of an adult when she spoke. "He's right. We all want Galina to be able to keep her chickens because we like her, and we know she likes her chickens. But if we set emotion aside, they have to be gotten rid of." Galina's hand went up to her mouth, as if to cover her feelings.

Everyone was nodding their heads, but I said, "No. She has six chickens, right? Let her keep one, and give one to each of five families who live closest to her. That way it seems normal if everyone has one chicken. If the Germans want them, they'll just take them, but because it's only one chicken, no one will stand out. In the meantime, Miss Galina makes an agreement with these families. They will receive so many eggs a week that the hen lays for taking care of it. She gets the rest to sell, like always."

"With the promise that they'll give back the chicken when the Germans leave," Polina chimed in.

"Yes," I agreed, happy to have her on my side. "Isn't that a better solution?"

Petr stared at me curiously. "Yes, it is. Galina, what do you think?"

Even across the room I could see her relief. "It answers all of the problems."

"Assuming the Germans are defeated and there is an end to all this." It was Polina again. She seemed to possess a confidence I'd rarely seen in girls my own age. Was this the same girl who just yesterday had so much fun sledding with me?

"That's settled," Petr said, looking satisfied. "Now, Ivan. Galina tells me you are leaving in a few days. If I'd known that —"

"No," I interrupted him. "I'm sorry, but I can't. I'm staying here, if Miss Galina will have me. If not, maybe one of you will let me stay with you."

"Ivan, I promised your mother," Auntie said.

My mind was made up. The minute I met Petr, I knew I was going to join the fight. "I will explain it to her. It's not your fault. This is my country, and I'm going to fight for it."

"You understand the danger?" Petr said. "The Germans don't care if you're a child. If they find out you're a partisan, they'll kill you all the same."

"I understand."

"You are welcome at my house," Galina said. "I'm sorry about the confusion last night."

"Then that's settled, too," Petr said. "If Yeshka's information is correct, there's not a lot of time. Galina, explain your duties to Vera. Decide how she can best help you. Yeshka — your orders are clear. Polina, show Ivan the book. Teach him as much as you can, as fast as you can. In the meantime, I'll figure out where we can use him."

Everyone nodded and prepared to leave. "Polina," Petr added, "take Ivan through the tunnels before you go."

"Come on," Polina said, excitement in her voice. "This is amazing." She led me into a bedroom to the right of the fireplace. It was an oddly shaped room because the cabin itself wasn't square, and its rear portion was built into the low hillside, making it look like it conformed only to the whim of the builder. I imagined this provided warmth and insulation in the winter and coolness in the summer.

I watched carefully as Polina opened a closet door, although it was the shortest and most overstuffed closet I'd ever seen. It was hardly tall enough for me to stand up straight in. She pushed her way into the mess of shirts, coats, boots, fishing gear, hats, gloves, and assorted items of clothing on pegs that stuck out from the walls, until she'd cleared a small space on the left between the wall and the last item hanging.

"See this?" she asked, pointing to a knot about waist-high on one of the wooden panels. I nodded. "And this?" She pointed with her foot to a scarred section on the same panel about two and a half feet off the floor. "Press them both *at the same time.*" I watched as she used the heels of her hands to press the two spots. Nothing happened. "Sometimes it's a little stiff, depending on the weather." This time she pounded her hands against the spots. A narrow door opened a few inches. I couldn't believe it. Polina opened the door farther, but the space past it was almost pitch-black.

"Okay, now feel on the left wall just inside the door." I tried to reach around her, but my arm wasn't long enough; we changed places. "Feel it?"

"It's a box."

"Yes, full of candles. Underneath it is a smaller box full of matches. Take one of each and light the candle."

It was easy to find both items; I held one in each hand. "Where do I strike the match?"

"The front of each box is covered in rough metal. Strike it anywhere on either one."

Feeling clumsy in the dark, I felt for the front of the candle box and ran the match across it. A flame burst forth, and I lit the tall taper candle in my other hand.

"Good. Now light one for me from your candle. It saves matches."

Only once we both held candles, and Polina and I traded places so that she could lead, did I dare to look around me. We were in an arched tunnel about two feet taller than either of us and wide enough so that if I put my hands on my hips, my elbows were still an inch or two from either side. Every few feet there was a rough-cut log that went from floor to ceiling. Wedged in between them horizontally about every two and a half feet were shorter logs to support them; it made them look a lot like ladders. Running across the ceiling from side to side were not only more logs to support the roof of the tunnel, but bent branches that covered almost every inch of the arch, providing a secondary protection from cave-ins.

"What is this place?" I marveled.

"These are the escape tunnels. There are two of them. Watch your footing. We go forward ten feet, and then we go down five steps."

I held my candle in front of me, fighting my dislike of closed spaces by focusing on Polina and what she was saying and trying to take in every detail of my surroundings.

"Here they come," she said. "The steps are made of wood, so you don't have to worry about them being soft or crumbling." Her head sunk down as she said it, and I quickly searched for the first step so I wouldn't tumble over on top of her.

"Who built this?" I asked as we descended the steep stairs.

"Petr. Sometimes I think he's more mole than man."

"It's been just five months since we were invaded. He couldn't have made it in that time!"

"No. He started years ago, when the Nazis marched into Poland."

"But why?"

"He said he had a feeling that one day it would be Russia's turn. He was right. Petr's cottage is the safe house for our band of partisans. Ivan, what if the Germans had arrived this morning during our meeting — what would you have done?"

"Run, I suppose. Or waited till they checked our papers and seen what happened."

"Well, good luck with that," she said with a laugh. "While you were busy being polite to the invaders, I'd have been halfway through this tunnel on my way to freedom." She stopped as we reached the bottom of the stairs, and I saw that we were in a sort of round area big enough for maybe three or four people. There were two tunnels that sprouted off from it.

"Unbelievable," I whispered.

"You don't have to whisper today," Polina said, "although it's probably a good habit to get into."

"Where do these tunnels go?"

Pointing to the one on the left, she said, "That one goes west. You'll come out by the other side of the gully that Petr's house sits in. But you can't be seen from the house. The other one takes you north. It's the longest one, and you'll be going in the direction of the village."

"Let's go left," I said, still fighting a feeling of claustrophobia and wanting to breathe fresh air.

"Follow me." I kept my eyes on Polina's back as we entered the tunnel, and I remembered an old trick my mother had taught me. I pretended there was a bright blue sky above me with white fluffy clouds floating gently by. It's amazing how powerful that image was, and how different my whole body felt just pretending I was in a ditch with blue sky above, rather than in a tunnel surrounded by earth. But it required a lot of focus and determination to keep it in my mind.

"Almost there," Polina said a short while later. "See that post on the left, the one painted red? That tells you you're about twenty feet from the exit, and to be on the alert for the door."

"How do you know that no one's watching on the other side?"

"You don't. But you'll see. Petr made it blend into the earth so well, it's sometimes hard to find from the outside even when you're looking for it."

A few seconds later, Polina said, "Okay, I'm going to stop now. You stop, too. I want to show you something." I did as she asked. "Look at that." She pointed to the end of the tunnel, where red paint had been used to outline the door. "When you get to the door, stand close to it, grasp the handle, and then blow out your candle. See on the left? It's a candle box and a matchbox, just like at the entrance. That way, if you come *in* this way you'll have a candle, too."

"Smart," I said, still in awe of all the planning, intelligence, and sheer hard work that had gone into making the tunnels.

Polina blew out her candle. "Make sure it's out before you put it back in the box," she warned me. I hesitated to extinguish mine. "It's okay. We'll be outside soon." I counted to three and blew it out, then felt for the candle box and put it on the pile of other candles. We stood in a blackness so complete, I reached out and touched Polina's back to make sure she was still there.

"Always open the door as slowly as you can. There's an evergreen in front of it that gives us protection. But still . . . if you're in this tunnel, you're probably running for your life, so be careful." Seeing the first sliver of the deep blue dawn gave me relief beyond words; it reminded me of how comforting it was to have had the door open a crack in our closet at home when we waited out that first bombing raid.

"Slowly, slowly," Polina said as she gently pushed the narrow door open just wide enough to slip through. I followed her out of the tunnel; air had never tasted so sweet. As she'd said, a tall evergreen blocked us from being seen by passersby, though not completely. "If someone is after you, it's best to crawl out. Get under the tree if you have to, like I showed you the other day."

"Okay." I followed her about twenty feet from the tunnel entrance.

"Turn around. Can you see the door?" she asked.

I looked back, knowing the tree marked the spot, thinking it would be easy to find. All I saw was a sloping, crumbling end to a mound of earth that flowed naturally from the hillside. "You'd better show me." We walked back together. The entire time I searched for the outline of the door and never found it.

Polina motioned toward the hillside. "Petr takes paper, mud, and leaves and molds them right into the earth, like a sculptor. Then he paints it or colors it until it looks completely natural. See this? It looks like a rock that's sticking out of the side of the dirt. Pull it, and that will open the door; it's the handle." I eyed her skeptically, not sure I believed her. "Go on. Try it."

I did as she said, and sure enough, the narrow door opened to reveal the darkness within. "Amazing."

"Now, let me show you how to get back to the front of the cabin from here." Polina ran through the snow, and I followed. "Wait till you see the book."

"The one Petr mentioned?"

"Yes. I'll show it to you when we get to my house. Everything you ever need to know in the whole wide world is in that book."

"What's it called?"

"You'll see. First I have to show you the other tunnel."

We entered through the side door to find that only Petr remained at his cottage; the others had gone. We went through the other tunnel, and I memorized the place it could be accessed from the outdoors. Again, Petr had so cleverly disguised the entrance that it was invisible at first glance, at least to a city boy like me. I hoped that if I ever needed to enter one of the tunnels from the outside I'd be able to find it again.

A little while later, as we walked back toward the village from near the stream, Polina said, "There's a lot to teach you."

"From the book, you mean?"

She nodded.

"What's the name of the book?"

She hesitated before answering. "I guess I can tell you now. But you can never repeat it. It's called *The Deadly Partisan*."

CHAPTER 15

POLINA HAD GONE TO GREAT EFFORTS TO HIDE HER BOOK. IN A CORNER OF THE MUSTY BASEMENT OF HER HOUSE, SHE PUSHED ASIDE A HEAVY-LOOKING BARREL. KNEELING DOWN, she lifted a piece of the floor under it. The *thud* it made when she set it down made me think she must be very strong. She reached into the space and pulled out a small book, its cover gone.

"Always arrange things so that if you hear someone coming you can make things look normal quickly," she cautioned me as she pushed the barrel nearer to the hole and moved the piece of floor to partially cover it.

I nodded, feeling alert, anxious to know what Polina knew.

She thumbed through the book, which measured about three by five inches. "Is that *The Deadly Partisan*?" I asked.

She looked up at me. "Don't say its name so easily."

"Why is it so much worse to be a partisan than a soldier?"

"Because we're an unknown," she answered, continuing to skim through the book. "We're unpredictable. They don't know who we are or what we'll do."

"Do the Germans know children act as partisans?"

"Probably. Our job is to make sure they don't know that *these* children are partisans."

I gazed over Polina's shoulder as she skimmed the index. "This whole first part is about guns and hand grenades and bayo-nets. We've only got a little time. . . . Let's pick three things."

What a smart girl, I thought, *a natural leader.*

"I'm going to teach you how to disarm someone who's attacking you with a knife. Then ... how to use wire against a motorcyclist, and ... oh, how to tie the five basic knots. Very important."

She put the book down. "I'll be the knife attacker first, then you. If you feel what it's like as the attacker and the one being attacked, you'll understand it completely."

She grabbed a rough piece of wood about nine inches long from a stack of odds and ends in the corner. Bending her knees slightly, she glided first to the left and then to the right, as if she were stalking her prey, almost circling me, using the wood as a stand-in for a knife. I moved along with her, keeping my distance, trying to figure out how she would attack me first — aiming for my stomach? My throat? My arm? Suddenly, she leapt at me, her right hand holding the "knife" high. It looked like she meant to bring it down with all the force of her body into my upper chest.

I turned to my left to run away and felt a stab on my right shoulder almost immediately.

"Bad move," Polina said matter-of-factly as she walked away from me, her body looking completely relaxed and in control. "First of all, you offered no defense. You didn't even try to disarm me. Second, if you're going to run, turn in the direction of your dominant hand — right, in your case — so that if you get knifed in the shoulder like you did just now, at least you'll be able to use your good hand and arm. Because your attacker will try to knife you more than once, just to be sure."

"Sure of what?" I rubbed my shoulder. Polina had hit me pretty hard with that piece of wood.

"That you're dead. And you would be if you'd really met an enemy like me."

Her skill and the feeling of vulnerability I felt being such an easy target made me determined to learn quickly.

"Listen carefully," Polina said. "Here's what you do when someone has a knife and they're attacking you overhanded, like I just did. Okay: The knife is coming down at you. You put both your hands up to catch the arm at the wrist. Keep your right hand higher than the left, but just a little. Here, you take the knife. We'll do it in slow motion. Come at me, that's it. Now, as you're bringing it down, my hands go up so they're in a sort of V or U shape. You're going to use your thumbs — because they're so strong — and you're going to hook the right one into the crook of your attacker's pinkie, and your left thumb into the same place but on his ring finger."

Her hands were up to catch my downward thrust. They were amazingly strong. "Do you feel where my fingers are?"

"Yes."

"I'm going to press hard while I pull your arm to the left."

"Not too hard," I said, still feeling a dull pain in my back from her first demonstration.

"Don't be a baby," she said as she pressed her thumbs hard into the tender joints that connected my pinkie and ring finger to my hand, pulled me with incredible strength to the left, and threw me to the ground before I could so much as yell.

I lay on the floor staring up at her, stunned. "How did you do that?"

She smiled proudly. "Just like I told you. Hands catch the arm in a V, thumbs in the two sockets, press hard, pull left, and throw to the ground." She was sort of bouncing on the balls of her feet like a skinny little boxer, proud to have her opponent on the ground.

"Let's try it again," I said. On our first attempt I forgot to push my hands up hard, and she got me in the shoulder again. But I remembered to turn right, so she got the other shoulder, and just barely.

"You move fast, that's good," she observed. "One more time. Forget I'm a friend. Forget I'm a girl." It wasn't easy to think that way, but I closed my mind to emotion and had her on the ground in seconds. I stood tall, smiling down at her. She slowly rolled on her side, pushed herself up on her elbow, and gasped for air.

"Oh, Polina!" I knelt down next to her. "I'm sorry. I didn't mean to hurt you!"

It took her a few more seconds to catch her breath. "It's all right," she said finally. "You knocked the wind out of me. You learn fast." We smiled and even laughed a little, and our eyes met; I think at that moment I had her full acceptance into their little group.

"There's another way to do it," she said, struggling a little as she got to her feet.

"Is it harder or easier?"

"Both."

"Do you want to rest a minute?"

"Don't be ridiculous." This time she had me catch her knife-holding wrist with one arm, grab her other elbow, and pull her toward me. If the attacker was short enough, I was to thrust my head up under his chin and knock his head back. If he was tall, I was to aim for his solar plexus, right where the ribs separate.

"This one's easier," I said, after trying it a few times both as attacker and victim.

"Yes, but it's a little more dangerous, because instead of throwing your attacker away from you and to the ground, you're pulling him toward you. You're using your own body as a weapon."

I nodded, thinking how much different it would be in real life to fight off an attacker. There was the element of surprise, the fear I might be feeling, the strength of my opponent, his training, how fast it happened, and my memory of how to disarm him that would all come into play.

"You mentioned knots earlier," I said. "Why do I need to know about knots?"

"Because you can do anything with knots. You can tie a wire between two trees across a road where you know an enemy motorcyclist will pass. You tie it at the height of his neck. He can't see it, but it will knock him off his motorcycle. If you don't know your knots, you'll miss your chance."

I couldn't help but smile. "So warfare is really about knowing how to tie knots?"

"Precisely! First, put the book back. Move the barrel back on top of it, and then I'll teach you the hitch knot. It's so useful. If you want to —"

Suddenly, the basement door creaked open. Our heads snapped toward the top of the stairs. "Polina, is that you?" It had to be her mother. The voice sounded clouded and scratchy, like it wasn't used much.

"I'll be right there!" Then, in a whisper, she said, "Ivan, put everything back, and then go to Miss Galina's. We'll practice more later. Wait one minute after I've gone, then leave by the back door. Don't say good-bye, and don't let my mother see you."

I nodded, and she ran up the stairs. I counted to sixty and slipped out of her house unnoticed. My life as a partisan had begun.

CHAPTER 16

I HEARD THE DEEP RUMBLE OF GUNS IN THE DISTANCE JUST AS I REACHED GALINA'S BACK DOOR. GALINA AND AUNTIE HOVERED IN THE KITCHEN, STANDING NEAR THE STOVE, involved in what looked like a tense conversation. They stopped talking when I entered and turned toward me as if they had something to say.

"Hello, Ivan," Galina said gently. "Sit down. We've had some news."

"Yes?" I squirmed in my seat.

"Kirill from the bakery just came by."

"And . . ."

Galina seemed like she couldn't get the words out, and so Auntie said them for her. "They're coming."

Those two words went like lightning through my veins. In Leningrad, the German soldiers were an unseen enemy, attacking from above. In Vilnov, the soldiers would march in, or ride into town in their tanks. They would be individual men, with faces, and guns at their fingertips.

"When?" I asked.

"Kirill said they were about five miles away."

"Does everyone know?"

"Kirill was running from house to house. They probably know by now." The boom of an artillery gun filled the air.

"It's really happening," Galina said in a hushed voice.

"What should we do?" I asked, suddenly feeling like I wanted to run. But where? Where would we be safe? There was no such place in our part of Russia.

"We stay put," Auntie said firmly. "We keep ourselves strong, and we stay calm."

Galina nodded. "Our valuables are hidden. Our papers are in order. What am I forgetting, Vera?"

Before Auntie could answer, another artillery shot shattered the silence; Galina let out a little cry. "Sorry," she said, covering her mouth.

"There was no impact!" I said excitedly. "Did you notice? Neither time. Just a boom. They didn't shoot a shell or it would have exploded. It's not an attack, it's a warning. They're letting us know they're on their way."

Auntie nodded. "He's right. We sit tight. Have your warmest coat hanging next to the door, and put your warmest shoes on."

"Why?" I asked.

"If they take us away, we'll be warm. It could be the difference between life and death."

We were prepared as Auntie suggested within minutes.

"Now what?" I asked as we stood in the hallway. We'd just hung our warmest coats on pegs Galina had hammered into the back of the front door.

"Take half of our food, Galina, and hide it. Same with the fuel, if you can. Quickly. Ivan, help her. I'll stand here as a lookout."

Galina and I rushed to the kitchen. She opened a cupboard, and I reached up to take a sack of flour from her that she'd slipped off the highest shelf. "There's a little cellar I dug just outside the door of the chicken coop. The few valuables I have are there already — my father's pocket watch . . . Anyway, we can hide a lot in there." She pulled a box of salt and a tin of oil off the shelf. "Grab the box of sugar on the first shelf and follow me."

We rushed out into the cold morning, our arms full, toward the eight-by-eight-foot coop. The chickens clucked and fussed and flapped their wings as we approached. "No time to find new homes for you now, my dears." Galina kicked aside a bale of hay to the left of the coop door to reveal a battered piece of wood with a thin six-inch piece of leather nailed to it to be used as a handle. She pushed away straw with her foot, bent down, grabbed the handle, and opened the top all the way so that it lay flat again on the ground.

The space was about three feet by four feet wide and about three feet deep. "Wow. I could fit in there," I said, amazed.

"Let's hope you never have to." She was already on her knees, reaching deep into the space and setting in the items she'd brought. The bottom and the sides of the little cellar had been lined with wood. A few of her personal items were tucked away in one of the corners.

We made two more trips, then Galina stood in front of one of her cupboards and said, "We'll hide only half of what we have."

"Why not all of it?"

"Because it wouldn't be believable."

"To who?"

"To a soldier sent to our house to take our food. We'd have to have some. If we had no supplies, they'd know we were hiding all of them and *really* start to look hard."

"Makes sense. What about our fuel?"

"We'll do something similar. We'll leave half of it in the woodpile outside the door. The rest we'll hide in groups of two or three — under the snow at the base of trees, near the chicken coop, a piece or two on the roof. You make it look casual, like you forgot to include them, or it's something that just fell from a tree."

We were startled by the sound of the front door opening and closing, and froze in fear. Auntie appeared in the doorway. Galina covered her heart with her hand. "You gave me a fright."

"I'm sorry, Galina. I went out to see if I could learn anything."

"And?"

"I stopped someone who was running west down the main road. He said soldiers and tanks were at the eastern edge of the town."

"That's only about a mile," Galina said softly. I barely heard her because another artillery boom interrupted us. "Quickly, both of you, let's get our fuel hidden. The Germans will be cold *and* hungry if we have anything to say about it."

We worked furiously for the next half hour. Thoughts kept circling through my mind: What would the first German face I saw look like? Who would it belong to? Would he be young? Old? Pretending to be friendly? Holding a gun? Shooting me on sight, and therefore the last thing I'd ever see on this earth?

In my wildest dreams, I never imagined the man I would actually meet, the man whose face was seared in my brain, the man who would haunt me for the rest of my life.

CHAPTER 17

THAT DAY PROVED TO BE ONE OF THE LONGEST DAYS EVER.
ABOUT AN HOUR AFTER WE'D FINISHED HIDING OUR FIRE-
WOOD AND FOOD SUPPLIES, GALINA PICKED UP HER PHONE
to call her neighbor.

"They must have cut the phone lines," she said quietly as she
replaced the receiver.

"Of course," Auntie said. "The less we know and the less we
communicate with our neighbors, the more powerful they become."

We sat in Galina's front room, looking out her big window for
any kind of activity. There was none, only sound. And the sounds
were confusing. Even two blocks away from the main street we
could hear the deep rumbling of the German tanks and trucks.
Of course we couldn't see anything, and there was no one to tell
us what was happening.

Never had time passed so slowly. Each minute felt like ten
with the anxiety, anticipation, and inactivity. Hour after hour
dragged by. Each of us took a book from Galina's overstuffed
bookcase, but none of us could concentrate, and we continued to
stare out the window for any sign of what was to come.

By afternoon I felt like I'd been in prison for a week. Leaving
the house was out of the question; staying in felt like torture. I
was weary from doing so little.

Finally I asked, "Would it be all right if I played my concertina for a while?"

The two women searched each other's faces, uncertain about

the answer. "What do you think, Galina?" Auntie asked, a doubtful look on her face.

Galina thought for a moment. "The neighbors on either side of us are too far away to be bothered. The Germans in town won't hear a note."

Auntie hesitated. "You don't think it will draw unwanted attention to the house?"

"I think it will be fine," Galina said.

"Thank you."

I went to my room, pulled my concertina out of its leather case, and slipped my hands through the straps. My fingertips caressed the buttons as if I'd been without it for a year.

Back in the living room, I began to play. The first notes of the melody felt as sweet as my mother's touch, pure and all-encompassing. I played a mournful folk tune my mother loved, the story of a traveler far from home. Of course I didn't sing it, but I felt it in my very bones. I must have played it for six or seven minutes, eyes closed, completely absorbed in the music.

But . . . what was that sound? I knew I hadn't hit a wrong note. There it was again. I opened my eyes and stopped playing. I knew exactly what it was. Not bothering to put down my concertina, I ran to the front door and threw it open. There, yapping at me, was the furriest, most beautiful German shepherd puppy I'd ever seen.

"Hello!" I cried, dropping to my knees. "Who are you?" I stared at her golden face as I set aside my concertina and petted her with both hands, soon feeling the lick of her tongue as she said hello in her own way.

"Auntie! Miss Galina! Come look — you won't believe it!" I turned to look at them over my shoulder as I continued to pet the thick, soft fur of my new friend. When they entered the hallway, their faces didn't reflect joy or happiness or surprise. They stared past me, shock and fear in their eyes.

I turned back toward the door, following their gaze. From my place on the floor, the first thing I saw was the perfectly polished black knee boots, with traces of dampness from the snow. Tilting my head back, I took in the blue-gray uniform under an open black leather coat, the peaked cap crowned by an eagle with its wings spread, its claws firmly grasping a circle emblazoned with a swastika.

I stopped petting the dog and stood up slowly. I swallowed hard. The first German I was to meet face-to-face was a Nazi officer. He wasn't too tall, but even with his overcoat on I could feel the strength and power underneath. His angular face was handsome, I suppose, although his skin was ruddy and rough-looking. His sharp eyes seemed to take in everything at a glance. I noticed there were three soldiers waiting at the bottom of the steps for him, rifles draped across their chests. Fear fluttered in my stomach.

"I see you've met Zasha," the man said in perfect, unaccented Russian. "I hope we aren't disturbing you." Zasha darted inside and ran through the house. I dared not follow her. I think we were all too stunned to respond. "I am Major Axel Recht, the commander of the troops currently occupying your town," he continued. He waited for a response, but we had none. "As my men and I walked past your house, we heard lovely music being played." My cheeks burned; I felt as if I'd signed a death warrant for us all. "Was that you, young man?"

My concertina lay on the floor next to me. "Yes, sir," I answered, trying to keep my voice from quavering.

"Music isn't something we hear much of in war. Would you mind if my men and I came in and listened while you played?" I looked to Galina and Auntie for direction.

"Of course, sir," Galina answered for me. "Please come this way."

The armed men jogged quickly up the stairs. As they did, another soldier came running from the side of the house, yelling to them in German. To my surprise, the other guards laughed in response to whatever it was he said. A smile even played across Major Recht's lips. I soon understood why. The soldier climbed the stairs holding another German shepherd puppy in his arms, who squirmed and fought to be set free.

After a brief exchange in German, the fourth soldier set the puppy on the floor. The commandant said, "And this is Thor." Thor's face was as dark as Zasha's was golden, and he was bigger and more muscular. He barked twice as if in greeting, and then trotted off toward the kitchen. The major stared at me. "Well?"

"Oh, yes, I'm sorry." I led the officer and his men into the living room; Galina motioned for them to be seated. None of the soldiers removed their rifles. Two sat down and two remained standing, one of them behind the major. Auntie and Galina huddled together just inside the door to the living room. I held my concertina and stood very still facing the men, who looked alert and dangerous. I was terrified of them, especially the commander, but I was also thrilled that there were two precious dogs roaming the house.

"There was a wonderful accordionist in our company," Major Recht said, "but unfortunately he was lost in action." I saw an emotion pass over his face so quickly — in the blink of an eye, just like it's said — that I was shocked I saw it. It was deadly anger, presumably because the accordion player was killed. It reminded me of the first thing Petr taught me at the partisan meeting: keep your thoughts private and your expression blank.

"What is your name, young man?"

"Ivan," I said, remembering how Petr said never to give more information than you're asked.

"What were you playing when we interrupted you?"

I had to think for a minute because I was still so stunned by what was happening. " 'Winter Moon.' "

He nodded. "Play it again."

I glanced at Auntie and Galina, but only out of nervousness; there was no question about refusing his request. Their expressions were set in a deliberate blankness. I let my fingers find their places on my concertina. This was one of the first songs I'd ever learned. I could play it in my sleep, which would give me time to think.

The first moody, minor chords filled the small parlor. As casually as I could, I examined the four guards of the Nazi commandant. They were massive men. Not just tall, but imposing, beefy. Their bodies seemed ready and anxious for a fight. When the one nearest Axel Recht adjusted his cap, I noticed that he was missing most of his ear. Where was all this leading, I asked myself, desperately searching for an answer. Should I play poorly and disappoint him and hope he'd never come back? Or should I . . .

In a flash of insight, I knew what I needed to do. I'd just completed the first verse of my song — *perfect timing*, I thought. I closed my eyes and let my body sway as I began the second verse, making it a little louder and a little syncopated.

I felt more than saw the slightly startled reaction of my audience. Now I began to move as I played, strutting like a dancer might, making the impassioned faces that Alik used to tease me about, twirling around as I came to the chorus. I ended the song with a dramatic hold on the second to the last chord, and when I hit the last chord, I dropped to one knee and held it for several seconds.

The men applauded and murmured their appreciation. Axel seemed never to take his eyes off of me. I rose and took a bow, bending at the waist toward the men, and then toward Auntie and Galina just so I could catch a glimpse of them. Auntie and I locked eyes. She knew what I was doing, I could feel it. I turned away from her and smiled modestly at the Nazi soldiers. "Thank you."

The clapping must have drawn the attention of the dogs, because they came running into the living room. The men, any one of whom looked like they could fight off a group of attackers with their bare hands, murmured and smiled as soon as the dogs appeared, making little clicking sounds with their mouths, and bending over and motioning with their hands so the dogs would go to them. To my great surprise, the one the major had called Zasha ran over to me. Standing on her back legs, she put her paws on my leg and begged to be picked up. Thor noticed and came over to sniff me closely. The soldiers looked disappointed.

"They like you," the commander observed. Suddenly I didn't want them to like me. They were his dogs, after all, and

I didn't want to find out what he'd do to me if he was jealous of the attention they were giving me. I petted Zasha's head, but also tried to push her gently away from me. Thor had already moved on to see who Auntie and Galina were.

"So, Ivan, how many songs would you say you know?" Axel Recht asked. He sat in the most comfortable chair in the room looking completely relaxed, as if he owned the house and had hired me for the evening's entertainment.

"Oh." I sighed. "So many . . . I've been playing since I was six. I would say a hundred or more. I've never tried to count."

Axel made a slight nod of approval. I tried to memorize his features: the light, observant eyes, the strong nose that was turned down at the end as if it had been injured and never repaired, the high cheekbones. If I had to use just three words to describe what was expressed in that face, they would be *intelligence, decisiveness,* and *cruelty.*

He said something in German to his guards. They looked at me and nodded their heads almost imperceptibly.

"I know one German song," I offered, wishing desperately I could understand what had just been said.

The commandant's eyebrows went up in surprise. "Really?"

"Yes. Our music teacher taught it to us. 'Stille Nacht' in German. In Russian we call it 'Silent Night.'" I swear one of the guards lit up like a child.

"It's Austrian, actually," Axel corrected me, "but close enough."

Never had a musician wrung so much feeling out of that simple lullaby as I did that night. Christmas was less than a month away; I'd always heard it was a particularly important holiday for the Germans, and that this song was sung all through the

Christmas season. It also calmed down the dogs. They lay quietly at my feet.

When I was done and the last suspended chord resolved, I knew what was coming. I'd tried to make it happen with my playing, and I thought I'd succeeded. Axel stared at me after I'd finished, then turned to Auntie and Galina. "Where are his mother and father?"

"They are deceased," Auntie lied smoothly. "I am his guardian until he is eighteen."

"How old is he?" His questions had a cool detachment to them.

"Almost thirteen," Auntie answered. Her demeanor was composed but deferential, a perfect combination for this strange and potentially dangerous encounter.

"And you are . . . ?" he said to Galina.

"I am her sister-in-law," she answered simply.

He nodded and stood up, glanced briefly at his guards, and then smiled politely, if briefly, at Auntie and Galina. "Ladies, thank you." He slipped on the black leather gloves he'd removed and walked into the entry hall; his men followed. Two of them picked up Zasha and Thor and held them tightly. Then Axel said, "We're going to take Ivan with us."

Galina's eyes grew wide; she opened her mouth as if to speak, but then closed it.

Auntie met his gaze and said, "For how long, sir?"

He studied me for a moment. "I don't know. For the evening, for a day, for a month? My men could use some entertainment. They've been fighting hard." Again, I caught a flicker of emotion, this time disdain, as if he could hardly make himself waste his time on explanations to two old women.

"We are happy to share him with you. His music always makes everyone happy. But . . . but he is such a comfort to us here."

He stared at her and then let out a little sound that was like a suppressed laugh. "Prepare him to go."

"I'll only be a minute," I said, and went into my room. Auntie followed.

"Let's get your toothbrush, some warm socks, and your sleeping clothes," she said, loud enough so that the men in the hall could hear. Then she whispered to me, "You did this on purpose, didn't you? You *want* to go."

I nodded and whispered back, "I played hard so they'd want to hear me more. I'm going to spy on them." Even as I said it I got a sinking feeling in my stomach. Who did I think I was to go walking into Nazi headquarters and expect I could be of any use to my countrymen?

"Don't forget some warm underwear," she said loudly. "But why? You don't even speak German," she whispered in my ear.

"I know, but if I'm there I can see things, I can make guesses about others, I can tell the partisans what's going on." I grabbed my duffel bag and began stuffing a few necessities into it.

"Take your knife; put it in your boot. Come back here the minute they let you go," she said quietly.

I nodded my head, reached under the mattress where I'd hidden the knife, and then froze as a terrible thought shot through me. "What if they don't let me go?"

I saw the fear in her eyes, too. "If they don't, I'll march in there and get you!" She put her arms around me and held me tight.

"Whatever happens, I'll figure out a way to get back here." I slung my bag over my shoulder.

"Here's your concertina case. Your coat is hanging on the back of the front door." She kissed my forehead; there were tears forming in her eyes. "Hurry, before he changes his mind."

Or before I change mine, I thought, but I knew it was way too late to turn back now.

CHAPTER 18

THE SNOW CRUNCHED UNDER OUR FEET AS AXEL LED US NOT TOWARD THE CENTER OF TOWN, BUT WANDERING THROUGH THE VILLAGE, CAREFULLY OBSERVING EVERY-thing. At first he allowed the dogs to run free, then ordered one of his men to put them on leads. Neither Zasha nor Thor seemed happy with limits on their explorations. He didn't stop at any more houses, but talked often with his bodyguards, and occasionally asked me a question.

"Ivan, what is on the other side of this forest?" He pointed in the direction of the path Polina and I had taken on the day we went sledding and I first met Petr.

"I don't know, sir. We only just arrived, and I don't know the area that well."

He continued to look around him. "Really? In my experience, twelve-year-old boys know their surroundings better than most."

"I do know there's a hill not far away where I've gone sledding with my friend."

"You see, you do know something. Tell me more."

"About . . ." My heart jumped at every question.

"This town, these people." He wanted to turn me into a collaborator, when all I wanted to do was be a spy.

"Many of them left for Moscow."

"Moscow?" he repeated, as though he found it laughable. "Our troops are just twenty miles from Moscow now. And where did you live before you came to this . . . *charming* village?"

"Leningrad."

"Ah, Leningrad." I hated hearing the word from his mouth, remembering all the needless suffering his people had rained upon us. "You're lucky to be here. There's not much of it left, from what I hear."

"But, sir, why has the city been targeted? It's full of women and children."

He stopped walking and turned to me. His guards seemed like they were disturbed by his action, and of course they couldn't understand us because we were speaking Russian.

"Never question me," he said sharply, the heat of anger beneath his words. "I don't care if all the people and buildings in Leningrad are destroyed. That is our objective."

Those words assured me that I'd made the right decision to enter the enemy camp if I could help rid my country of our savage invaders. He didn't speak to me again until we were approaching the town square. The sight was amazing and frightening. Everywhere I looked was a tank or a troop truck, even two large artillery guns. If they had belonged to the Russian army, I would've done anything to get close to them and examine them. But these machines were here to kill us, and so I tried to memorize their details, their shapes, and their functions so I could give the information to Petr.

I noticed that all the men we passed saluted Axel quickly when they saw him. There was something else in their response: fear. He wasn't just the officer in charge, a man of authority and power. I'd sensed cruelty in him only minutes after meeting him. The soldiers unwittingly confirmed it.

The Germans had occupied what looked like the largest building in town for their headquarters. It was the two-story brick building painted pale yellow that Polina had showed me, the one she said we'd explore soon, and it hummed with activity. I was at a terrible disadvantage not being able to speak German. From what I could observe, most of the rooms or former offices had been turned into sleeping quarters for the soldiers, while others had the look of command centers, with tables, desks, and chairs.

The sight of Zasha and Thor brought smiles to the faces of almost everyone we passed. Many of the men glanced at me curiously, or with confusion, or even hostility; maybe not only because I was Russian, but because I wasn't being treated as a prisoner. The men exuded confidence and a sense of superiority. And why wouldn't they feel that way? I asked myself. So far, they were the winners, conquering almost everything they'd set their sights on. They also had the well-fed, well-cared-for look that I'd noted in the soldiers with Axel. These men were not to be underestimated.

Finally, we entered what I assumed was Axel's command center, if only because it was the biggest room we'd seen. One of the guards helped Axel with his coat and pulled out a chair for him behind a large desk. He quickly began to sift through a stack of papers laid out in front of him. I stood near the door and watched, trying not to get in anyone's way or do anything wrong.

A makeshift bed of blankets had been created for Thor and Zasha in the corner. They settled themselves in the blankets, pawing them first into a more comfortable arrangement.

Already my ears were tired of the harsh tones of German, my spirit jarred by the sight of Nazi uniforms and insignias. This was the belly of the beast, and I had purposefully taken up residence here. I started to feel the kind of fear I'd had before I crossed Lake Ladoga, that I might die before I had a chance to grow up.

"Ivan."

I flinched. "Yes, sir?"

"Play."

I took my concertina out of its case and slipped my hands through the straps. I'd already picked out the songs I would play him, beginning with a Ukrainian melody the janitor of our apartment building had taught me. As I played those first chords, I could feel myself back in the basement of our building in Leningrad, watching and listening as he instructed me. I reminded myself that we each had our own way of fighting our enemy. My mother's was to work in a factory that made tanks. Auntie's was to take responsibility for someone else's son and to help the partisans. Petr, Galina, Yeshka, and Polina had committed themselves to being secret citizen soldiers. I played my concertina for a Nazi officer and hoped to learn something useful.

I played off and on for most of the afternoon, responding to Axel's terse "stop" or "play" as he wished. Just two guards stayed with him, but they were vigilant. One was posted outside the door; the other one watched every person who entered for every second they were there and monitored activity in the streets when they were gone. If someone did manage to make his way into the room to harm Axel, he'd be dead before he reached his target.

When dinnertime came, I was told by Axel to stay put and watch the dogs. As hungry as I was, I couldn't have been happier. I sat down next to the dozing puppies. Zasha rolled on her back, and I petted her tummy. I swear her face shone with some kind of light from deep inside her; she had what Auntie would have called an old soul. Her face and chest were covered in golden fur, perfectly accented by black fur around her mouth, in a little widow's peak on her head, and around her eyes.

Thor managed to wriggle himself between me and Zasha to receive his share of attention. It was easy to tell them apart. The fur on Thor's muzzle and face was black, all the way to the tips of his ears. One ear stood at attention, and the other flopped softly down. In spite of my surroundings, I laughed and was filled with a kind of peace. For the next twenty minutes, I played with them in their bed, rolling around with them, scratching them behind their ears, petting them in long strokes from head to tail. We were lying together contentedly when the door opened. The dogs and I sat up immediately, although I'm sure they didn't share the fear that filled me.

Holding two bowls of food in his hands, a man with a white apron over his uniform entered the room and kicked the door closed behind him. To my surprise, he smiled and spoke to me in German as he set the bowls down for the dogs. He talked sweetly to them as they ate.

"I'm sorry, I don't speak German," I said to him in Russian.

"Fritzi," he said, patting his chest.

Relieved, I did the same. "Ivan."

"Good, good," he said in Russian.

"You speak Russian?"

"Little bits. Good doggies, huh?" he asked, motioning toward them. Thor had finished his meal and was making an effort to eat some of Zasha's. She deftly moved her body to keep him at bay while she finished.

"Good doggies," I concurred.

Fritzi frowned as he looked around the room. "No watering?"

"No," I said, having noticed there were no water bowls, but not yet bold enough to bring it to Axel's attention.

"Ah." He sighed. "I'm getting." He disappeared, but was soon back with bowls of water for the thirsty dogs, who drank deeply from them. After Fritzi left, the dogs seemed content to rest. We cuddled together in their nest of blankets on the floor and fell asleep.

★ ★ ★

I was awakened by the sound of Axel arguing with someone. The room quickly filled with bodyguards and other soldiers. The dogs ran to Axel. His ranting stopped temporarily as he bent over to pet them and pick up Zasha, then started up again. It was then that he noticed me in the corner. "What are you doing in the dogs' bed?" He sounded annoyed.

I stood up. "I'm sorry, sir. We were taking a nap together. After their dinner," I added, hoping he'd remember I hadn't eaten. He didn't.

The door opened and, still speaking Russian, he said, "Now what?" A soldier brought him a letter, which he read as he put Zasha down. The soldier remained at attention. Axel threw the letter down on the desk and looked furious. He snapped at the soldier, who promptly left, and I noticed the guards exchanging glances. Axel seemed like one of those volatile people whom those around him had to cater to or risk being his next target.

When two more people came to see him a few minutes later, he pushed Zasha and Thor away from him in irritation. "Ivan! Take care of these dogs, for goodness' sake!"

I jumped up and tried to corral the puppies over by their bed, but they were restless, and I thought I knew why. "Sir, may I take the dogs outside to do their business?"

"Go! And don't you dare let them get away from you!"

I clipped the leads the German soldier had been using onto their collars and went out to the hall. I remembered where the side entrance was where we'd come in earlier and went that way. No one asked me any questions or tried to stop me.

After we'd left the building and were halfway down the stairs, I heard a dreadful, loud torrent of German that I knew was aimed at me. I stopped instantly. A soldier rushed at me from the sidewalk, his rifle up and ready to fire. Three more soldiers came running to help him.

I raised my hands, a lead still in each one. The dogs pulled to go forward. "Axel Recht," I said, as loudly and clearly as I could, hoping they'd understand that I was there with his permission. "Axel Recht." The soldier stepped closer, speaking to me in German. "Russian!" I said. "I'm Russian. I don't speak German." He gave a command to one of the other soldiers, who ran toward me and grabbed the leads from my hands. I closed my eyes, afraid he might hit me, but the blow never came.

When I opened my eyes, the soldier with the rifle was yelling at me again, and making a twirling motion with his hand, indicating I should turn around. Keeping my hands in the air, I turned and walked back toward Axel's office. I could hear the tap of the dogs' nails on the hard floor and knew they were close behind us. It gave me comfort to know I hadn't been separated from them.

The guard outside of Axel's room showed no indication that he recognized me. In fact, I thought I saw a hint of a smile, as if he found my predicament amusing. He knocked on the door, opened it, and in we went. There was a quick exchange in German, with Axel's temper soon on display. I could practically feel the guard who'd stopped me shrinking in front of his tongue-lashing. Thor took the opportunity to relieve himself on the leg of Axel's desk.

Axel's face became flushed with anger, and he raced around to pick up Thor. He never stopped yelling at the soldier, and when Thor continued to urinate after Axel picked him up, I thought his head would explode.

"Ivan! Get something to clean this up! Now! Oh, my boots . . ."

For a moment I was afraid he would hurl Thor across the room. "I've got him!" I cried, reaching over to take the dog from his hands. "Where can I find rags, soap, and water?"

"Do I look like a janitor?" he shouted. "Go to the basement. Find Fritzi."

I ran out and down the nearest flight of stairs to the basement, Thor still in my arms. At the other end of the hall there was activity of some sort. I ran toward it.

It turned out to be a cafeteria or dining room of some sort. A half dozen men in white aprons were clearing the tables and putting food away. Fritzi stood in front of a stove, talking to another man.

"Fritzi!" I called out, and ran toward him.

"Ah, Thor! Ivan," he said in greeting.

"We — I mean, Axel needs towels, soap, and water for me to clean up after the dog."

"Bathing?"

"No, no. Bathroom. Thor went to the bathroom."

Minutes later I was on my knees cleaning up Thor's mess. Only Axel and the bodyguards remained. "Those soldiers thought you were trying to steal my dogs," he told me with a dismissive laugh as he stared out of an open window and lit a cigarette. After a pause, he added, "I'd put you in one of our uniforms, but you're too small." The thought of wearing a German uniform was repellant. Axel sat down at his desk. "I'll write a note on my stationery. If you're stopped again, show it to the soldiers."

Once I was sure the floor and desk were spotless and no odor remained, I stood in front of Axel. "Shall I try to take the dogs out again, sir?"

"Don't *try*, do it." He thrust a piece of paper toward me. I barely glanced at it, but saw it contained a short message handwritten in German. "If you're stopped again, show this. And don't lose it, because you won't get another."

"Yes, sir." I folded it carefully and put it in my shirt pocket. The dogs and I completed our walk without any problems, although we did receive a dirty look when we passed the soldier who had first stopped us.

When we returned to Axel's room, Fritzi was collecting the blankets and bowls from the corner. I stopped, alarmed, not understanding what was happening. Fritzi saw us. "Follow me!" he said with a smile, and headed for the door.

I turned to Axel. "Sir?"

He didn't look up from his reading. "You didn't think you were going to sleep in this room with me, did you?"

"No, sir," I answered, trying to hide the relief I felt at the chance to get away from him.

"Take your things. Do whatever Fritzi tells you."

I got the dogs on their leads and took my belongings, saying, "Thank you. Good night, sir," and followed Fritzi out the door. What joy I felt in the hall, as if a thousand-pound weight had been lifted from me. Zasha and Thor pulled hard on their leads to follow Fritzi.

As we descended the stairs to the basement, I said, "Fritzi, who's been taking care of the dogs?"

He shrugged. "Soldiers."

"No one special?"

He shook his head. "Only me. I cooking for them! Two days."

I'd been curious about when the dogs arrived and why they were there in the first place. As pets for Axel? I knew groups of soldiers often kept stray dogs they found at the front as mascots and companions. But puppies during active fighting? Ones · that looked like they were special, the best of their breed? If I could find the right moment, I'd ask Fritzi to tell me what he knew.

The long corridor was lined with doors on either side. "Opening, please?" Fritzi said, pausing in front of one of them about halfway down. His hands were full with the dogs' bowls and blankets. I opened it, but before he entered, he said, "No. Wrong." I peeked in; it looked like a storeroom full of brooms, mops, shovels, and buckets. "Maybe next." We backtracked to the room behind it, and I rushed to open the door for him.

"Yes! New home, doggies!" He set Zasha's food and water dishes on one side of the room and Thor's on the other side. The back wall of the room was dominated by two metal desks, with several layers of chairs piled on top of them. Fritzi arranged the blanket beds for the dogs under the cutout spaces in the middle of the desks, providing them with a protected, sheltered area.

I made a little pantomime with a few words to show him I would be sleeping there, too. "Bed?" I asked. "Pillow? Blanket?"

"Bed," he repeated, and sort of shrugged, like that might be a hard order to fill. "Pillow? Yes, no. Blanket? Yes."

"Thank you." I put my hand over my heart to show him how much I appreciated anything he could give me.

Fritzi made another trip to fill the dogs' bowls with water and bring them a treat of bread and butter. He even managed to find an inch-thick pad for me to use as a mattress. It was barely long enough, but would protect me from the cold floor. As Fritzi was saying good night to us, I told him I hadn't had anything to eat since lunch. Ten minutes later he brought me a dish of hot stew and bread and butter. He watched me eat it, laughing as Zasha and Thor demanded that I share it with them. And, of course, I did.

After settling the dogs in their beds for the night, I lay in the dark thinking of all the things that had happened in that one day: becoming a partisan and learning some of their secrets, preparing Galina's house for the German occupation of the town, Zasha coming to the front door, meeting Major Recht and his bodyguards, playing my concertina for them, being taken to Nazi headquarters, being frightened to death when the soldier aimed his gun at me, and finding myself at the end of the day with the two most beautiful dogs in the world asleep in a storeroom.

As I drifted off to sleep, I heard a sound like a moth fluttering its wings against a window, a gentle, rhythmic tapping. My weary mind was still trying to place it when I realized it was the *click* of little nails against the hard floor.

"Zasha? Thor?" I reached out in the darkness and felt the caress of fur on my fingers. I couldn't tell which of the dogs it was. Lifting my blanket, I said, "Okay, come here. You can sleep with me tonight." Without hesitation, the dog crawled under my blanket and settled against my abdomen.

As I was moving to make more space, I heard the telltale sound of another lonely puppy making its way toward us. "We're over here," I said with a laugh, reaching out to guide the dog. I knew immediately it was Thor, because he was bigger than the first one, who I now knew to be Zasha. Thor found a place against my chest where he was comfortable, and I covered all three of us with the blanket. "Good night," I whispered.

CHAPTER 19

"GET UP! GET UP!" THE OVERHEAD LIGHT SEARED MY EYES. I COULDN'T SEE THE PERSON WHO HOVERED OVER ME, BUT I KNEW IT WAS AXEL. MEMORIES OF THE PREVIOUS DAY LIT up my tired brain just as I felt the movement of puppies against my chest and heard their faint moans of waking.

"Where are my dogs?" he demanded. "They're gone! *Where are my dogs?*"

I sat up, pulling the blanket back to reveal Thor and Zasha. "They're right here, sir."

I could see his face now, the anger changing to relief, then to something I couldn't quite read. He bent down and picked up Thor.

"You will not sleep in the same bed with my dogs again. Do you understand?"

"Yes, sir. I set up their beds for them, but they wanted —"

"I don't want to hear your idiotic excuses. I won't have them sleeping with a Russian. Their job will be to hunt Russians when they're older. I can't have them confused."

Zasha was licking my hand. I quickly turned her around and pushed her gently toward her water bowl. Rage sparked in me at the idea of their being trained to hunt my fellow countrymen, but I tried to ignore it as I said, "You're right. I shouldn't have let them sleep with me."

"Of course I'm right. You are not their master — I am. Get the other dog and follow me." Zasha was a little skittish and tried to run under the desk, but soon I had her in my arms.

"I'm thinking of changing their names," Axel informed me as I ran to catch up with him. "Hansel and Gretel sound more German, don't you think? And more amusing."

"Of course that's up to you, sir," I said diplomatically, thinking not only what an awful idea it was but of his terrible temper. "Although dogs do learn their names very quickly. Changing them now might confuse them. It could slow down their ability to learn."

He didn't respond, but I could see his body stiffen. "I'll make the decision before the day is over. Do not refer to them by their names until then."

"Yes, sir."

We entered the cafeteria, which was already bustling with preparations for the morning meal. "Fritzi!" Axel called out to the cook. He held Thor high, smiling proudly. Fritzi looked up and stopped stirring what looked like a huge pot of oatmeal; a smile spread across his face. Soon Fritzi and the other cooks had gathered around Axel. They laughed and talked and reached out to pet Thor, while Zasha sat at Axel's feet.

I couldn't understand what they were saying, although the names *Thor* and *Hansel* and *Zasha* and *Gretel* were repeated several times. Finally, Axel shrugged and placed Thor down. Then he said to me, "The consensus is that Thor and Zasha are stronger names." It seemed so obvious. Even I knew that Thor was the name for the Norse god of thunder. It was the perfect name for the lively, bold puppy. And Zasha was a Russian name, one of the nicknames for Alexandra.

I couldn't help but hope that every time Axel uttered her beautiful Russian name it would taste bitter in his mouth.

Fritzi put down bowls of chopped meat and oatmeal in the corner for the puppies. They ate quickly and looked up at Fritzi expectantly when they were done.

"Oh, no, no more," Axel said, "or you'll both be looking like fat Russian peasants." He scooped up Thor. "Get Zasha. Follow me."

We went back to the storeroom. "Get your concertina. We'll leave the dogs in here for now," he said, closing the door to the windowless room without saying good-bye.

"Are we . . . Are you just going to leave them there alone?"

"Are you *questioning* me again, Ivan?" He strode down the hall toward the stairs; I rushed to follow.

"No, sir, it's just that I was thinking . . ." I hesitated because, in truth, the idea was still forming in my brain somewhere. Several seconds went by.

"Apparently you're not actually thinking," he said as he reached the stairs.

Then it hit me. I knew. "I was thinking that I could train the dogs, sir. Back in Leningrad I was well known for being the best dog trainer in our apartment building."

"In your entire apartment building? Imagine that," he said sarcastically, jogging up the staircase.

It was a lie. I'd taught Olga's dog, Oskar, a few tricks and watched occasionally as Georgi trained Leonid, but I knew I could figure it out.

"As much as I'd like to take advantage of your *gift*, what I'm sure is your *genius*, I have made other arrangements for their training. We start this morning."

"Maybe I could help that person," I said as we reached the first floor. Something in me knew that I had to be with those dogs to protect them.

"I can't imagine he'll have any need of your help. Now, quiet."

Ten minutes later I watched Axel shave in a large, tiled lavatory, standing shirtless in front of one of the mirrors. I played the concertina for him near the door. He said he liked the way the sound reverberated and echoed in the room. I'd never seen a grown man shave, and I watched with interest as he foamed the soap in a cup with a brush, spread it carefully, and expertly removed the hair with a straight razor. But the thought of learning about shaving from a Nazi filled me with anger, not just for myself, but for all the Russian boys who had lost their fathers at the hands of the army that surrounded me.

Many men came in and out to prepare themselves for the day. Every one of them acknowledged through the tone of his voice or the way he moved his body that Axel was the man in charge. When they spotted me, they spoke to Axel, probably asking who I was. I could tell they were pleased with having music; some even nodded to me in greeting with smiles.

When he was done, I followed Axel back to the cafeteria where breakfast was being served. He went directly to the head of the line. There seemed to be endless pots of food filled with things we hadn't seen in Leningrad in months. I envied and hated our enemy all at the same time.

He glanced around the room and pointed to a place near the wall. "Go over there. Play for everyone while I eat. Fritzi will give you breakfast afterward."

"Yes, sir." Then I took a deep breath to gather my courage and said, "I keep thinking about the dogs. I'd be more than happy to stay with them during their first training session. It would be no problem. I —"

He closed his eyes, as if his anger was building. "Not only do I not want you with us, you will leave this building when you have finished playing. You *will not* return until noon when their training session is over. Do you understand me?"

I opened my mouth to speak, but knew if I uttered another word about the dogs there would be trouble. I nodded.

I positioned myself where Axel had told me to stand and began to play "My Sunflower," the song Alik and Misha and I had been working on the day of the first heavy bombing. It helped me put the dogs out of my mind temporarily and focus on the necessity of memorizing everything around me so I could tell Petr: the number of men, what their uniforms looked like. There was hardly a wounded man in the room. Most looked healthy and confident. They chatted happily and laughed often. *Doesn't one of you have a pang of guilt about invading our country?* I wondered. *Do you know about the siege of Leningrad, of what your fellow soldiers are doing right now to us, as you feed your faces and look so satisfied?*

"Ivan!" It was Axel. "Softer." I nodded, only then realizing my anger and tension had been expressed in my playing.

Forty minutes later, when the room was almost empty and Axel had dismissed me, I packed up my concertina and asked Fritzi if I could have something to eat. He fed me well and asked about the dogs. I told him that Axel was going to start their training that morning.

155

"Good!" Fritzi exclaimed. "Good dogs for guarding. Everything they find." He smiled at me like we should both be happy for their glorious futures. It was the guarding and finding I worried about. I felt certain that to make the dogs capable of such things they would have to be exposed to cruelty themselves. You don't create a vicious guard dog, one taught to hunt human beings, by gentle coaxing. You create it through fear and brutality.

My distress must have been written all over my face. Fritzi said, "You sick, Ivan?"

"No, I'm fine. Just thinking. Thank you, Fritzi," I said, holding up the rolls he'd wrapped in butcher paper for me to take with me.

Once I was out of sight of the soldiers guarding headquarters, I ran all the way to Galina's. Auntie and Galina were out near the chicken coop searching for eggs. They both gasped when they saw me.

"Ivan," Auntie whispered, "come in the house." We hurried into the kitchen, where I'd barely set down my things before the two of them began hugging me and fussing over me. They both had tears in their eyes.

Auntie shook her head as she gazed at me. "After you left I worried I would never see you again. How could I ever have explained it to your mother?" She closed her eyes.

"Sit down. I'll get you breakfast," Galina added.

"I've already eaten." I held up the parcel of food. "And look — soft rolls!"

"How do you know they're not poisoned?" Galina asked, frowning.

"I don't. But Axel told me to be back by noon, so I don't think they'll kill me just yet. He seems to be in charge of everything here. What's happened since I left yesterday?"

"We went to see Petr early this morning to tell him they'd taken you."

"What did he say?"

"He said if they let you go, or if we found out anything about you, to go see him immediately."

"All right. But what happened here, in the town? Did any of the Germans come to tell us what we can do and what we can't do?"

"No. Galina has heard they sometimes go through the neighborhood with a loudspeaker, telling everyone to report to their headquarters."

"Other times they come to the door. They look at everything you have and take what they want." Galina shrugged, her eyes wide. "It's only what I've heard; I don't really know. We should be prepared for anything."

"I'm going to go see Petr now. He'll figure out something important for me to do while I'm there," I said, pushing myself away from the table. "I have to be back there in just a few hours, and I can't be late." I ran out the back, never having taken off my coat, and barely saying good-bye.

CHAPTER 20

ON MY LONG WALK TO PETR'S, I KEPT A KEEN EYE OUT FOR MOVEMENT OF ANY KIND OR SIGNS THAT SOMEONE MIGHT BE WATCHING ME. I SAW ONLY BLUE SKY AND THE QUIET blanket of snow that covered everything.

I passed near the crest of the hill that Polina and I sledded down. I wanted so badly to slide or roll down it or to play in the snow, but thought to myself, *No, you're a partisan now. Partisans don't make snow angels on their way to meet their group leaders.* It filled me with a sense of purpose and determination.

I knocked once on Petr's door, just as Polina had done yesterday morning. There was no answer. Stepping back to see if smoke was coming from the chimney, I saw there was none. I looked around, uncertain what to do, when I saw one of the curtains that covered the front windows move slightly.

The door creaked open, although I couldn't see anyone behind it. I slipped quickly into the cottage.

"Wrong knock." It was Petr's voice. Like the last time I was there, my eyes had to adjust to the dim light before I could make out his face. "One knock is for a meeting. One knock, count to three, then two knocks means 'I have to talk to you.'"

"I'll get Polina to teach me the others."

"Good. What do you have to tell me?" He lit a long pipe, and I sat down in a rough wooden chair near him. I began my story about how Zasha had come to Galina's door, of Axel and his bodyguards, of Thor, of playing music for them, and of Axel's decision to take me to headquarters. I poured out as many details as I could remember about the guns, other weapons, and soldiers I'd seen. I even told him about sleeping with the dogs, and about the soldier outside the building who'd stopped me from walking them.

"You're brave," he said simply. It was an unexpected compliment from a man I guessed didn't give them out often.

"Thank you."

"Once you're in their territory, your options are limited."

"What do you mean?" A little ripple of anxiety shivered through me.

He shrugged. "If they go to your house, catch you on the road, you can run, or at least try. If you're in their camp, well, you're their prisoner even if they haven't put the handcuffs on yet."

"I'll remember that."

"What did you learn of Major Recht?" Petr had an intense way of looking at you, like he knew your words before you spoke them.

"He seems to be in charge of everything. He speaks perfect Russian; his guards don't speak any. He seems very smart and . . ."

"And what?"

"Cruel. It was nothing he did exactly. I just saw it in him. He tries to hide it, though."

"What does a twelve-year-old boy know about such things?"

"I saw it. It passes over his face in an instant, even less."

Petr nodded slightly as he lit his pipe again. "Axel Werner Siegfried Recht was, until recently, a lieutenant colonel in the German army. He was demoted when his superior officer found out Axel was spending a great deal of time with the officer's wife."

"So you know of him! But why would they send a colonel to little Vilnov? It's not like we're Moscow or Leningrad."

"I think that's the point exactly. He's being punished."

"Oh. How did you know all of this?"

"Information is power. Any bit of news or even rumor a partisan hears he passes along. You'd be amazed what we know."

"Like what?"

"Like what I just told you about Recht. We know other things. For instance, he likes whips. In fact, he's an expert with a whip."

Something deep inside of me was so repelled by the thought that my stomach contracted as if I'd just seen a snake. Using a whip was different from using a gun. It seemed to me you had to enjoy inflicting pain to use a whip.

"I didn't see one," I said, my mouth feeling dry. "How do you . . . how do you defend yourself against someone with a whip?"

"I don't think you do. And they say the pain is . . ." Petr must have realized how his words were affecting me because he changed the subject. "Why has he let you go?"

"He hasn't. I'm supposed to be back at noon. I don't know what will happen after that. He even gave me a letter," I said with a little laugh, "so that if another one of his men stops me or wants to shoot me, they'll know I have his permission to be there."

Petr stood up very straight and leaned toward me. "Do you have the letter with you?"

I nodded, unbuttoned the upper left pocket of my coat where I'd put it for safekeeping, and handed him the folded letter. He took it over to the window where, although the curtains were drawn, there was a little more light.

"Oh my God," he muttered, and he looked up at me, his eyes burning with excitement. "Do you know what this means?"

"Yes, that I can go there again, and —"

"It means we have official Wehrmacht letterhead *and* a copy of the seal and signature of a high-ranking officer!"

"Let me see!" I peered over his arm as he read it a second time. I hadn't even looked at it when Axel gave it to me. His handwriting was even and precise. The letterhead had the insignia of the double eagle. Beneath it in an almost medieval-looking print were several lines of German I couldn't read, except for an address in Berlin.

"What does it say, Petr?"

He shook his head. "My German is poor, but it doesn't matter. What *does* matter is that we can get Yeshka to copy it —"

"The boy I met at the meeting?"

"Yes, the printer's son. You see this seal?" I nodded. "It's carved from hard rubber. Yeshka and his father are so good, they can make a copy of Axel Recht's personal seal!" He could barely contain his excitement, and kind of shook his head as if he'd just come in from a snowstorm. He must have seen my confusion. "You don't understand, do you?"

I shook my head.

He held the letter up. "With this letterhead, seal, and signature, the partisans can create other letters full of bad information, wrong directions, impossible orders, anything you can imagine."

"Oh!" I was starting to get the idea.

"The partisans have lots of uniforms they've taken off dead German soldiers. With a uniform, official-looking letterhead, and a seal . . ." He stopped, a smile spreading across his craggy face. "We can cause the Germans a lot of trouble."

I felt so proud, so grateful that I'd been able to provide something useful to the partisans.

"When did you say you have to be back there?"

"Noon."

He folded the letter and slipped it in his shirt pocket. "We're going to go see Yeshka and his father now. There's no time to lose."

CHAPTER 21

"PETR," I SAID AS WE MADE OUR WAY THROUGH THE WOODS TOWARD THE VILLAGE, "WHY AREN'T YOU IN THE ARMY?"

"I KNOW YOU WILL FIND THIS HARD TO BELIEVE," HE answered with a half grin, "but I am too old."

"What about Yeshka?"

"Too young." We crested the last forest hill and stopped to catch our breath.

"You mentioned his dad. . . ."

He laughed. "That answer is more interesting. He's missing part of his trigger finger. Printing accident."

"I'm so sorry." Maybe I was being too inquisitive, but I wanted to understand who the partisans were.

"Why do you want to know these things?"

"Well . . . it's all new to me, and . . . and how did you know I wasn't a spy or something? You welcomed me so easily into your little group."

He nodded as he scanned the open space we were about to enter. "Two reasons: Galina, and what you said when we met."

"About?"

"You told me about the three partisans you met. If you were a spy or a traitor, you never would have mentioned them. Besides," he added, bending over to brush the snow off the bottom of his pant legs, "we need every bit of help we can get. Now, pay attention. I want you to count to a hundred, then follow me. Knock only once; someone will answer the door." He took his first long stride toward the town.

"Petr, wait, just one more question."

He turned and looked at me as if to say *This better be good.*

"I have a knife, right here in my valenki. Do you think they'd punish me if they find it when I'm at headquarters?"

His expression was instantly serious. "Let me see it." I slipped the slender hunting knife out of my boot and handed it to him. He held it in the palm of his hand horizontally and sort of bounced it, as if feeling its weight and balance. "I love these Finnish knives. Keep it. Don't let anyone see it. Who knows? You may need it." Before I could ask him *why* I might need a knife at headquarters, he was off, and I began to count to a hundred. I almost lost sight of him once I neared the town because he turned two corners so quickly.

A few blocks later, he entered a small house on a corner. Two minutes after that I went to the same house, knocked once, and waited. The door was opened by a sturdy-looking man with a bald head and ink-stained hands, wearing a leather apron. He had a broad smile on his face.

"Well done!" His congratulatory slap on my back was so strong, I stumbled a few feet forward. "I'm Josef. You know my son, Yeshka." Yeshka stood next to a lamp, examining my letter closely with Petr.

"Ivan," he greeted me with a smile. "This letter is incredible. How long can we keep it?"

"I have to be back at noon."

He and his father exchanged a look. "Let's get going," Josef said with enthusiasm. It was only then that I noticed that the entire inside of their house was a workplace, with a small printing press in the main room. The sound of more machinery seeped in from an adjacent hall.

"Should I wait here?" I asked uncertainly.

Petr shook his head. "Too many of us in one place."

"Come back at eleven thirty," Josef said. "If we're not finished, you'll have to bring it back tomorrow."

"What if I get stopped before then?" I asked Petr, feeling the full weight of the Nazi presence in a new way without my letter.

"Then you're just like the rest of us," Petr answered, moving toward the door.

I caught the looks on Josef's and Yeshka's faces: serious, angry, determined. "Axel Recht," Josef said, and mimicked spitting on the floor. "Come on, son. Let's create a few problems for Recht to deal with."

He and Yeshka disappeared down the hall as Petr and I hovered near the front door, preparing to leave. "You go first this time, Ivan. I'll follow in a few minutes. Go to Polina's. Ask her to —"

"Petr . . . wait. You know the dogs I mentioned?"

"Yes?" He looked preoccupied as he peered out a window near the door.

"Well, I was thinking they could be of some use to the partisans."

A little laugh escaped him. "What?"

"Yes. Axel's going to start their training today. They're going to be trained to hunt Russians."

"Of course. What did you expect? The Germans are well known for training their dogs to do their dirty work for them."

I stared down at the floor, trying to form my thoughts and feelings into some kind of clear picture. "I asked Axel if I could help the trainer. He said no."

"Ivan, why are you worrying about dogs at a time like this?"

"Because they're innocent!" It came out forcefully.

"Lower your voice," Petr said with a frown.

"And they're captives, too, just like us in Vilnov! He's going to turn them into vicious hunters that will be used to hurt us. It . . . it would be sort of like capturing a weapon."

He gave me his full attention now. "Capturing? Ivan — are you thinking of stealing his dogs?"

Maybe I only understood it at that moment, but it felt inevitable. "Yes, I am."

Petr glanced around the room with a look of disbelief on his face, as if trying to find someone to share it with. "Let me see if I understand you correctly." His voice oozed sarcasm. "You, a twelve-year-old boy, are going to smuggle something out of Nazi headquarters that belongs to the man in charge?" I opened my mouth to explain, but he continued. "And not just an item you could slip into your pocket. No. Two living creatures that could betray your plan with a mere whimper or bark at the wrong moment?" His voice grew louder. "Not even full-grown dogs, but *puppies!*"

"But, Petr —"

"And for what?" He sounded almost outraged.

"Listen to me," I said calmly. "We could train them — *I* could train them. The partisans could use them just like other armies use dogs." He exhaled impatiently. "They could deliver messages, and . . . and we could use them to guard safe houses like your house! You'd know in advance if anyone was near you."

"So they would bark and let everyone know where the stolen dogs were?"

I felt so passionately that my idea was good, but of course I hadn't had time to think it through. "I don't know. What I do know is that we will hurt the Nazis if we steal them. They'll have two fewer weapons with which to track down and kill our people. And we will have saved two innocent dogs from being turned into monsters." Nothing changed in Petr's stern expression, but I was almost sure I caught a light in his eye, as if the idea had taken hold and he was turning it over in his mind. But before I could continue trying to persuade him, Yeshka came into the room holding Axel's letter in his hand.

"Oh, good. You're still here. Petr, you speak a little German, don't you?" he said.

"Very little."

Yeshka held out the letter so that both of us could see it. "I can't quite make out that word." He pointed to something Axel had written. Petr squinted and peered at it.

"Well, it could be . . ." He turned to me. "Ivan, I've got something for you to do, something *reasonable*. Go to Polina's. She's got a Russian–German dictionary, I'm almost sure. Bring it back here."

I nodded. "Anything else?"

"Yes. For now, do what Axel tells you to do. Get away as often as you can, and report what you learn to me. I'll talk to some of the others in our group. We'll try to figure out the best way to use you while you're there. Don't do *anything* I haven't told you to do." He eyed me meaningfully. "And have Polina show you some maps; familiarize yourself with the area. Start looking around you for places where you can hide. All over. At Galina's and Polina's, down by the tunnels, inside and outdoors. You want to have some places you can go if the Germans are ever chasing you." That hadn't occurred to me. "Didn't you say you had an uncle nearby?"

"Southeast of Sviritsa."

"That's quite a distance. Make sure you know how to get there, just in case."

"In case of what?"

He actually laughed, and then said, "This is war, Ivan. Anything can happen."

"Petr," Yeshka whispered, sounding like he could barely catch his breath. Both of us looked at him, then followed his gaze. Two Nazi soldiers were coming into view in the window on our left.

"Quick," Petr hissed. "Give Ivan the letter back. Put it in your pocket, Ivan."

I felt almost paralyzed, but I folded the paper and slipped it into the pocket of my coat. I glanced quickly at Petr and Yeshka. No one spoke, but I saw the looks of fear and resolve on their faces.

Without a knock, the front door suddenly burst open to reveal the pair of Nazi soldiers.

"Stay where you are!" one of them yelled in heavily accented Russian. We froze as the man drew his pistol. "Hands up! Move back." We did exactly as we were told.

CHAPTER 22

THE SOLDIERS WERE YOUNG BUT HAD HARD, SERIOUS EXPRESSIONS ON THEIR FACES. ONE OF THEM CARRIED A LARGE LEDGER, BUT IT DIDN'T STOP HIM FROM QUICKLY drawing his gun, too.

The man who spoke first looked at the machinery in the room carefully. "What is this place?" he demanded.

"It is a printing shop," Yeshka answered slowly, hands still in the air.

"Where is the owner?"

"He's in the back. It is my father. Do you want me to get him?"

"Don't move. Is anyone else in the building besides him?"

"No."

"What about your mother? Where is she?" he asked suspiciously.

"She died giving birth to me," Yeshka said.

"We'll search for ourselves in a minute. If you're lying, you'll be the first to die. Call your father. Tell him to get out here."

"Papa! *Papa!*" he called loudly. "We have German soldiers in the front room. They want to see you."

I stared nervously at the door to the back area, praying Josef wouldn't do anything foolish when he saw us being held at gunpoint. But Josef was no fool. He walked slowly through the door, his hands empty and visible. He put them in the air and joined us in our line facing the soldiers even before they commanded him to do so.

"What do you print here?" the soldier asked loudly.

"We have a little newspaper, *The Voice of the Village*. Our modest press has printed it for the last five years."

"What else?"

"Oh . . . handbills for village events. Memorial cards for deaths . . ."

"There is to be no more publication of your newspaper. Is that clear?"

"Yes, sir. Ah, may I ask a question?"

The man hesitated. "Quickly."

"May my son and I work on our other orders?"

"No. As of this moment, everything in this house belongs to the German army."

"But we sleep in the back," Yeshka protested. "This is also our home."

"Yeshka," Josef said softly to silence him.

"Step forward," the soldier told Yeshka in a deadly calm voice. "That's right. Keep your hands up."

Yeshka took a deep breath and raised his head slightly as he moved a few steps toward the soldier. The man slipped his gun into his left hand, made a quick advance on Yeshka, and punched him as hard as he could in the stomach.

Yeshka moaned, bending over with the pain, almost falling to the ground.

"Stand up straight," the soldier snapped at Yeshka. "It looks like you're going to have to find another place to live. Do we understand each other now?"

Yeshka nodded as he struggled to stand up, suppressing a groan. I don't know how I kept my cry of fear and horror in my throat. I forced myself to hide my thoughts and feelings as Petr had instructed me; only the tremble in my hands betrayed me. Poor Yeshka stepped back next to me in line, barely able to stand up straight or raise his hands above his waist.

The soldier turned his attention to Petr. "Who are you? What are you doing here?"

"I'm just an old bachelor, sir. I came to see my friends. To share some tea. To hear the news." His tone was deferential, his face a mask of dullness.

"And are you aware, *old bachelor*, that the German army now occupies this town?"

"Yes, sir, I've heard the guns."

The man pointed at me. "Is this your son?"

"No, sir."

Suddenly I became the object of his interest. "Why are you here?"

Remembering Petr's advice to answer only what you're asked and not to elaborate, I said, "He's my friend," and nodded toward Yeshka. He said something in German to the man who carried the ledger and went off to search the rest of the house, his movements echoed by the crush of his heels on the wooden floor.

When he returned he said, "You are to give this man your names, addresses, ages, and occupations," and indicated the soldier with the notebook.

Petr stepped up to the man. "I am Petr Ostrov. I live in the glen to the . . ."

The soldier seemed uncomprehending, and spoke to the other man in German, confirming my suspicion that he didn't speak Russian. The soldier who had hit Yeshka grabbed the man's ledger and the pencil he held out for him impatiently and said, "Name!"

Once Petr had given him his information and it was my turn, I panicked, realizing I didn't know Galina's address. I could admit the truth, but I had a feeling it would arouse his suspicion, and lead to something bad. Remembering the responses of the soldiers at headquarters, I took a chance. "When I was with Major Axel Recht this morning, he told me I should show the letter he gave me to any soldier who stopped me."

The man's eyes widened, fear flashing over his face. "Major Recht? What do you . . . How could you . . ." He stopped and turned to tell the other soldier something in German. The man looked as incredulous as his partner. Then the first soldier snapped, "Letter."

I pulled the letter from my pocket and handed it to him. Both soldiers hunched over it and read, looking up at me and the rest of us when they were finished. Their expressions were different, more subdued. The tone of voice the soldier used was still demanding, but now contained the slightest hint of courtesy.

"Major Recht has made his wishes clear. However, we are not released from our obligation to record your personal information."

Taking another chance I made up an address, while giving my real name, which they'd already seen in the letter. When I was done, the soldier glared at Yeshka and Josef. "You two — I want your names and ages. Report your new address to headquarters the minute you have relocated."

"Yes, sir," they mumbled.

"I will be checking. If it's not there in two days, I will come and find you."

The tiny bit of leverage Axel's letter gave me also provided me with the nerve I needed to ask a question. As politely as possible, I said, "Sir, I was wondering . . ."

"Yes?"

"What should we expect to happen next?"

It was obvious he didn't want to explain himself or his army's requests to a small boy, or probably to any Russian, for that matter. "As with any occupied town, we are taking inventory of the population and any goods and services that might be of use to our army."

"Thank you," I said as humbly as I could manage. "When I see the major this afternoon I will tell him how well you treated us."

I saw the look of fear again in his eyes before he said, "Now all of you — get out!"

CHAPTER 23

WE WERE ABOUT THIRTY FEET FROM THE HOUSE BEFORE ANY OF US SPOKE. "NAZI FILTH," JOSEF SPAT, PUTTING HIS ARM AROUND HIS SON'S SHOULDERS.

"Our coats are back there, Papa; our money, our papers. Everything."

"Don't worry about that now, Yeshka. I felt so powerless when they hit you! I wanted to —"

Petr interrupted him. "You did the right thing, Josef. One word from any of us would have resulted in a beating. Or perhaps even death."

"Whoever thought little Ivan and his letter would have saved us?" Yeshka asked, attempting a smile.

"Only for the moment," Petr said seriously. "They don't see us as humans. If they don't kill or starve us first, they'll soon decide whether we could be useful as slaves and send us to Germany to work in their factories."

"Really?" I was incredulous, never having heard of such a thing.

"Unless they think we're partisans," Josef said. "Then they'll just kill us and save themselves the trouble of having to send us anywhere."

"Ivan," Petr said, "go to Polina's house until it's time for you to go back. Have her show you the maps and hiding places like we talked about. Josef and Yeshka, go to my house. Josef, take the western route, Yeshka, the eastern. I'll go to Galina's, wait fifteen minutes, and then follow you to the cabin. There are warm clothes in the closet; help yourselves." Yeshka and Josef left us and went in separate directions. They looked so cold and vulnerable without coats on.

Petr turned around suddenly and, in a loud, raspy, urgent whisper, called, "Josef! Josef!" He must not have heard him because he continued on his way west as Petr had instructed. When Petr turned back to me, there was a look in his eyes I couldn't read. Frustration? Anger? Alarm? I wasn't sure. "Let's walk a little faster" was all he said.

"I can't believe my letter helped us!" I said proudly. "They're scared of Axel, you could see it."

Petr put his hand on my shoulder. "I know. You did the right thing. It got us out of there before they could ask us more questions. The problem is," he said with a sigh, "that now they'll remember you. They'll repeat the story to their comrades. You've been marked, not only by Axel, but by those men."

I was confused and a little scared by his comment. "So what if I have? The only reason I'm at headquarters is to learn whatever I can for the partisans. Isn't that worth being marked?"

"Yes," Petr said slowly, deliberately. "But it makes your time there limited. Whatever good you're going to do for our cause is going to have to be done very, very soon."

"How soon?"

"Five, six, seven days? You've seen how volatile Axel is. And although I'm sure your concertina playing is amazing," he said with a small smile, "he'll tire of it soon and be done with you. The novelty will have worn off."

Even as I listened and recognized the good sense in what he said, I kept thinking about the dogs. I dared not mention them again just yet. "If I have only days . . ." I took a breath as the strange truth of that sunk in. ". . . then you'd better figure out how I can help, and fast."

"There's someone I'm going to talk to. His name is Lev; remember that in case he approaches you directly or you find him at my house. He's a brilliant partisan leader, one of our best. If he tells you to do something, do it. Understood?" I nodded. "If only you were older," he said, a smile creeping across his face. "Oh, the things I'd have you do to Recht!"

"Isn't there money we can steal from him? Think what a help it would be to the partisans who live in the woods. Blankets, food, weapons . . . or if we had intelligence that arms were arriving, we could intercept them."

"If you spoke German, you might be able to overhear something like that. Chances of Axel sharing that information with you in Russian are zero."

We turned a corner, and Polina's house came into view. "When will I see you again?" I suddenly felt a rush of anxiety, not knowing when I'd be able to get away from Axel.

Petr stared at the snow-covered ground. "I don't know. Take every opportunity to get away, but nothing foolish, nothing that would make him suspicious. In the meantime, I'll talk to Lev. There's got to be something. . . ."

The faces of Zasha and Thor came into my mind so strongly, it was as if they were right there in front of me. It made me find my courage. "Petr, I'm twelve," I said. "Which means I don't really know how to use a gun, and even if I did, I don't think I could kill a man." I paused. "But I am fully capable of injuring

Axel in another way. I really think you should reconsider my idea about —"

"The dogs?" he interrupted me, sounding impatient.

"Please, listen to me. It's not just about hurting Axel and preventing the dogs from being wrongly used — it's about helping the partisans."

We were just a few houses from Polina's. Petr surprised me by saying, "What would you do with these dogs?"

"I'd take them up to my uncle Boris's cabin."

"Even assuming you could steal his dogs out from under his nose, how would you get the dogs out of Vilnov without being seen?"

"I know someone with a sleigh who I'm pretty sure we could count on." I was thinking of Vladimir, of how he'd helped the partisans, of his invitation to visit him. "He lives near Kobona." I rushed on. "I know what you're thinking: Why risk so much just to steal two dogs? Isn't there something more important we could do? Think of it this way: First, it would make Axel so mad, it would distract him from his other duties. Distracted men make mistakes, lose their tempers, miss important details. Second, we could breed them to help the partisans; train them to send messages, sniff out bombs and soldiers. They're the best alarm system in the world. If the enemy was approaching a partisan camp, the dog would know about it long before they arrived." I'd said most of this before, but there was something different this time. Petr slowed our pace to extend our conversation.

"There are many potential problems, and you can't do it alone."

"I have to. I wouldn't want anyone else to be in danger."

"Don't play the hero, Ivan. It will get you killed. If you do go north with them, I'll be going with you."

"But what would the others do without you here?"

"I'd be back as soon as you're settled at the cabin. Someone else would be in charge when I'm gone. I'm not saying yes. You are not to do *anything* until I give the word."

I nodded nervously. "I couldn't do anything anyway. I don't have a plan yet."

He sort of laughed. "Yes, I'm aware of that."

"There would be so many details to work out."

"I'm aware of that, too. If I do get approval from my higher-ups , . . I have to admit it would give me great pleasure to stick a knife in Axel Recht's heart this way."

"I'm not sure he has one," I offered.

"You know what, Ivan? I almost wish you hadn't thought of this."

"Why?" We were in front of Polina's and couldn't linger together without drawing attention to ourselves.

"Because it's just so tempting. Saving those poor animals, hurting Recht. And it really is a clever idea to breed dogs for the partisans. It might take a while in the beginning, but this war could drag on for a very long time."

After my initial pride and happiness at having come up with the idea, I suddenly felt the full weight of the terrible consequences if something went wrong.

"That's right, Ivan," Petr said, as if reading my mind.

"What's right?"

"There can be no mistakes." He walked on toward Galina's and never looked back.

CHAPTER 24

GUESSING THAT POLINA'S FAMILY KNEW THE NAZIS WERE
GOING FROM DOOR TO DOOR, I WENT TO THE BACK DOOR SO
I WOULDN'T SCARE THEM.

"Yes?" a nervous-sounding voice replied to my knock.

"Polina, it's Ivan. Let me in."

"Go away. You can't come in."

I thought maybe I didn't understand her correctly. "Polina, don't be afraid. It's me, Ivan. I'm coming in."

The sound of running and then water were the first things I heard. "Polina, is that you?" I half whispered, slipping in the door and closing it quickly behind me. She didn't answer. I tiptoed down the short hall and into the kitchen. Polina was standing at the sink, her back to me. She held something to her face.

"Why are you here?" she demanded.

"What's wrong? Did something happen?"

"No. Go away." She hunched over slightly, as if to shield herself as I approached her. My heart was pounding. I remembered her strange mother. Could she have hurt Polina in some way?

"Why are you hiding your face?"

"I'm not." Her voice sounded choked with emotion.

"Petr sent me. I have to talk to you." *Maybe that will reach her*, I thought.

"I can't."

"Why not? What is going *on*?" I demanded in frustration.

She put down the cloth she'd been holding to her face, laying it on the sink. Slowly, she turned around to face me.

I gasped. "Oh my God." The left side of her face was so swollen, it distorted her features. Red and purple swirled under her skin, and a two-inch cut between her temple and her eyebrow was still moist with blood. I stepped toward her, my arms out to hug her.

"Don't touch me," she said pleadingly. "It will hurt too much." Her eyes glistened with tears.

"Who did this to you?" I asked as a cold fury spread through me.

She looked in my eyes a long time before answering. "You know who, and you know why."

"Why?" I could barely get the word out.

"Because they can."

I understood perfectly. We were in the power of our invaders, our occupiers. There would be no punishment for any of their hideous actions, and there would be no justice. There would only be more gratuitous violence, until it turned into torture, and then death. We were at their mercy, but they had none.

"Would it hurt to sit down?"

Polina laughed in spite of herself, even though I could tell it hurt her. "No, Ivan, it wouldn't. They only hit me in the face." I sort of laughed, too, as much as I could with sorrow in my heart and anger in my gut.

I pulled a chair out from the kitchen table for her. Polina, who I had last seen looking strong and agile in her basement when she taught me some secrets of hand-to-hand combat, now seemed almost waiflike, her dark hair in braids, an oversize sweater hanging from her thin frame. She sat down tentatively on the edge of the oak chair.

"I'm so sorry. I guess I couldn't have come at a worse time. . . ."

She shook her injured face slightly. "It's okay. Is there something you want to tell me? Has someone else been hurt?" Looking almost panicked, she added, "Or captured?"

I looked down and said simply, "The Nazis paid Yeshka and Josef a visit while Petr and I were there."

"Oh, no." She covered her mouth with her hand. "Is everyone all right?"

"Yeshka was hit very hard in the stomach." Polina moaned sympathetically. "He's okay, we're all okay, but they threw Josef and Yeshka out of their house and said they couldn't go back."

"What are they going to do? That's their business, and —"

"Petr will take care of them, but there's more. Petr wants you to show me maps, local ones, but also ones that show the area on the eastern shore of Lake Ladoga. He said I need to find some places to hide. He wants me to be familiar with this area so that if someone is chasing me —"

"Why would the *Germans* be chasing you?" She fixed her fierce brown eyes on me.

"He said you could help me."

She sat back in the chair. Although battered, the look in her eyes was clear. "You didn't answer my question."

I stared at the table, uncertain how much I should tell her about Axel's letter, the plan to copy the letterhead to make other fake letters, and my idea about stealing Axel's dogs. Hadn't I been told that the fewer people who knew about something, the less trouble anyone could get in?

"No, I didn't," I said evenly. "I'm a partisan now, just like you. I can't answer all questions I'm asked."

She smiled, although her swollen lip made her look like a fighter who'd lost his big match. "I knew you had the makings of a good partisan! I just didn't know you would learn so quickly."

"I would like to tell you everything, but —"

"No, don't. But I can tell you what I know. That you were taken right out of your house by Recht."

"How do you know about that? I thought we were supposed to keep things to ourselves."

She shrugged. "Not *everything*, or we couldn't work together as a group." Leaning toward me, she said, "I have an idea. He took you because you play the concertina, right? I play the violin a little, although I admit not very well. What if I went with you next time to play for Recht? We'll play duets. I know some German, and maybe I could understand —"

"No, no, no, Polina, no, no, no." I said it softly, but my conviction was strong.

"Why not?"

"You don't understand. He's a terrible man. He's dangerous. He's . . ."

"What did you see?"

"Nothing yet. But it's there in his eyes. He's a cruel man, and very powerful. Everyone seems like they're afraid of him."

"It's because I'm a girl, isn't it?" Her battered face suddenly flushed with anger.

"Well, yes, sort of. You don't belong there with all those men."

"Oh, and you do?" She grabbed the edge of the table and gave it a shake in her frustration. "Look at me. I survived my encounter with the German army. No one can count me out."

"What I mean is that I can fit in because I am a man."

"You're a boy," she corrected me.

I decided not to be offended. "Yes, I am a boy. But my birthday is soon. I'll be thirteen. That's almost like a man."

She rolled her eyes impatiently.

"Polina, please," I implored her. "The Nazi headquarters is no place for a girl. Do you know where I serenaded the men this morning? In the lavatory!"

She laughed and closed her eyes, as if finding the idea funny and embarrassing at the same time.

"You see?" I said, anxious to join in with her laughter. "No place for a girl."

"I could have stood outside, maybe. . . ." For the first time I thought about how many things girls weren't allowed to do. Here was Polina, so brave and capable, so smart, but she could never do what I did by going with Axel, no matter how much more experience she had than me.

"It's all right. I can do other things."

"Yes!" I agreed with enthusiasm, inspired by the defiant look on her poor injured face. "Like teach me how to get around without being noticed and find places to hide."

She nodded, and I saw a little of her pain and frustration leave her, replaced by determination.

"I'm a good hider, Ivan," she said proudly, "but let's start with maps." She went to another part of the house and returned with paper and pencil. In a sure hand, she began drawing an area map of Vilnov, with the main streets marked, along with the positions of houses I knew.

"Draw in Petr's cabin and the tunnel exits."

She looked up at me, pencil poised over the paper. For a moment I saw her injuries as if for the first time and was filled with sympathy for her. "If I do that, you have to memorize this map and destroy it before you leave."

"Oh. Of course. Just draw it, Polina. We'll burn it later."

For the next ten minutes, we went over the map. It helped me understand the relationships of the places I knew to one another. With another map from an atlas she showed me an overview of the area between Lake Ladoga and Vilnov, which included Kobona, where Vladimir lived.

She pointed to a spot on the map. "Of course you go west, but . . ." She looked at me thoughtfully. "If you're going to Kobona, you won't be taking the roads, will you?"

I shook my head. "No."

"Because you'll be . . . escaping."

"Yes."

"Wait here." She disappeared. When she returned she had something in the palm of her hand that she stared at as if saying good-bye. Holding her hand out to me, she said, "Here. Take it."

It was a compass, silver and round, hardly a half an inch thick. The markings on the inside were remarkably detailed. It was beautiful.

I picked it up out of her outstretched hand. "Really? Are you sure?"

She nodded, looking a little bit sad. "I won it when I was ten."

"For what?"

"For being the fastest runner of my age for fifty miles around!" She was clearly proud of her accomplishment.

"That's incredible. I can't take your prize." I tried to hand it back to her; she shook her head no.

"If you're going to Kobona or . . . or wherever else you go, you'll need a compass. Especially if you're on the back roads or in the forest."

"Thank you." I closed my hand around it and felt its coolness, its weight and texture. "When the war is over, I'll return it to you. I promise."

"I'm holding you to it. That means you'll have to stay alive."

"Polina, does your mother know that you're a partisan?"

She laughed. "No! She'd kill me. You're so lucky that your auntie and Galina understand."

How sad, I thought, that her own mother didn't appreciate the strong, brave daughter who had so much to offer. After another quick look at the map, we talked about hiding spots. I told her about Galina's wood-lined hole in the ground just outside the chicken coop, where she hid some of her food and valuables. "Perfect," she responded. "That's a new hiding place for me. I'll keep it in mind, especially now." She picked the map up off the kitchen table. "Do you want to look at it again?"

"No. I have it memorized."

She took it to the sink, lit a match, and touched it to the bottom corner of the page. When it began to flame, she dropped it into the sink, watching as it consumed itself, then she rinsed the ashes away with water.

There was a noise that startled us both so much, my hand jerked and I almost dropped the compass. The front door slammed. All I could think of was the Nazi soldiers.

"Mama?" Polina called. There was an inarticulate reply. "Ivan, go."

She followed me to the back door. As I reached for the door handle, she said quietly, "I forgot to say *sir* to the man who was interrogating me."

I burned with hatred for the occupiers. Looking at my friend, I saw it in her eyes, too.

CHAPTER 25

I KNEW THINGS WERE GETTING WORSE VERY QUICKLY WHEN I WAS STOPPED THREE TIMES BY GERMAN SOLDIERS ON MY WAY BACK TO THEIR HEADQUARTERS. EACH TIME I SHOWED my letter, and each time I saw the same reaction of surprise and fear. When I arrived Axel was alone, seated at the desk, looking at a small pile of photographs.

"You're late," he said without looking up.

"Yes, sir. I would have been on time, but the soldiers kept stopping me."

He smiled at me. "That's why we'll win the war, my little friend. We plan ahead." Then his smile twisted into something malevolent. He pounded his fist on the table, hitting it once with every word as he yelled, *"YOU — ARE — NEVER — TO — BE — LATE — AGAIN!"* It was like being blown over by a sudden foul wind.

"Yes, sir," I mumbled. "Sorry, sir." I was already so upset from seeing Yeshka hit for no reason by the Nazi and poor Polina's beaten face, it was all I could do to remain calm and normal-looking. I began to take my concertina out if its case. "Is there anything special you'd like to —"

"No. No music now."

"Yes, sir," I responded, packing it back up. I looked around uneasily. What was I supposed to do? "If — if you don't mind my asking, how did the first lesson go with the dogs and the trainer?"

"I don't know. They haven't returned yet."

I stood in silence for another minute until I remembered that the room I slept in with the dogs could use some cleaning. "I was wondering, sir, if —" A scream came from just outside the window, a terrible cry of pain. "What's that?"

Axel was studying a photograph carefully, holding it just a foot from his face. "What's what?" He looked up as if he were just hearing it. "Oh, that. A man is being punished for disobeying an order I gave him. Ivan, come here. Look at these pictures. They're of Thor and Zasha's parents."

I approached him reluctantly. As I caught my first glimpse of a photograph of a beautiful, full-grown German shepherd, another scream pierced the air.

I jumped back. "What are they doing to him?"

"Go look," he answered nonchalantly, picking up another photo. I shook my head. I almost couldn't stop shaking it. "I insist." He fixed me with a hard stare.

"Yes, sir." Slowly, I eased toward the large window. It looked out onto a street where two sawhorses had been set up at the curb with a board laid between them, forming a crude table. On the table, stretched out on his stomach, hands above his head, was a German soldier. Another soldier held his ankles, and another held his wrists; a third man, large and stocky, held a whip. Just as I realized what was happening, the man with the whip raised it high and brought it down with all his might on the back of the man's legs.

That scream was worse yet. I gasped loudly.

Axel laughed. "Do you see the men watching the punishment?"

I'd barely noticed that twenty or so men were gathered in back of the man with the whip watching the proceedings. "Yes." I could barely get the word out.

"They'll remember it. Just like you. And when they think of disobeying me, or doing something they shouldn't, they'll remember that man and what he sounded like. You won't forget him, will you, Ivan?"

Before I could answer, the man screamed again and cried out for them to stop. Tears formed in my eyes; rage filled my heart. "Never," I choked out.

"They will continue until I tell them to stop, but a half dozen lashes is usually enough." He stood in front of the window and watched dispassionately as the man received two more ferocious strokes of the whip. I trembled as I stood next to him, forcing myself to keep my eyes open so he wouldn't use that as an excuse to prolong the man's misery. He knocked hard on the glass with his knuckles. The man with the whip looked up, and Axel nodded.

I must have been holding my breath, because a gush of air rushed from my lungs when I realized it was over. Just as my body relaxed and I turned away from the window, there was another nerve-shattering cry from the poor man below. A garbled noise escaped from me.

Axel barked out another horrible laugh and slapped his thigh. "That's the one I enjoy the most: the one he isn't expecting, the one that comes after he thinks it's over." He sighed happily. "Come here, Ivan. Look at the pictures with me."

I stood up straight, filled with hatred for this cruel man, closed my eyes, and refused to let him see how repugnant he was to me. Breathing deeply, I leaned over the table and said, "Show me, please, sir."

He spread the dozen or so pictures out and pointed to one of two adult German shepherds. "These are Thor's parents, Bruno and Freya."

"Beautiful," I murmured, glancing at Axel, hoping I looked like I had already forgotten about the man outside.

"Thor will be a champion, I know it. Bruno is known for strength and speed; Freya for her cunning. Thor will be superior in every way." He looked at me and smiled brightly. "Like all of us Germans!"

I hoped my forced smile let him think that I agreed with his absurd and grandiose claim. "And here" — he pointed to another photo — "are Zasha's parents, Konrad and Gerta. They're both known for their good dispositions."

"Zasha does seem very sweet —"

The door burst open and Thor and Zasha ran in looking like they were being chased by the devil himself. They scurried around the room as though looking for a hiding place. They found one behind a tall wooden storage cabinet.

Striding in after them was an athletic man, one who looked like he spent most of his time outdoors hunting and fishing. He was dressed in an officer's uniform, his broad shoulders straining the seams of the jacket and his pants tucked neatly into his tall boots. He carried a thin, flexible training stick in his hand. I loathed him on sight.

Axel stood up, smiled, and conversed with him in German. He even tried to coax Zasha and Thor out of their hiding places, getting down on his knees and reaching under the cabinet. The dogs pressed their little backs hard against the wall, lifting up their paws repeatedly as Axel tried to grab hold of them.

I eyed the other man, and he caught me. He yelled at me in German. My hands went up defensively, and I said, "Russian! Russian!" in German — one of the few words I knew. His eyes narrowed, and he turned away just in time to see Axel dragging poor Thor out from his hiding place. He whimpered and struggled to get away; Axel's tone with him was friendly and kind, but Thor seemed terrified.

"May I help, sir?" I asked.

"No," he snapped, "they're being trained." After a few exchanges in German between the men, the trainer walked over to the cabinet and with some effort, managed to move it far enough away from the wall to grab Zasha. She squealed and writhed, trying to escape his grasp, but he held tight.

Oh, how I wished I could understand the conversation that went on between the two men. I hated both of them for the way they were handling the dogs, as if they were things, possessions, soulless creatures to be molded into slaves, robots, performing clowns.

They let the dogs back on the floor. To my joy and horror, they ran to me; Zasha standing on her hind legs begging me to pick her up, Thor trying to make himself invisible behind my legs. I stood as still as possible with my hands pressed against my legs. I didn't dare move toward either dog, although I so desperately wanted to.

The men stared at us, Axel with a frown, the trainer with disdain and arrogance. He pulled a lead out of his pocket and without a word attached it to Zasha's collar and took her from me. She cried and turned her head back toward me, looking frantic. I wanted to snatch her away and run for the door, but I could do nothing. I tried to comfort Thor by mumbling soothing things to him, never taking my eyes off the trainer.

He led Zasha around the large room in a circle while talking to Axel, as if explaining something to him. She kept turning around to find me and Thor. Every time she did, the trainer yanked her head back by her poor little neck. It's a miracle he didn't snap it.

I swallowed my anger and helplessness for Zasha. The trainer stopped suddenly, pulling Zasha back as if she, too, should have known to stop, then tapped her rear end hard with the training stick. She yelped and trembled. If this horrible pantomime went on much longer, I didn't know how I was going to stop myself from running over, wrestling the stick from his hands, and using it on him. I knew Thor would be next. As a male, there was a chance he would respond to the whip hand with a bite. What terrible consequences that would bring I couldn't imagine. *What can I do? What can I do?* my mind screamed again and again.

There was a knock at the door. "What?" Axel said impatiently. A young soldier entered, a letter in his hand. Axel took it, frowned, and then handed it to the trainer.

Within seconds his face grew pale, his expression pained. He dropped Zasha's lead, and she ran over to be with me and Thor. He was soon in an animated discussion with Axel. Finally they saluted each other, and Axel patted him on the back sympathetically just before he rushed out of the room. I felt Thor's body relax and Zasha's breathing become calmer the instant he was gone.

Axel sighed loudly, his exasperation clear. "His son was wounded," he said, as if to himself, but it was also meant for me. "So what! Thousands of men have been wounded, and their daddies don't go running off to put bandages on them. We've captured Stalin's own son. And do you know what Stalin did?" He looked at me as if expecting an answer.

"No, sir." I didn't even know his son had been taken prisoner.

"Nothing! Absolutely nothing." He closed his eyes and shook his head in frustration. "And now I have two puppies who must be trained and a trainer who's too busy being a nursemaid to do his job!" He was practically yelling by the end of his sentence.

I didn't say a word. The next move had to come from Axel. If he didn't remember that I'd claimed to know how to train dogs, surely he would notice how they'd run to me for protection, how even now they crouched next to me on the floor.

He sat down, and then immediately pushed his chair back noisily from his desk. "We're going for a walk. Bring the dogs."

I slipped on my coat, attached Thor's lead, grabbed Zasha's, and ran into the hall after him with the dogs close at heel. The two guards outside of his door looked momentarily surprised and confused, but sprang into action, one taking his place in front of Axel and the other in back of me.

You've got to show him, Ivan, I said to myself. *Show him what you can do with these dogs. This is your chance. If he won't trust you with the dogs now, you'll never be able to save them from the terrible future he has planned for them.*

CHAPTER 26

"TAKE THOR OFF OF HIS LEAD," AXEL COMMANDED ME AS SOON AS WE WERE OUTSIDE. WITH ALL THE ACTIVITY SUR- ROUNDING THE BUILDING I THOUGHT IT WAS A TERRIBLE idea, a dangerous one for Thor. But we were all under his power, and so I did as I was told.

"Let's run!" he said to Thor, and set off down the sidewalk, looking over his shoulder several times to see if Thor was follow- ing him. He wasn't; he was too excited by the new environment to do anything but sniff and mark his territory. One of the guards said something to Axel that he answered in a sharp, dismis- sive way. I got the feeling Axel was making their job of guarding him much harder. The curious stares of several soldiers who were outside shoveling snow and tending vehicles confirmed this for me.

Axel bent down and called, "Here, Thor, here, boy." This time the puppy ran to him. I was relieved; I didn't trust Axel not to hurt the dogs if they did something to displease him. "Take off Zasha's lead. Call her and see if she'll come to you."

I did as Axel requested. Zasha immediately stood on her hind legs and put her front paws on my leg, begging me to pick her up. I brushed them off gently and ran about twenty feet before turn- ing around and calling, "Here, Zasha!" But there was no need. She was at my feet, having followed me from the moment I ran from her.

Axel noticed. "She likes you. Don't forget what I said: You are not their master."

"Yes, sir. I think she followed me because she's cold, that's all."

"She's about to get a lot colder. We need to start their conditioning. Make them stronger. Tougher." He ran ahead of me, Thor following in his footsteps.

"I'm not sure I understand," I cried as I rushed after them, making sure Zasha was at my heels.

"You told me you and your friend went sledding somewhere near here."

"Did I?" I answered weakly.

"Show me that place. It will do them good to climb up and down a hill."

My mind was screaming inside of me, *No! No! Don't take him there. Don't take him anywhere near Petr's house or the tunnels!* What I said was, "We don't have a sled."

"We're not going to be sledding, you idiot. These are dogs. You're going to lead us to that area." We'd already left the main square behind, and were half walking, half running in the direction of the forest to the south.

This was terrible. Petr, Yeshka, and Josef were all at Petr's cabin. Polina had called it a safe house. For all I knew, other partisans were there, too. "It's quite a distance from here," I said. "Maybe too far for the puppies."

I started to pick up Zasha, but Axel snapped "no" just as my fingers touched her fur. "That's the whole point — to make them strong. Muscular. Hardened to the elements."

"Yes, sir." We walked in silence for the next few minutes. I tried to walk at a pace that wouldn't be too hard on the dogs. They were already showing signs of tiring with the effort of walking in the snow. Axel either didn't notice or didn't care.

"Tell me, Ivan. How would you begin their training?" Surprise and fear hit me simultaneously. If Axel knew I had only taught some simple tricks to dogs in our apartment building and was unqualified in any other way, I dreaded what he might do. I regained my footing by reminding myself I was a performer, only now without an instrument in my hands, and assumed an attitude of confidence and knowledge.

"Well, sir, training a dog is like building a wall — you do it methodically, brick by brick. Training is serious business. Routine is most important. I think you made a wise decision in creating their own quiet room for them." He looked pleased to hear his wisdom praised. "May I say something else, sir?"

"If it's reasonably intelligent."

I breathed deeply as I prepared to deceive him. "You may remember that I have trained many dogs, and . . . and in my opinion, the trainer I saw today was doing everything wrong."

"Oh, *really*?"

His sarcasm wasn't followed by an order to stop talking, so I rushed on. "Yes, that kind of cruelty will only hurt and confuse them. They may obey under the threat of pain, but they will never be loyal, never love you. They may even try their best to get away from you."

He stiffened and said curtly, "I've always had kennel men train my dogs. I never inquired about their methods as long as they did their job."

"I think I could train them — and quickly — if you'd give me that opportunity. I'm already sleeping in their quarters. I'll feed them, walk them, clean up their messes, train them. You'll see them every day, but with none of the . . . unpleasantness animals can bring with them."

"So." He sort of laughed. "You will be the nanny, they will be the children. You will bring them to their father for his pleasure — clean, fed, and well behaved. When I am done, you will take them back to the nursery, like good children! Hmmm . . . possible." Then the harsh, threatening tone returned as strong as ever. "But only for a short time! When they are fully trained, they will stay with me. That's when I will introduce them to the combat specialist who will turn them into proper German soldiers."

"Of course, sir," I answered deferentially, but suddenly knowing that no matter what, I was going to rescue those dogs, whether Petr would help me or not. We marched on for another fifteen minutes until we reached the place where Polina and I had gone sledding.

"Beautiful!" Axel exclaimed as he stood at the top of the hill. "And look — a little stream. Perfect." The bodyguards looked less than charmed and never stopped scrutinizing the landscape, as if expecting to see sharpshooters in the trees.

"Thor and I will race you and Zasha to the stream. Go!" Axel skillfully managed the first steep fifteen feet of the hill without falling. Thor rolled, and ran, and rolled some more, but seemed to relish the adventure. One of the guards muttered something under his breath that I knew was a complaint about Axel; I pretended I hadn't heard it.

Zasha huddled next to me, shivering. "I'm sorry, girl. We've got to do it. Come on." I carefully maneuvered down the first five feet or so of the hill and waited for her to follow. She looked to each side of her, obviously reluctant to join in our supposed adventure. "*Please*, girl. Don't give him an excuse to hurt us." Zasha took a tentative step, and once she made it down to where I stood, we were able to get down the long slope without a problem. Both bodyguards followed, muttering what I think would be understood as curse words in any language.

Thor looked like he was enjoying himself. He was curious about the stream, running alongside it, stopping to smell it here and there, twice skittering out onto the ice. It appeared to be frozen in most places, but not all. There were darker patches near the middle where it still ran. I worried that Thor would fall through the ice if he wasn't careful, but something else was bothering me more. Thor was heading in the direction of Petr's cottage.

"Wait up, Thor!" Axel cried with a laugh, running after him. "Ivan, hurry!"

I waved to let him know I understood. Thor ran farther and farther west toward Petr's, with Axel not far behind. I racked my brain for some way of bringing them back toward us. I thought of pretending I'd sprained my ankle, but Axel wouldn't care; nothing was going to interfere with his fun. I picked up a handful of snow thinking I'd lob a snowball at Thor, make him remember me and Zasha and want to play with us. But he was too far away now, and if I hit Axel by accident, I'd be in serious trouble.

"Will you hurry up?" Axel yelled. We ran as well as we could in the snow.

I was breathless by the time I reached his side. "Maybe we should turn back, sir. The dogs are still so young."

"Nonsense. Look at Thor. As curious as a cat, strong as a tiger." He looked at Zasha and whisked her off the ground almost before I knew what he was doing. "And you, my pretty . . . what are you made of?" He tossed her in the snow in front of him and began to chase her. I followed them.

Her instincts took over, and she ran. At first she followed the same path as Thor, but as we came within twenty yards of where the stream angled to the south, she charged over it. Axel stopped. "Go get her."

"Zasha, no!" I ran after her, jumping easily across the three-foot-wide stream. Now she seemed like she thought it was a game and ran in an arc back toward the creek, but not so close that I could catch her.

She made it easily across the ice, closer now to where the stream turned south. It was wider there, the jump more difficult; I didn't trust the ice to hold my weight. "Zasha, please," I called, dropping to my knee and extending my open arms to her. But my pleas meant nothing compared to the fun she was having running back and forth, and she paid no attention to me.

"Get control of the dog," Axel yelled at me. Zasha made another run across the creek. I rushed after her. This time the water was too wide to jump. The ice must have been as thin as a frost covering, because it cracked almost immediately when Zasha's paws touched it.

She looked shocked and struggled to get her balance, to get back on top of the ice and out of the water that was quickly engulfing her. She cried out in fear.

"Zasha!" I slammed my feet down through the ice and cold water until I reached her. The stream was just eight or ten inches deep. I was protected by my galoshes, but Zasha was already soaked up to her neck. She lashed out with her front paws, reaching for the bank, succeeding only in splashing freezing water on her face and head.

I grabbed her by her sides, lifting her up and out of the water as I stepped back on solid ground. She was soaked; there was no way I could set her down in the snow.

"Look what you've done!" Axel scolded me as he reached us. "If anything happens to that dog, you will pay dearly."

I held her at arm's length as the water dripped onto the ground and she tried to shake it from her.

"I'm so sorry. I . . ." And then I did the only thing I could think of — I unbuttoned my coat, held her cold, wet body against my warm chest, and buttoned my coat back up. Within seconds it felt like it was me who'd fallen through the ice.

Axel was furious. I think if Zasha hadn't been so close to my face, he would have hit me. Instead, he shoved me with broad hands that felt like bricks against both of my shoulders. I cried out as I fell down in the snow. Pain shot up my back as I landed, but I managed to hold on to Zasha and keep her safe in my coat.

"Good. I hope it hurts. It's going to hurt a lot more if that dog catches a cold. And if she *dies* from that cold . . ." His face was distorted with rage. "Take her back. Now! And if you think your stupidity is going to ruin Thor's exercise, you are mistaken."

"Yes, sir. I'm so sorry."

"Sorry," he spat. "Get out of my sight."

I struggled to get up and headed back up the hill as fast as I could. The only good thing about Zasha's accident was that it kept Axel from continuing in the direction of Petr's house.

But if Zasha wasn't dried and warmed soon, she would catch a cold or even pneumonia. My life wouldn't be worth much if that happened. There was only one way we'd both have a fighting chance; we'd have to stop at Galina's, dry Zasha, and change my clothes. If it was done quickly and we made it back to headquarters before Axel arrived, he probably wouldn't punish me for doing it without his permission. Remembering the whipping of the man outside his window, I prayed he wouldn't.

I unbuttoned the top two buttons of my coat, just enough so that Zasha could see where she was and what was going on around her. She squirmed and repositioned herself. I held the bottom of my coat tightly against her so she wouldn't fall to the ground.

"I'm sorry, girl. You'll be warm soon, I promise." She trembled, but made no sound. We were on flat ground now. I trudged through the foot-high powdery snow as quickly as I was able. My chest felt bitterly cold. The water had dripped down onto and even into my pants, making every part of me ice-cold except my feet. Between Zasha's weight, the cold, the wetness, and keeping her from falling out of my coat and into the snow, my shoulders became more hunched, my posture worse, my walk stiff and awkward. I kept my focus on putting one foot in front of the other, head down, knowing that just a little farther there was help and warmth for us both. Maybe that's why it took me a moment to realize someone was calling, "Ivan! Ivan!"

I wanted to cry with relief when I saw it was Auntie rushing toward me, with Galina not far behind. Neither of them had coats or hats on; they must have seen me from the window and realized something was wrong.

"What happened?" Auntie cried as she neared me. Then I heard her gasp — she must have seen Zasha. "We're wet, Auntie, and very cold. Help us get in the house." Until I saw her and

Galina, I hadn't realized how desperate I felt. Auntie was at my side, slipping her arm around me, bustling me toward the house. Galina supported my other arm, after a squeal of joy when she saw Zasha's head peeping out from my coat.

"Where is Major Recht?" Auntie asked quietly as we started up the back steps. "Does he know about this?" There was an edge of fear in her voice.

"Yes, but he doesn't know I'm here. We have to hurry." Auntie closed the door behind us, but not without a backward glance to make sure no one was following or had seen us.

CHAPTER 27

AUNTIE AND GALINA LED US INTO THE BATHROOM, WHERE AUNTIE HELPED ME OFF WITH MOST OF MY HEAVY, DAMP CLOTHES. SHE BROUGHT ME DRY UNDERWEAR, SOCKS, PANTS, a shirt, and a sweater, and waited outside while I changed.

In the meantime, Galina wrapped Zasha in a big towel and took her to the kitchen to dry her in front of the wood-burning stove. When we joined them a few minutes later, Galina was rubbing Zasha's wet body vigorously and talking to her in a singsong voice. "Yes, you're going to be so nice and dry, and then I'll find something good for you to eat, and then —" She stopped when she saw us. "She is the prettiest little dog I've ever seen!" Her happiness filled the room; the Tsarina was nowhere in sight.

"Sit down," Auntie said gently. "You need something warm in you."

"As soon as she's dry, we have to go," I told them. Galina's smile wilted a little, but she continued to feed wood to the stove and to dry Zasha.

"Tell us quickly: What happened?" Auntie sat next to me and took my hand.

As fast as I could I told them about the room I had with the dogs, the horrible trainer, the sledding trip, and how Zasha fell through the ice. Auntie got up twice to look out the back window as I spoke, saying she didn't put it past Axel to make another surprise visit.

"Petr was here," she said. "He told us about the letter and the visit from the soldiers."

"It was horrible! The man hit Yeshka as hard as he could, and for no reason." Auntie nodded empathetically, squeezed my hand, and leaned back in her chair. "And — you don't even know this — some other soldier hit Polina! In the face! Poor Polina."

Galina shook her head in anger. "Hitting little girls. What's next? Incarcerating babies?"

"There's something else," Auntie said. My heart stopped as the two women exchanged a knowing glance. It was clear that she didn't really want to say what was on her mind. "They've taken Josef."

"Oh." I sighed and smiled in relief. "You had me scared there for a minute. No, Auntie, he's safe. I walked with him and Petr and Yeshka almost all the way to Polina's. The soldiers let us go."

She looked down. "Yes, I know."

"Then why would you think —"

"Because we saw him," Galina interjected, gently rubbing Zasha's front paws dry.

"Petr was still here," Auntie said, "when Josef walked right past the house with his hands tied behind him."

"Followed by two soldiers," Galina said, "with their guns drawn and aimed at his back."

I wanted to cry. Yeshka, Polina, Josef, even me, and the dogs, of course; our lives so quickly changed, brutalized at the hands of our invaders.

"Petr had a guess about it," Auntie said.

"What was his guess?" I asked.

"He thinks Josef went back to the house to try to get something and was caught."

"Petr told him to go directly to his cabin!" But I remembered what Yeshka said, that their papers and everything were left behind at the house.

"I know," Auntie said. "But people, even partisans, do what they think is right in a war, not always what they're told to do."

I put my head in my hands. "Poor Josef. Poor Yeshka."

Galina was tenderly drying Zasha's ears. "We may as well tell him the rest."

"Oh, no — there's more?" I was incredulous.

Auntie delivered the bad news. "The fighting's gotten much worse in Tikhvin."

I thought of the three partisans we'd met who were on their way there. "What does that mean for us here in Vilnov? We're already occupied."

"It depends on who wins. If we recapture Tikhvin — and it seems that we might — the Germans here will probably leave to join the fight, but . . ."

Galina finished the thought for her. "But not before they destroy our town in retaliation. At least that's what I've heard they do." Knowing Axel even a little, I could picture it clearly, the soldiers going from house to house with torches or hand grenades and throwing them into each one.

"And killing us?" I asked bluntly.

"Probably," Auntie answered. I appreciated her honesty.

"And if they win?"

Galina looked disgusted. "Look what's happened here already. Life can only get worse."

"Either way," Auntie said, "we need to get out now, before the situation becomes even more volatile."

I studied Galina as she wrapped Zasha in a fresh, dry towel and held her near to the warm stove. "Did I tell you that Axel told me he's going to turn both dogs into beasts to hunt us in our own country?"

"Oh, Ivan," Auntie said. "You're so young to have seen all that you've seen."

I looked at each of them carefully. "I know, but that's not what's bothering me." They waited for me to go on. "I can't leave here without the dogs. I just can't."

An uneasy silence filled the room. "What are you saying?" Auntie asked.

"I'm not sure, exactly. I don't want to do anything stupid or put anyone in jeopardy, but I couldn't live with myself if I abandoned them to Axel."

Auntie's kind eyes looked pained. "We're going to have to leave here very soon, Ivan. That plan cannot include two dogs. Certainly not *those* dogs."

"But Auntie, you won't even put a bird in a cage because you think it's cruel. Look at her!" I pointed at Zasha, who eyed us attentively. "Would you leave her in the hands of the German army and their vicious ways?" I was quiet, and then walked over to the stove to join Zasha and Galina. I rubbed Zasha's head, and she licked my hand. "I can tell you one thing with certainty: I am not leaving this town without Zasha and Thor." I let those words hang in the air.

"Have you mentioned this to Petr?" Galina asked.

"I have. He's ambivalent, although at first he said no."

"But he hasn't given his approval?"

"No, he hasn't." I took stock of the cozy kitchen, of the warm refuge where I'd hoped to stay for a while, knowing now that very soon I'd be gone.

"All of us need to leave this town soon, no matter who wins at Tikhvin," Galina said. "We need to do it fast and in a coordinated way. We must all leave at the same time, but go in different directions."

"Who do you mean when you say *we*?" I asked, stroking Zasha.

"You, me, Vera, Petr, Yeshka, and Polina."

"Are there other partisans in Vilnov?" I'd never thought to ask.

"We're the only ones left." She said it with a wistful smile.

"What about Josef?"

"I don't know." No one spoke, but I was sure his capture and possible punishment weighed heavily on all of us.

"I need a coat and my valenki," I said. "If we aren't back at headquarters soon, Axel will be mad."

Auntie quickly helped me find the few last things I needed, including an old overcoat of Galina's to replace my wet one. We hovered together at the back door, reluctant to say good-bye. In my heart I knew that hard choices and difficult paths were close at hand. *How close?* I wondered. Hours? Days? Certainly not weeks. If I wanted to survive and help see my friends and the dogs to safety, I couldn't be Ivan the Not-So-Terrible anymore.

I said good-bye, picked up Zasha, and left the house with a fire in me that I knew wouldn't be put out until I had fulfilled my mission.

PART THREE
ESCAPE

CHAPTER 28

THE GUARD OUTSIDE THE MAIN DOOR OF HEADQUARTERS LOOKED STERN, BUT INSTEAD OF GREETING US WITH QUESTIONS OR A RIFLE, HE HELD OUT HIS HANDS, AS ANXIOUS AS a child to hold the puppy. Within a few seconds he was rubbing his finger along the side of her face and talking to her. She obliged him by licking his hand. He laughed and talked to me. All I could do was encourage him with smiles and hand gestures.

"Making friends, I see," Axel said as he ascended the steps to the front door, startling us both. The guard looked terrified, pushed Zasha back into my arms, snapped to attention, shouldered his gun, and saluted. I couldn't understand what Axel was saying, but it sounded like harsh scolding; the young man's face burned red.

"Follow me," he snapped. I set Zasha on the ground, and we trailed in his footsteps along with the two bodyguards, into the building and then into his room. Thor was tucked under Axel's arm, and judging by the way he squirmed to get down and play, he was happy to see Zasha and me.

Axel said something to one of the guards, who immediately took Zasha's lead from me, put Thor on his, and left the room. "So . . ." Axel said, pulling off his black leather gloves and dropping them on the desk. "Zasha is now dry and well, I presume?"

"Yes, sir. I hope you don't mind, but I went to my house to dry us off and get warm again."

He nodded as he threw his overcoat onto a chair. "What was the reason for the problem at the front door?"

211

"There was no problem, sir; the guard was just being friendly. If there had been, I would have just showed him my . . ." That's when I remembered.

"Go on."

"I, ah, I just realized that I forgot to put your letter into this coat pocket." My mouth suddenly felt so dry, I could barely get my words out. "Because my other coat got wet. . . ."

He nodded and strolled to the window. When he turned to speak to me, there was a look in his eye I couldn't read.

"You forgot," he said softly. "You forgot the one thing that would keep you safe in the face of an occupying army?"

"I'm sorry, sir. I was only thinking of making sure Zasha got dry, and . . . and getting her back to you."

He sort of smiled and took stock of me as he walked slowly toward where I stood in front of his desk. "What does that say about you, my little Russian friend?"

"I don't know what you mean, sir."

He began to walk around me in a circle. I felt his eyes on me, his surgical examination, even when I couldn't see him.

"It might mean you're simply careless and forgetful. That's plausible. But you strike me as a precise type of person. I can hear it in the way you play music."

"Thank you."

"I'm not complimenting you. Precision can also make a piece of music sound wooden. I'm talking about your character." He completed his circle and stood in front of me.

"Are you the type of boy who would sell your letter for a few rubles?"

"No, sir! You can go home with me right now and you'll find it there in my pocket, just like I said." A prickly, hot feeling was making its way up my neck and into my face.

"A letter like that would be very valuable to some people."

"No, I —"

"For example, to a man who wanted to kill me. He'd merely pretend to be you, enter my chamber here" — he made a sweeping gesture with his arm — "and shoot me. Of course he'd be dead in seconds, but still, there is always some fool who will volunteer for the job."

"I swear, sir, it's right there in —"

"But I don't think you are the sort to be bought with money. No, you're . . ." He looked me up and down. "You're the type to be motivated by ideas and sentimentality."

"Please, sir, I'm just twelve years old. All I want is for the war to be over and to go back to Leningrad."

He made a mockingly sad face. "Sorry. It won't exist by the end of the war. Forget about Leningrad. You'll all be working for Germany by then, anyway. We'll put you where we need you."

He turned away, and then back to me, as if something had just occurred to him. "There's another possibility." He paused for so long, my hands became moist and clammy. "You're with the underground."

"No!" My response was so vehement, he looked startled. "I'm not. I would never be — I'm just a boy." I willed my face to stay still, to not give me away.

He walked to his desk. "Children are sometimes used by the partisans. I've never seen it myself, but one hears rumors." He pulled something out of the desk drawer that I couldn't see until it was in his hand: a coiled whip.

"Oh, no, please no," I said, pleading, tears tumbling from my eyes. "I haven't done anything, sir. I was forgetful, that's all. I was thinking about the dog."

The long lash of the whip uncoiled and rested innocently on the floor. "I used to be very good with one of these." Axel snapped the whip at the far corner of the room. I gasped. "Quite a sound, don't you think?" He smiled a twisted, sadistic smile. "Crisp. Crackling."

I stood with my hands at my sides, tears flowing down my face. My heart was racing. If he lashed out at me, there'd be no way to escape. The thought of the whip slicing my skin made me light-headed.

"There was a time I could snap a cigarette out of someone's mouth without ever touching their lips." He snapped the whip again, in a motion like a fisherman would make casting his line into a stream. The *snap* exploded dangerously close to my ear. The beginnings of a scream escaped my lips before I could help it. He laughed softly. I didn't move. I couldn't move. "You wouldn't want me to practice with you, would you, Ivan?"

I shook my head, my answer a whisper. "No, sir." He cracked the whip once against the ground; it moved like a snake. He began to coil it into a circle over his left hand.

"Well, I think we understand each other." He gave me a quick, closed-mouth smile. "We'll be leaving soon. Our army is needed elsewhere. You may be going with us. I haven't yet decided."

"Yes, sir."

His stare was hard. I gazed into those impenetrable eyes. "That sounded a little too easy. What about your aunt or guardian or whomever she is? What about your precious Leningrad? What about your *patriotism*?" He'd moved closer and closer to me with every question until I could smell his harsh, metallic breath.

I cleared my throat, willing myself to stop crying and sound reasonable. My voice wavered a bit as I said, "I am a good Russian, but I also want to live."

Something in my answer pleased him. He grasped my right shoulder. "Good boy. We've cleared that up. Now go see that the dogs are fed and dry. See if Fritzi can find a brush so that you can start grooming them. I'll want you back in here by six o'clock with your concertina — *and* your letter."

He turned away from me and I left him, muttering, "Thank you, sir," a half dozen times. I don't know how I made it down to the basement, my body was shaking so hard. My legs felt like they had turned to rubber and could barely support me. Suspicion about me had wormed its way into Axel's mind. It would stay there, and probably get worse. Certainly he'd be watching me more carefully.

Petr had warned me that we had a limited amount of time with access to German headquarters. And Axel had just confirmed it with his talk of leaving Vilnov.

CHAPTER 29

I ENTERED OUR BASEMENT ROOM. ZASHA AND THOR WERE THERE WAITING FOR ME JUST INCHES FROM THE DOOR. TURNING ON THE LIGHTS, I COLLAPSED ON MY BED WITH the dogs, almost crying with relief. They seemed to understand something was wrong and made repeated efforts to lick my face.

"What are we going to do?" I asked them. More than anything, I needed time to think, but there wasn't any. My finger caught on something in Thor's fur. It was a burr, and it didn't come out very easily. Remembering what Axel had said about grooming them, I said, "I'll be right back."

Out in the hall I stared at the four doors on our side of the hall that led in the direction of the cafeteria. Which one had Fritzi opened that was full of cleaning supplies? I was still so shaken from Axel's whip demonstration that I didn't want to be caught doing anything that looked suspicious. *Axel told you to start grooming them*, I reminded myself, so I investigated the room next to ours.

"Oh." I sighed in relief, turning on the light and closing the door. This was the one. The room was jammed with janitorial and cleaning materials; rags, brooms, mops, shovels, and other similar items were piled everywhere. The smell of ammonia made me sneeze. "What about brushes?" I murmured as I began searching through the mess methodically.

When I found some buckets near the corner, I hit pay dirt. There were no fewer than four hand brushes resting in one of them, the kind you use when you're cleaning the floor by hand.

The bristles were stiff and rough. I'd have to use them gently on the puppies. Smelling each one, I picked the smallest; it seemed the cleanest and least used.

There was a closet in the corner. Peering in, I saw what looked like cleaning uniforms hanging from several hooks. A few mud-covered pairs of galoshes lay on their sides on the floor. I couldn't help but wonder what had happened to the workers who once spent their days cleaning the building before it had been abandoned and the Nazis had arrived. *Don't think about that now,* I told myself, the way I did when thoughts of my mother and Leningrad pushed their way into my mind.

The dogs were happy to see me return, and didn't seem to mind being brushed. In fact, they fought each other for the prized spot on my lap. "We're going to start your training," I told them as I finished brushing Thor's tail. "And you're going to learn so fast!" My plan was to work with them for an hour, then go to Galina's and retrieve my letter. Once that letter was back in my pocket, I'd never let it go again. I didn't want to do anything that would make Axel want to take his whip out of that drawer again.

With so little time, I wanted to focus on the most important commands for the puppies. But which ones were they? Whatever plan was ultimately put in place, the one thing I would need from the dogs was silence. I sat cross-legged in the middle of the room. Thor had focused his attention on one of my shoes, while Zasha crawled into my lap, around my back, and into my lap again.

"So," I said out loud, "are you ready?" Both dogs glanced at me, but continued with their play. "I need to teach you to be quiet. But I can't do that until I teach you to speak." Just then I heard two voices in the hall and the clatter of something heavy being dropped on the floor not far from us. The dogs and I froze and stared at the door, but no one entered. Hammering began almost immediately; I hoped the added noise wouldn't distract the puppies too much from what I needed to teach them.

"Thor!" I said. He turned to look at me, recognizing his name. "Speak!" As soon as I said it, I barked two times. Both dogs regarded me as if I'd grown an extra leg. "Speak!" I barked again. Thor made whimpering sounds, as if he wanted to join in the fun. I reached out, held him lightly by his shoulders so he would have to look at me, and said, "Speak!" Again, I barked. This time he whined loudly and yawned in the way dogs do when they seem uncertain about a situation.

I petted his head. "Good boy. Speak!" Thor whined, yawned, and barked. "Good boy!" I was ecstatic. Of the five times I asked him to speak after that, he barked three more times.

Zasha had not looked at all pleased after my first bark, and had trotted off to smell the pile of chairs that lined one wall.

"Zasha, here, girl!" I snapped my fingers. She inspected me briefly — I knew she understood her name — but turned back to sniffing the legs of a chair. "Zasha!" This time she lifted her head, turned left, then right, as if to see who had called her, and then slowly walked toward me, sitting down about two feet in front of me.

"Zasha — speak!" I repeated my barking sounds. Thor barked once, but Zasha said nothing.

"Speak!" I cried, thinking maybe it was better to use one word. Thor barked loudly. "Good boy!" I petted him as I said it. Just as I was about to try it on Zasha again, she barked. "Good girl!" I scooted onto my knees so that I could reach her and pet her. Since the moment I met them I knew both Thor and Zasha were good-hearted dogs, smart dogs. But Zasha always seemed to me like she was more thoughtful, if you could say that about a dog. Like now, when she listened as I taught Thor, learning easily and quickly before it was even her turn.

For the next ten minutes I repeated this exercise with the dogs. The sounds of hammering continued. Although I was curious to see what was going on, teaching the dogs was my priority, and so I resisted. The only problem was when I said "speak," now they both barked, but it was still progress. It encouraged me to move on to step two.

As I considered how I was going to do that, Zasha rolled over; Thor pawed at her as if he wanted to wrestle. He barked sharply at her several times. "Thor — quiet!" He looked at me curiously, but obviously couldn't understand the new command. When he barked again, I said, "Quiet!" and gently put my hand around his muzzle. He didn't like that one bit and shook my hand off.

Zasha was on her feet, alert, watching us closely. Thor barked again as if in protest. "Quiet!" I said, and for a few seconds held his muzzle shut. There was a glimmer in his eye like he might be putting the sound and the action together. I let go quickly, not wanting to hurt or frighten him. Just as I was about to try it out on Zasha, someone opened the door. My body tensed and I jumped to my feet, hoping that if it was Axel he wouldn't find fault with me or the room or the dogs when he entered.

It was a soldier. He laughed when he saw the dogs and said something to me in German. I felt my hand go to the pocket of my coat where my letter from Axel should have been. I responded in Russian, and he shrugged as if he understood that I couldn't converse with him. Thankfully, he seemed more interested in whatever he was doing than in finding out why a strange Russian boy was down here. The dogs ran out the open door.

"Zasha! Thor!" I got up and ran after them. They were already greeting and being petted by a second soldier. He laughed and talked with the other soldier who had come to our room.

They'd attached two metal brackets on either side of the door just down the hall from our room. I stared at them, wondering what they were for. A long metal bar lay on the ground, along with a door handle.

I clapped my hands. "Thor! Zasha! Come!" I walked backward toward our room, but the hall and the two men were more interesting. Thor trotted off toward the cafeteria, and I ran after him. The men laughed and resumed their work.

I reached Thor just as he discovered a garbage bin that interested him. "Oh, no, you don't!" I picked him up and carried him back quickly to make sure Zasha wasn't getting into any trouble. When we got back to the hall, I was relieved to see that one of the soldiers was holding and petting her. The other was on his knees fitting the new lock into the door, screwing it securely into the heavy wood. Pulling a key from his pocket, he tested the lock and door twice.

I watched and petted Thor as the man picked up the metal bar from the ground and laid it across the door, resting it in the metal brackets. It was a barrier. The room was being fitted as a place to lock someone up. My heart constricted. Would they be doing that to all the doors in the basement? Would I soon be locked into our windowless room?

I stared at the simple security devices, my mind racing, hardly realizing someone had called out loudly in German. But the soldier holding Zasha had heard and quickly placed her in my arms. The sound of footsteps filled the air and drew closer. I hoped no one heard me gasp or saw the look of recognition on my face before I was able to set it in a blank stare.

Not far from us were two guards and a prisoner, his hands tied behind his back. His hair was tousled, as if he'd been in a fight. The dark stains on the front of his shirt confirmed it; I'm sure they were dried blood. His lower lip looked like it had been split by a fist, and he didn't seem all that steady on his feet. The guards spoke briefly with the soldiers who had been preparing the room. They lifted the metal bar off and opened the door. Just before the prisoner was escorted in, his hands were untied. He rubbed his wrists vigorously and glanced at me briefly before he walked into the room. I watched as the door was locked and the bar put in place, then took the dogs back to our room.

I stood there, breathing heavily, scared. The prisoner had recognized me. Somehow, I had to get to Petr and let him know that Josef was being held just feet from me.

CHAPTER 30

I RAN ALL THE WAY TO GALINA'S HOUSE, FRIGHTENING BOTH GALINA AND AUNTIE AS I BURST IN THE BACK DOOR LIKE A WINDSTORM. THEY CAME RUSHING INTO THE HALL from their bedrooms.

"I'm sorry," I panted. "I need something I left here." I bent over, hands on my knees, trying to catch my breath. "Petr . . . Where's Petr?"

"I'm not sure," Galina said. "We haven't seen him since he was here earlier."

I stood up straight, saying, "I'll be right back; wait here." I ran into my room where I'd hung my coat over the back of a chair. The letter was exactly where I'd put it and was dry. What a relief it was to slip it into my shirt pocket.

"Something unbelievable happened," I told them as I came back into the hall. But behind Galina I could see into her room, where a suitcase sat open on her bed. "Where are you going?"

Galina looked at me, perplexed. "Don't you remember, Ivan? We talked about how we all had to get out before the Germans decide to . . . decide to . . ."

"I'm getting my things ready, too, Ivan," Auntie added.

I had to suppress a smile or they'd think I'd lost my mind. But I had something planned that I thought would make all of my fellow partisans happy. I just couldn't share it until I spoke with Petr. "Here's what's happened." I told them about Josef being held just two doors down from me. I said I had to go see Petr immediately.

"Are you sure it was Josef?" Auntie asked. "You only met him once."

"Positive. And I know he recognized me."

Galina shook her head, smoothed a strand of hair off of her face, and sighed. "Why didn't we all just leave the moment we heard they were coming?" She looked upset.

"I want you to promise me something," I said.

"What is it?" Auntie asked.

"Promise me you'll do whatever Petr tells you to do."

"I don't understand," Galina said.

I reached out and touched her arm. "I don't, either! Not yet. None of us will until I speak with him. Just promise me."

Auntie, who'd known me almost all of my life, trusted me. "I promise."

Galina said, "Petr understands what's going on better than any of us. I'll do whatever he says."

I walked toward the back door. "I don't know exactly when I'll see you again, but I think it will be soon." I stopped and contemplated the two generous, resilient women who watched me, their confusion obvious. "Thank you, Miss Galina, for your hospitality. Auntie, don't forget to pack my bag, too!"

I was out the door in seconds, on the long trek to Petr's cabin.

★ ★ ★

I used the knock Petr had taught me the last time I came to see him. The side door opened just wide enough for me to get in.

"Polina!" I said in surprise. Seconds later, Yeshka and Petr came into focus. "Why are you all here? Has something else happened?" I tried not to stare at Polina's swollen face, which even in the dim light looked painful.

Yeshka sounded forlorn when he said, "Isn't what's happened bad enough?"

"Sit down, Ivan," Petr said, moving the few chairs he had closer to one another. "We were just beginning to discuss our plans for leaving Vilnov."

"Petr —"

"Hold on." He held out his hand to silence me. "Don't give me your opinion until you've heard all the facts."

"But Petr —"

He interrupted me. "I've talked to Lev. He's been fighting with a group of partisans near Tikhvin. It's his opinion the Russian army has the upper hand in this battle. Everyone seems to think we will be winning it back soon."

"How soon?" Polina asked.

"A week, perhaps. Lev thinks it's only a matter of days, but that may be overconfident." When he stopped to light his pipe, I thought I wouldn't be able to keep my news in for one more second. "Either way, we've got to speed up our departures."

"If we don't?" Yeshka asked.

"They burn the village and kill most of us first before they leave. It's their scorched-earth policy. You boys might be lucky enough to be sent to Germany to work in their factories until you die from exhaustion."

"Why take the time to do that if you've just lost a battle?" Polina asked.

"Punishment," Petr answered simply.

I stood up. "I have to tell you something *right now*. I've seen Josef."

Yeshka jumped to his feet. "What?"

Polina and Petr seemed almost as surprised.

"Yes, and I have information that must have to do with what's happening in Tikhvin. Axel said that they will probably be leaving soon."

Petr sat back in his chair, stunned.

"Listen," I said, "I only have a few minutes because I have to be back there very, very soon."

"Did he . . . had they hurt him?" Yeshka asked.

"I couldn't tell." It was a white lie I could live with. Why make Yeshka feel any worse than he already did? He put his hand over his heart and looked relieved. "Here's what I do know: He's being kept two doors down from where I sleep. His room has no windows, a thick locked door, and a metal bar in front of it." Yeshka began to pace back and forth. "But," I said emphatically, "I've been in the room next to his, the one between us. It's a utility room that has a closet in the back."

"And?" Petr said, like he could hardly wait until the words were out of my mouth.

"I'm not sure, but I'm guessing there's one on his side, too. You know, so that they share a wall. If he can dig a hole in the closet that's big enough to slip through —"

"Oh!" Yeshka gasped.

"— to get into the closet in the utility room, I think I can get him out of the building."

"How?" Petr demanded.

"I take Axel's dogs out to do their business. There are janitors' clothes in the closet. We'll dress him in some of those, put a rag in his pocket and a broom in his hand, and he'll walk out with me and the dogs."

"Then what?" Polina said sharply, but I could tell she liked the idea.

"And how does he make a hole in the wall?" Yeshka frowned.

"Polina, I don't know. That's why I'm here. And we've got just ten minutes to figure it out. I can't be late getting back there *no matter what*," I said emphatically, thinking of the whip in Axel's drawer again. "To answer your question, Yeshka, I'm going to slip this under the door for your father." I reached into my valenki and pulled out my knife. He smiled, and his eyes shone.

"We don't have that kind of time. They built things to last back then. It could take him a week to dig through plaster with a knife like that," Petr said. "I'd like everyone to be gone tomorrow night." Polina, Yeshka, and I exchanged disbelieving glances. "But," he added, getting up, "if he had your knife and a few more tools, he could do it." He disappeared into what I thought was the kitchen. I couldn't see him, but we could hear him as he rifled through drawers. When he returned, he held up a thin saw blade about eight inches long in one hand, and in the other an object that looked like the back side of a hammer, just the claw part.

"This blade will cut anything but stone," he said, handing it to me, "and this little beauty is meant to break up hard, impacted dirt. It will pull out plaster fast. Just catch the ends of the claws on the surface and pull."

Yeshka was so excited, he practically grabbed the hammer claw out of Petr's hand. "Perfect!"

I stared at the tools. "I can slip my knife and the saw blade under the door to him. But that thing is too thick, it won't work."

"You could do it from your side of the closet, Ivan!" Yeshka exclaimed. "You work on your side, he works on his — it's twice as fast, and he's out!"

I was silent for so long, Petr said, "Ivan?"

I looked at my new friends, my brave friends, and said, "I can't."

"Why not?" Yeshka demanded, an edge in his voice.

"Because . . ." I hesitated, wanting to make sure I was telling the truth. "I'm pretty sure I can manage to get the tools to Josef. I think I can get him out of the building. I'm not *brave* enough to risk being caught in the closet helping him dig a hole in the wall. When I am there, I don't have much free time away from Axel or other soldiers. It'd be too easy for me to get caught."

"He's the only family I have! You have to help," Yeshka said. "Please, Ivan."

Polina got out of her chair and went over to Yeshka, who leaned his arms and head on the mantel of the fireplace in despair. She laid her hand on his shoulder. "It's a lot to ask."

He spun around to face us, tears in his eyes. He opened his mouth to speak, but only sobs came out. Collapsing in a chair, he hid his face in his hands and cried.

"I'm sorry," I said softly. "I just can't."

Petr went back into the kitchen. When he came out, he held a broad, flat tool in his hand. Giving it to me, he said, "This is used for smoothing out putty and plasters that you use to fill in little holes in walls. If I can crack the handle off of it, Josef can use the edge of this putty knife to dig through the wall. It won't be fast, but this thing is strong."

Yeshka looked up, his face wet with tears, his expression hopeful. "I can get the handle off. Do you have a hammer?" He followed Petr into the kitchen. We heard two blows and the sound of wood cracking.

When they came back into the living room, Petr had two dish towels with him. "I'll wrap everything up so you won't get cut." I hadn't really thought about the fact that I'd have to walk all the way back to my room with a knife, a saw blade, and part of a putty knife in my boots. Petr packed them in well for me after a couple of false starts.

As he was doing that, Polina said, "What happens once you're outside the building?" My heart sank as I remembered we hadn't yet discussed it.

"I have about three minutes left before I have to leave," I said.

No one spoke. Petr lit his pipe again and said, "Let me think." I knew it was unreasonable, but I wanted to cry out, *Just tell me what to do! I have to go!* The next two minutes of silence dragged on. I could feel myself getting antsy, desperate to leave so I wouldn't be late. Polina and Yeshka must have known that this was how Petr's mind worked, because they sat calmly and didn't say a thing.

Finally, Petr put his pipe down, leaned forward, put his elbows on his knees, and said, "This is what we're going to do."

Minutes later I was on my way back to headquarters, thinking Petr was the smartest man who ever lived.

If all went as planned, in three nights' time I'd be on my way to Vladimir's with Auntie, Petr, and the dogs, and from there to Uncle Boris's in the woods. Josef and Yeshka would join a partisan group near Tikhvin run by Petr's contact Lev. Polina and her mother would go to Kazan with Galina.

It has to work, I said to myself with every step forward in the snow. *It has to work, it has to work, it has to work.*

CHAPTER 31

IT WAS ALMOST TOO EASY. I MADE IT BACK TO THE ROOM WHERE THE DOGS WERE WAITING FOR ME WITH NO PROBLEM, EVEN ARRIVING A LITTLE EARLY. ZASHA AND THOR were restless after my absence. I gave them each a hug and a kiss, and then quietly let myself into the room next door.

Hiding the tools would be simple; in fact, they'd be hiding in plain sight because they looked like tools a janitor would use. There were two pushcarts toward the back of the room. On the lower shelf of one of them was a metal pail that held half a dozen miscellaneous items: rags, a long-handled brush, a bottle of yellow liquid cleanser. I think there was even a screwdriver in there.

Kneeling in back of the cart in case someone came in, I carefully extracted the saw blade and metal piece Petr had given me from my valenki. Lifting a rag, I placed them behind it. They clattered against the metal bucket. My heart stopped and I froze. I think one of the dogs may have barked. I stuffed Petr's dish towels behind them so that would never happen again. Later that night, when I was sure everyone was asleep, I would sneak back in here, retrieve the tools, and give them to Josef, along with my knife.

By the time I had the dogs on their leads and arrived at Axel's door, concertina in hand and letter in my pocket, I was feeling almost confident.

That wouldn't last long. Axel and two other men were deep in conversation, standing over several maps on the desk. Without even looking at me, Axel said, "Sit there," and pointed to a chair by the door. "Keep the dogs on their leads."

Zasha and Thor squirmed like toddlers. They made small sounds of protest that drew dark looks from Axel. Twenty long minutes went by.

Suddenly Axel said something loud and angry, hit the edge of one of the maps with the back of his hand, and stomped over to the window, where he stared out, arms folded across his chest. I caught the look the two men exchanged, one of frustration tinged with fear. They rolled up their maps and were out the door without another word.

"Why are you here?" Axel asked without turning around.

"You asked me to be, sir. You wanted me to play for you tonight."

"Then why have you brought the dogs? Can't you see I'm busy now? Take them downstairs. And be quick about it."

I did as he asked. As we went down the stairs to the basement, I noticed something that I'd given little attention to before. It was a double door that led to an outside staircase. I looked around to make sure no one was watching, then opened it. The dogs were thrilled, thinking I was taking them out for a walk; I was thrilled because it gave me an idea.

★ ★ ★

It was many hours before I could try out my idea, because Axel made me play until midnight. It was exhausting. Something was definitely going on, because men went in and out all evening, talking earnestly with Axel, making notes, standing over large maps, pointing at various spots, and tracing routes with their fingers. Axel had instructed me to play slow songs, very softly, in the far corner of the room. It made it impossible for me to see any-thing specific.

If only I'd been able to speak German, maybe I could have learned something valuable. But even without understanding the language I observed other things, like Axel's terrible temper, how he often raised his voice, and how he moved slowly and with a sinister demeanor toward whomever he was talking to. All his adversaries backed off, except for one. When that man, who looked intelligent and of a rank at least approaching Axel's, raised his voice in response to Axel's anger, I thought the men would come to blows. Axel won the battle after he grabbed a chair and hurled it across the room. It hit the wall and landed at the feet of one of the guards, who looked as if he might shoot it if it came any closer.

Axel seemed to thrive on conflict. He looked energized and excited during and after his most intense exchanges. In contrast, I was fading, having eaten almost nothing all day and my body now used to having meals again. But I knew better than to ask Axel if I could have some dinner.

Finally, just after midnight, only Axel, a guard, and I were left in the room. Axel clapped his hands together. "Well done," he told me. "The music was a perfect backdrop for my meetings."

I smiled, trying to hide my exhaustion. "Thank you. Sir, I wonder if I might ask a question."

"Yes, yes." He waved a hand at me like I should hurry up and ask.

"I wanted to know if I could use the door downstairs near our room to take the dogs in and out for walks and to go to the bathroom."

"Why do you want to use that exit? Are you too lazy to come upstairs?"

"No, sir. It's just that I want to start training the dogs to do their business outside. They're puppies, so they need to go a lot. I thought I could train them better — and faster — if I could bring them in and out quickly and often."

To my utter surprise, he stretched his arms above his head and said, "You're a hard worker, Ivan, unlike most of your countrymen. Yes, you can use the door. There's a guard there at ground level. I'll have one of my men talk to him so he won't shoot you by accident." He yawned and said something in German to the bodyguard who sat nearby. "And Ivan." I stopped and turned to face him. "Don't think that because you work for me it gives you any special privileges."

"No, I never . . ." My cheeks grew flushed.

"Dismissed. Get out." I followed the guard through the door, trying to make sense of Axel's last remark. Hadn't I already seen firsthand what he could do with a whip? Why had he found it necessary to tell me I didn't have special privileges? It was the second time I'd felt Axel was suspicious of me.

The guard showed me no friendliness. He was all business when he took me outside and spoke with another guard, who sat near the ground-level entrance to the side stairs.

That guard seemed like a man who wished he were elsewhere. I pointed to myself and said, "Ivan."

He nodded his understanding and said, "Dieter," and tapped on his chest a few times. The other guard rolled his eyes as if he couldn't believe we were engaging in civilities given our different circumstances in the war. He said something to Dieter that sounded critical. To my surprise, Dieter snapped right back at him, as if he wasn't afraid. The guard stormed off. Dieter murmured something at his back that I'm sure was a curse word. When he spoke German to me, I shrugged and shook my head to let him know I didn't understand.

A big piece of our escape plan had just been put in place with the unwitting assistance of my enemy. Now I could come and go with the dogs as I pleased out the side door, from the basement to ground level. I was fairly sure Dieter wouldn't trouble me, and that soon seeing me and the dogs go in and out would seem normal.

That acceptance would be critical when three nights from now the dogs and Josef and I went for a late-night walk. There was much work to be done before then. It would start in a few minutes when I made my first contact with Josef.

CHAPTER 32

THE HALL WAS DARK, STILL, AND COLD. I LEFT ZASHA, THOR, AND MY BOOTS IN OUR ROOM AND TIPTOED INTO THE UTILITY ROOM NEXT DOOR. I RISKED TURNING ON THE LIGHT because it would be impossible to dig the tools out quietly if I didn't. Wrapping my knife and the tools in Petr's dishcloth before I left served three purposes: It stopped the metal from clanging together, it hid them if someone found me before the transfer, and it was also my excuse for being in the hall at that hour; I'd claim I was there to clean up the mess one of the dogs had made.

My nerves were steady as I reached Josef's door and lay down on the cold, hard floor. Positioning my mouth as close to the crack under the door as possible, I whispered, "Josef. Josef." There was no reply. No sound came from the room, either, no snoring, no rustle of movement.

"Josef," I said a little louder. Still, no answer. I lay quietly for thirty seconds, listening for any sound, inside the room or out. With my right hand I knocked as gently as I could, using the knock Petr had taught me that means *I need to talk to you*. There was no answer. Suddenly, I was fearful that he'd been transferred somewhere else. Then I heard a little moan, the kind people make in their sleep when they roll over.

"Josef! Josef!" I said again, louder this time, and then tapped rapidly on his door, using the partisan knock at least three times. Now there was movement inside; I knew he'd heard me. "Josef. Josef, it's me, Ivan."

There were more sounds from inside; I could tell Josef was getting into position to speak to me. "Ivan! What are you doing here?" His lips couldn't have been more than six inches away from mine, although separated by an impenetrable boundary. I could hear him easily.

"Petr sent me. Josef — are you all right?"

"I've been better." If we hadn't been in such a serious situation, I would have laughed at his bravado.

"What happened? Why did you go back to the house?"

"I'd already started copying Axel's letter. I hid it in an envelope glued to the bottom of the table, but I couldn't be sure they wouldn't find it." I felt terrible when I heard this. He'd gone back so I wouldn't be in danger. "You know how they are, Ivan. They don't forgive, they don't forget."

"Oh, Josef. Thank you. Did you . . . were you able to . . ."

"Don't worry. It may give me indigestion for a while, but it's gone. They found me just as I was finishing my last delicious bite."

I was momentarily stunned as I realized what he was saying. I said thank you again, but I don't think the words could express how relieved I was.

"Now, to what do I owe this unexpected visit?" Josef asked.

"We're going to get you out of here. Listen carefully. I'm going to slip three items under the door. Move your face away now. They're sharp."

"Okay." The knife went in first, and barely made it through the space between the floor and the bottom of the door, although it looked almost an inch high. The blade was next, and then the flat piece of metal.

"Did you get them all?"

"Yes! Yes! What do I do now?" It was only at that moment that I had the horrible realization that I hadn't actually seen a closet in this room. It was merely my guess based on how apartments are laid out as mirror reflections of one another.

"Do you . . ." I could barely breathe. "Do you have a closet in your room?"

"Yes."

"As you face the back of the room, what side is it on?"

"The right."

My relief was enormous. "Are you sure?"

"Yes, I'm sure."

"This is what I want you to do. With these three tools you can dig a hole in the closet big enough to crawl into the room next door. You'll come out in a closet just like yours."

"All right."

"Tonight is Tuesday night. You've got to have it done by Friday night. Do you think you can do that?"

"I *will* do that."

"At ten P.M. I'll be there waiting for you. There's a janitor's uniform that you can change into. You and I will walk out of the building with two dogs on leads. I know the guard at the exit I use to take the puppies on their walks. It'll probably be easier for you to sneak out with me and the dogs." The cold floor was starting to make my stomach ache. My lips kept brushing against the ragged edge of the door, and saliva collected in the corner of my mouth. "Yeshka will be waiting in an alley a block and a half away with warm clothes. You and Yeshka will then take separate routes to Petr's. Do you understand?"

"Every bit. Words have never sounded so sweet! What about you?"

"Polina will be waiting for me and the dogs. Don't worry about that. Just get the hole dug."

"I'm going to start right now."

"Josef — wait! Do they come to your room at specific times?"

"I don't know yet. I haven't been here long enough."

I gasped, thinking I heard a sound coming from the kitchen. "I have to go. Be there at ten o'clock three days from now."

I got up slowly, quietly, and walked on my tiptoes, my limbs stiff from lying in such an odd position on the cold floor. As I reached out to open the door to my room, someone called, "Ivan!"

"Ah!" I cried, an involuntary expression of fear. I turned around toward the cafeteria. A dim light was now on somewhere farther back in the kitchen. Fritzi stood there staring at me, a glass in his hand. He must have gotten up for a midnight snack. Even from a distance I thought I could see a look of curiosity on his face.

I held up the dish towel and said, "Thor made a mess. Don't worry. I cleaned it up. Hope I didn't disturb you." Not waiting for a reply, I went into my room, shaking.

Had he seen me on the ground? Would he believe my story about being there at that hour? Throwing my arms around Zasha and Thor, who had gotten up to meet me, I made soft crying sounds, though no tears came; they came from fear, relief, and fatigue. I stacked two chairs in front of the door so that if Axel came in again unexpectedly in the morning, I could get the dogs out of my bed before he saw they were there. Then the dogs and I snuggled together under a blanket.

How would we ever make this plan work? When I first heard Petr's idea I was ecstatic. It sounded so simple, elegant even. Now it seemed like there were so many things that could go wrong. I went through the details once more in my mind, step by step. Josef and I and the dogs would leave through the basement door. Pretending to go on a walk, we would head down Kirov Avenue for one block, turn right, and turn right again at the alley. Josef would get some warm clothes from Yeshka and leave with him. Polina and I would secure the dogs in the crates and sacks on two of her sleds, then rush to Petr's. Auntie, Vladimir, and Petr would be waiting with the sleigh to go to Kobona. We'd rest there for a night or two if it was safe enough, and then go on to Uncle Boris's.

Every nerve in me was on high alert, and yet just yards from me, Josef was already hard at work digging his way to freedom. It was a good plan, I told myself, a good plan. I fell asleep counting all the things that could go wrong, one after the other, like so many sheep. They seemed endless, and they haunted my dreams.

CHAPTER 33

IF IT HADN'T BEEN FOR THE DOGS, I THINK I MIGHT HAVE GONE A LITTLE CRAZY. ONLY FIVE DAYS AGO I'D LEFT LENINGRAD; SO MUCH HAD HAPPENED SINCE THEN, IT FELT like a month. I'm sure my mother didn't have Axel Recht in mind when she sent me across the ice road to "safety." And yet here I was, a sort of prisoner with special privileges in the very heart of darkness.

On the second morning I awakened at headquarters, Axel was gone. No one could really understand me except Fritzi. But after seeing him last night as I crept back into my room, I wanted to keep my distance. I asked one of the men in Axel's office through pantomime when Axel would be back by pointing at the wall clock and the major's desk. All I got was a look of annoyance. It was the best thing that could have happened. Now I could give all my attention to training the dogs.

With Axel's letter securely in my shirt pocket, I left to go outside with them through the side door of the basement. Dieter was gone, another soldier in his place. I walked right up to him, showed him Axel's letter, and let him pet the dogs. I *wanted* him to notice us. Until we escaped from this place, my goal was for the sight of me walking the dogs to become commonplace.

Petr's instructions for the night of the escape were for me to go down Kirov Avenue just outside headquarters for one block, turn right, and then turn right again when I reached the alley. Polina would be waiting. Today would be my first dry run.

Thor and Zasha couldn't have been happier. Thor sort of leapt every few feet as if in joy, anxious to be running and having fun. A light snow began to fall. I walked toward the street I thought was Kirov — Petr had described its position to me — but, as in Leningrad, all the street signs were gone.

"Let's see if we can figure this out," I murmured to the dogs, walking faster, anxious to get to the corner to see if there was an alley where Petr had said there would be. The dogs fell into a walking rhythm together like they were little huskies pulling a sled. How beautiful it was to look down and see them ahead of me, the snowflakes landing on their thick fur, their bodies moving with such coordination and grace.

"Let's turn here," I said as we reached the corner. "That's it." We passed a well-tended house and its snowy garden before we came to an alley. My heart beat fast as I thought about how we would be here again in two and a half days under the cover of darkness.

The alley was like a narrow road; no German vehicles were going to come plowing down this little lane. We walked past the back of the first house and I saw immediately why Petr had picked his spot. A garden shed belonging to the second house abutted the alley, perfect for hiding behind. If unlocked, a shelter for a quick, private change of clothes.

"I think it's going to work," I whispered to the dogs, so excited to have a clear picture of it all in my mind. "Now we can go walk!" They pulled me back to the street and right, taking up just where we'd left off.

I was thinking so intently about what I would teach Zasha

and Thor as we walked briskly through the light snow that when someone came up behind me and spoke, I jumped.

"Ivan, it's only me," Polina said, looking concerned and casting a watchful eye around her.

"But why are you here?" I said, my heart pounding. "I was doing a practice run with the dogs. Is everything okay?"

"Keep walking normally," she instructed me. "If we're stopped we say I'm on my way to Galina's house to see if the chickens have laid any eggs." She patted the handle of the wicker basket resting in the crook of her arm, a kerchief neatly folded on the bottom.

"Why are you here?"

"I'm practicing," she said brightly. Her face was less swollen, but the cut above her eye still looked new.

"Me, too. Do you have information for me?"

"Not much. I've been walking the west side of the village from below Petr's up to the German perimeter in the north."

"And?"

"There doesn't seem to be anyone guarding the southwest area. Yes, it's remote and hilly, but . . . I keep asking myself why the security is wide open there. It makes no sense."

"Unless . . ."

Polina stopped walking. "Unless what?"

"Unless that's the direction they'll go when they leave."

Her bright eyes reflected the excitement within her. "That's what I've been thinking! They don't want to waste manpower in the west. They probably think the people of Vilnov won't go that way under any circumstances. There's nothing in the west to go to! A twenty-mile strip of land, then Lake Ladoga, then Leningrad. And who in their right mind wants to go to Leningr — Oh, I'm so sorry, Ivan. I didn't mean it in that way."

"It doesn't matter. You're right. The city is half dead. I don't even know if my mother . . ." I couldn't make the words come out of my mouth. Polina slipped her arm through mine, and we walked in silence until I regained control of myself.

"What effect does this have on our escape route?" I asked finally.

"I think it means that if you go west and then north — and stay off the roads — you'll have a good chance of making it. Just make sure you leave before they do."

"Have you nailed the boxes to the sleds yet?"

"I have. They're all ready for the dogs. You look so worried, Ivan."

"I am! The idea of stuffing the puppies in potato sacks and then putting them in boxes on your sleds is pretty . . ."

"Imaginative?"

I laughed and looked down at the dogs, who were busy smelling the bottom of a tree. "Yes."

"And makes the dogs suddenly disappear?" she teased.

"That, too. And you promised to cut lots and lots of airholes."

"Already done."

I'd noticed that Polina hadn't acknowledged the dogs at all yet, except for watching them as we walked. "Do you want to pet them?" I asked.

"Yes," she said softly, looking at them. "But I shouldn't. I can't let my heart get attached to anything right now. It's like I'm protecting it."

"I understand," I said softly, and I did. At that moment I realized I would soon lose Polina, and some of my other new friends. It was almost more than I could stand; I'd been torn away from so much already. And even though Polina and I hadn't been friends that long, it still hurt. "Polina, do you think we'll ever see each other again?"

"Maybe someday, when the war is over." She looked at me sadly when she said it.

"It might not be over for years." I felt desolate.

Her eyes glistened. "I wish there were no war. Sometimes I just want to be a normal girl worrying about normal things."

I smiled. "Fortunately, you're one of the least normal girls I know. Wait — I'm not sure that came out right."

She laughed. "It's okay. I think I know what you mean."

"I'm starting to feel better," I said. "This plan is coming into focus. I meet you in the alley, the dogs go into the sacks in the boxes nailed to the sleds. We take the path near Galina's down to Petr's. From there, Vladimir drives us to his place."

"That's where Petr is now," Polina said.

"So no one knows if Vladimir has agreed to help us?"

"No, we don't."

My emotions seemed to sway like branches in a strong wind. I was feeling doubtful and fearful again.

"Just two more days, Ivan."

"Two more days."

We said good-bye, but when she was just a few feet away from me I said, "Polina, what if someone chases us? What do we do?"

"You let go of the sleds and you leave the dogs. You run for your life down to Petr's."

Did she really expect me to abandon them? Axel was a punisher. If I wasn't there to satisfy his vengeance, I had no doubt he'd take it out on the dogs.

"Maybe Josef and Yeshka could help us."

Polina took a few steps toward me. "They have their orders. We have to make our part succeed by ourselves."

That was the truth; there was no more to be said. Polina turned and left.

★ ★ ★

After I'd walked with the dogs another twenty minutes, I returned to headquarters and dug something out of my duffle bag. Fritzi had shown me a small bathroom off the kitchen. I took it there and hoped no one would come in for the next few minutes.

I laid my father's shaving kit on the side of the sink, carefully pulling out a brush and a straight razor. I took off my shirt and ran the water until it was hot, letting it clean and soften the brush. Swishing it around on the soap, I foamed it enough that I was able to cover my face in a thin layer of soap suds. Taking the razor carefully in my right hand, I scraped my face from the top of my right cheekbone down an inch or two at a time until I reached my jawline.

I observed the results. My skin looked damp and clean. I repeated the process on the other side, cutting myself twice. Droplets of blood oozed out and dotted my skin. Above the lip and the chin were the hardest, and I cut myself some more.

Finally, when I was done, I cleaned my razor and brush, rinsed my face, dried it lightly, and stared at my reflection in the mirror. Bits of blood still oozed; others had congealed.

You're a man now, I told myself. *A man acts bravely even when he's afraid. Do this for your mother and your father. Make the family line of Savichev proud. Do it for Leningrad and all the hungry people fighting for life. Do it for the partisans. Do it for Zasha and Thor and the good lives they'll have away from Axel Recht. Do it for the generations of puppies they'll give life to. Do it so you can look yourself in the mirror and be proud.*

I was ready now, my energy focused, my motives clear.

CHAPTER 34

On Thursday, the day before our escape, Axel still wasn't back. As curious as I was about where he'd gone, I was secretly relieved. It would be so much easier to escape if he wasn't here. All day I'd worked with the dogs on simple commands: come, sit, stay, go. They were tired of it. Zasha finally just lay down on her bed and ignored me. Thor was still ready to learn, but often he pawed at the door to our room as if the reward for even the tiniest bit of learning was a long walk.

I waited until about three P.M. to go and check on Josef's progress. The kitchen staff would be on their break between lunch cleanup and dinner preparations.

Taking Petr's dish towel with me in case I needed it again as a cover story, I let myself into the utility room. I wasn't too nervous about being caught in the main room. There were a lot of legitimate reasons I could invent for being in there that wouldn't arouse suspicions.

But the closet . . . If I were found in there and Josef had made progress with the hole, it'd be all over. We'd both be dead. To make it worse, there was no light in the closet. If I wanted to see, I had to leave the door open and get light from the main room.

I opened the closet door and got down on my knees. There it was, the outline of a narrow, dark space that started at the floor and went up about six inches. It was only about a foot wide. If Josef started this on Tuesday night and this was all the progress he'd made by Thursday, he'd never get out by tomorrow.

I got my head as low to the floor as I could and whistled softly through the hole. After a few moments I heard what I was almost sure were footsteps. Within seconds I heard his voice.

"Is that you?" he asked, being smart enough not to use my name.

"Yes. The hole looks good, but . . ."

"I know. It's not big enough. I'm grateful for the tools you gave me, but they're just not strong enough. And I have to be very careful about not making too much noise."

My heart beat faster. "There's so little time. . . . What are we going to do?"

"Are there any other tools you can get me? A hammer, a screwdriver, something heavy. Whoever built this building did too good of a job!"

"Let me look around." I was filled with frustration and fear as my role in helping Josef expanded. And yet if Josef hadn't been worried about the copy of my letter being found, he wouldn't be here. Petr had been very clear that my participation in Josef's escape was the reason he'd given his okay to stealing the dogs. He understood they provided the cover we needed to get out of the building. Closing the closet door, I began a methodical search of the clutter in the utility room. There were some things that would have been helpful, like a shovel, but it would have been too noisy, and impossible to get to him.

Brooms and mops had sturdy wooden handles, but again, there was the noise to consider. He needed something smaller to gnaw away at the wall. There had to be something. . . . I remembered the screwdriver I'd seen when I hid the tools. Pulling it out,

I saw that it had a sturdy red wooden handle, a strong shaft, and a flat blade.

Taking it back into the closet, I slipped it through the hole to Josef. It was weird to be able to see his fingers as he accepted it. "You have to make this work, Josef," I said, feeling desperate as I looked at the pitiful, rough opening.

"Don't worry, Ivan," he said confidently. "I'll think of my Yeshka with every stab I take at that wall. I will be ready tomorrow night."

I wished I felt as confident as he did. There were so few hours left. What would we do if he couldn't get out? I tried to imagine what I'd do if roles were reversed, if Yeshka were at headquarters passing tools to my imprisoned mother. I'd probably say to him what he said to me: "She's the only family I have! You have to help."

Focus on what you can do something about, I told myself, and left to work on commands with Zasha and Thor for the rest of the day.

★ ★ ★

I lived in constant worry about when Axel would return. In just another hour, I planned to leave this place forever.

As nine P.M. approached, I looked again at the few items I'd brought with me, knowing I'd have to leave some of them behind. The letter from Axel was going with me, of course, and Polina's compass. My concertina and my father's shaving kit were non-negotiable. The kit I was able to stuff in a side pocket of my jacket. The concertina I'd have to tuck between my belly and my coat and hope the fit was tight enough to hold it.

Zasha sat in front of me, demanding that I pet her. Every time I stopped she pawed at me for more. I think Thor knew something was going to happen. Instead of being his usual rambunctious self, he lay close to me as if to say *If you need help, I'm here.* Their leads were out and ready to go.

Soon Josef and I would leave through the side basement door with the dogs. How many times had I reviewed what would happen once we were outside? Three dozen? Or four? It felt like a hundred. I paced nervously in our room. *What am I forgetting?* I asked myself. I knew the answer, and *forgetting* wasn't the right word.

It was Josef. I hadn't been in to check on him since yesterday, half out of fear of being caught, half out of knowing that digging the hole was something he'd have to accomplish himself.

It was Zasha and Thor who alerted me — jumping into standing positions, ears up, tails trembling. They heard and felt the surge of energy and activity before I did. I poked my head out the door and saw that people were rushing around in the kitchen area. What was going on? I closed the door behind me to keep the dogs safe and ran to see if I could find Fritzi. He and a dozen others were pulling supplies from shelves and refrigerators as fast as they could.

"Fritzi, what's wrong?" I asked.

He shook his head, opened one of the refrigerators, pulled something out, and promptly dropped it on the floor. It shattered. He yelled as if someone had pinched him, and then began talking to himself in German. It almost sounded like he was crying.

"Fritzi, what's wrong?" I said, louder this time, as I went over to help him clean up the mess. Four more people ran into the kitchen, two of them speaking to Fritzi at the same time, looking almost as distraught as he did.

"Fritzi!" I practically yelled it so that he would focus on me. "What happened?"

I could see him struggling to find the Russian words. He stood up and looked deeply upset as he said, "Tikhvin! Tikhvin bad! Germans leaving now helping. Hurry," he said, motioning toward the other men who were grabbing utensils and pots and pans out of drawers and cupboards. He bent down again to clean up the mess at our feet. Shouts and the clamor of men on the floor above us grew louder. The whole army was on the move.

"Fritzi — where are the Germans going?"

He blinked his eyes rapidly and shook his head to show me he didn't know. "Going now."

When I started to speak to him again, one of the other men yelled at me. I don't know what he said, but he looked angry and annoyed and swung his arm toward me like I was a fly. The message was clear: *Get out! Get away from us!*

Just as I was turning to leave the kitchen, Axel came flying down the stairs. "Ivan! Get your things. We're leaving. Where are the dogs?"

"In their room."

"I'll get them."

I stood there openmouthed, not knowing what to say to deter him. He was halfway across the kitchen before he was intercepted by someone who needed his attention. They spoke rapidly in German.

Maybe he wouldn't notice if I snuck away in all the chaos. Five steps later, he yelled, "Ivan! Be in my office in ten minutes with the dogs."

"Yes, sir," I said, and ran not to my room, but to the utility room. I prayed Josef was ready; we had to leave now. I flipped on the light and threw open the closet door. There was Josef, lying down on his back, his body stuck partway between his closet and the one I was in. He'd made it in just past his shoulders.

"What happened?" I cried. "How long have you been here?"

"About three hours," he answered with some effort. "Help me."

I was so shocked by what I saw, it took me a moment to comprehend it. "Okay, okay," I muttered. "Stay right there." I think I heard a weak laugh as I tore out into the utility room. I grabbed a rag out of a pile of them and a shovel from the corner.

"This would be so much easier if I could use your arms for leverage," I mumbled, kneeling down. But I knew if Josef had decided to come through the hole arms first, it would have made his rib cage bigger. Which would have meant he'd have to make the hole bigger as well, and there just wasn't time. I sighed and said, "I'm going to put this cloth over your face so you won't be hit by the plaster. Turn your head to the left, all right?"

"Okay." Whatever noise I'd make didn't matter anymore; it was already coming from every direction. I hit the sharp blade against the wall about six inches above Josef's face. Very little happened. I tried again and heard a slight crackling sound. The third and fourth blows brought an actual horizontal crack. Josef said something, but I didn't want to stop and ask. He could talk to me when he was free. I hit the wall again at the crack. Fine white dust began falling. I slammed the shovel into the wall a dozen times before actual pieces crumbled. Leaning the shovel against the wall, I clawed at the plaster with my hands. Within two minutes there was about four inches of space open above Josef's chest.

I took the towel off his face. "Ah, thank God," he said. "I could hardly breathe."

"I'm sorry, but we need to get out of here. The army's leaving right now. Can you move?"

"I'll try to push myself toward you with my heels. . . ." He closed his eyes, he made grunting sounds, but he didn't budge. "Go, Ivan. Save yourself."

I ignored his remark. "Josef, try this. Can you roll on your side just a little? That will make you less wide on the sides and wider at the top where you've got some room now."

"I've been lying here a long time now. I'm not sure."

"I'm going to help you." I couldn't get my hands into his armpits from underneath, so I stood over him and pushed my hands into the almost nonexistent space between his arms and torso and pulled him away from the wall with all my might. Before I let go, I was almost certain I'd felt some movement.

"One more time. Try to roll slightly on your right side. Push with your heels. Okay? Go!" I pulled and strained; he pushed and struggled to roll himself over.

"Ah!" I cried. We'd moved him an inch or so. "Do it again!" We tried even harder, if that was possible. If we could just get him angled a little more, past his muscled arms, he'd make it.

"I'm going to get out, aren't I?" he said, almost to himself.

"Yes. Two more pulls and your elbows will be through. I know it. Let's go. Push!" We gave it our all, and I don't know who was happier when Josef's elbows cleared the opening and he was able to slip his hands up. He used them to push against the wall; his waist appeared, then his knees, and then his feet.

He sat on the floor for a minute as if in a daze. "Thank you, Ivan. I know you could have run, I know you could have left me. . . ."

"That's not what partisans do, is it? That's not what you did."
I patted his shoulder. "We're not out of here yet. Can you stand?"
It took him about thirty seconds to feel secure on his feet. "There
are the janitors' uniforms." I nodded to several hanging on hooks.
"Put one on, and put those galoshes over your shoes. My room is
right there," I said, pointing in back of me. "I'm going to get
ready. Come in as soon as you're dressed."

"Okay." When I was halfway across the room, he said, "Ivan,
your knife!" The tools I'd given him and my knife lay on the
floor near the corner. "At least I remembered to throw them in
here first before I got stuck." He smiled.

It felt so good to have my knife again. I slipped it into my
valenki and left. The echoes of activity from the kitchen and the
floor above filled the hallway. Slamming the door behind me, I
stood staring at Zasha and Thor although barely seeing them, my
mind was racing so fast.

It was more than an hour before we were supposed to leave.
Nothing that we so carefully planned was going to happen. Josef
and I would have to get out of the building with the dogs on our
own, in the middle of the chaos, with every soldier awake and
alert and no one on the outside to help us.

And who would be leading the charge, making sure every
man and every thing was where it was supposed to be? Major
Axel Recht. The same man who expected me to be arriving in his
room any minute with his dogs.

"We're going now," I said aloud, unbuttoning my shirt and
grabbing my concertina. I pushed it up beneath my undershirt
and gasped as the cold metal edges of the case hit my skin. I put
the flat part against my stomach and slipped my coat on to cover

the bulge. I felt in my pockets for my gloves and pulled my hat down on my head until it covered my ears.

The dogs were at my feet making little whining and moaning sounds. "You have to be very good and very quiet," I said as I knelt down and clipped their leads to their collars. It wasn't easy with the concertina in the way. I petted each of them and said a few soothing words.

As I looked around one last time to make sure I hadn't forgotten anything, Josef entered the room. "Are you ready?" I asked.

"I've never been more ready for anything."

"Stay at my side. Try to look natural."

Josef nodded.

"Quiet," I whispered to the dogs as I turned off the overhead light. I opened the door; the hall was empty. We scurried toward the side door. The cold hit us like a slap, and it was snowing. *Good*, I thought, *it might help obscure us.* "Quiet," I cautioned the dogs again, and we walked up the stairs quietly and slowly.

There were men running everywhere, yelling to one another, trucks and other vehicles roaring into action. Dieter, the guard whose duty it was to protect this side of the building, was standing next to the cab of a truck, engaged in an animated conversation with the driver.

We hurried from the building and across the street to Kirov Avenue. No one seemed to notice us. If they had, I would have waved and then ignored them as if I didn't understand that they wanted us to stop. If they caught up with us, I would have pulled out Axel's letter and tried to convince them I was walking the dogs one last time before we all left with them for the new location. If they asked about Josef, I'd say he was someone assigned to help me with Axel's dogs. Hopefully, if that happened, that lie would buy us enough time to escape.

Kirov Avenue was dark, and the snow acted as a thin veil. The farther we got from headquarters, the faster we moved. We were passed by at least four different vehicles, including one tank, but no one stopped or tried to speak with us.

"What's the plan?" Josef asked softly, his eyes darting around.

"Turn right at the corner. We're going to go in the alley and hide until Yeshka and Polina arrive."

I was getting nervous. Even though we were out of sight of the activity on Kirov Avenue, we didn't know what would happen next because we were an hour early. "See that shed?" I said. "If it's unlocked, we'll wait for them in there."

The dogs trotted along unconcerned, having been here a few times already on our many walks. We got to the shed, looked around to make sure no one was watching, and opened the door. I almost screamed. There were Polina and Yeshka, standing in the dark not three feet from us.

"Papa!" Yeshka said in a voice barely above a whisper. "Get in."

I stood outside, uncertain whether I should take the dogs in. Polina said, "Wait, let me take the sleds out." After a quick hug with Josef, she maneuvered the two wooden sleds, now modified, out into the snow.

"Good-bye," we whispered to our friends. "And good luck." I closed the door so Josef could make his quick change into warmer clothes.

"Ivan, you put the dogs in the sacks, okay?" Polina said. "They don't know me." I nodded and gave her Thor's lead.

I decided to put Zasha in first because her temperament was a little more mellow than Thor's. At least I thought so, until I tried to get her into the burlap sack full of airholes that would act as her protection for the next hour.

She fought me hard, twisting, jumping, and in every way refusing to cooperate. "Zasha, please," I begged. "It's only for a little while."

"Ivan, hurry."

"I'm trying." It was useless. "Let me try Thor," I said, after another minute of struggle. If possible, Thor was worse. He'd seen Zasha's response; if she hated the idea, he was determined to hate it even more.

"Why is there all this activity?" Polina asked as I tried once more to slip the sack over Thor's head.

"It's Tikhvin. I couldn't understand exactly, but I think they're going there to join the fight. Remember? Petr said he thought they were losing that battle."

A sound of deep fear escaped from Polina like it was her last breath. "We have to go. Right now."

"But I can't yet. . . ." Yeshka and Josef emerged from the shed, touched us each on the shoulder in farewell, sprinted into the alley, and disappeared.

"Now, Ivan," Polina said in a deadly calm voice. "We have to go now."

"But I can't get them in the bags!"

"Leave the bags, leave the sleds. It'll be too slow. Walk to the street *RIGHT NOW*." Her tone was so authoritative, so certain, that I abandoned it all immediately, held fast to the dogs' leads, and walked quickly with her to the street.

"Turn right. We'll follow the rest of the plan," she said, looking straight ahead. "Walk as fast as you can, but don't run." We'd made it almost to the corner when someone screamed my name.

"Ivaaaaaan! Halt or I'll shoot!"

That voice would haunt me forever.

Time seemed to slow down as I looked behind me and saw Axel, a gun in his right hand, running toward us at top speed. He didn't have a coat or hat on — he must have gone to the basement to find me and the dogs and realized what I'd done.

"Run, Polina!" I cried. We ran as fast as we could over the snow-covered ground, the dogs in the lead. I held tight to my concertina with my left hand so it wouldn't fall out. We were almost a block ahead of Axel, but he was a grown man, and battle hardened.

Zasha kept turning around, as if she knew something was terribly wrong and I could explain it to her. It slowed us down. Twice I almost tripped over her. Polina noticed. "Give me one of the leads!"

"No!" I cried, afraid I might drop it, afraid I'd be separated from Polina and one of the dogs, afraid it would give Axel a chance to get even closer.

The shot Axel fired broke the silence of the night air like the *crack* of his whip. "He'll kill us, Polina. Faster!" I felt blind with fear as my legs pumped harder and harder. The dogs were swift and light on their feet, but they were still puppies. If Axel followed us all the way to Petr's, they'd tire and stop.

"Stop! You Russian swine . . . pig . . . I will kill you!"

Panic was building within me. "Polina, where should we

go?" I panted. "We can't lead him to Petr's. He'll find and kill everyone."

Axel fired again. I swear I felt it rush past me, just inches from my arm.

"Go to Galina's," she cried softly. "We'll hide in the hen coop."

"No, he's been there. He'll find us."

"Then there's no choice. We go to Petr's."

"We'll never make it before he catches —"

There was a strangled cry, and as we were about to round a corner I stole another glance back at Axel. He'd fallen. But he lay on his belly in the snow, both hands gripping his pistol. He fired off three more shots, hitting chips off of a brick building not seconds after we'd passed it.

"I'll find you," Axel screamed. "I'll find you. And when I do, I'll kill you! Do you hear me? I'll kill you!"

"Don't listen, Polina. We'll head for the north-facing tunnel, the one hidden by the five trees."

"He could follow our trail there in the snow."

"Do you have a better plan?" We were running so hard and fast, our words were coming out unevenly between our short gulps of breath.

"The north tunnel," she agreed. We ran for our lives. There were no more shots fired at us. Although I was fairly sure Axel had stopped chasing us after he fell, I dared not turn again and lose even a few seconds of our lead or risk falling myself. The dogs were tiring, but I cajoled, encouraged, and half dragged them down the hill until we reached the entrance to Petr's north tunnel.

Only then did we stop and peek out from the small grove of trees to see if Axel had followed us after all. In the dark, through the falling snow, I could see nothing out of the ordinary, no movement, no sound. We did our best to quickly cover our footprints around the entrance and make it look natural by brushing the snow with a branch Polina broke off of an evergreen tree. After fumbling for the handle, we pulled open the entrance to the tunnel as quietly as we could and shut ourselves into its pitch-black silence. I struck a match against the rough surface of the candle holder, illuminating Polina and the dogs. They were all breathing heavily and looked a little disoriented and relieved.

"You go first," I told Polina as I handed her my candle and lit another for myself. "If Axel follows us in here, I have a knife with me. I'll protect you."

"It's all right, Ivan," she said softly. "I think we're safe."

I nodded my head to reassure her, while knowing with certainty that Axel's declaration that he would find me and kill me was not a threat. It was a promise.

CHAPTER 35

PETR HAD OBVIOUSLY HEARD US IN THE TUNNEL, BECAUSE WHEN WE FINALLY EMERGED FROM THE CLOSET IN THE BEDROOM AND WENT INTO THE LIVING ROOM, WE WERE GREETED by four people, each of them with something in their hands they could use as a weapon, poised for battle.

"Ivan!" It was Auntie, standing off to the side holding a ski pole, its spike ready to impale anyone foolish enough to attack. Petr lowered a chair, and Vladimir a walking stick, with sighs of relief. The other man, who had a kerchief covering most of his face and a rifle in his hand, hesitated.

"Polina, dear," Auntie said, putting down the pole and embracing her.

"What's wrong with your stomach?" Petr demanded. I unbuttoned my coat, clasping my concertina to me. "What happened? Why did you need to use the tunnel?"

I explained briefly and assured him that Yeshka and Josef had gotten away safely.

"Yes, they've been here and gone already."

"Good." I sighed in relief. "Nice to see you, Vladimir. Petr, who is this?" I asked.

"It's okay," Petr answered. "He's one of us. Lev, this is Ivan." With just a hint of hesitation, the man pulled his scarf down around his neck. His face was weatherworn, and a thick stubble covered his cheeks and chin. I extended my hand and he took it.

"Is he coming with us?"

"No. He came to warn us. The fighting at Tikhvin is getting worse. He came to tell everyone to get out of town now."

I nodded. "I think it's even worse. The Germans are already preparing to leave tonight." The adults exchanged worried looks.

"How can you be sure?" Lev demanded.

"I was there when they got the news. They're leaving as soon as they can get out."

"They'll evacuate to the west," Petr said, the anxiety in his voice clear. "We have to leave. Now!"

Lev agreed. "They can't go south, or east because of Tikhvin. There's no reason to go north."

Petr was already striding across the room when he said, "We're leaving in three minutes. Anything not in the sleigh by then stays here."

The sleigh was waiting about fifty feet from Petr's front door, obscured by a turn in the road and a cluster of pine trees. Just a few trips back and forth to the sleigh for the things not yet packed ate up those precious minutes. Thank goodness Lev and Polina were there to help.

We stood catching our breath. Only the dogs seemed excited by our adventure, although they were skittish about getting anywhere near Nesa, who must have seemed like a strange giant to them.

"We have to go," Auntie said urgently. "I'll get in first, then we'll get the dogs settled.

Vladimir climbed in the driver's seat, and Petr sat next to him. I helped Auntie into the back and then handed her the dogs.

As Lev exchanged a last few bits of information and advice with Vladimir and Petr, I turned to Polina. "I have your compass with me," I said softly.

She looked like she was struggling to control her emotions. Then she leaned over and grabbed me in a fierce hug. In a whisper, she said, "Promise you'll bring that compass back to me!" Before I could answer, she turned and ran back toward Petr's house and disappeared.

"Ivan," Auntie said, "we have to go!" I nodded and climbed into the sleigh, glancing back quickly, hoping I'd catch a glimpse of Polina, but she was gone. Zasha and Thor made it clear immediately that they wanted to be on our laps. Auntie and I were firm, positioning them again and again under the blankets at our feet until they accepted that's where they'd be staying.

"Good luck, my friends," Lev said, stepping back from the sleigh. "Don't let the Germans see you. If they do . . ." He hesitated. "Run for your lives."

CHAPTER 36

THE SNOW HADN'T STOPPED FALLING SINCE MY ESCAPE FROM HEADQUARTERS, ALTHOUGH IT WAS LIGHTER NOW. I LEANED UP CLOSE TO SPEAK WITH PETR AND VLADIMIR TO ask about our route to Kobona.

"Will you go directly west, Vladimir?"

"Not exactly. We'll go north, then west, then north, then west. That way if two different people saw us and reported our direction, they could easily contradict each other and cause confusion. I'm also staying off the roads whenever possible."

It was a silent journey; no sleigh bells jingled on Nesa's harness, and none of us spoke much once we left Petr's. His rifle rested on his knees; two more sat on Auntie's lap under the blankets. Our rush from headquarters to Petr's was an unexpected blessing; the dogs had exhausted themselves and fallen asleep.

The first twenty minutes were uneventful. We were approaching the main east-to-west road, the road the Germans were almost certain to use when they retreated. It would take only a few minutes for us to cross and disappear into the forest, but those few minutes might be the most dangerous of our journey. I was listening hard for any unusual sound.

"What was that?" I said, half to myself. Was I the only one who heard it? "Vladimir, turn — now — into that gully," I whispered as loudly as I dared.

He didn't question me, and with a pull of the reins guided Nesa down a small hill at the edge of the meadow. There were few trees; the hillock provided our only protection from someone on the road spotting us.

"What did you hear, Ivan?" Auntie asked once we came to a stop.

"Motors, rumbling. The same sounds I heard outside headquarters."

She nodded and put her arm around me. "We haven't come this far to be careless now."

Vladimir climbed down and stood next to Nesa, holding her reins and petting her head. It was decided that Auntie and I would stay where we were to keep the dogs quiet, and Petr would see if he could find out what was happening. On his knees, with his rifle in his hand, he crawled to the lip of the hill. We sat motionless in the falling snow, listening to what were clearly the sounds of the German army abandoning Vilnov. It was cold and hard to sit still. Just when it seemed that we'd heard the last of them, another contingent of noisy vehicles would rush by. We must have been there an hour before Petr carefully crawled backward down the hill and came to talk to us.

"This could go on for some time," he said, looking almost as pale as the snow, and very, very cold. "I don't think we should leave until fifteen minutes after we've seen our last vehicle."

"I agree," I said, "but we have to take turns or you and Vladimir will freeze." All of us were covered in about a half inch of snow, like so many statues in a garden; and it didn't look like it was going to be letting up any time soon.

Petr looked doubtful, but I jumped down from the sleigh before he could protest. "Take my seat, get warm, and we'll trade places in another hour if we're still here. Be careful of the dogs," I warned him.

Auntie slipped out of her side of the sleigh and said something to Vladimir. He shook his head. Auntie put her hand on his arm and talked to him some more before he handed her Nesa's reins and climbed in next to Petr in the back of the sleigh.

"You're no good to us if you're frozen to death," I said, making sure they covered themselves in the thick blankets all the way from the neck down, and that the dogs didn't awaken.

"I'm worried about Nesa," Vladimir said. "We can't keep her standing in the snow for too much longer." Petr and I nodded without answering. If we were lucky, we would be on our way soon and wouldn't have to formulate a plan for Nesa at all.

I lay on my stomach on the hill; it was freezing. Every five minutes or so I crept carefully to the crest of the tiny hill and peeked out to see if the German army was still on the road, then crawled back down. At least it kept my blood moving.

It surprised me at first that the Germans, so well known for their discipline and organization, hadn't left Vilnov in one long column, in an orderly retreat. The possibility of losing Tikhvin must have frightened them deeply to respond so quickly, and a little haphazardly.

After twenty silent minutes went by, I shimmied down the hill, hoping Petr would agree with me that it was time to go.

"I was just going to come and get you," he whispered, climbing out of the sleigh, stiff from inactivity.

Vladimir leaned toward me. "I'm worried about Nesa. We have to get her out of the cold."

"As soon as we're clear of the gully, we have to go as fast as we can," Petr said softly. "There's a forest about a quarter of a mile away, on the other side of the road. We'll head for that."

Vladimir smiled patiently. "That's where I was going when we stopped. I'm not sure Nesa will be able to run immediately. We'll see." As he left the sleigh, I saw two small lumps appear under the blankets on the floor. Zasha and Thor were awake.

"Petr, can I let the dogs stretch their legs and go to the bathroom?"

He shook his head. "There's no time. Maybe once we're in the forest."

Vladimir examined Nesa's feet and rubbed her ankles with his bare hands. Settling himself on the front bench, he said, "I think she can run," but his tone was uncertain. Nesa proved her master wrong and set off at a good pace, increasing it quickly as though happy to be free and moving again.

There was a rise in the land where the road cut through, so we didn't see the wooden box upended on the road until we were racing past it. I stood up quickly, as did Petr, trying to see what it was that had bounced out of a German truck and lay waiting to be claimed.

It was dark and hard to see, but Petr said, "I think it's a box of bullets. Vladimir, go back. Ivan will help me load it into the sleigh."

"No," Vladimir said. The sleigh quickly cleared the road and glided down the modest embankment on the other side. The forest lay just beyond a small meadow.

"Vladimir — we need those bullets. Go back," Petr insisted.

The sleigh rushed forward. "If I stop on the road and a vehicle comes, we're all dead."

"We haven't seen a German in almost thirty minutes," I argued.

Petr looked furious, but Vladimir continued quietly, "I will stop when I find a place in the forest where we can't be seen. One of you can go back for it."

Petr shot him an angry look. Vladimir simply flicked Nesa's reins to make her go faster. Petr had no choice but to sit back down and go along with Vladimir's decision, although he was clearly none too pleased about it.

"Ivan, look," Auntie said. I turned to look east toward Vilnov. A cloud of black smoke was rising high into the sky. "They're burning Vilnov on their way out."

I thought of all my friends who were planning to leave by dawn. Had they escaped? Were they in danger? "What about . . . our friends?"

Auntie shook her head. "I don't know." Axel knew where Galina lived. I was certain that if any house was burned that night, it would be hers, the place where he'd first found me. Petr reached out and patted Vladimir's back, like a reminder that we were all in this together. Vladimir urged Nesa on toward the forest.

In another minute we had penetrated the forest deeply enough that we couldn't be seen from the road. Petr turned around. "Ivan, you and I will go. Those boxes can be heavy."

We couldn't have been more than fifty feet from the sleigh and nearing the edge of the forest when we heard a low whistle. Petr and I froze. "It's Vladimir," Petr whispered.

"What's wrong?" I turned back toward the sleigh, and even in the darkness, through the light snow, I could see movement. The dogs had gotten loose and were running toward us. Behind them Auntie and Vladimir were doing their best to catch them.

"The dogs! Petr — go after the one on the right." I ran toward the one on the left, who I soon realized was Zasha. She looked happy and excited to be out in the snow and moving. As I got closer to her, she changed course, as if to engage me in a game of chase.

"Zasha! Here, girl!" I called softly. She ran farther, ears back, tongue out, happy as any puppy could be. "Please, Zasha," I pleaded, "come here." I was terrified she'd get so far away from me that she'd get lost.

Her desire to run and play won out over her desire to please me or obey the commands she'd been responding to so well back at headquarters. I desperately wanted to know how Petr's rescue of Thor was going, but I dared not look away from Zasha for fear I'd lose sight of her.

I ran as hard and as fast as I've ever run, but she was faster. I finally caught up to her when she stopped to smell something around the bottom of a tree. Whatever she smelled must have been awfully interesting, or maybe she was tired, because she let me pick her up without protest.

"Oh, you bad, bad dog," I said, holding her in my arms as she licked my face. What I really meant was, *Don't ever scare me like that again. If I lost you, I don't know what I'd do.* She panted happily after her run, and seemed content to be placed in Auntie's arms when we arrived back at the sleigh. Petr arrived a minute later stroking Thor's head and settled him into the blankets.

"He's got spirit," he said. "I only caught him because he let me!" I think the scare and the exercise actually did us all good: Everyone was smiling and talking and laughing softly. We'd made it across the main road and were well on our way to our destination.

"All right, Ivan. Let's get those bullets," Petr said. We walked at a good pace out of the forest and out into the meadow. It was beautiful and quiet.

The box weighed more than we'd anticipated. We could lift it, but it was too heavy for us to carry back to the sleigh. We knelt next to it on the road; Petr sighed. "If Vladimir has rope with him, we can tie it around the box and around our waists and drag it back to the sleigh."

"Is it worth the delay?" I asked, tired and anxious to be on our way.

"There are bullets — hundreds of them, maybe thousands. Not a gift a partisan can easily turn down."

"Will they fit our rifles? What if they don't?"

"We have hundreds of rifles we've taken from dead German soldiers. We can use them, all right." As he got up, moaning a little as he did so, I heard another sound.

"Petr — someone's coming!" He froze. I knew there wasn't time to make it back to the safety and cover of the forest. Petr was looking around frantically.

"Run to one of those trees," he said, pointing to a few birch trees scattered along the edge of the meadow between the road and the forest. "Lay flat on the ground and sort of curl yourself around the base of the tree." He began to run, and I followed. "If we're lucky we'll blend in like patches of ground underneath the trees. Thank God it's dark and snowing," he said, panting as he ran, "or we might be dead men soon."

I was faster so I let him take the nearest tree and I ran to one not far behind it, taking a couple extra seconds to position myself so I could see the road. Petr's idea was a good one; the human body can quickly fade into the background when lying down. I even threw some snow over myself to make it look more natural.

Finally, a jeep came into view. It carried four men. They must have been freezing because the jeep had no roof or sides and was completely open to the elements. The brakes whined and it came to a halt. *The box,* I thought. *Of course. They'll take the bullets with them.* Their conversation floated across the meadow to us. I could see the men, but not very clearly. All four got out of the jeep. Two of them lifted the heavy box, and a third quickly went to help them.

The fourth man strode up and down the road as if looking for something, then stopped to light a cigarette. Even before that flash of illumination showed me his face, I knew who it was.

Like a sinking ship's captain, Axel Recht was the last one to leave. He stopped, staring out across the meadow in our direction. I could barely breathe. What would I do if he suddenly came running toward us? I had my knife in my boot, but it was no match for a gun. As far as I knew, Petr was unarmed, his rifle waiting for him in the sleigh. Axel tilted his head back, as though smelling for his prey, trying to pick up the trail of its scent in the air.

I forced myself to hold still, willed myself not to shake. If the dogs hadn't delayed us we'd probably be dragging the box right now, easy targets in the open meadow, Zasha and Thor lost to us forever.

Just as the soldiers deposited the box in the back of the jeep, I heard more conversation. The men joined Axel at the edge of the road. He pointed at the ground. Our footprints! The sleigh and horse tracks were all there to be read and followed, although he couldn't know it was us.

One of the men ran down the embankment about ten feet and stopped, but craned his neck as if looking for something. A conversation ensued between him and Axel, and he pointed toward the forest. After some hesitation, Axel said something and the man returned to the group.

I exhaled the breath I'd been holding. They talked for another thirty seconds or so, gesticulating toward the forest where Auntie, Vladimir, and the dogs waited. Then, to my great relief, all four of them got back in the jeep. But the one in the front passenger seat, who I knew was Axel, stood up and stared out across the meadow before they drove away.

"Zasha! Thor!" he cried. My heart froze. I listened hard for a bark, a whine, a yap, anything that would give us all away. "Zasha — come! Thor!" He called again, crisp and commanding. Another thirty seconds passed in silence. Finally, he sat down and the jeep roared back to life and headed west.

Petr and I lay still for ten more minutes on the cold, hard, damp ground. Then we half walked, half ran to the safety of the forest.

"It was Axel," I told him.

"You can't be sure; it's too dark."

"No, I'm sure. I'd know him anywhere."

"Well, whoever he was, he didn't come after us."

To myself I thought, *If he'd come down from the road instead of sending one of the others, we might not have lived to tell the tale.* What were his last words to me? *I'll find you. And when I do, I'll kill you.*

Now he was in retreat, minus his dogs and me, his musical performing monkey. How long before he forgot us? I wondered.

The war provided so many important distractions and challenges on a daily basis that surely we'd fade from his memory soon.

But something told me Axel's anger, hatred, and desire for revenge would burn like an eternal flame, ready to spark into a wall of fire to destroy the boy who had deceived him if he ever had the chance.

CHAPTER 37

I COULD SEE PART OF LAKE LADOGA FROM MY ROOM AT THE BACK OF VLADIMIR AND HIS WIFE NATALYA'S HOUSE. IT LOOKED AS FROZEN AND FORBIDDING AS THE DAY I CROSSED it with Auntie. For the last two days our hosts had fed us and warmed us in front of cozy fires and under thick comforters. They made me feel so welcome that I wanted to stay, to forget my idea of being a partisan, to abandon my plan to breed the dogs to help our underground army.

If I'd had a magic wand, I would have made my mother appear, and Alik and Misha, Polina, too, and Galina to keep Auntie company. We would all move into a big house together and wait out the war. But no magic wand appeared. The talk on that second night of our stay was of the best route to Uncle Boris's cabin. Vladimir would take Petr and me there in the sleigh. We'd start out several hours before dawn to avoid drawing attention to ourselves, and hopefully arrive just as the sun was breaking the horizon.

The worst part for me was saying good-bye to Auntie. She was like my second mother, my aunt, and my grandmother all in one. She'd taught me about the world, helped me see and understand things, made me feel safe, and helped me to be brave. For the time being, she would stay in Kobona with Vladimir and Natalya. We'd make a long-term decision soon.

Petr had committed himself to staying with me "for a while." He said, "I have responsibilities to so many. We'll get you settled in with your uncle, and then we'll see." So it was no surprise that when we said farewell to Natalya and Auntie my heart felt like it was made of lead. The best thing I can say is that I held back my tears.

All my comfort and hope came from the dogs, nestled on the floor of the sleigh under several blankets. As Petr, Vladimir, and I drove north, I thought about what a short time ago I'd left Leningrad, and how much had happened. I didn't feel like the same boy who'd waved a tearful good-bye to his mother; I felt so much older.

Soon we'd have Uncle Boris to deal with. He wouldn't recognize me, I was certain; too many years had passed. What if he thought I wasn't his nephew, but an impostor? He might be terribly upset or frightened by our plans for breeding the dogs, think it too dangerous, and ask us to leave. Or the cabin could have burned down, or be empty. Uncle Boris could have passed away, for all I knew.

I felt like Vladimir was reading my mind when he said, "I'm coming in to meet your uncle."

"Why?" Petr and I asked at the same time.

"Because you don't know much about him. You can't be sure of your reception." We nodded silently. "I'd never forgive myself if I just dropped you off and he turned you away with nowhere to go, no food, and two little puppies. I'm meeting this fellow."

Hours later, after a few wrong turns, we finally found his sturdy-looking wooden cabin, with a slim stream of smoke floating out of the chimney.

"Let's all go to the door with the dogs. I want him to know immediately what he's getting into," I said as the sleigh pulled to a halt.

"Why not?" Petr asked. Vladimir shrugged, as if to say it was fine with him. If anyone heard us arrive, there was no sign of it. Petr held Thor, I held Zasha, and Vladimir stood next to me as I knocked hard three times on the cabin door.

A man of medium height opened the door, his thick hair a silvery gray, his eyes kind, a long-stemmed pipe in his hand.

"You're not my uncle Boris!" I exclaimed. Petr, Vladimir, and I glanced at one another in surprise.

He smiled and said softly, "No, I'm not. You're his nephew?" I couldn't place his accent.

"His great-nephew."

"Please come in out of the cold."

"Can we bring the dogs in?" I asked.

His smile deepened. "If you didn't I would be very disappointed." He held out his hand to each of us as we entered. "I'm Taavo," he said. I thought that might be a Finnish name, but he didn't look Finnish. "Make yourselves at home."

The cabin was warm and inviting; a fire burned low in a stone fireplace. Before I sat down, I asked, "Is it all right to let the dogs down?" Although the dogs had relieved themselves as soon as we got out of the sleigh, I didn't want an accident to make Taavo mad.

"Of course!" He had such a serene look on his face, such a calm air about him, that it made me feel more peaceful. "What are their names?"

"The darker one is Thor. The one with the golden face is Zasha."

He bent over in his chair, stretching his hands out so the dogs would come to him. When he made a funny *chkkk* sound out of the side of his mouth, both of the dogs turned to him. Zasha trotted over to him, while Thor continued to sniff around the cabin. Taavo rubbed Zasha's head and scratched behind her ears and under her chin. "Who does this dog belong to?"

We hesitated, exchanging awkward glances. "She belongs to me," I said finally. "Both of them belong to me." He nodded, but I sensed his skepticism.

"Maybe you should tell Taavo why we're here today, Ivan," Vladimir suggested, as if he was anxious to understand this new turn of events. Petr nodded his head slightly to give me his okay.

"Yes. Well," I began, looking him in the eye, "my name is Ivan Savichev. I am the great-nephew of Boris Savichev, who lives here . . . or used to live here. When the bombings began in Leningrad, I was sent by my mother to live with my uncle until the war is over."

Although Taavo seemed like he was listening, most of the time he kept his eyes on the dogs. He said nothing. After almost a minute went by, I said, "So . . . where is my uncle Boris?"

He smiled kindly. "It's hard to say." I sensed Vladimir and Petr were feeling impatient with his vague reply. "I'm sorry," he said, shaking his head and closing his eyes for a moment. "I haven't seen a dog in months. I miss them so much. . . ." His voice trailed off.

"What do you mean?" Petr asked, speaking for the first time.

"Yes, I should explain," he said softly. But first he offered us tea, which we refused. We were more interested in understanding why he was here, and where Uncle Boris was.

"Your uncle is my dear friend," he began. Thor was now at his feet, sniffing his rough shoes. He petted him as he continued.

"I came to know him when he first began coming on our winter migrations."

"Migrations?" Vladimir said.

But I thought I understood. "Are you a Sami?" It was the name for the nomadic northern folk who migrated anywhere from Russia's Kola Peninsula across the tops of Finland, Sweden, and Norway.

He nodded. "Your uncle was born in the wrong place. He should have been born one of us, in one of our tents. He is a man made for the north, for quiet, and for hard work."

"I didn't know the Sami welcomed strangers into their groups," Petr said, looking skeptical.

Taavo smiled. "Not many want to join us. It's a hard life."

"Where did your paths cross?" Vladimir wanted to know.

"He saved my life. Someone had set a bear trap under the snow. There are many who do not welcome us, you know."

I nodded, having heard that the nomads were not always wanted on the lands they crossed and on which they fed their reindeer herds. There were rumors of confrontations and violence.

"What happened with this bear trap?" Petr asked.

"I stepped right into it!" Taavo laughed. "If not for your uncle Boris freeing me, I would have frozen to death."

"He just came upon you out in the middle of nowhere? Didn't your own people notice you were missing?"

"Oh, yes, I'm sure they noticed, but it happened during a terrible ice storm. My band was traveling west, trying to outrun it."

"So they abandoned you?" Petr asked bluntly.

"Not exactly. If they had stayed and looked for me, everyone would have been in danger." Vladimir, Petr, and I exchanged uneasy glances again. "If you live in the north, you understand these things. I have no bitterness." Although I was sure I would have had bitterness to spare, I tried hard to accept his tale without judgment.

"How is it Boris found you?" Vladimir asked.

"He had just joined us," Taavo said with a faint smile. "He told me later he had gotten turned around in the storm when he was out hunting and wasn't sure which direction to go in. When he saw me, he thought I'd been sent to find him! Lucky for both of us in the end."

"What happened after he rescued you?" I asked

"He took me all the way down here to his cabin and tended to my wound."

"And obviously," Vladimir said, motioning toward Taavo, "you've now healed. How long ago were you trapped and injured?"

"Five winters ago."

Now I was really confused. "Then why are you still here? And where's my uncle Boris?" I was starting to wonder if everything he said was nonsense and he'd somehow stolen my uncle's cabin, or even hurt him.

"It turns out I was born in the wrong place. Just like your uncle Boris." He laughed, as if enjoying a good joke.

"You traded places," Petr said quietly.

"Yes."

"But, but . . ." I stuttered, so many questions in my mind that I couldn't get them out. "What about your family?"

"I am a widower in my eighth decade. We had no children. The weather, the work . . . it was all getting to be too much for me. I felt like I was becoming a burden."

I leaned back in my chair, closed my eyes, and sighed. It was one thing to come to the house of a family member, who was also Russian, and tell them of your plan to breed dogs for the partisans. But Taavo was a stranger, and a Sami. There was no time for Vladimir, Petr, and I to develop a cover story for our being there, or for having two perfect purebred German shepherds in an area where such animals were not only a luxury, but would probably be resented, even hunted, because of their German heritage.

"So you came here to live with your uncle?" Taavo asked, interrupting my thoughts.

"Yes. But now . . ." There was silence. Both Petr and Vladimir were frowning, looking as disconcerted as I felt.

"I would welcome your company."

I didn't answer right away, but when I did, I told him what to expect. "My friend Petr may come and go. My aunt will visit regularly, and Vladimir, too. It's too much; we can't impose on you. Plus, there are the dogs."

Taavo started to speak, but Petr interrupted him. "Where were you born, Taavo?"

"It's hard to say. I was born east of the lake near where Finland, Norway, and Russia all meet."

"But which country were you born in?"

He smiled. "I don't know. The Sami have land markers to find their way through the snow; mountains, rivers, and meadows. Settled people have borders. Somehow, I was never able to see the borders, so I don't know where I was born exactly. I just say 'in the far north.'"

"Which has no borders and extends over four countries," Vladimir said.

"Yes."

"Whose side are you on in this war?" Petr asked bluntly.

"No one's."

"That's not possible!" I exclaimed. "Russia was invaded. You live here. You have to be on our side."

He shrugged. "Wars come and go. I stay out of them."

I decided I would have to take a risk. "We are army men, the underground army, that is. We want to breed these dogs so that we can use their offspring to help our soldiers in the field."

Taavo looked at the dogs, and then at us. "You want the dogs to be soldiers?"

"Not these two, but any puppies they might have."

Taavo shook his head. "That's a bad idea."

"Why?" I demanded.

"For many reasons. Mostly because it's not fair to them." He gazed at me calmly.

"Why not? All the armies use them! Dogs like to perform tasks. It can help us win the war."

He shrugged. "They are your dogs. You can do as you please with them."

"But you don't approve," Petr said.

"No. You're right that dogs like to perform tasks and please their masters. But you're wrong to ask them to do it at the price of their lives."

Vladimir leaned forward. "Certainly dogs risked their lives every day for you on your migrations in the north."

"They did," he acknowledged, "but it's different. They were part of our family, almost as much as our children. We all depended on one another. Sometimes the adults would go hungry to make sure the dogs were fed."

"But still," Vladimir insisted, "you risked their lives."

"You're correct — there are special dangers in the north because of the cold. But no one shoots bullets at them."

"Someone set bear traps," Petr said.

"Yes, they did. I'm glad it was me and not one of the dogs who was caught. The dog would not have survived."

The entire time he spoke, Zasha and Thor competed for his attention. Finally, Zasha jumped into his lap. I'd always believed animals had a deep and quick sense about which humans were good and which were bad. Zasha's action told me a lot. It emboldened me.

"I have a proposal. I will live here until my uncle Boris returns, as my mother requested, and my friends will visit, as I told you before. Perhaps you could help me train the dogs, but not for any type of work with the partisans."

Taavo sighed and stayed quiet for a few moments before he answered.

"Train them for what?" Taavo asked.

"Uh . . . to be good dogs."

"No. That's not enough; they won't be happy. They'll have nothing to do," he answered.

I eyed Vladimir and Petr, thinking of how much we'd gone through to get to this point, how it seemed to be slipping away.

"I have an idea," Taavo said as he stroked Zasha's head and Thor pawed at his leg to be picked up. "These dogs are shepherds. That's what they're bred for, that's what will fulfill their nature."

"And?"

"I propose that we teach them, help them to be the best shepherds they can be."

"And then?"

"Then we have some decisions to make."

"Like what?"

"We can rent their services out to farmers, or shepherds, to guide and guard their flocks. Dogs are getting scarce now, so I've been told." His words reminded me that in Leningrad I hadn't seen one for two months before I left. He continued before any of us could respond. "We could give the money we made to this army of yours."

"Ah!" Vladimir exclaimed. "Not a bad idea."

"I'm sorry," I said firmly. "The dogs aren't going anywhere without me. I'd never see them again."

"I think Ivan is right." Petr sighed. "But the general idea is good. What other ideas do you have, Taavo?"

He laughed as Zasha licked his face; I felt a little jealous. He thought for a moment and said, "We could buy our own sheep and let the dogs herd them. We could sell their wool and give the money to your army."

"Will sheep do well in this climate?" Vladimir asked skeptically.

"I don't know," Taavo answered.

"What do sheep eat?" Petr asked. "It could be expensive."

Taavo shrugged, but smiled. "I don't know. I'm just trying to come up with an idea that's better than yours!" Then he laughed as Thor jumped on his lap, pushing Zasha off. "You couldn't turn these dogs over to soldiers. Those men are good, but hard. They'd use the dogs as they saw fit."

I shook my head. The idea sounded awful. How could I not have thought it through? Still, I said lamely, "Not Thor and Zasha, just their puppies."

"Oh, I see," he said softly, as if to indicate we both knew I now had no enthusiasm for it.

"Do you have a garden, Taavo?" Petr asked.

"Oh, yes. Although until spring we'll be eating what I preserved from last year's harvest."

"Why did you want to know, Petr?" I asked.

"Because the partisans also need food. And although Taavo's idea about herding is a good one — it's too complicated." He cleared his throat. "Here's what I propose. How much land is here, Taavo?"

"About five acres, but I can only plant one."

"Why?"

"Because there's just one of me!"

"Is the rest of the land good for planting?"

"Most of it."

"That will be our contribution to the partisans — food."

"But there will be only Ivan and me," Taavo said. "At best we can tend two acres."

"What about the dogs?" I asked, trying to get my mind around this new turn of events.

Petr looked excited. "I can send men up here, men who need a break from the fighting. They'd welcome the chance to work outside in the sun with the crops, and with dogs as their companions."

"What about the dogs?" I asked again.

Taavo spoke before Petr could answer. "We could begin to train them as farm dogs. As for breeding — why don't we let nature take its course? Let's see who these two are when they're a little older. Sometimes, dogs raised together act more like brother and sister and won't breed."

I felt a peacefulness when I heard his thoughts. "I like that idea a lot." I could see that Vladimir and Petr did as well. "This changes everything. I've never done any gardening or farming. But I know I can do it." I walked over and picked up Zasha, who was sniffing at the logs next to the fireplace. "Could . . . could my aunt come up here and live with us?"

Taavo shrugged. "I don't see why not. The cabin is small, but I can sleep in this room."

"Or we can build another room! Or two, because we'll have the partisans coming up to help us."

"I hate to ask this," Vladimir said, "but what if the Germans get this far north?"

"Wasn't it you who said improvising is what makes a partisan so effective?" Petr answered.

Vladimir looked pleased. "That sounds like me — and true, too!"

I hadn't felt this happy in a long time.

Petr looked serious when he said, "Taavo, how often do you go to town?"

"Once a month or so."

"Do you have friends there, or among your neighbors?"

He shrugged and looked uncertain. "People are polite to me, but they're just acquaintances. No one comes to visit, if that's what you mean. We're far from the town. Isolated."

"Do they know about your arrangement with Boris?"

"I don't think so. I never discussed it with anyone."

I interrupted, remembering what he'd said earlier. "But Boris visits during the year; someone must see him coming and going. They're used to the fact that you live here. So no one's suspicious of you, or watching you. When does Boris visit?"

"It depends on the weather. May or June, usually, and October. Oh," he added, as he pushed tobacco into his narrow pipe bowl, "I go back with him to visit my people for about a month each time."

"How do you get back here after your visit?" Vladimir asked.

"Boris brings me back down!" Taavo laughed and shook his head. "I think he's trying to make up for all those years before he became a nomad."

★ ★ ★

Vladimir left an hour later. Petr stayed that night, but now that Taavo was there, and he didn't have to worry about me, he wanted to go back and see what had happened in Vilnov. "We saw the smoke," he reminded me. "I have to see what was burned . . . and who escaped."

"When will you come back?"

Quoting Taavo, he said, "It's hard to say. But you two can get started without us."

"Not until the winter has passed," I said. "I don't know anything about seeds, and planting, and . . ."

"There are the dogs to train, Ivan. And didn't you talk about adding rooms on to the cabin? Surely you can start on that even though snow is on the ground."

"Yes, I suppose so," I said, suddenly overwhelmed with all the things that had to be done, although each one excited me.

"And your auntie Vera will be coming up soon, I'm sure." That thought filled my heart with joy. "Christmas will be here in no time. Go find a tree to bring into the cabin! There's plenty to do."

That night Petr, the dogs, and I all slept in the same room on two comfortable, straw-filled mattresses. "Petr," I said, just after he blew out the last of the candles that lit our room. "Do you really think this will work?"

He laughed and sighed. "It's hard to say."

PART FOUR
REVENGE

CHAPTER 38

It took about a month for us to get the news of what had happened in Vilnov the night the Germans fled. Sheer luck saved every one of my friends. Galina was out searching for the Tsarina when she saw Polina and me running for our lives. She even heard the shots shortly before we came into view. Galina made sure that she, Polina, and Polina's mother were on their way to Kazan to her sister's within the hour. Petr said many, many fires were set. Polina's house was badly damaged, but Galina's house managed to escape the torch.

A week after my arrival at Uncle Boris's cabin, Auntie came to live with Taavo, me, Zasha, and Thor. At the end of that desperately cold winter, spring arrived in a way I'd never seen in Leningrad. The way delicate blades of grass pushed up through ground that had so recently been frozen solid was awe inspiring. Birds I'd never known existed filled the air with beautiful songs I'd never heard. The smell of wildflowers, the gurgle of creek water rushing over smooth stones, the very sweetness of fresh country air made every day a happy and rich experience.

Zasha and Thor loved the open space and being surrounded by loving people. They grew quickly from playful puppies into bright, responsive, and loving dogs. When Taavo told me he'd helped train some of the dogs when he lived his nomadic life, I didn't understand its significance. I soon found that he understood dogs on a very deep level, as though he could read their minds and reveal their true thoughts and feelings.

"It's not hard," he told me. "You just have to listen and watch carefully."

Even though I'd considered myself capable of becoming a good dog trainer, compared to Taavo I knew almost nothing. But I was so motivated to train the dogs, to make them happy with their lives, that I learned quickly.

"You're their parent, their leader," he told me repeatedly. "Act like it. You're not their friend."

"Yes, I am!" I insisted.

"Not if you want them to respond to your commands." It took a while for that to sink in, because I wanted nothing more than to be their best friend. Finally, I learned to make the distinction, and the dogs thrived.

Within a few months, Galina and Polina and her mother had returned to Vilnov from Kazan. Polina came to visit and stayed for two weeks. I think she would have loved to move in, but she knew her mother couldn't manage without her, and there was a lot of work to do to repair their damaged home. Even though we worked hard on the farm, I hadn't had such happy and carefree days since before the war.

In May, Petr arrived with the first two partisans. Each had been living in the woods while fighting for almost a year. They seemed haunted and withdrawn, in desperate need of time in the country to heal their battered bodies and spirits. They helped Petr build a long room onto the back of Boris's cabin that would easily sleep four people, six if they didn't mind being crowded. I saw the life come back into the partisans as the sun, air, rest, and wholesome food worked their magic on them.

In late June of that first summer, my uncle Boris appeared. I don't think he uttered more than two words for the first few minutes after Taavo, Auntie, I, and two barking dogs greeted him at the front door, so great was his surprise. He'd arrived midday when both partisans were hard at work, clearing brush and stones from his land to make it ready for more planting. Petr was hammering up on the roof of the new room, while Auntie, Taavo, and I were busy making jam from the wild strawberries that seemed to grow everywhere. It must have been quite a shock to see his home in such a state of change and activity, and full of strangers. Taavo wisely suggested that Boris have lunch first, and then we'd explain everything to him afterward.

After he'd cleaned up and eaten, all of us except Petr and the two partisans gathered in the living room. The dogs had calmed down, and Boris called for them to come to him as he settled in his chair. They were curious and friendly, letting him pet them.

"So," he said, "does someone want to explain to me what's going on?"

I stared at my uncle, who I hadn't seen since I was about five years old. He was shorter and thinner than I remembered him. He also seemed calmer, a little like Taavo. Maybe the lifestyle of a Sami did that to you; maybe their simple, demanding way of life made them see things more clearly than the average person with their complicated or cluttered life.

Because my arrival had brought all the changes to his home and land, I answered Boris. "Uncle, you probably don't remember me. I am Ivan Savichev. My father, Edvard, was your nephew, the son of your brother."

He looked startled, his head jerking back slightly. Squinting, he looked at me intently, as if to find the child within the thirteen-year-old boy. "Yes . . . yes, it is you." He hesitated before asking, "How is your mother?"

"I don't know. Her factory was being evacuated to the Urals and I was unable to go with her. Leningrad was dying . . . there was no choice. My mother sent me here. Taavo was kind enough to take me in, along with my family friend, Vera Raskova."

Looking a little confused, he said, "And the men outside — who are they?"

Taavo, Auntie, and I exchanged brief glances. We'd talked about telling Boris everything when he returned, but suddenly it felt like too much to share all at once. Petr appeared in the doorway. Holding out his hand, he said, "I'm Petr Ostrov. You must be the Uncle Boris I've heard so much about."

Boris still looked slightly bewildered, and suspicion lurked behind his eyes. "Who are the other men?"

"They are partisans. We are all partisans, except Taavo," I said.

"You're just a boy!"

"I am still a partisan."

"You, too?" he asked Auntie, looking doubtful. She nodded and smiled proudly.

Petr took over. "Ivan's aunt and I brought him here to deliver him into your care at his mother's request. When we met Taavo and saw the use to which we could put your land for the good of Russia and the partisans, we went to work. I apologize for such presumption on our part." He paused as Boris studied him. "If you want us to leave, of course we will respect your wishes."

What else could he say? We'd moved into another man's house and were working his land like it was our own. Although we all knew Boris was the owner and would return, we'd grown to think of it as Taavo's place, and even as our own.

"Taavo," Boris said, still looking unsure about what he should do, "tell me what you think."

The gentle Taavo smiled. "Our home is happier and fuller with our guests. They've improved everything. The cabin is bigger, we're turning all our land into space that can be planted and cultivated. And . . . although I don't want to involve myself in wars, I am happy to help Russia for all she has given to me."

"We plan to give most of the harvest to the partisans," I said. Boris frowned, but I attributed it to the fact that all of the information was new to him and probably hard to take in all at once.

Zasha began to growl, her body suddenly tense, and stared hard at the door. Thor barked and rushed toward it. We heard a faint knock. "What now?" Boris said, half to himself.

I stood in front of the door, facing the dogs. "Down!" I cried. They sat, but didn't take their eyes off the door. I opened it slowly, just wide enough to peek out.

There stood a stout woman with a scarf covering her head, with wisps of gray floating out. She looked startled as I said, "Yes? May I help you?"

"Oh!" She held a bowl covered with cheesecloth in her hand. "I thought . . . I thought I'd bring some borscht to Boris to welcome him home." She studied me. "Who are you?"

"I am Ivan, his great-nephew. Come in." I opened the door with another order to the dogs to come to me. We stood off to the side as the woman entered the room full of people.

"Boris," she said in a kind of cooing voice, "I thought I saw you on the road this morning." She held out the covered dish. "I know how much you like my borscht!"

Boris looked pained, but said, "Thank you, Mrs. Chemakova. How thoughtful of you."

Taavo seemed as if he was trying not to laugh as he said, "Thank you for your generous gift. I'll take it to the kitchen."

"So, Boris, who are your visitors?" She inspected us curiously. This was the moment of truth. How he answered would dictate our future.

After a lengthy pause, he said, "Relatives and old friends. This is my neighbor, Mrs. Chemakova."

Auntie held out her hand and introduced herself, as did Petr, saving Boris from having to remember their names.

"And who are the men outside?"

"My sons," Petr lied coolly. "Too young to join the army, but farm work will strengthen them for it." He smiled like a proud father. I had the feeling she didn't believe all that was said, but she acted pleasantly.

"And these dogs! Have you ever seen such beautiful dogs? German, aren't they?"

"Yes," I replied.

"Doesn't it make you nervous having German dogs?"

"No. Why should it?"

She looked at me like I must be dim-witted. "Because we are at war with them."

"Dogs are dogs. That they were originally bred in a particular country has no significance." I tried not to sound as defiant as I felt.

"Yes, well . . . We're short of dogs up here. It seems like the war has taken away even our smallest pleasures. Tell me the minute they have puppies. I would love one, even if it is German. Think of all the work I could get it to do!"

I nodded mutely with a half smile as that last sentence rang in my mind. That attitude made it certain that Mrs. Chemakova would never be the lucky recipient of one of the puppies we hoped Zasha would have one day.

"Well," she said at last, turning to Boris, "you must be tired after your trip. How long will you be here this time?"

Boris got up, walked toward her, and led her to the door. "I'm not sure. Thank you so very much for your delicious soup. And for stopping to say hello." He opened the door, but not before she gave us all another inquisitive glance over her shoulder.

"Yes, I'll come back! Would tomorrow be too soon?"

"Thank you, but I have many matters to settle that will require my attention for . . . for some time. I'll call on you just as soon as I'm able." He smiled, and she had no choice but to leave.

He closed the door, then leaned back against it, sighed, and closed his eyes. When he opened them, he looked at us and laughed. "The widow Chemakova has convinced herself that I am husband material. I can't imagine why!"

"She has a sixth sense, like a dog," Taavo said with a smile. "She knows when you're here."

"God help me," he muttered, and for the first time he stood tall and looked clear-eyed and commanding. "You're all welcome to stay. Just don't advertise your presence. If you'll forgive me, I'll be sleeping in a tent outside." Taavo nodded as if he'd expected as much. "If I don't speak to you, please don't be offended. I'm just not used to . . . to civilization anymore."

"Would you like some of that borscht?" Taavo teased.

"Hate the stuff," he muttered as he turned and went outside.

"I guess that means we can stay," I said.

Everyone appeared pleased except Petr, who said, "She could be a problem."

"Who?"

"The widow Chemakova." I wasn't sure what he meant exactly, but realized I had a tight, dull ache in my stomach that began the moment I saw her.

★ ★ ★

Not long after Boris's first visit in June of 1942, a letter from my mother arrived. My joy lasted for days. She was safe in a small town in the Ural Mountains, still working eleven hours a day, but alive and well.

In my response, and my only letter to her, I pretended to be someone who was temporarily taking care of Boris's land, telling her he didn't know anyone named Ivan Savichev. It was in my handwriting, of course, so she would know it was me, assuming it reached her. Her letter was dated four months before its delivery, so I couldn't be sure. Not writing to my mother or getting any letters from her was one of the hardest parts of the war. What a relief it would have been to be able to hear from her, to reassure her that even after all this time I was okay, and to share my experiences. But writing her would have put too many people in danger. Our farm would have been an enticing target for rogue German units, or even individual soldiers who lingered behind the lines. We were not only a refuge for partisans, the scourge of the German army, but we also supplied their small bands with food.

Those first two years at the cabin went by quickly, with partisans coming and going, seeds planted and vegetables harvested, and friends coming to visit. Zasha and Thor grew into strong, healthy adult dogs, although no puppies were born.

I didn't mind what others might call isolation in the country because most everything we did helped the war effort, but without the danger of bombs, starvation, and being a fighting partisan. I grew four inches, developed strong arms, and played my concertina at night, even composing songs now and then. Axel Recht sometimes haunted my dreams, but as the Russians pushed the Germans farther and farther west, my worries lessened.

Then, in January of 1944, the blockade that had starved Leningrad was broken. For the first time in two and a half years, more than a trickle of food and medical supplies would reach the city. My impulse was to go back immediately, but I realized I could best serve Russia by staying where I was and continuing to do what I did until the war was over. I'd heard Vladimir say once it was estimated that more than a million people had died during the worst of the siege. My mind couldn't grasp it, and so I pushed it aside as well as I could, along with images of Alik, Misha, and my other friends. The siege being broken didn't mean the war was over; far from it. But it did mean that Hitler had failed to destroy Leningrad, and that hopefully one day it would be a city again.

Our lives at the cabin, or what we now called the farm, went on as usual, even after the good news about Leningrad, for another year and a half. Uncle Boris visited twice each year, in the spring and·the fall, and Taavo went with him for a month afterward to visit his old friends and family who still followed the reindeer. Vladimir and the others from Vilnov visited; Petr came regularly to bring more partisans for recuperation, guide them back to their bands, and see that the harvests went to those who needed them most.

One unexpected danger came from deserting German soldiers. As 1945 dawned and the war looked like it could end soon, deserters and stragglers were reported more and more often. Mostly they were scared and hungry men who didn't want to die in the fierce fighting that was destroying the once mighty German army. Other times, knowing they were sure to be defeated, they killed as many innocent Russian civilians as they could before being killed themselves.

As Petr predicted, the widow Chemakova had proved to be an annoyance, like a pebble in your shoe that you can't shake loose. She showed up uninvited every few weeks, wanting details about everyone and everything. We even found her once in the small barn we'd recently built examining our harvest. Auntie was best at handling her and deflecting her questions, but there was one topic with which she was obsessed: when Zasha was going to have puppies.

No one had ever promised her a puppy; I knew I'd never give her one. And for reasons unknown, Zasha had never been pregnant. By the last days of the war, in May of 1945, Zasha was three and a half years old. "It should have happened before this," Taavo said many times. "She may not be destined to be a mother." Although I would have loved puppies, Zasha and Thor were enough for me. I loved them more than I could ever say.

It was Mrs. Chemakova's obsession with puppies, a stranger she met, and Zasha's first pregnancy that all came together at the same time and brought with them events that would change everything.

CHAPTER 39

IT WAS A GOLDEN JUNE TWILIGHT; THEY LASTED FOREVER AT THIS TIME OF YEAR. PETR AND I SAT UNDER THE TREES IN FRONT OF THE CABIN IN ROUGH-HEWN CHAIRS ONE OF the visiting partisans had made. Zasha and Thor lay on the soft ground in front of us cleaning themselves, yawning, and napping.

Boris and Taavo had left the day before to go north to visit Taavo's family. Auntie was staying with Vladimir and Natalya for a week or two. It was almost six weeks since Germany surrendered. The last of the partisans left the farm shortly after receiving the good news. Petr and I were doing something we'd all but forgotten how to do — we were relaxing and enjoying ourselves.

He asked me about my plans.

"I know I'll go back to Leningrad. I'm a little unsure about when," I said.

He smiled and puffed on his long-stemmed pipe.

"And what about you, Petr?"

He shrugged. "I'll carry on as before. At least I won't have to be digging any more tunnels!" He laughed. Now that the war was over, he laughed more often; he'd even shaved his beard and cut his hair. "What will you do in Leningrad?"

I shook my head, having no real answer. "I don't know. I'm sixteen now, but I missed all those years in school. I used to think I wanted to be a musician, but now . . . I'm not sure I could ever feel that lighthearted again."

He didn't answer right away. "Haven't you ever listened to Beethoven? I don't think being lighthearted is important. You might even play better now because of all that you've been through."

I smiled. "Maybe. I've also thought about training dogs. Did you know there's a school for training dogs near Moscow?"

"Really?" He carefully filled his pipe bowl with tobacco.

"They train them for military duties. I'm sure I could learn some valuable things. But I'd only train dogs on my own for individual people, not for military work."

"Taavo taught you well." I knew he was referring to Taavo's refusal to train Zasha and Thor or their puppies for military purposes because it wasn't fair to them. I agreed with him, which meant I probably wouldn't last a day at the dog school.

"Of course now that Zasha's expecting puppies it's going to be a while before I go anywhere." She turned at the sound of her name, gazing at me with her soft brown eyes before laying her head back down.

"Finally," Petr said. "I wonder why it took so long."

I got up and knelt by Zasha, petting her head and her tummy as she rolled over. I could feel the small lumps inside her.

"Oh, no," Petr said.

"What?" I automatically felt for my boot where I still kept the knife Auntie had given me so long ago. I saw the pained look on his face and followed his gaze down the long drive that led from the cabin to the public road a half mile away. There were two figures in the distance, one I now knew well: the widow Chemakova.

"Not again!" he said. "I thought we were safe for a while with Boris gone."

"Zasha!" I said in a panic. "I don't want Mrs. Chemakova to know about the puppies."

"Put her in the barn. We'll tell her she's sick."

"Zasha, come!" We ran around the cabin and out to the small barn. Now there were only some barrels of potatoes in there, the last of the fall apples, and shelves full of vegetables and fruits we'd canned. I arranged some hay in the corner, and Zasha happily lay down on top of it. "Don't make a sound unless you want Mrs. Chemakova to have your firstborn." She slept more than usual these days and seemed content to be left in the quiet barn.

By the time I got back to Petr, he was standing with his hand under Thor's collar, and Mrs. Chemakova and her companion had almost reached the cabin. He was a middle-aged man in a blue coat that reached the tops of his knees and looked like it had seen better days.

"Hello, hello!" she chirped. "I'd like you to meet my new friend. His name is Petr, too!"

"Petr Gribovich," he said, holding out his hand to Petr and me. "Pleasure to meet you." His face was red with broken capillaries, and his hair looked like it could have used a good washing. Thor sniffed him with interest, and he petted Thor without hesitation. Mrs. Chemakova greeted Thor and asked where Zasha was.

I pretended like I hadn't heard her questions and said, "Please, sit down."

Before she settled into her chair, Mrs. Chemakova said, "I brought something." My stomach involuntarily contracted as I thought of the endless bowls of borscht and sauerkraut she'd brought for Boris, none of which he ever touched.

"Yes?" I said politely.

Out of the pocket of her wide skirt she pulled a bottle. "Vodka!"

"Glasses! We need glasses!" Petr Gribovich said, a little too enthusiastically.

"Wherever did you find vodka?" Petr asked as he got up to go get the glasses.

"It was market day in Sviritsa." She sighed contentedly. "Thank goodness things are getting back to normal. There's been almost no vodka for sale for . . ."

"Forever!" Mr. Gribovich said, looking like he'd already had his share before he arrived. The gray-haired Mrs. Chemakova looked at him flirtatiously. Maybe she'd given up on Boris and had set her eyes on Petr Gribovich.

"There I was at the market this morning, looking at the potatoes, minding my own business, when this charming man approached. He said, 'Did you know it takes an entire bushel of potatoes to make one bottle of vodka?' "

"I have no idea how many bushels of potatoes it takes to make a bottle of vodka," Mr. Gribovich said. "But I did know that I wanted to meet the lovely lady at the potato stall."

Mrs. Chemakova practically blushed. "It's so nice to have company again after all these dreadful years of people leaving and going off to who knows where."

"How well I know. I hope to see my wife and family again one day."

A frown creased the widow's forehead.

"Were they in Leningrad?" I asked.

"Oh, no — thank heavens! Although I last saw them when I left for Leningrad. I tried to get my sister out over the ice road that first winter."

"Were you able to?"

He waved his hand dismissively. "It was much too dangerous. These are things a boy of your age wouldn't understand."

I think I did understand. He'd left his home about the same time I was forced to leave mine. The difference was that I wanted to go back, and apparently he didn't. I think Mrs. Chemakova understood, too, because she was suddenly smiling again.

Petr returned with four glasses and a little table he placed near our guests. Mr. Gribovich was out of his seat, very interested in how he might help. He took over hosting duties, pouring generous helpings in three of the four glasses. "And you, lad? Are you old enough to drink?"

"I don't drink, thank you."

"Suit yourself." He tipped off the other glasses to the rims. "More for us!" he said to Mrs. Chemakova with a little shrug of the shoulders. Some of it spilled on her skirt as he handed a glass to her. "To Russia!" he said loudly. "And to our brave, brave men!" He threw back his drink, and it was gone in one gulp. He shook his head as if to clear it as the alcohol did its work.

Petr and Mrs. Chemakova repeated, "To Russia!" and took modest sips. Mr. Gribovich quickly refilled his glass and sat down.

"There are so many men coming home!" she went on. "We must have seen two dozen of them at the market."

"Two dozen," Mr. Gribovich repeated, gazing up happily at the twilight sky.

"Remember that one poor boy, Petr? Every single finger on his left hand was gone. Only the thumb remained. Imagine!"

"Imagine," he responded, draining his glass and getting up to pour another.

"And remember that other man? Sort of handsome. I would

have thought he was an officer, but he was wearing a private's uniform."

"I don't think I do," he answered, holding up the bottle to see how much was left.

"That's right, it was before I met you. What a lovely man! He made me think of you, Ivan."

"Why is that, Mrs. Chemakova?" How I wished they'd go away and give us back our peaceful night.

"Because he loves dogs." She sipped her vodka.

Unexplainably, a little stab of fear hit my heart. "How did you happen to be talking about dogs?"

She shrugged and smiled. "I don't know. It's my opinion that those boys have been away from home for so long, they just want to talk. You know, normal talk: dogs, horses, the weather."

Petr must have understood what I was feeling. "How old was this man?"

"Oh . . . I don't know. Everyone is younger than me now! I couldn't really say."

"You do yourself an injustice, my dear lady," Mr. Gribovich said. "Anyone with eyes can see you're not a day over . . . forty!" She giggled like a schoolgirl, and he poured himself another drink.

I pressed her. "And what exactly did he say about his love of dogs?"

"What? Oh." She reluctantly turned her attention back to me. "He said he always had dogs, before the army and the war and all. He especially loves German shepherds. 'Even after fighting all those Germans?' I asked him. He insisted he did, and went on and on about them until I finally said, 'I happen to know two of the finest German shepherds in this part of Russia!'"

"You did?" My mouth had gone dry; my heart pounded.

"Yes! I said that right here in our cozy little corner of the country we had prize specimens. I told him that when Zasha had puppies, I have the pick of the litter! Where is Zasha?" She looked around her, as if she'd just noticed that she wasn't there.

"She's got an upset stomach. I put her in the barn to rest." I closed my eyes, and the breath seeped out of me as I asked, "Did you mention the dogs by name?"

"Well . . . I'm not sure. I think so. I mean, their personalities are so distinctive, and their names suit them so well."

Petr leaned forward. "Did he also want a puppy?"

"He certainly did. Of course I told him I had no idea when any would come, that it had been three and a half long years since you'd arrived and no puppies yet." She sipped her vodka. "But I remain hopeful."

"Did you tell him where we lived?" I asked, almost afraid of the answer.

She made little movements with her mouth, as if to indicate that my question wasn't important. "I told him where *I* lived because he said he knew all about plumbing. You know how much trouble that pump in the front gives me. I said you had the farm to the north."

"Do you think he'll visit?" Mr. Gribovich asked, maybe afraid of a potential rival.

"I certainly hope so. If he does, I'll bring him over to meet Thor and Zasha. It would make that poor soldier so happy."

I stared off into the distance of the dim light. It couldn't be, I told myself. The chances of that man being Axel Recht were too slim. The Germans had been pushed back all the way to Berlin, and the war in Europe was over. An officer like Axel would probably have been taken prisoner. Russian soldiers were returning by the truckloads now. We'd found two camping at the far end of Boris's property near a creek just a week ago. I'd even had a conversation with them about dogs because Thor was with me. No, I decided. The chances were too slim.

And yet . . . something in me was deeply frightened. I glanced at Petr, caught his eye, and could tell the same thoughts were gnawing at him.

Maybe we'd grown too complacent in our country retreat. Although we'd sheltered dozens of partisans and heard the stories of their exploits, it all seemed farther and farther away, especially as the fighting moved west.

Mr. Gribovich pulled out a deck of cards from the pocket of his coat and slapped them down on the table. "Who wants to play? A ruble for every ten points."

"I do, I do," Mrs. Chemakova cried, clapping her hands.

"A penny for every ten points and we'll play," Petr said, drawing his chair nearer to the table. I think we both realized that Mr. Gribovich wasn't going anywhere until that bottle was empty. Best to play a few hands and get it over with.

Mrs. Chemakova's companion was an enthusiastic but terrible card player. He lost hand after hand, seeming to get more determined to win and more drunk with every hand. One thing he could do was arithmetic; he added up what he owed to each of us with precision every few minutes. After an hour, the twilight had deepened so much that we either had to stop playing or invite them in. There was no way I was going to prolong their visit; besides, I was pretty sure Mr. Gribovich had emptied the vodka bottle with his last pour. He stood up and stretched. "What a lovely evening. The best I've had in quite some time. What do I owe you, boys?"

"Two rubles," Petr said, repeating what the other Petr had said just a minute earlier. He plunged his hands into his pants pocket and made a face as if to say he was surprised his hand came out empty. He repeated the performance with his left pocket, then patted his chest to see if there was anything in those pockets.

"This is most embarrassing," he said. By now he was slurring his words. "I must have left my wallet somewhere, or dropped it. I can't imagine. . . ."

Mrs. Chemakova looked concerned. "Maybe it slipped out when you took off your coat at my house."

"I certainly hope so. I feel terrible," he said, looking from Petr to me. "Here." He took off his coat and held it out for Petr.

"No, no, really, it's fine. It's just a card game. Consider the debt forgiven."

Mr. Gribovich looked solemn and stood up very straight. "I am a man of honor. A man of honor always pays his debts." He shook the coat as he held it out, demanding that it be taken. "When I come back here with two rubles, I will gladly accept my coat in return." I cringed at the thought of another visit.

"Done," Petr said, accepting the coat. "In fact, I have to do some business tomorrow that will take me by your house, Mrs. Chemakova. I'll stop by then."

"That's just fine," she said with a smile, getting up from her chair. "We don't see nearly enough of any of you." She sort of wagged her finger at me and added, "You'd better go take care of that dog, young man. I don't want anything happening to her!"

"Yes, ma'am." I returned her smile, wishing desperately for them to be gone.

"Try it on," Mr. Gribovich told Petr. I actually saw Petr's shoulders slump a little, as if he, too, was at the end of his patience. He slipped the coat on, held out his arms, and then turned around so that his tormentors could have a full and satisfying view.

"Looks better on you than it does on me!" Mr. Gribovich joked.

After endless good-byes, apologies, and promises to see one another the next day, our uninvited guests finally left. Petr and I stood together for a few minutes watching them disappear down the road, fearful they'd find a reason to come back. Even Thor seemed restless, and twice jumped to his feet, tense and still, ears up, as if he heard something. I assumed it was Mr. Gribovich's out-of-tune singing, which floated back toward us.

"It actually does look good on you," I told Petr with a laugh as we gathered the glasses and went back in the cabin. Thor stopped and turned around quickly just before he went over the threshold. He emitted a low, brief growl, but then moved into the house. I surveyed the woods from our door carefully and saw nothing out of the ordinary.

"I'll go check on Zasha," Petr said. "I need a little walk to clear my head after all that nonsense."

It couldn't have been more than thirty seconds before I heard a bloodcurdling scream. "Ivan! *Ivaaaaaan!*"

Some instinct I'll always be grateful for told me to leave Thor in the house. I rushed out to find out what made Petr scream as fast as I could, but in my heart, I already knew.

CHAPTER 40

ZASHA'S BARKING SOUNDED ALMOST HYSTERICAL. THOR HOWLED AND BARKED IN RESPONSE. AS I RAN TOWARD THE BARN, I HEARD THE MUFFLED SOUNDS OF MEN GROANING, moaning, and grunting as they do when they're engaged in hand-to-hand combat.

I burst through the door and my worst fears were confirmed: Axel Recht and Petr were wrestling on the floor.

"Ivan! Get his whip!" Petr cried. I couldn't see it in the dim light. "By Zasha." The words were almost unintelligible as he gave all his strength and attention to his struggle with Axel.

There it was! I ran around the two men, resisting an almost overwhelming urge to jump on Axel's back and help Petr. I picked up the whip, gripped it tightly, and with all my might I snapped it at Axel. A second before it would have sliced his back, he rolled off Petr. The tip of the awful thing caught the top of Petr's boot, but even that much made him scream in pain.

"You!" Axel screamed. "You filthy, thieving scum!" He lunged for me. I lashed the whip again, but Axel knew his weapon and knew how to avoid its sting. He dove onto the floor toward me, like he was sliding on ice, and knocked me over. I heard Zasha squeal. I must have hit her as I fell, but it all happened so fast, I couldn't be sure.

Axel was on his knees, crawling on top of me, where I would have been trapped and pummeled by endless blows to the head if Petr hadn't taken the whip I'd dropped and looped it over Axel's head and around his neck. There was a gurgling sound as Axel felt the leather noose slip around him. Instead of grabbing the whip, he turned his head to the right, tilted it up, let his body go loose, and slipped to the floor and out of it.

He was on his back. Before he jumped into a standing position, he lashed out with his heavy-booted feet and landed one kick on my right hip and another in my ribs.

"Agggg!" I cried, certain I'd heard something crack.

Axel lunged for the whip that was still in Petr's hands. Petr held on tight with his left hand and smashed Axel hard in the face with his right, not the expected blow to the chin, but a fist held high and brought down hard on Axel's nose.

Axel screamed as blood gushed from his face. Then, like an enraged bull, he put his head down and charged Petr, pushing him backward until he tripped and fell. As Axel raised his boot to stomp on Petr's stomach, I remembered the knife in my boot. I was up and had it out in seconds. Petr was rolling like a log to get out of the way of Axel's foot, and as he stood up, grabbed a hoe that was leaning against the wall and swung it wide. Axel ducked just in time to keep from getting his head smashed in. The whole time we fought, Zasha barked and barked, but never attempted to join in or intercede.

Petr swung and missed again as I approached Axel from behind, knife in hand, ready to do whatever was necessary. The whip was at my feet. In an instant I flung it up into the rafters toward a small loft where we stored hay. It disappeared. I had to do it. Axel could do so much more harm to us with it than we could possibly do to him.

"Ivan — take Zasha and run!" Petr yelled as he swung the hoe again. The agile and battle-hardened Axel avoided it easily, then spun around toward me, grabbed me by the wrists as if the knife weren't there, and swung me around so that we had traded places, putting me in the direct line of Petr's next swing. Petr must have seen it in a flash because he let go of the hoe as if it were on fire, and it merely hit my shoulder on its way to the ground.

As Petr rushed past me to attack Axel, he screamed again, "Take Zasha and run! Save Zasha!" Axel was crushing my wrists; I could see his clenched teeth and feel the shudder of his arms. I would lose my grip on the knife in a few more seconds and it would be his. Remembering what Polina had showed me that day in her basement, I pulled Axel closer to me, put my head down, and then butted him under the chin, hitting him hard enough in the windpipe that his hands loosened. He choked for breath and was momentarily rendered helpless.

Still holding my knife in my hand, I ran to Zasha, took her by her collar, and was going to make a run for the side door. She pulled against me, still barking, as if her fear was too great for her to move, especially in her state. I was vaguely aware that Petr and Axel were again engaged in hand-to-hand combat, Axel obviously having regained his breath.

"Zasha, please," I begged, as she fought against going anywhere. I would need all the strength I possessed to get her out of that barn. There was a rope hanging from a nail just a few feet away. I grabbed it, but to tie it around her collar I had to take the knife out of my hand. For the briefest moment I laid it down close to my knee on the floor. With the knot secure, I reached down for my knife just as another hand snatched it away. It was Axel. Petr was on him in a minute, and they tumbled to the floor.

Something in Zasha's mind changed, because she was suddenly pulling me toward the door nearest us.

"Oh, no, you don't!" In a quick backward glance, I saw that Axel had the knife in his left hand; that was good, because Axel was right-handed. Petr was astride him and had the advantage, but Axel still managed to free his arm enough to swing and cut Petr's left upper arm. By the sound of Petr's cry, it was deep and painful. Hitting his target made Axel lose control of the knife, and it clattered and skittered over the rough wooden floor.

Petr screamed at me. "Go!"

It was then that I made a terrible mistake. I hesitated. Zasha was at the door, more than ready to leave. But I couldn't abandon Petr to the vicious Axel; I had to help him.

I rushed to the other side of the room to get the knife. An iron hand gripped my ankle as I neared it, and I fell fast and hard to the ground. It must have been the angle at which I fell, or the handle of the hoe, or . . . I'll never know. Whatever my head hit, it knocked me unconscious.

★ ★ ★

When I woke, it was dark and quiet. For a moment I couldn't figure out where I was; then it all came back to me. But why had Axel left me alive? Or maybe he was on the run, chased by Petr and Zasha?

"Ahhh," I moaned as I moved. In the panic of the fight I'd ignored my injuries. My ribs now reminded me something had probably been cracked, and my hip hurt so badly where Axel had kicked me on the joint that I limped when I was finally able to get to my feet.

"Petr!" I called. "Zasha!" It was too quiet; I knew they were gone. "Think!" I commanded myself, breathing weakly, feeling nauseated. *Thor*, I thought. *Get Thor. Get Auntie's pistol. Find them. Kill Axel.*

I limped to the house, holding my ribs and moaning with each step. When I was within ten yards of the cabin I heard Thor whine and then bark. It was the sweetest sound in the world; I had to stop myself from weeping.

Once in the house I went first to the kitchen, throwing water on my face. Ignoring Thor's cries, I went to the living room, took Auntie's gun out of a cabinet, filled the empty chambers, pocketed the extra bullets, and tucked it in my belt. I grabbed Thor's lead from the hook where it was kept near the front door. Finally, I opened the door to the bedroom where I'd kept Thor.

He bounded at me, practically knocking me down. He yelped and cried and licked my face until I did weep, but only for a moment. Wiping my eyes with my sleeve, I said, "No time for that now, Thor. We have to find Zasha and Petr."

First we went to the barn. There on the floor was what I was looking for: the knife that Auntie had given me, the knife that had injured Petr. I wiped the bloody blade on the straw where Zasha had lain. I tried not to think of the fact that it was Petr's dried blood that still stained the blade when I slipped it into the sheath sewn to the side of my leather boot.

I didn't know which direction to go in, but something told me that if Petr was being chased, he would have run with Zasha deep into the fields and into the forest, not toward the road. That is, if it was Petr who had the choice, if he and Zasha were still alive.

I had Thor's lead in my left hand and took the pistol out of my belt with the other. If I saw Axel, I'd unload every bullet into his evil self.

That chance never came. I combed the fields. After trying to be quiet and stealthy for the first half hour, I began to call out Petr's and Zasha's names. No answer came.

Then Thor seemed to pick up a scent and dragged me down a narrow path into the woods. He must have smelled Zasha. There were no signs that I could read to tell me if they had passed this way. It wasn't like a detective novel where drops of blood or torn bits of clothing conveniently point you in the right direction.

We walked deep into those woods for an hour. Dawn had come, but revealed little. When we came to a stream, Thor drank deeply and sat down, staring across it. Then he looked at me as if to say, *They're gone.*

We turned back, walking in a zigzag pattern to cover as much ground as possible. There was nothing. Later, as we approached the cabin, I knew what I had to do. Axel might be dead . . . or he might be alive. I was no longer safe here.

It took me ten minutes to gather a few things for my journey and feed Thor. I looked around the little cabin that had been my home for three and a half years and said good-bye. It was the third time in my short life that I was forced to leave a home where I was happy and wanted to stay.

Thor and I took a side path south. It might take an entire day, maybe more, to reach Vladimir's house. I didn't care. It was our only choice. It was our only hope. I might have to run away at this moment to save Thor's and my life, but as soon as I reached Vladimir's I knew he and Auntie would help me formulate a plan to find Zasha, to find Petr, and if Axel was alive, to find him, and if necessary, to kill him.

I wouldn't stop until it was done.

CHAPTER 41

IT TOOK US ALL DAY TO REACH VLADIMIR'S PLACE. I LOST TRACK OF TIME. IN MY HURRY TO LEAVE I HADN'T THOUGHT TO BRING WATER OR FOOD. WE FOLLOWED THE MAIN ROADS, but always walked a good forty or fifty feet from them. Not only did I not want to be seen — in the unlikely event that Axel and Petr headed south — but I didn't want anyone to see Thor, either.

My fear was soon justified. We were on a section of road that was impossible to follow with our forty-foot buffer. We had to walk along the soft dirt shoulder for about half a mile. It was an isolated area; I hadn't seen a farmhouse or a vehicle of any kind for miles.

A low rumble announced the presence of an open-backed truck coming toward us. Next to the driver sat two women. The back part held six or seven children, who caught a glimpse of us as they drove by. None of them looked older than twelve. Once they were behind us, I heard a high voice cry, "Traitor! Traitor!" I was so horrified, I couldn't help but turn around and stare. The screamer pointed his finger at us. Soon he and all his friends were chanting, "Traitor! Traitor! Traitor!" Their voices grew fainter as they sped away. Thor and I didn't stop running until we were able to get off the road again and maintain a safe distance from behind the veil of scattered birch trees.

The injuries I received when Axel kicked me settled in as dull, constant pain. I could tell Thor was tired and hungry. Several times we rested, especially when we crossed streams and creeks, but never for very long.

By the time we got to Vladimir's, it was early evening. We heard laughter floating out of the open windows, along with the smell of dinner cooking. We went to the back door and knocked.

"Ivan!" Auntie exclaimed when she opened it. "What happened? Are you all right?"

It was only then that I let myself feel my pain, my hunger, my weariness, my upset. I collapsed against the door frame. "Thor needs water," I answered. "Do you have some food you could give him?"

"Yes, yes," Auntie said, her distress clear. "Vladimir! Natalya! Come here!" As she filled a bowl of water for Thor and a glass for me, Vladimir and his wife came rushing into the kitchen. They gasped when they saw us.

"What happened?" Vladimir demanded, sounding almost angry. Natalya was wetting a dish towel that she quickly and gently applied to the side of my head that I'd hit when I fell. It occurred to me that I must look pretty awful after the fighting in the barn and the long hours on the road. Vladimir pulled a chair up next to me and took my hand. "Where's Petr?" He must have feared the worst.

"I don't know. Axel Recht found us. There was a fight. I was knocked out. They were all gone when I woke up."

"Zasha, too?" he asked quietly. I nodded, leaned back in my chair, and stared at the ceiling. "Do you think . . ."

"No. Petr fought so hard, he can't be dead. He just can't."

Auntie put a bowl of stew on the floor for Thor and one on the table for me. "How did Axel find you?" she asked.

"The widow —"

"I *knew* she was trouble the minute I saw her!"

"— was talking to a stranger at the street market in Sviritsa. He mentioned how much he loved German shepherds —"

"And she said she knew two of the best!" Auntie finished for me.

"We should have made you more secure up there," Vladimir said, looking anguished.

"Nothing short of a barbed-wire fence would have kept her out," his wife said dryly, having had several interactions with her.

"Was Petr injured?" Auntie asked, putting her hand on my shoulder.

"Yes. A deep cut on his upper arm." I felt fear ripple through the room. A cut like Petr's wouldn't kill you, but the germs that caused infection could.

Vladimir stood up. "We have to find him. I'll go get Josef and Yeshka. Polina, too. Natalya, pack some food for me. I'm leaving now for Vilnov. Ivan, you eat and rest. I'll bring them back here. We'll leave for the cabin before dawn."

I nodded, so weary I could barely speak. "Zasha will be so tired. We can't let her lose her puppies." My voice cracked. "Petr was so brave. . . ." Tears leaked out before I could stop them.

Vladimir slipped his arms through a coat Natalya handed him. "Sit and eat, then rest. But be ready to leave when I return. We'll take Thor with us."

I did as he asked. Auntie awakened me at three A.M. and helped me prepare for our journey.

Coming down the stairs ten minutes later, I saw the sweetest sight anyone could have asked for. Yeshka, Josef, and Polina stood waiting for me. Polina grabbed me in a giant hug and held me tightly. "Don't worry. We'll find them." I hugged the others, who whispered words of encouragement before we headed outside, where Vladimir was preparing a cart with an open top and benches built into the sides.

"Ready?" he asked, turning around to look over the good friends who had come to help us.

"Ready," came the murmured replies.

So began the hunt for Zasha and Petr.

CHAPTER 42

IT TOOK ALMOST FOUR HOURS TO REACH BORIS'S CABIN. A
WAVE OF FEAR SWEPT OVER ME AS WE PULLED UP TO THE
FRONT. IT WAS POSSIBLE AXEL WAS INSIDE, OR WATCHING
us from nearby.

I'd reviewed the details of the fight with them, and my search
for Petr and Zasha. Our first step was to spend a short time going
over some of the terrain I'd already explored. I think Polina was
right when she said that after having been unconscious, I might
have overlooked details I would normally have noticed.

"How should we do this?" I asked. "Polina, why don't you
start in the farthest field and work your way toward the center?
Keep Thor with you. Yeshka, Josef — you take the fields that
begin next to the well. Vladimir, let's you and I search every inch
of the cabin, the barn, the loft, and anywhere someone could hide
on the grounds from the front door to the main road. We'll all
meet back here in about an hour."

"Are everyone's guns loaded and ready?" Yeshka asked. We all
answered yes. They had brought five rifles with them from Vilnov.
I still had my knife and Auntie's gun, but the rifles made me feel
safer.

After the nerve-racking experience of scouring the interior
spaces and the front grounds, we met up with our friends. They'd
come up empty-handed, too.

"Okay," I said. "The forest. You've all been here before, but
maybe not into the wilderness behind the farm. It's standard terrain,

similar to the woods near Vilnov. There's nothing to distinguish it that I know of."

"Isn't there a creek or ravine or something about three miles east?" Yeshka asked. "I'm sure I saw it once."

"Oh, right. I forgot. It's not too far east of here. Do you and Josef want to explore that?" I asked. Yeshka nodded. "Polina, why don't you go —"

Vladimir interrupted me. "I'm sorry, Ivan. I don't mean to criticize your plan, but . . ." He looked around and motioned with his hand. "This is serious wilderness. Any of us could get lost and never be found. I propose that we stay together. It may not be as efficient, but we reduce the possibility of harm."

Yeshka put his hand on my shoulder. "He's right. We all know how easy it is to veer off course in the woods. Besides, if Axel is as dangerous as you say, he could overcome two of us. But five? No."

"Do you think we should call out their names?" Josef asked.

"I think so," I said. "They've been without food and water for many, many hours, unless they found some in the woods. There's the lack of sleep, Petr's cut . . ."

"Come on," Vladimir said. "Let's find them."

We began to search the forest by going east and slightly south. They were the least challenging paths — no big hills or gullies or other impediments to a fast escape. We all agreed that our own instincts would have led us in this direction if we were running from an enemy. An hour passed, then two. We rested and had a few bites of food from the pack that Vladimir carried. He never complained about the extra weight from the containers full of water.

I scanned the sky for vultures. "I've been looking for them, too," Polina said softly as we prepared to resume our search. I pretended not to understand.

"Let's go toward the water," I said, picking up my rifle. "Petr knows of the creek, I'm certain. He might go that way for water, and to clean his wound." The others agreed, and we adjusted our course. The ground became hilly, just enough to make walking twice as tiring as it should have been. We stopped again in less than an hour for water and a short rest. To our left the land rose steeply. Although I didn't think I'd been in this exact spot before, I was fairly certain the creek was nearby.

"Do you think Petr would have gone that way?" Josef asked as we prepared to resume our search, pointing to the short, steep hill.

I shook my head. "I don't think so. Why would he go up at this point? He would have been tired by now. Petr's smart. He'd be looking for a way out of the forest."

"How much farther does the forest go?"

I looked around me. "I'm not sure. I think there are some farms farther east and south."

"Did Petr know that?" Polina asked.

"I think so. Why don't we go that way?" I pointed southeast. "It looks like the forest is a little thinner there, too." As I took a last drink of water and poured some in my hand for Thor, I noticed that Polina was climbing the small hill to the north.

"Polina, come," Vladimir called. She continued to walk to the edge of the top of the rise. I was deeply tired; my ribs hurt, my head throbbed. I wanted our efforts to be focused and was the tiniest bit annoyed that Polina was delaying us. Then, as I gazed back toward her, I remembered everyone had come at a moment's notice, ripped out of their warm beds, to help me and Petr. It made me think of the night Polina and I had run from Axel, missing his bullets by who knows how many inches. Even now I carried the compass she gave me years ago. She insisted, saying it was good luck. My impatience dissolved, and I felt nothing but gratitude toward her.

"I think you're going to want to see this," she called to us over her shoulder. We exchanged quick, nervous glances and rushed up the hill to where she stood.

It turned out to be a precipice, not the crest of a hill. Below, lying next to the small stream, was Axel Recht. His right arm was angled from his body in such a way that I knew it was broken. He lay so still, he could have been dead, or he could have been unconscious.

"Oh my God," I murmured. The others looked stunned. I scanned the terrain quickly. "Down there! About thirty feet that way it looks like we can get down to the creek level."

The adrenaline pumped so hard in my veins, I no longer felt my injuries. If we found Axel, it meant we might be able to find Petr and Zasha. We scrambled down the hill and, led by Polina, jumped the last three feet to the muddy creek bank. When we were within about eight or nine feet of Axel, we stopped as one, and I asked Vladimir to hold Thor's lead. I slipped up to the front of the group to stare at Axel.

He lay with his feet pointed toward us. It was only then I noticed that his left foot was bent oddly and was probably injured, too. His eyes were closed, his lips parted. We inched closer, until I stood about two feet from his boot.

"Do you think he's dead?" Vladimir asked from his place at the back with Thor. The creek bank was narrow, and we were standing single file. "I can't quite see."

"I don't know," I answered.

"If he's not, I'll gladly finish the job," Yeshka offered.

"Ivan, kick his boot," Polina said. "See if he responds."

I didn't want to touch him with any part of my body, so I pushed the top of his right boot sharply with the muzzle of my rifle. There was no response.

"Check his pockets," Josef said. "Make sure he doesn't have a knife or a pistol."

I nodded. "I don't think he does," I said, easing my way along the narrow bit of earth between the bottom of the hill and his body. I bent over to feel in his pants pocket. "If he did, I'm sure he would have used them in the —"

Axel's left hand shot up and grabbed me from behind the neck. He pulled me down with great strength toward him. His fingers began to squeeze my throat.

I was so startled that no sound escaped me for a moment, and then it was a strangled gurgle because of the bent-over position of my body and his fingers cutting off my air. I slammed my right hand down to stop the forward motion, but my elbow bent easily; I was clumsy because my rifle hung awkwardly from my shoulder. I tripped on Axel's body as I moved my feet in a space too narrow for them. I fell on Axel, my rifle between us. Its barrel hit my sore ribs, giving Axel a momentary advantage.

Strained, groaning sounds and a foul odor emanated from his mouth. He pulled me closer in his iron grip. Why wasn't anyone helping me? I thrashed, trying to pull free of his hand. But it was impossible.

Then, in a motion so swift it seemed to come out of nowhere, a rifle butt came down hard on Axel's forehead. The *crack* of the wood hitting his head, his moan of pain, and the loosened grip came all at once.

I scrambled awkwardly off of him in fear and relief. My heart raced, and my breath came in short, ragged bursts. My throat throbbed, and I gasped in deep breaths. I stared down at him to make sure he wasn't moving. Only then did I notice it was Polina holding the rifle that had come to my rescue. "Thank you," I murmured, putting my arm around her shoulder. "What now?" I asked the others, listening to Thor's whine, knowing he was anxious to break away and come see what had happened.

Vladimir peeked around from his position in the rear to answer. "It's tempting just to leave him. I think we should, but only if we cover him in honey first, so we can be sure he attracts the bears."

"Are you sure you don't want me to finish him off, Ivan?" Yeshka offered again.

"We're not murderers, Yeshka," his father said softly.

"But look what they've done to our people!" he cried, although I think we all knew Yeshka wouldn't kill him unless it was a fair fight.

"What do you think, Polina?" I asked, in deference to the fact that her quick observations and actions had saved me from Axel.

"There's a small army depot in Sviritsa. I say we turn him in to the Russian army there."

I nodded. "Let the army do with him whatever they do with other prisoners of war. But . . ." I glanced up at the steep hillside, and then at the quick flowing stream on our left. "What about Petr and Zasha?"

"It's your decision, Ivan. We can leave Axel here and continue to search, or we can take Recht to the depot and then start again."

Yeshka leaned around Polina to catch my eye. "Maybe we should split up. You and I will push on, and the others can deal with Recht."

I stared down at the unconscious man who was seriously injured. But something in me knew better than to *ever* underestimate Axel, even in a situation where someone who didn't know him might call him "harmless." I squeezed my eyes closed in frustration. Because of Axel, my time in Vilnov ended, and I was forced to flee to Boris's cabin. Fear that he'd find me had haunted me ever since that night. Now he'd caused the disappearance of a good friend and a dog I loved beyond words. There was no way I'd take even a small risk now that we had him under our control.

I cursed silently and said, "We'll get rid of Axel, then we'll start looking for Petr and Zasha again. Let's make it quick."

"How do we get him back to the cabin?" Vladimir asked.

"On a stretcher," Polina answered confidently. "We'll have to make one." She looked at each of us carefully. "Vladimir, I'm going to need your coat. Yeshka, Josef, your shirts, please. Does anyone have a hatchet with them?" None of us did. "We need a sturdy piece of wood — a fairly straight branch about three inches thick and about nine or ten feet long. If you can't find one, break or shoot it off of a tree at the trunk, and we'll strip it of its other branches."

I didn't know how Polina would be able to make a stretcher out of the materials she requested, but I remembered how she told me she knew how to make snowshoes and snow masks, and had no doubt she could do it. In less than twenty minutes, it was done.

The two shirts were tied together to form a crude sling, and then tied near to the ends of the pole. Vladimir's coat went under Axel in the opposite direction, giving support to his lower torso, and was tied in a knot at the middle of the pole.

To make sure he was unconscious, Polina poked Axel hard enough that he would have reacted. When he didn't, Polina, Yeshka, Josef, and I lifted him and laid him in the sling. We made no attempts to put splints on his injured arm or foot. The four of us would take turns carrying him; Vladimir and Thor would lead the way.

It was a grueling trip back to the cabin. For two and a half hours we sweated and strained, lifting and maneuvering his body through the forest and finally back to the farm. I resented every minute that took us away from finding Petr and Zasha. Yeshka and I carried him on the last leg of our journey. I made it on willpower alone, determined not to collapse so close to our goal.

We set him on the ground at the well in back of the cabin. After getting shirts for Yeshka and Josef from the cabin and drinking our fill, we loaded Axel onto the wooden floor in the back of Vladimir's wagon. It was then that he regained consciousness.

"Ivan," he moaned. It was almost inaudible, but made me jump in fear. "I was good to you. Help me."

I stared at the prostrate figure. "Where's Zasha? Where's the man who was with her?"

"Who is Zasha?" came the enfeebled answer.

"Liar. You remember my name and that you were 'good to me,' but you can't remember who Zasha is?"

"I'm an old man. I'm battle weary. . . ."

"Where are they?" I shouted.

"I could make him tell us," Yeshka said, and climbed into the cart. The rest of us followed and sat on the built-in benches on the sides of the wooden vehicle. Axel lay at our feet, surrounded. Vladimir kept Thor up front with him.

I shook my head. "I don't think you can," I said, knowing Axel well enough to understand that anything he told us would be a lie. I swear a smile flitted across his face.

"Should we bind his hands and feet?" Josef asked.

Because of his injuries, we tied only his right foot to his left hand. "We still have to keep a close eye on him," I said after Yeshka tied the knot. Axel closed his eyes and seemed to fall asleep.

Not too long after that, as we lumbered down the empty road, Axel opened his eyes. He looked at me and said clearly, "You know I'll find you."

"You won't be finding anybody," Polina said sharply as she untied the scarf around her neck. Getting down on her knees, she lifted Axel's head from the back — none too gently — took her scarf, and tied it like a gag around his mouth. He stared wide-eyed at the sky.

★ ★ ★

In another half hour, we delivered him to a startled army officer in Sviritsa. "But he's in a Russian uniform!" the man exclaimed.

"And he speaks perfect Russian," I said. "He'll try to convince you it's all been a terrible mistake. Give me some paper, and I'll write down his full name for you, and the time period when he was in charge of the German occupation of Vilnov."

It took another fifteen minutes for them to decide what to do with him before they would let us depart.

"Just don't let him go," I said for the tenth time as we waved farewell. We climbed back into Vladimir's cart. This time, Thor sat in the back next to me. As Vladimir turned us around in the right direction and we went south, I said half to myself and half to the others, "Where are Petr and Zasha?" Thor looked at me when I spoke Zasha's name.

"He'll head for Vilnov," Josef said. "It's the logical thing."

"If he's strong enough to make it that far." I hated the sound of my own words.

We had about four hours on the road ahead of us. "Why don't you all spend the night with us? Everyone's tired. Natalya will feed you well. I'll get you back to Vilnov first thing in the morning, and we'll begin our search."

"No!" I cried. "No delays."

"Ivan," Yeshka said, putting his hand on my shoulder. "You've been hurt; you don't look well. Vladimir's right. When we get back to his house, we'll look at some maps and see if we can figure out the most likely direction Petr might have gone. There's a lot of land between the cabin and Vilnov. He could be anywhere. We have to think clearly and be methodical."

Polina declared, "Only time will tell."

It might seem like an obvious response, but she was right. We knew nothing; we had only our common sense and our guesses to go on. Time *would* tell, but it was the one thing we didn't have. Who knew exactly what injuries Petr — or Zasha — had suffered at Axel's hand after I was knocked unconscious. Time was the one thing they didn't have, either.

CHAPTER 43

BY THE TIME WE REACHED VLADIMIR'S, I WAS FEVERISH AND DIZZY, ALMOST FALLING TWICE ONCE I WAS OUT OF THE CART. THE OTHERS LEFT FOR VILNOV TO CONTINUE THE search without me. I stayed at Vladimir's house for a week to recuperate: from exhaustion, from my injuries, from the trauma of someone trying to kill me, and from losing Zasha — words I could hardly bring myself to say.

It was a strange week, filled with fitful sleep, nightmares, hopes, healing, and a sense of being lost. Sometimes I wasn't sure if I was dreaming or awake, like the time with eyes wide open I petted Thor, asked him how the puppies were doing, and called him Zasha.

Our friends kept us apprised of their efforts. They searched every place they could think of between the cabin and Vilnov, but found nothing. Polina suggested that they go back to Sviritsa, track down where Axel had been sent, and demand answers from him. No one supported the idea. I appreciated her determination, but also understood it was an indication of desperation, that it meant there were no more leads to follow.

During that week I often walked along the shore of Lake Ladoga. Summer was in its full glory, the skies filled with birds, the cold blue water rippling in the wind. It helped me to think, to come to a decision I knew I had to make. Finally, late one morning as I sat on the shore watching storm clouds blow off to the west, I decided I was going back to Leningrad. Immediately. And I was taking Thor with me.

My decision came only after accepting the fact that continuing to search for Petr and Zasha was a waste of time. If they hadn't been found by now, there was a reason. If Petr was alive, he would contact one of us as soon as he could. If we never heard from him, I had to accept what that meant, too. It was possible I would never know what happened. It might remain a mystery that haunted me forever. My heart ached at the very thought of them.

Vladimir promised to contact Taavo and my friends in Vilnov and let them know I was returning to Leningrad. I reminded myself that we would be separated by only seventy-five or eighty miles. How far from home it had felt that first night when we knocked on Miss Galina's door; another world, a million miles away. They could visit, maybe meet Alik and Misha — that is if . . . I wouldn't think about that now.

I struggled a lot over the decision to take Thor. Selfishly, I never wanted to be separated from him again. He was my rock, my companion; he was my tie to Zasha and the memories of our time together. Some might argue that to take him from the home he knew on acres of beautiful countryside was wrong, especially considering we'd be living in an apartment in Leningrad. But our world at the cabin had been shattered; it would never be the same. It might hurt Thor even more if he was separated from the one person who most loved him and had been a constant in his life.

I was forced to confront another difficult truth. I was sixteen now and had lived my life independently since I was twelve. There was a good chance that living with my mother — who might still think of me as her twelve-year-old Ivan the Not-So-Terrible — would be too difficult for either of us. I smiled as I fantasized about living in Auntie's old apartment, since she wasn't ready to return to the city yet, and my mother living downstairs in hers. Maybe it wasn't a bad idea; close to each other but with some distance. First I had to find out if our apartment was even still there. Thor's presence would create an extra challenge because of her allergies to dogs and cats.

Many tears were shed as Auntie and Natalya bustled around the kitchen, packing food for our trip. Neither of them thought it was a good idea, and they didn't spare me their strongly worded opinions.

"It's too soon," Natalya said firmly. "Let the government get some systems in place to support reconstruction."

Auntie agreed. "For all you know, you'll be homeless by tonight! How will you eat? Where will you sleep? Who knows if any of our friends survived?" She looked troubled, and she was right when she demanded, "What about water? Electricity? Food? I don't think it's fair to Thor, either." That stung a little, but I knew Thor and I belonged together, now more than ever.

"It can't be worse than when we left, Auntie," I argued. "No one will be bombing us night and day."

"Yes, it could be worse. You'll be trying to make a life in the rubble and destruction they left behind."

"You're right," I said quietly. "But they *did* leave. We won. I want to help Leningrad heal, and I think . . . I think it will help heal me."

She sighed in frustration and continued preparations for our trip. Vladimir seemed to understand more, and simply went outside to prepare Nesa for our drive to the departure dock on Lake Ladoga. How different this crossing would be from the one Auntie and I made in the frozen winter of 1941!

There wasn't much time before we left; I was not looking forward to our final good-byes. I sat down on the sunporch to do the last thing left to do before my journey home: write a letter to my mother.

My mother and I had exchanged only one letter each in three and a half years. Because of my involvement with the partisans, it had just been too dangerous. Although illogical, I felt guilty about it, even angry sometimes because it hurt not to be able to communicate with her.

I sometimes dreamed that she'd just show up at the cabin one day. I'd look down the long drive and there she'd be, waving to me, smiling, calling my name. Axel's reappearance had destroyed that dream. At least for now, I didn't want her near the place where such an awful thing had happened. Maybe it was a weakness in me that I couldn't accept half a dream — just me and Thor to welcome her, without Zasha — but it was more than I could face.

I'd almost trained myself not to miss her. Almost. As the possibility of seeing her came closer, the yearning that had been bottled up in me threatened to rise up like a flooded river to overwhelm me. I had to keep that contained for just a little longer.

Thor wandered out onto the porch and sat beside me. He had a way of finding me when he knew I needed him. I petted him for a few moments and felt the soft brush of his fur through my fingertips. Finally, I picked up the pen.

Dear Mama, I wrote. The pen hovered above the paper for a long time before I put it down. I picked it up and put it down several more times before I realized it was impossible to tell her in a letter what I really needed to share with her. It would have taken a book, one that started on the dark, cold morning we parted and ended when Petr and Zasha disappeared. I needed to look in her eyes to even begin to explain why I was going back to Leningrad now without her and to tell her all that had happened that made that decision inevitable.

And what about her? I wondered. We'd heard stories that when the factories were moved to the Urals, many had been set up outdoors as soon as the equipment arrived, but before buildings were found to house them. I'd been thinking so much about myself that I hadn't stopped to fully consider her sacrifices. Would I find her exhausted, worn out? Old before her time? We'd missed out on each other's company for three and a half years. She'd missed seeing me grow up. There would be a lot of catching up to do.

It wasn't only Leningrad that had been under siege. The lives of all of us had been held hostage, starved, and ravaged by the war. Now it would be up to each of us to figure out how to take what had been broken and put it together in a way that fit the new realities that faced us. But I was ready to accept that challenge.

When I arrived and knew that our apartment was still there, I would write to her. From Leningrad. It was time to go back to where I'd started — my life had come full circle.

I petted Thor one last time and stood up. "Come on, boy. We've got a long road ahead of us. It's time to go home."

RUSSIA AND WORLD WAR II

IN HIS BOOK, *MEIN KAMPF*, ADOLF HITLER MADE IT CLEAR THAT HE SAW RUSSIA AS THE PERFECT PLACE FOR EXPANDING LIVING SPACE (*LEBENSRAUM*) FOR THE GERMANS, WITH THE RUSSIANS ACTING AS their slaves. Although the two-volume book was published in 1925 and 1926, well before Hitler came to power, this was a consistent theme in later speeches he gave. Because of this, World War II, or what the Russians call The Great Patriotic War, meant something different to them. If the Russians lost, it would mean not only devastation, but enslavement.

And yet, less than two weeks before Hitler started the war by invading Poland in 1939, he and Joseph Stalin signed the Nazi-Soviet Nonaggression Pact, promising not to attack each other. Germany waited only twenty-two months before breaking that promise; they invaded Russia on June 22, 1941. Which is how Russia began the war on the side of Germany but ultimately ended up fighting alongside the United States and the rest of the Allies.

Knowing Stalin had killed 80 percent of his military leadership as part of the Great Purge a few years earlier, Hitler assumed the Soviets were weak and that victory would be easy. And at first, it was. Within two weeks of the initial attack, Russia had lost as many men as America lost in the entire war. In another month, the Germans were halfway to Moscow. Three million Russians died in the first three months. The British were pressured to help, but they were under a German siege of their own. The Americans were reluctant to enter the war — until they were bombed at Pearl Harbor by the Japanese on December 7, 1941. But the Americans didn't fight in a full-scale ground invasion of Europe until D-Day, June 6, 1944, and their troops never made it as far as Russia.

After entering Russia, the Germans had to fight on two fronts simultaneously: in Europe and in Russia. And the deeper they went into Russia, the harder it was to supply their troops with food, ammunition, and medical treatment. One of the biggest problems for the Germans was the weather. The heat and dust of summer caused their tanks to use twice as much oil. Only 3 percent of the Russian roads near its borders with Europe were paved, and those were soon destroyed by tanks and other heavy vehicles. The unpaved roads turned into deep trenches of mud and water after the autumn and spring rains, making them nearly impossible to use. That first winter of 1941, the temperature fell as much as fifty degrees below zero at night. It was so cold that guns wouldn't fire and engines froze while running — even anti-freeze was found frozen solid. Because the Russians had cold weather lubricants, they were able to take the discarded German weapons and vehicles and use them on their enemy. Though the German forces were spread thin and faced many obstacles, they still managed to leave a path of destruction across Russia and occupy many towns, such as happens in the fictional village of Vilnov in *Finding Zasha*.

In between the German invasion in 1941 and D-Day in 1944, two important events stand out in Russia's struggle: the Siege of Leningrad and the Battle of Stalingrad. During the Siege of Leningrad, called the 900-day siege, although it actually lasted 872 days, a million and a half people starved, froze to death, or were killed by German bombs. A young girl named Tanya Savicheva kept a diary during the first winter and spring of the siege. In it she lists the names and dates of death of her family members. In her last entry she wrote, "Only Tanya is left." She was evacuated to a children's home in 1942, but her body had been so weakened by what she'd suffered that she died two years later. In honor of her, Ivan shares her last name.

The city of Tikhvin was a critical rail supply line between Moscow and the eastern shore of Lake Ladoga. If the Russians controlled it, supplies could be sent to Leningrad. Unfortunately, the Germans captured it on November 8, 1941. The battle for Tikhvin referred to in *Finding Zasha* is the one in which the Russians won the city back on December 9, 1941. This was an important victory for the Russians — both morally and strategically.

The Battle of Stalingrad took place from August 1942 to February 1943. The Russians fought relentlessly for every street, building, floor, and room. The very word *Stalingrad* has come to stand for courage, tenacity, a ferocious refusal to give up. Then–British Prime Minister Winston Churchill called the battle the "hinge of fate." Most historians consider Russia's win at Stalingrad to be the turning point of the war.

The partisans, who play a big role in *Finding Zasha*, were a key part of the war effort. The first year, they were disorganized and poorly armed, but by the end of the war there were ninety thousand partisans working behind enemy lines. They disrupted supply lines, destroyed communications, blew up railroads, provided reconnaissance, and generally made the work of the German army much more difficult. With the German army split between two fronts, it could be hard for them to fight back against these attacks. One effective method they often used was to burn the surrounding forests in order to smoke out the partisans. However, if even one Russian citizen committed an act of arson against the Germans, they would shoot eight hundred civilians in retaliation. That action, and others like it, outraged the population, who then joined or assisted the partisans.

The Partisan's Companion, after which *The Deadly Partisan* in *Finding Zasha* is modeled, was published by the Russian government late in 1941. For the purposes of this story, the publication happens a few weeks earlier. *The Partisan's Companion* illustrates combat techniques and survival tips, such as telling a soldier he can live on thinly sliced frozen fish, claiming it melts in the mouth like ice cream. Amazingly, as of the publication of *Finding Zasha*, an edition of the original *The Partisan's Companion* is still in print.

The story of Russia's part in the war is also one of devastating statistics: Twenty-five million Russians died, twenty-five million more became homeless, and thirty million were wounded. The Battle of Kursk between the Germans and the Russians lasted from July to August in 1943 and was the biggest tank battle in history, with about six thousand tanks, two million troops, and four thousand aircraft. Eighty percent of Germany's losses happened on the Russian front. Russians made up 40 percent of the deaths in the war. Fifty million people died worldwide as a result of the war. Without Russia's contributions and sacrifices, it is not at all certain the Germans would have been defeated. Along with the other Allies, the world owes them a great debt of gratitude and honor.

A BRIEF WORLD WAR II OVERVIEW

1939

August 23 — The Nazi-Soviet Nonaggression Pact is signed by Hitler and Stalin.

September 1 — Germany invades Poland.

September 3 — Britain and France declare war on Germany.

September 17 — Russia invades Poland.

November 30 — Russia invades Finland.

1940

March 12 — Russia's war with Finland ends.

May and June — Germany invades and occupies France and the Low Countries.

May 10 — Winston Churchill becomes Prime Minister of Britain.

May 26 — Germans defeat the Allied forces at Dunkirk, France. However, 338,000 trapped Allied troops are rescued from the beach by hundreds of civilian boats sent from Great Britain.

June 10 — Italy enters the war on the side of the Axis powers and declares war on France and Great Britain.

June 22 — France signs an armistice with Germany. A collaborationist government is set up in Vichy, France.

Mid-July to mid-November — The Battle of Britain.

September 27 — Germany, Japan, and Italy sign the Tripartite Pact, an economic and military alliance.

1941

February 12 — German Afrika Korps deployed to Northern Africa to help the Italians fighting against Great Britain.

Early 1941 — Yugoslavia, Greece, and Crete attacked by Germans.

June 22 — Hitler attacks Russia in Operation Barbarossa.

September 8 — The Siege of Leningrad begins.

December 6 — Russia counterattacks at Moscow. This is the first major German defeat.

December 7 — The Japanese attack the Americans at Pearl Harbor.

December 8 — America declares war on Germany and Japan.

December 9 — Russians recapture Tikhvin from Germans.

December 11 — Germany and other Axis countries declare war on America.

1942

Early 1942 — Japan invades the Philippines, Indonesia, Malaysia, Burma, and others.

January 20 — Details for the "final solution" are drawn up by the Nazis at the Wannsee Conference.

February 15 — Singapore is captured from the British by the Japanese.

June 3 to 6 — The Battle of Midway. America defeats the Japanese navy.

August 23 — The Battle of Stalingrad begins.

October to November — British Allies win at El Alamein.

1943

February 2 — Russians win the Battle of Stalingrad.

May 12 — Axis forces surrender to British and Americans in North Africa.

July 5 — The Battle of Kursk begins.

July 10 — The Allies invade Sicily.

July 25 — Benito Mussolini is forced to step down as dictator of Italy and is hidden away to keep him out of German reach.

August 17 — The Battle of Sicily is won by Allies.

September 3 — Italy surrenders, joins the Allies.

September 12 — Germans rescue Mussolini and set him up in Northern Italy.

November 28 to December 1 — Roosevelt, Stalin, and Churchill meet in Tehrān, Iran.

November 6 — Russians liberate Kiev.

1944

January 27 — The Siege of Leningrad is broken.

June 4 — Rome is liberated from the Germans.

June 6 — D-Day. The Allies attack Germany in Northern France.

July 20 — Hitler survives "Valkyrie" assassination attempt.

August 25 — Paris is liberated.

October 20 — Americans land in the Philippines.

October 20 — Japanese navy pilots begin kamikaze attacks.

December 16 — The Battle of the Bulge in Belgium's Ardennes forest. Allies win.

1945

January 27 — Russians liberate Auschwitz.

February 19 — The battle for Iwo Jima begins.

March — Americans closing in on Berlin from the west and Russians from the east.

April 12 — U.S. president Franklin D. Roosevelt dies. Harry S Truman becomes president.

April 16 — The Russians reach Berlin; it is fully surrounded by the 25th. They meet with American forces on the 27th and cut the German army in two.

April 28 — Mussolini is captured and killed.

April 30 — Hitler commits suicide.

Early May — Germany surrenders in various countries.

May 8 — Victory in Europe declared (V-E Day). Allies formally accept unconditional surrender.

May 9 — Germans surrender to Soviets. Russia and Europe marked this event on different days due to the difference in time zones. It was the 8th in Europe when this happened, but the 9th in Russia.

July 26 — The Potsdam Declaration is issued, calling for the immediate surrender of Japan. Japan refuses.

August 6 — The first atomic bomb in history is dropped on Hiroshima.

August 8 — Russia declares war on Japan, invades Manchuria.

August 9 — A second atomic bomb is dropped, on Nagasaki.

August 14 — Japan agrees to surrender.

September 2 — Japan's formal surrender. Official end of World War II.

ACKNOWLEDGMENTS

JODY CORBETT, WHO EDITED *SAVING ZASHA* AND *FINDING ZASHA*, DESERVES CREDIT FOR MAKING THEM BOTH BETTER BOOKS THAN I COULD HAVE MADE THEM WITHOUT HER. SHE WORKS HARDER THAN ANY TWO people, reads faster and more deeply, and has the best ideas to make a story come alive. Thank you, Jody, for your kindness, your generosity, and for sharing your incredible talent and love of books.

Many thanks to my literary agent, Marlene Stringer, without whom Ivan, Zasha, and Thor would not have found a home. I'm sure I'm not aware of even half of the work you do behind the scenes, and all the stress that entails. But I know that you will always tell me the truth and give me reason to hope. Thank you for being there.

Thank you to the children who have taken the time to write to me. I love your e-mails and letters, and I am thrilled to know we are sharing a story together. I particularly like it when you give me suggestions about what to write about next and what to name the animals!

My husband, Arthur, will always get a special thanks for going to his studio so that I can write, even when he doesn't feel like it. That is the very definition of a good man.

Lastly, to the people of Leningrad who were there during the siege: You were in my heart and mind as I wrote and read about that terrible time. I hope that in some small way I have helped people remember what you endured.